ACCLAIM FOR *STUPID AND CONTAGIOUS*

"STUPID AND CONTAGIOUS is anything but stupid and completely contagious. Infectious, riotous, and hip beyond belief, it's a great read."

—Isabel Rose, author of *The J.A.P. Chronicles*

"A witty romantic comedy debut."

—*Kirkus Reviews*

"Smart and feisty! Milk-snorting funny and playfully intriguing! Love it!"

—Karen Salmar... of
How to Be Ha...

"Insanely funny and outrageou... ...ND CONTAGIOUS effortlessly captures the glorious awkwardness of becoming who you are, finding that special someone who drives you crazy, and ultimately following your dreams wherever they may take you."

Erica Kennedy, author of *Bling*

"Caprice Crane rocks! This is the best book I've read in a long, long time. Sharp, original, and wickedly funny, this is a must-read. I absolutely loved it."

—Johanna Edwards, bestselling author of
The Next Big Thing and *Your Big Break*

"Caprice Crane's writing is so cool I feel like the geek girl stalking her locker, trying to slide a mix CD through the slats before she spots me. STUPID AND CONTAGIOUS is hilarious and insightful. A book with its own soundtrack, this is one not to miss."

—Pamela Ribon, author of *Why Girls Are Weird*

"Caprice Crane brings her respect for music and all of its universal sentiment into her stylish, page-turning, sharp-tongued debut novel."

—Liza Palmer, author of
Conversations with the Fat Girl

Stupid ⟶ and Contagious

Caprice Crane

NEW YORK BOSTON

5 Spot
Hachette Book Group USA
1271 Avenue of the Americas
New York, NY 10020

Visit our Web site at www.5-spot.com.

5 Spot is an imprint of Warner Books, Inc. The 5 Spot name and logo are trademarks of Warner Books, Inc.

Printed in the United States of America

First Edition: May 2006

10 9 8 7 6 5 4 3

Library of Congress Cataloging-in-Publication Data

Crane, Caprice.
Stupid and contagious / Caprice Crane.
p. cm.
Summary: "A romantic comedy about two twentysomething neighbors on a mission to find the founder of Starbucks"—Provided by the publisher.
ISBN-13: 978-0-446-69572-5
ISBN-10: 0-446-69572-6
1. Starbucks Coffee Company—Fiction. I. Title.
PS3603.R379S78 2005
813'.6—dc22 2005023575

Book design and text composition by Nancy Singer Olaguera/ ISPN Publishing Services

For my beautiful mother, Tina Louise, the eternal optimist . . . whose outer beauty is eclipsed only by her exquisite inner . . . who's been my biggest fan and cheerleader for my entire life. Your belief in me and unconditional support have inspired me, kept me going, and taught me faith. I love you with all of my heart.

Acknowledgments

Mom (Tina Louise), Dad (Les Crane), Stepmom (Ginger Crane), Grandma (Betty Yaeger), my dogs (Chelsea and Max), Jennie Abrams-Trager, Walter Afanasieff, Jeremy Armstrong, Jenny Bent, Cristina Brascia, Danielle Brisebois, Allison Burnett, Stephen Cabot, Adam Carl, Michelle Chydzik, Dahlia Cohen, Alex Coletti, Robert Cort, Jim Cotter, Tajma Davis, Denise Diforio, Steve Dirado, Amy Einhorn, Endeavor Agency, Ellen and Irwin Frankel, Glen E. Friedman, Jonathan Fuhrman, Gillian Garrett, D. B. Gilles, Jeff Goodman, Emily Griffin, Gary Helsinger, Kevin Hershey, Andy Kaplan, Devon Kellgren, Scarlett Lacey, Erik Lautier, Adam Levine, Brian Lipson, Melissa Lipton, David List, K. E. Macey, Nez Mandel, Nathalie Marciano, Cade McNown, Tracey Mikolas, Jill Morris, John Nutcher, Brigid Pearson, Dizzy Reed, Joel Rice, Kevin Roentgen, Amanda Rouse, Penina Sacks, James Schiff, Lisa Singer, Lou Stalsworth, Jason Steinberg, Makyla Stone, Sky Stone, Sarah Tomkins, Trident Media, Robert Trujillo, David Vanker, David Veloz, Joe Vernon, Amanda Voelker, Fran Warner, Warner Books, Elly Weisenberg, Andrea Wells (my third-grade teacher), and Harley Zinker

Stupid ——→ and Contagious

"This song explains why I'm leaving home to become a stewardess."

—Anita Miller, *Almost Famous*

"Yeah, well, sometimes nothin' can be a real cool hand."

—Luke, *Cool Hand Luke*

Heaven

My name is Heaven Albright and my husband of two years is cheating on me. I'm only twenty-five and you can argue that getting married at twenty-three is young, but I'll argue right back that people marry out of college and even high school, so considering that, it's not so young. Anyway, young or not . . . the bastard is cheating on me. After I gave him the best years of my life.

He's cheating on me with someone he works with. A girl from his office who he didn't even think was cute at first, but after months of working long hours together and cultivating inside jokes, and commiserating over bad cafeteria food . . . they're bumping uglies. It sickens me to even *think* about it. He'd always be so happy when he came home late from work, and you'd think I would have caught on because *nobody's* happy when they have to stay late at work. But I thought he just really enjoyed his job. Or maybe he *was* pissed off, but the minute he walked through the door and saw me, his bride of two years whom he loved and adored, all the day's annoyances would disappear. Poof.

But no. He would come home all smiles because he'd just gotten his rocks off with some little skank who probably wore twinsets and laughed like a hyena at their stupid inside jokes. I hate twinsets, with their matching fabric and color coordination and phony reserve. It's a known fact that twinsets are one of the most easily removed garments there is. Her name is probably Megan or Jessie, and she's probably a couple years younger than me. She's like me two years ago, but in a twinset. He's re-creating me even before I've had a chance to become the tired, old, sexually reluctant "ball and chain." I resent that. I'm not *old*.

Marriage sucks. People who tell you that you stop having sex after you get married are right. You just don't have it anymore. It's not like you say your *I-do*s and immediately stop. It takes a little time. Of course there's the honeymoon, and the first few months of playing horny housewife and helpful handyman, or slave girl and surprisingly warmhearted barbarian, or Winnie the Pooh and the Magical Honeypot. But after a while you stop shaving your legs, and he stops noticing, and it seems more practical to try to get a good night's sleep.

• • •

Brady

My name is Brady Gilbert, and I hate the window seat. Airplanes in general are a pain in the ass, and when I clearly stipulate that I want to sit on the *aisle*, a window seat is a personal affront that my secretary will be hearing about. If I had a secretary.

I'll just sit here and *will* nobody to sit in the aisle seat. That way I'll not only have the aisle seat, but I'll be able to achieve that almost-but-not-quite-comfortable sleeping position that inevitably ends up with a dead arm, stiff legs, and dried drool at the outer corner of my mouth. In front of complete strangers, no less.

Don't get me wrong . . . sure, it's nice to look out a window. But at what price? Do I want to have to ask permission every time I need to take a piss? It's like needing a hall pass in school, but worse. These are strangers. And when I got a hall pass, I didn't inconvenience anyone. But to go to the bathroom on an airplane, I have to make awkward small talk and offer the obligatory apologetic shrug to a guy who's been hogging my armrest. Then he gets up just enough to let me squeeze by. He'll sigh as he gets up, not trying to make me feel guilty per se, but more like "Oh, these old bones of mine," which is crap unless he's over eighty. And he's not, he's just annoyed.

Then to add insult to injury, as I maneuver out of the "now more room than ever before" four inches of space, I hold on to the tacky fabric headrest of the seat in front of me and get a glance from that person, too. I'm making enemies left and right. Flight attendants hate me, too. Me and my devil-may-care bladder. Then when I come back, I have to do the dance all over again. Heaven help me if it's a three-seater with a middle seat. Not to mention the etiquette question of which way to pass my neighbors—crotch first or ass first?

I hate the window seat. So I wait, and I *will*. People are still boarding, but so far, so good. I've spotted the token hot chick that's way out of my league anywhere but in my overactive imagination. This is going to be a long flight. There is always that one hot chick, no matter where you're going, domestic or international, and never in the seat next to you. Or me.

Well, this flight's no different. In walks our token goddess of flight, and I shift all my willpower to connect her ass with the seat next to mine. Nothin'. But she smiled at me, or at least I think she did. Maybe she was smiling at the flight attendant who'd just given her an extra blanket. Just because.

• • •

Heaven

If it sounds like I'm okay with my husband cheating on me, it's because I've worked hard at it. And not in the way that you might think. You see, I'm *not* actually married. And nobody is cheating on me. I'm engaged. I'm getting married in eighteen months. I do these little mental exercises every now and then to prepare myself for anything that might come up in life.

Unfortunately, you caught me when I was smack-dab in the middle of one, so we sort of got off on the wrong foot. I'm still me, and everything I told you up until the married-with-the-cheating-husband bit was true. Just not that part. I guess that's where we started, so you really don't know me at all. But you have to admit, I was handling it fairly well. Which I think I can attribute to my exercises. Had I never done this and found myself in the position of having a cheating husband, I don't know how I would deal. Luckily, I am now prepared.

So let's start over. I'm still Heaven Albright, still twenty-five years old. I'm five foot six and I weigh about one hundred thirty pounds. One twenty-five. One twenty-five on a good day. One thirty if I'm PMS-ing. One thirty if I'm depressed or indulging a little too much in things like wine or pizza or raw cookie dough. One thirty most of the time. I have medium-length dirty blond/light brown hair. It's that store-bought highlight thing. Kind of rootsy and tricolored, but not in a punk rock kind of way. Or like pasta, for that matter. Okay, sometimes I may top out at one thirty-five. And five feet five inches if you wanna get technical.

I've always thought I had somewhat chubby cheeks, but I think I finally see some cheekbones coming through. And not by sucking in my cheeks when I look in the mirror. I never quite got that whole thing. Whenever I'm washing my hands in a public bathroom, nine times out of ten, the woman next to me sucks her cheeks in when she looks in the mirror. What are these women doing? Trying to look thin? Like a fish? Like *Zoolander*? If they're not going to keep that face on when they leave the bathroom, what exactly does the exercise gain them? If it's just for fun, then, hey, I'm all for it.

When I say marriage sucks, I don't mean it *sucks,* so much as I don't really know if it sucks or doesn't. I've heard good and bad. My feelings about marriage are mixed, or should I say mixed-up. My parents were split before I even knew what a split was. So, while I'm speaking with authority, I have no experience with marriage or married parents, to say nothing of marital bliss.

My first memory of the male/female dynamic would be enough exposure to hold me through several years of high school.

When I was about eight years old, Pete, my neighbor from down the street, used to lurk outside my house for hours on end. Sometimes I'd come out and play. Sometimes not. He was relentless in his pursuits, and with me . . . persistence often pays off.

One day, when I was picking flowers from my neighbor's garden to make a bouquet for my mom, Pete followed me for half an hour without saying a single word. And I ignored him.

When I started to go back to my house, he finally spoke up and asked what I was doing later. I told him I was going out to dinner with my dad. He asked if he could come. I said okay.

On our way to Santo Pietro's we were in the backseat of my dad's Camaro. My dad's girlfriend, Sandra, was in the front seat with her long blond hair and overgrown, feathered bangs, and all I could think about was the twisty garlic knots that we'd have at the restaurant. I didn't see my dad very often. I think it'd be safe to say the garlic knots were more familiar to me than my dad.

So there we were . . . me, dreaming of bread, Pete trying to get my attention. And the whole car ride I was trying to touch my tongue to my nose.

"I'll show you mine if you show me yours," he said. I shrugged and stuck my tongue out at him.

"You don't want to?" he asked.

"I just showed you!" I said, sticking it out again, this time bulging my eyes out at the same time.

"Not that," he said. And then he looked down and yanked at his zipper.

"I don't think so," I replied, wondering how much longer to Santo Pietro's.

"I'll show you mine anyway?" he offered.

"Okay," I said, looking out the window, watching my dad navigate the twists and turns of the canyon.

Without a second thought, Pete unzipped his fly and pulled out his johnson, not even bothering to unbutton the top button. He just pulled it through. It was thin. It looked like a misplaced pinkie.

But more important, my tongue was now only a teensy weensy bit away from my nose. I gave it one last try, curling it upward, stretching it, reaching . . .

Then BOOM. From up front, a thunderclap shook the car in the form of my dad yelling. I don't remember what he said as he caught Pete in the rearview mirror, his penis on casual display as though it were a Peking duck hanging in the window of a Chinese restaurant, but I know the sheer force of it practically blasted me out of my seat. To this day, the mere sight of a penis makes my ears hurt a little.

My dad turned the car around immediately and took Pete home, and then he took me home. No garlic knots. I was devastated.

• • •

Brady

And then he comes. The jerk-off that is about to claim the seat next to mine. My aisle seat. No chance of there being *two* beautiful women on this plane. Not with my luck. Luck being a relative term, because lately I haven't had any. I'm the Siegfried and Roy of luck. Not in the smash-hit-show-on-the-Strip-for-fifteen-years-running sense, but rather in the this-thing-that-supposedly-loved-me-is-dragging-me-around-by-my-jugular-like-a-rag-doll-and-fighting-off-efforts-by-stagehands-to-rescue-me sense.

I look in the mirror and I know I'm not in the top 1 percent. But definitely top 10 percent. Or maybe 20. Certainly no worse than 30. Anyway, I clean up nice. I'm a good enough height that I don't automatically get ruled out for dates on that alone. In some cases, it may have even been the *only* attraction, which is not to say I'm super tall—luckily, I'm just tall enough. It's like that sign in front of the dangerous rides at the amusement park: You must be *this* tall to get on this girl.

Some girl once told me that I have a cute smile. But there was a time immediately after the Rolling Stones' *Tattoo You* came out when I thought it could have been made better with the addition of a diamond in my front tooth, à la Mick Jagger.

I have what has clinically been described as "dating disorder," characterized by a series of medium- to long-term relationships, suffering from sore tempers, abraded vocal cords, and the occasional fractured heart.

First there's Sarah, a particularly severe case. But we'll get to her later. She was only the most *recent* in a series of troubling episodes.

My mom says it's temporary, but looking at her and my dad, I sometimes think my romantic problems are congenital.

Their idea of a good time is finding the thousand ways they can spend entire evenings in separate rooms without saying a single word to each other—though the house I grew up in had exactly five rooms spread across 1,400 square feet. My dad says it's because I haven't met the right girl yet, but sometimes I think maybe I've met her five times already but ended up staring at her friend all night and asking *her* out, the one who would eventually steal eighty dollars out of my wallet to pay for a bikini wax, which I never got to see.

It's not all my fault, though. I've had a substantial selection of the crazy and the cruel. There was Jill Perczyk, who broke up with me on New Year's Day and then called me three weeks later to ask how much the DVD player I bought her for Christmas was, because she couldn't determine a fair price to ask on Craigslist.

There was Courtney Goodkin, who scolded me good-naturedly about paying more attention to my dog than I paid to her, *then* revealed her true nature by leaving a twenty-four-ounce bar of dark baking chocolate in her purse by my dog's bed one night—a gift he eagerly consumed. A sleepless thirty hours and five hundred dollars in vet bills later, Courtney was but a bittersweet memory.

And then there was Wendy Richtor, whose name couldn't have been more fitting. If a devastating earthquake measures an eight on the Richter scale, the Wendy earthquake of '92 registered a twelve. She was beautiful. She had long, wavy strawberry-blond hair and milky-white skin. Her long, willowy arms were like stretched-out vanilla taffy, and to be lost in them was better than any sugar high I'd ever experienced.

I met her at a Pearl Jam concert, which made me feel like it was destiny. I loved Pearl Jam and she loved Pearl Jam, and I loved her and she loved me. It was perfect. Like Eddie Vedder brought us together. Eddie sang the words I wished I could tell the girl I thought I'd never meet. And there she was . . . singing along to every word. And it's not that Pearl Jam was any more amazing than anyone else. I think we just liked who *we* were when they were who *they* were. If I could stop time at my last moment of purity and innocence, it would be right then.

Wendy warmed my heart, earned my trust, touched my soul, and then touched me in a lot of other places. And right after we'd slept together for the very first time she looked up at me with her chocolate-brown, trustworthy doe eyes and said, "I've got herpes. I thought you should know."

"I guess this is me," the interloper says, and I nod as he sits himself down and gets situated. "I'm Marc."

"Brady." We shake hands. His hands look like oversize pancakes. Did I mention I also hate germs?

Now I want to wash my hands. I'm not obsessive-compulsive, and I don't mean to come off sounding like a wuss, but there's like zero air pressure in here, and the air is all recycled. It's basically a germ factory, and I can't afford to be sick when I get home. Not because I have anything important going on. In fact, that's just it. Nothing's going on, and I've got to *get* some things going on. God, I want to wash my hands. We haven't even backed away from the gate, and already the bathroom thing is coming into play. I'll just suck it up and wait.

• ● •

Heaven

I'm not a list-maker. I'm not overly organized. I'm not what some people would call "anal retentive." And I'm definitely not the kind of person who makes air quotes when she says "anal retentive." That said, I've made two lists in my life that give a little insight into who I am. Not much, but a little.

One list is the "People I Hate" list. The other is the "People Who Are Not Invited to My Funeral" list. I used to update and revise the "People I Hate" list regularly, but truth be told, it hasn't been updated in years. It's been so long I don't even know where it is or who was on it. Except for G. E. Smith. I know he was definitely on it. So I can safely say it hasn't been updated since G. E. Smith was part of the *Saturday Night Live* band. I don't know him personally, in case you were wondering. I just always hated the way he mugged at the camera like a skeleton in heat.

The whole funeral thing isn't as morbid as it sounds. I don't have a disease or a death wish. In fact, I plan on living a very long life. It's just that in the event some freak accident happens, I want to be prepared. And I want to make sure certain people don't show up and pretend they were my friends and act all sad and so forth. I have to assume I'll have a bird's-eye view of the whole thing, and watching people I dislike feigning sadness at their loss would just bug the hell out of me. I want to be able to enjoy my own funeral. I think I deserve at least that.

Life doesn't always work out the way you think it will—sometimes you walk into the restaurant thinking salad, and end up with nachos and a greasy Reuben. I went to Emerson College. I double-majored in economics and political science. After graduating with a BS degree, I got a job with one of the top PR firms in New York, which specializes in entertainment.

What public relations and economics/poli-sci have to do with one another is absolutely nothing, but during my last semester I got rejected for an internship at the governor's office, and ended up interning at the PR firm. They loved me there and offered me a job at graduation. A job I gladly took. Within three years I was dealing with all their major clients. Within four years I was making six figures and living in a kick-ass apartment with rooftop access.

And as I prepped myself for a major book signing with one of our clients—Tommy Lee of Mötley Crüe—I had every reason to believe I was one more "attagirl" away from being made a partner.

So there I was. Twenty-five years old. Soon-to-be-married almost PR mogul.

• • •

Brady

As it turns out, Marc and I both flew out for the South by Southwest Music Conference. This is the one place where everybody who's nobody in the business goes to realize just how small we really are next to the true luminaries and visionaries, who seem to be stacked like cordwood about the place. And this is an indie conference. It's not like the Rolling Stones are there performing. Still, it's the people who rule *my* world and I always come away feeling like a peasant, wishing I had more than my slop bucket to peddle.

"Leaving a day early, huh?" he asks.

"Yeah."

"First time at South by Southwest?"

"I've been every year since they started," I admit.

"Cool, man. See anything good?" This is the exact conversation that I do not want to be having with a total stranger. Especially a stranger that looks almost identical to me. Thirty-something, hair slightly thinning although neither of us has admitted it yet, and dressed like a teenager. Band T-shirt, ugly-yet-cool button-up shirt over it, Diesel jeans, and sneakers.

"Couple good shows," I say. "Mostly letdowns."

"I hear ya." I desperately want to get out of this conversation by putting on my headset and becoming one with my trusty iPod. "MyPod," as I call it. I don't want to talk to Marc about bad-joke bands with one great song, who all suck live but get good press from assholes who don't know shit about music but think they're supposed to like it. No, that is not what I want to talk about. I don't want to talk at all, in fact.

So here we do the classic dance of not wanting to be murdered in your sleep by an irate seatmate but not wanting to be *too* friendly so you can't zone out and ignore them for most of the trip. "Wasn't Cat Power amazing?" he asks. Here it goes. "I saw Liz Phair at the Cat Power show. She was standing in front of me in the tightest jeans you've ever seen. All of a sudden she feels herself up. I swear to God, dude. It was unreal. Like I'd willed her hand to grab her own ass. It was truly a beautiful thing."

I just don't feel much like dancing. I pull out my iPod, pop the headphones on my ears, take a quick glance back at the hot chick, and settle in for the ride. And then . . . Marc pulls out his iPod.

Right then I take a good look around the plane and start to freak out. Everyone else on the plane looks just like me. Except the hot chick. The closest thing to compare it to would be a complete and utter Malkovich moment. The entire plane is filled with twenty-eight– to thirty–something guys who undoubtedly fancy themselves the lead characters in a Nick Hornby novel.

They all look the same, dress the same, talk the same. They all have their iPods on and *Q Magazine* in their hands. And worse—I know most of them or know who they are or know someone who knows them. They probably all think they have a chance with the hot chick, too.

Suddenly I get this vision of the entire plane full of geeks re-enacting the scene from *Say Anything,* except instead of boom boxes they're holding iPods over their heads à la John Cusack, blaring "In Your Eyes" in an earnest attempt to win her heart.

This actually makes me laugh out loud until I look into my bag and cringe when I realize that I too have a copy of *Q Magazine* and the latest Nick Hornby book. Fuck me, I think. If I could shred and burn them with my mind, I would.

I decide to do the crossword puzzle instead. That will surely make me feel superior. Who am I kidding? I'm just another overgrown indie-rock kid, fighting the good fight against the corporate behemoths of radio. At what point should college radio no longer matter? Is there a cutoff? How many years, post-college, do I get to cultivate the whole music snob thing? I don't want to be thinking about this shit. This is all Marc's fault. And worse, now I have to pee.

• • •

Heaven

I worked at Schiffman Morton PR. Affectionately known as S&M PR, it's one of the top public relations firms in New York. Greg Schiffman and Lisa Morton started the firm two years before I came on board and have an amazing array of A-list clients. You could look at them in one of two ways: as scrappy, brilliant, driven entrepreneurs who cut their own path in a tough business, or as conniving, backstabbing frauds whose ticket to success was Lisa's dad's position as senior VP of corporate affairs at Chase. As far as I was concerned, the jury was still out.

Greg put me in charge of the *Tommyland* book signing because he knew I had a borderline obsessive affinity for music. And because he had walked in on some interns the day they watched the Pam and Tommy sex tape in the office, and Greg didn't want to be in the same room as a man he'd seen honk a boat horn with his penis. I, however, was excited about the prospect.

I got to Astor Place and Lafayette and was struck by the proximity of two different Starbucks. I wondered if I stood at the exact midpoint between the two, would I be sucked into a coffee vortex and emerge a superhero . . . Caffeine Queen—able to wage at least six different arguments simultaneously, stay awake for weeks at a time, and strike down foes with the sheer force of my pee.

I could tell the book was going to be a grand slam when I could barely squeeze past the groupies and fans lined up around the block. Girls in Mötley Crüe baby-doll T-shirts that barely covered their breasts, and guys with almost forgivable mullets. Almost.

I walked into the Barnes & Noble and saw the table set up.

But there was a pink tablecloth. Pink streamers. Stacks of books, sheathed in pink. Pink ribbons *everywhere.* What was up with the pink? Tommy Lee *dated* the singer Pink, but working *that* angle seemed like a stretch.

As I stepped closer, I noticed that the pink ribbons were actually the single-fold Breast Cancer Awareness ribbons, and with each step I took toward the table I found it harder to swallow and got that panicked feeling in my gut—the same feeling I got when I was caught stealing bubble-gum-flavor Bonne Bell lip balm from Rite Aid when I was eleven years old.

The big pink 45-by-30-inch sign read: *Farewell My Breasts.* Unless Tommy was giving up on women with fake double-Ds, there had been a huge mistake.

After running around frantically for what seemed like an hour (but was really only three minutes), I found the woman I dealt with on the phone, Jeannie Sayer. She stood in black high-waisted trousers, which left only about two inches for her blouse. Her hair was salt-and-pepper, and her whole face came to a point, like a bird beak.

"Hi, Jeannie, I'm Heaven," I said in a saccharine-sweet voice to hide my panic. "We spoke about the *Tommyland* signing?"

"Right," she chirped. "We're looking forward to it! He seems like a real pip!" she said with a knowing glance. "Did you want to take a look around before the big day next month?"

The words "next month" were like an air horn going off in my ear. They echoed about seven times before I was able to recover. "No," I said, sucking the breath in through my gritted teeth. "The big day is *today.* In one hour, in fact."

Jeannie pulled out her Palm Pilot and then squiggled up her face when she realized they'd made a mistake.

"Fuck," I said. Jeannie winced more at my cussing than at the mistake, it seemed.

"Someone must have made a mistake. I guess . . . oh gosh . . . I must have made a mistake. *Farewell My Breasts* is next month," she said, meekly adding, "One woman's struggle with breast cancer."

I took a few deep breaths as I looked at the display. "I understand scheduling snafus. I do," I said. "And there may come a time in Tommy Lee's life when he struggles with breast cancer and writes a memoir about his brave journey. And when that book comes out, I'll be happy to set up a book signing here. But the book Mr. Lee has just written is about sex and drugs and the underbelly of rock and roll. And the hearty yet satisfying soup that you get when you blend the three together. There are two hundred people lined up outside to get *that* book signed. So if you could get the copies we ordered on or around this table in oh . . . say . . . the next twenty minutes . . ." But her darting eyes told me there was a huge problem.

"There's a small problem," she said. "When we order large quantities for book signings we have them delivered in time for the event. It's a matter of storage." She looked out the window at the gathering leather horde. "I *wondered* why the breast cancer crowd looked so . . . scruffy."

I wanted to scream. But I couldn't—because at that moment I needed heavy metal paraphernalia and two hundred *Tommyland* books.

"Here it is . . ." she said. "This is what confused me. Greg Schiffman sent me an e-mail that mentioned the reading, dating it next month. See?" She showed me a printout of Greg's e-mail, and my eyes grew wide as I saw it in black and white. The wrong month. So Greg screwed up *and* she screwed up. But none of that mattered right then.

"Where's the PA? Do you have a PA system?" I asked. She pointed to the front of the store. And the next thing I knew, I was standing on top of the front counter with the mic in my hand. "Attention, *all* personnel: Report immediately to the *Farewell My Breasts* display."

I marched over to the display in full drill-sergeant mode and saw the various employees gathered before me. About fifteen of them. All looking bored and annoyed.

"Hi, everybody. I'm Heaven Albright," I said in as sweet a tone as I could muster.

"Hi, Heaven," one or two of them said distractedly, like an unenthusiastic reply at an AA meeting.

"There has been a *really* big misunderstanding and I need you guys to take these books and put them somewhere safe." Now I seemed to have earned at least a glare from the majority of the group. "These are for next month. Today you've got Tommy Lee coming. I need all of these pink ribbons gone and . . . is there anything else we can put up?"

"We have some black garland left over from Halloween," offered a malnourished goth girl with a safety pin poking lewdly out of her eyebrow.

"Perfect. I'll be back in twenty minutes. When I get back I want this place to look like a headbangers' ball."

I bolted out the door and called Greg from the cab. I told him to send the fifty copies we had at the office over with an intern. I stopped at Borders and bought up all seventeen copies they had, then went to Tower Records and bought up all of their copies. I had Karen, my assistant, doing the same. By the time Tommy Lee sat his leather-clad self down . . . there were two hundred copies of *Tommyland* beside him, Mötley Crüe posters behind him, and an extra hot Starbucks latte in my hand, which his assistant requested ahead of time.

"This is for you," I said, handing him the Starbucks cup. His tattooed hand took the cup from my inkless hand, and he smiled at me. I watched as he took his first sip.

"Extra hot," he said with a nod of approval. And even though I knew he was talking about the coffee, I couldn't help but hope that he was referring to me.

I got back to the office, and as soon as I walked in, Lisa and Greg stopped talking. If I were the paranoid type, I'd have thought the hasty hush meant they were talking about me . . . but I'm not. So, as soon as Lisa walked out of Greg's office, I took it as my cue to go in and collect my praise. Greg saw me walking toward him and got this weird expression on his face. He barely looked at me. He awkwardly turned in to his desk, banged his knee, and tried to cover it up. Finally he looked at me.

"Anything you'd like to tell me about today?" he asked.

"Ugh!" I said. "It was a total cluster-fuck. They had the months confused and set it up for another book. But it turned out great, and they sold every copy."

"I didn't hear it was great. Tommy's assistant was there a half hour before and said the whole place was in a panic."

"It was nuts. They had only seven copies in the store and zero decorations, but I got the books in time—"

"I *sent* you the fifty copies," he barked.

"Fifty wasn't enough. I had to run out and buy another hundred and fifty."

"One hundred fifty hardcover books at full retail? And how'd you pay for them?"

"I charged them." What the hell? I had just saved the day! Why was he giving me attitude?

"On your corporate card?"

"Yes," I said. "Greg, what's the problem? We were twenty minutes away from a complete train wreck, and I got us out of it in record time. I still haven't caught my breath."

"Well, if you'd set it up properly, that wouldn't have happened."

"I did!" I defended. "This wasn't my mistake. The manager didn't even know what day it was."

"Heaven, we can't have this type of thing going on. Not at your level."

"What thing? Me saving *your* ass? You sent—"

"My ass wasn't saved. My ass was pretty much chewed off by Tommy's assistant. I'll be surprised if he ever works with us again." Greg looked out the window and clenched his teeth. Then he looked at me again. "I'm afraid there's no longer a role for you at Schiffman Morton."

I was stunned. "Is this a joke?"

"No," he said.

My heart was pounding. This couldn't be real. I looked at

him, waiting for the punch line. Nothing. He couldn't even look me in the eye. He was serious.

"Fine. I've worked my *ass* off for you every single day—including today . . . but fine—it's your name on the door, Greg." I started to walk out, but stopped short at the door. "What kind of severance package are you giving me?" I turned and asked.

"Severance packages are for people who are laid off. You are being fired for *cause*."

"What cause?"

"Gross misconduct."

"Misconduct of *what*?"

"Abuse of corporate funds. However, due to your previous good service, I'm not going to press charges."

"Press *charges*?" Was he insane?

"For the books you charged. I'll let it slide."

"How generous of you," I seethed. "Jesus, Greg!" and I started to storm out. "Press charges. What an ass," I said just loud enough for him to hear.

"Heaven?" he called out.

"What?" I said as I turned back.

"I hope there are no hard feelings."

"You've got to be kidding me," I said.

"I'm not," he said. I started on my way again, but he cleared his throat. "And I'll need you to surrender your corporate card. Now."

• • •

Brady

Sitting on a plane doesn't leave too many options for activity, so I start thinking about things that I'd blocked out for the week of the conference. Like the fact that Sarah's moving out. Well, that's not true. I'm moving out of the apartment, but Sarah is moving out of my life. Sarah didn't want to break up and refused to move out, so I'm the one who's going. It's like that *Seinfeld* where George was trying to break up with the girl and she just wouldn't let him. Only my efforts didn't end in half an hour, there was no laugh track, and I'm now being forced to give up the rent-controlled pad I've been in for seven years and move into a new apartment. The place that was mine before she got there, and was supposed to be mine long after she left. As they always do. Which is a real fucking drag. Losing the rent control . . . not Sarah.

You might ask how I can possibly give up rent control and to that I say: You haven't met Sarah.

Marc points out what he's listening to on his iPod. Ted Leo and the Pharmacists. This snaps me out of my brief escape from this plane ride from hell. I do not want to be this guy. I am nothing like this guy. But that Ted Leo album is fucking brilliant. *Fuck.*

Actions need to be taken. Number one on my list—new headphones. I'll get a big pair of black Sony Noise Canceling Headphones. That way, nobody will know it's an iPod I'm listening to. That white cord is a dead giveaway. Well, not anymore. I'm going to fix that fast. I am not going to be one of the pod people, or iPod people, as it were. At least as far as *they* know. Number two . . .

I just need to rethink everything. Like, why had I even bothered to go to SXSW in the first place? Did I go to discover Cat Power? To discover Liz Phair's ass? Actually, that I wouldn't have minded. But the rest? It's all bullshit. I went because everyone else was going. I went to see who had the best parties. I went to hang out with the same people I hung out with every other night in New York, but it would be different because we'd be in Austin, Texas. That changed everything.

Post 9/11, it's pretty common for me to size up the plane I'm on, just in case any terrorists might be onboard and wanting to start some shit. Usually I look around and pick out my wingman and a few backups. I can tell who would be able to throw down if need be. This plane is a lost cause, though. I am totally on my own. What are these indie-rock geeks going to do if the shit hits the fan? Strike up a conversation with one of them about Nusrat Fateh Ali Khan and then bore him to death? Fuck it. If it goes down, I guess I'll be the one. More important . . . if the plane goes down, who's gonna review the new Super Furry Animals CD?

"I saw Joe Levy when I was boarding," Marc says. So? "I asked him for an autograph." Is Joe Levy a fucking celebrity now? The scary thing is, he *is*. This Horshack-looking motherfucker has been on every single VH1 *Behind the Music* in the last five years. Just because he works at *Rolling Stone*, we get to watch him opine about Vince Neil killing Razzle and the gut-wrenching reuniting of Leif Garrett and the crippled guy. Or did the baby drown at Vince's house? No, Vince lost his baby to an illness, and somebody else's baby drowned at Tommy Lee's house. But Joe Levy has an opinion on each of these matters for sure. I make a mental note to keep my kids away from any and all members of Mötley Crüe. If I have kids.

The flight attendant walks over to me and leans in with a plastered-on smile.

"Did you need something, sir?"

"No." Did I mention I also hate being called sir? Can't she see my Mudhoney T-shirt? I am so not a "sir."

"Your call button is pressed."

"Sorry. Must have been an accident," I say apologetically. She turns it off. She hates me. As she walks away Marc puts up his hand to high-five. "What?"

"Bad skin, but I'd do her."

"I'm sure she'd appreciate you overlooking her acne."

My iPod goes back on. And remains on. I glance back at the hot chick. She knows she has it going on. Why am I even feeding her ego? Because she's there. And I'm a guy. Period.

I'm sure Marc isn't a bad guy. He's probably a lot like most of the guys I hang out with. He *is* most of the guys I hang out with. But for some reason, for the rest of my flight I hate Marc with all of my being. Any other day I'd have made nice, nodded yes, and drunk way too much Grey Goose with the schmuck. But not today. I am not only being confronted with the fact that I am absolutely not unique in any way whatsoever, I am disgusted by my entire existence. Who cares what shows I've been to? What electronic gadgets I have? How big my record collection is? If I've read the book before anyone else? As I think all of these things, I turn the page of my in-flight magazine and see an ad for a new gadget. A Game Boy Advance SP. And all I can think is, God damn, I want that fucking thing. So much for enlightenment.

Sitting in the cab on my way home from the airport, I feel a kink in my pocket. I reach my hand in and realize it's a few crumpled-up business cards. Some of the contacts I made at the convention. A life shrunk down to a 2-by-3½-inch rectangle of cardstock. I picked up several of these over the past few days, all of which will make their way to the stack of cards I already have on my desk at home. A sad, disheveled little pile of lives whose paths I will never cross again, because I will probably never take the initiative to enter the contact info into my PDA. I know this drill. I've got the stacks of cards to prove it. In nearly every case, the person's contact information outlives the relationship.

I don't know if I don't like throwing them away because this represents an actual person, or if it's because I just hold on to things longer than I should in general. But the end result is me on some Sunday, or at the beginning of a new year, going through them wondering, Who was X? Who was Y? What is Alberon Sound Concepts? Did I do business with Foam-All Carpet Cleaning at one time in my life? And what made me think the need for carpet cleaning would be so urgent at some point that I'd need their contact information by my side every waking moment?

The long-ago, faraway dream of the PDA was for it to be the one family room of my life, or maybe the kitchen—the one place where everyone came together—where we could find anyone with a few keywords or fragments of names. It inherited the mantle of touchstone from a little address book with Alice in Chains and Def Leppard stickers on the cover, which was literally disintegrating before my eyes. The contact information there was like a dwindling population of survivors on a raft, moving closer to the edge, a few disappearing each night or with each big wave—the last few finally leaping to safety into my first . . . Rolodex. Where half now sit, neglected, starving for attention. Totally isolated from their brethren on the PDA.

In truth, the move to the PDA served only to highlight the many dead ends I've come up against in my life. I spent the better part of two weeks after I got it, hour upon hour, pondering who should make the cut. I scanned the names of ex-girlfriends, ex-coworkers, and even ex-family. Well, maybe not *ex,* but gone. Like Uncle Stu. Insurance adjuster, husband, father, part-time genius.

Stu Gilbert was my favorite uncle. He was sort of a loner, so I didn't get to spend that much time with him—but whenever I did, it became an event. Once when I was a kid, we went out for a family dinner at the Wo Hop Chinese restaurant down in Chinatown. I couldn't quite master the chopsticks and was getting frustrated. Uncle Stu took the chopsticks out of their paper housing, folded the paper into a thick square, placed it between the two chopsticks, and wrapped a rubber band around that spot. The result was an easy-to-use all-in-one pair of chopsticks that didn't require balance or hand coordination—and hero worship.

Another time, when I was at Uncle Stu's house, he took me into his basement bathroom. I can see it now, with the gold-flocking wallpaper—and smell it now, redolent of the urine from a thousand near misses.

"Go ahead. Change the toilet paper roll," he said.

"But it's not empty," I said.

"I know," he said like a wizened Samurai master.

I removed it carefully, slid a new roll of paper on the holder, then compressed the ends of the holder between my thumb and index finger and prepared for the pinch. You know the pinch. Virtually impossible to avoid when you replace a roll of toilet paper, no matter how quick and catlike your release.

"Ha!" he said, seeming to relish my pain. "Now try with *this*." And he produced a holder of similar size but perforated with holes, stained with streaks of glue, and stuck through with a bent coat hanger as if it were a shish kebab.

I looked at it, then at him, wondering how or whether it worked. He took it from me, squeezed part of the coat hanger, deftly slipped on a new roll, and popped the whole contraption into the brackets with ease. I didn't get it. But this would turn out to be the Cushion Spring Pinch-Proof toilet-paper roll holder.

He was well on his way to earning his patent and approached a large manufacturer of toilet-paper roll holders about mass-marketing his innovation. Apparently the idea was a little too revolutionary. And rather than watching it undercut sales from their phenomenally successful finger-pinching models, they preferred to simply buy him out and keep his brainchild from ever seeing the light of day. No matter. He got a chunk of change and moved on to his next inspiration.

And such was the bond between us that five weeks after he died I received a check for thirty thousand dollars and a handwritten note: "Seed money for that scatterbrained music thing you've been talking about. Love, Uncle Stu."

So removing Stu from my PDA was unthinkable. Though by all counts, there's not much chance of reaching him at any of the numbers I have for him.

But many lesser personalities remain with much less justification. It's not really even that hard to delete people, but I just can't bring myself to do it. Who knows when one of these people might prove pivotal? Who knows when some neighbor's dog will barf up a shoe and I'll have a desperate need to reach out to Foam-All? So now I stare at the SXSW contacts, debating their entry into my Contact Hall of Fame. Some aggravate me. They only suggest to my paranoia that everyone else at the conference is racing along the road to success while I'm stuck in the starting blocks, having forgotten my running shoes. I'm half tempted to chuck the entire lot. I guess what the exercise has taught me is that people come and go. Maybe that's all right.

So I begin to look through these cards. And already I've forgotten who at least a third of them were. Someone once said, People come into your life for a reason, a season, or a lifetime. They forgot one other option: Some people come only to give us their contact information, let us know that we really need to get together sometime, and why don't we give them a call?

• • •

Heaven

I spent my first week after being fired getting reacquainted with the soap operas that I watched in college. The second week I vowed to go to the gym every day, but tapered off after day one. The third week I did a budget for myself and realized that I'd already been living above my means and that I needed a new job. Like, yesterday.

So now I'm a waitress. I work at Temple, which is a French-Vietnamese fusion restaurant, and it's extremely hip. I'm not even sure why they hired me, because I had zero waitressing experience, but I've been here for two months and I'm getting the hang of it. Mostly. The money's decent, but my bosses are assholes, and the clients aren't much better. I've served Demi and Ashton, Mayor Bloomberg, and Monica Lewinsky. I should probably clarify that the latter two were not at the same table. I should also clarify that the names I've singled out are not the assholes I spoke of. In fact, all four were quite polite and good tippers. But on average, people seem to think you are their servant. Granted, you are. But they also must think it's okay to treat their servants like shit. The jerks I serve pale in comparison to the jerks I work for. I work for a white guy named Bruce who thinks he's Asian, and a French guy named Jean Paul who thinks he's Steve McQueen.

Bruce will use any opportunity to yell at us, and he'll always make sure it's in front of customers and the rest of the staff. Jean Paul . . . for the most part, he just smokes cigarettes and sits on his Triumph 650cc, which is prominently parked outside our restaurant at all times. It's never good to interrupt his "cigaritual," as I like to call it. Jean Paul takes out a cigarette, packs it on his hand, then places it behind his left ear, walks outside, and cases his motorcycle as if he's never seen it before. Then he sort of leans on it as he pulls the cigarette out from behind his ear and lights up. He always closes his eyes for his first inhale and always exhales through his nose.

The restaurant has all these little quirks, you might call them. I really shouldn't be talking about them this way. If they found out, I'd be fired. But fuck it. I'm okay with that.

Marco is wearing an eye patch today. Marco is a busboy at the restaurant. He's been in America for only six months and seems to get into a lot of trouble. He's absolutely my favorite busboy. He's about twenty-four years old, with an overgrown bowl haircut. When he first showed up at work he had hair down to his ass, and Jean Paul told him he had to cut it if he wanted the job. So he did, but he hasn't cut it since. Marco is from Albania and he likes to drink. A lot.

A few weeks ago he comes into work all smiles and tells everybody about a woman he met over the weekend at some discothèque in his neighborhood. The fact that he was still using the word *discothèque* in the twenty-first century we'll leave alone.

"She was beautiful. And she said she wanted to make sex with me. So I took her home and she gived me a blow job." His English could still use a little work, but he spends every Sunday in English classes, and he's getting better. "And then . . . when I took off her underpants . . . she has a penis!" he says, still smiling and laughing at the audacity. We're all mortified and half wondering if he just saw *The Crying Game* for the first time. But no. Sadly, for Marco, he missed that one.

"What did you do?" we all ask simultaneously.

"What do you think I did? I told her to go home!" None of us laughed at him. I mean, *all* of us laughed at him, but we felt so bad for him that it wasn't really malicious laughter. And he's so unaware that he didn't really get that this isn't the kind of story you tell everyone at work on Monday morning. Or any morning, for that matter. You tell your best friend. Maybe. But now everyone knows. God bless him, he's not ashamed. As far as he's concerned, it's just another experience of all that America has to offer.

"What's up with the eye patch?" I ask.

"I lost it."

"What do you mean, you lost it?"

"I had a car accident, and it broke."

"What do you mean, it broke?"

"It broke!" he says, like an eye "breaking" is a common occurrence.

"Your eye?"

"It broke. It came out and got broke into a million pieces." I look at him, but before I can inquire further, a customer waves me over. Later, I found out that Marco has a glass eye. Or *had* a glass eye. When his face hit the dashboard of the car, his eye popped out and it broke. Apparently they're like seven thousand dollars and he can't afford a new one. Apparently *I'm* the only one who didn't know he had a glass eye, as well. I heard that once he asked another waiter to hold it, and the other guy took it—not knowing what it was—and then freaked out. I never got the privilege of seeing that. I guess a customer once did, though, and threw up. Which made another customer throw up, and made the majority of the restaurant *want* to throw up. They had to comp everyone who saw. Jean Paul and Bruce sat Marco down and told him if he ever took out his eye again he'd be fired. This all went down before I got hired. I always miss all the fun.

So to help Marco's cause, I take an empty Opus One wine magnum and place a sign on it. It says "Glass Eye for the Bus Guy." The "Queer Eye" reference is almost mean, considering the blow job, but it's a tip jar, and I place it prominently on the bar. If helping Marco get a new eye is my mission . . . then I'm gonna do it. Marco is so touched, he sheds a tear out of his one good eye. We hug, and I toss the first dollar into the magnum.

I spit in someone's Caesar salad today. I'm not proud of it. But I promise you . . . the customer was such an asshole, he deserved it. It was a preemptive but prophetic spit. He went on to leave me a five-dollar tip on a bill for one hundred seventy-eight dollars. *And* he complained about me to my manager.

Luckily, it was Jean Paul that he complained to and not Bruce. Jean Paul never cares when people complain. As far as he's concerned, the restaurant is so "in" right now that if someone's not happy, they can just go somewhere else and not take up space here. Anyway, Jean Paul had a cigarette in his hand when the guy called him over. He tells Jean Paul that my service was "poor" and my attitude so disgraceful, he was embarrassed to have brought clients here. I'll admit when I do something wrong, but this guy was on me from the minute he sat down. I did *nothing* to offend or embarrass him.

First, he snaps his fingers when he wants me to come over to the table. When I offer to tell him the specials he rolls his eyes and says, "Fine." Then as I'm telling him and his guests the specials he actually blurts out "Blah, blah, blah," while I'm talking. Stunningly rude. I mean, what is *that*? So, fine, I ignore it.

He was nasty the entire time, and I swallowed it and smiled. Even when he loudly announced that he dated a waitress once, but dumped her because it was embarrassing when people asked her what she did for a living. I chuckled at that. Maybe that was what pissed him off. I've developed the habit of smiling and sometimes even laughing when people go out of their way to be jerks. I find it amusing. Life's too short to get that worked up over nonsense, and when people freak out over virtually *nothing,* I can't help but laugh at them. Probably not the best idea, I know, but it's either that or letting them get to me, and there's way too many of them, so *amused* is what they get, like it or not. In his case *not.*

So I don't feel bad about the spitting. He deserved it. Okay, maybe I feel a little bad, but not that bad. Considering the fact that I know waiters who have wiped people's credit cards in their ass cracks and then handed them back to customers, a little spit doesn't seem so bad. Like everything that happens to us in life, it's all relative, and I try to keep things in perspective.

I feel awful about the spitting. I called my best friend, Sydney, and told her. She gave me a spiel about the karmic ramifications of what I did. She said I had just opened up the floodgates for some really bad juju. Actually, it's not that I feel worse about what I did or that I'm overcome with guilt, really. I guess it's that now I have to live in fear of bad juju. Which is worse. Now I can never eat in a restaurant again. Thanks, Sydney.

• • •

"La-di-da, la-di-da, la la."

—Annie, *Annie Hall*

"I'm not talking to you. Call me!"

—Neil, *The Big Picture*

Brady

I went back to my apartment today. Only just when I was about to turn the key, I remembered it's not my apartment anymore. So I leave, and I'm walking away from what *was* my apartment building, and my cell phone rings. I answer.

"I knew you'd change your mind," Sarah says. I look up and see her standing in the window. Her hair is pulled back in a ponytail, the way I always liked it. That is, back when there were things to like about her. "Less hair . . . more face," I'd always tell her. I wave hello. "I was just about to shower," she says. "Want to wash my back?"

"Hi," I say awkwardly. "Shit, Sarah . . . I'm sorry. I didn't change my mind. I'm tired. I just got off a long, annoying flight. I just came back here out of habit."

"Fuck you, then. I'm changing the locks." She hangs up, slams the window shut, and then flips me off with both middle fingers. I wave good-bye, feeling very, very good about breaking up, and head back to the subway.

Along the way I see an ambulance and a crowd watching as paramedics carefully lift someone onto a gurney. I shake my head in disgust and continue on. I *hate* that. People who slow down to see the crash or stop and stare at other people's misfortunes. It's morbid curiosity and bad karma. Who knows? Maybe someday they'll be carted off as other people watch.

However, there *is* one thing I always do whenever I see the wreckage of a car crash or the wreckage of the relationship I just left behind. I see the flashing lights on an ambulance and immediately start to think about how every moment in that person's life or my life has led up to this moment right now. How your whole life had to be measured out in such a way that you step out in front of the car at that very second. And for the person driving the car to be at that spot at that second. Right now I think about my life and how every single thing I've ever done has gotten me to right here. Walking away from a failed relationship and a cheap apartment.

And for some reason known only to God and the operators of torture chambers the world over, into my head comes "Unchained Melody" by the Righteous Brothers. A song destroyed—along with the art of making pottery—for a generation to come by the movie *Ghost.* A movie I was once forced to watch for the thousandth time by—you guessed it—Sarah. "Oh . . . my love . . . my darling . . . I've hungered . . . for . . . your touch . . ." The next line of the song is about how time goes by so *slowly.* Maybe it wouldn't go by so slowly if you could just . . . finish . . . a . . . fucking . . . sentence.

I think about the first time I fell in love with a girl and a song at the same time. The Beckets' house. They were friends of the family, and they still had a bad shag carpet. I was eleven and Sheryl Becket was thirteen. When I passed her room, she was playing "Cars" by Gary Numan, dancing around her room, singing along. She didn't see me, but I thought she was the most graceful girl in the world. With the most beautiful voice in the world. And I loved the song. Although, truth be told, it wasn't the best showcase for her teenage lyrical chops. Not only did that moment show me the hold that music could have over women . . . it made me want to learn how to drive.

I think about the first time I kissed a girl. Maggie Stanhope. She had a Band-Aid on her chin to cover a zit, and she thought somehow the Band-Aid was less conspicuous. We were thirteen and hanging out at her friend Monica Sellers's house. Maggie took me into Monica's closet and planted one on me. I can still taste her bubble-gum lip gloss. Elvis Costello's "Alison" was playing on Monica's radio. When he sang the words "My aim is true," I thought about what a target her lips made and that I should keep aiming my kisses right there at the bull's-eye. Now

I think about the promise that kiss held—and every other kiss with every other girl I kissed after Maggie—with a similar sense of hope, each one turning out progressively more disastrous.

I think about the first time I got fired from a job. I was washing dishes eleven hours a day. Day after day, in a non–air-conditioned kitchen. My clothes stuck to me. The only thing I was allowed to drink for free was soda water. Not soda. Soda *water.* And my boss would walk around every now and then and take a sip of my soda water to make sure it wasn't actually 7-UP. Every time he took a sip, I'd toss it because I didn't want his germs or God knows what else lurking in his mouth. One day he did a spot check and took a sip. I tossed it. Then, thinking he wouldn't check again for a while, I got a cup of 7-UP. Five minutes later he took a sip, and I was busted. I was so distraught that right after he fired me I ran to Kmart—it was the only place open past nine—and bought the new Tears for Fears album. When I got home, I played "Mad World" over and over again and wallowed in self-pity. I'd become a lonely traveler in a world of broken dreams, and no song seemed a better accompaniment on the journey.

All of my most significant moments somehow involved music. It's like my life was a John Hughes film and somebody had to put together the perfect soundtrack.

My first KISS concert. Which led to my buying an electric guitar. Which led to my starting my first shitty band. Which led to my finding out that girls are impressed by guitar players—even if they play in shitty bands. Which led to a career of helping *other* guitar players with *their* shitty bands. Which led to a 2002 New Year's Eve gig at Roseland and an unwarranted spirit of optimism at the moment a stranger named Sarah ran up to me at midnight and demanded that I kiss her. Which led to my kissing her, which led to my living with her, which led to my finding out what a screaming psychotic banshee she is, which led to my leaving her, which led to . . .

Well. To here. Right here, descending the steps to the subway, after being flipped off outside *her* apartment. A straight linear progression from then to now.

But you can see that it's not my fault. I should really blame KISS. Or John Hughes.

• ● •

Heaven

Last night there was a lunar eclipse. I set my watch alarm, but I've never been good at that, so it didn't go off. Then I was looking at my toilet-seat cover thinking I wanted to get one of those furry carpet covers, and for some reason it came to me . . . the lunar eclipse! I raced to my window, but my window is north facing, and directly north of me is a brick wall about seven feet away.

So I raced outside with a paper plate and a roll of aluminum foil, because those were the items I vaguely remembered from my fourth-grade science project involving lunar eclipses. Or maybe it was solar eclipses? Anyway, I didn't know what to do with them exactly, so I used the plate to sit on, in an effort to buffer the cold concrete, and I rolled the aluminum foil into a telescope. Then I realized that without lenses it wouldn't be good for much, so I turned it into a mini megaphone to bay at the moon.

I stayed up half the night, enchanted by a lunar eclipse I never got to see. The other half of the night I stayed up for a less enchanting reason. Some asshole in my building was screaming "Hello!" at 2 a.m. repeatedly. In the apartment *right next door* to mine. I don't know what the hell *that* was about, but I finally pounded on the wall and screamed back, "Yeah, hello! Can you please shut up now?" He yelled, "Sorry." And then he stayed quiet. Then I couldn't sleep for the next two hours because I started worrying, What if that guy was retarded? He must have been. What if he couldn't help himself . . . and I just told him to shut up. I felt awful. Completely guilty. I couldn't fall back asleep.

• • •

Brady

Last night there was a lunar eclipse. From all the press, you'd have thought a meteor was going to hit us. I looked all night . . . for someone who actually *gave* a damn.

It was my first night in my new place. It echoes. I don't know if it's a guy thing or what, but I had to test the echo from all possible angles of the apartment to see where it was best. All of my furniture is being delivered tomorrow, and then it won't echo anymore. So I had to take advantage of it while I had it.

Some bitch started pounding on the wall like a maniac to get me to shut up before I got to fully experience all possible echoes, but I did get my fair share in. Sorry I woke you and your twelve cats up, lady. Jeez.

It's weird sleeping in the new place. Sarah insists I'll be back, but there's no way in hell that's gonna happen. If I left a rent-controlled apartment just to get away from her, all bets are off that I'll be moving back in. I will not be getting back together with Sarah. I don't want to date anyone, period. This is going to be my time to be single. End of story.

• • •

Heaven

I think I'm suffering from toxic mold poisoning. I've been achy and tired and feeling like shit for months. I know some other people that had the same symptoms, and it turned out they had mold in their homes. My friend Deirdre had to move out of her house because of black mold. She and her boyfriend had been sick for months, and as soon as they moved they got better. They could have done mold removal, but they wanted to move anyway. I'm not moving. If I have toxic mold in my house I'll just have to get it removed. I hope it's not expensive.

I just ordered a mold test kit online for $29.95 from Mr. Mold. After looking it up online, I'm almost positive I have the black mold. This Web site lists all the symptoms. People who have it have at least ten of these symptoms:

1. Respiratory distress, coughing, sneezing
   - I cough, I sneeze.
2. Burning in the throat and lungs
   - Does acid reflux count?
3. Diarrhea, nausea, piercing lower abdominal pains, vomiting
   - I'll go with no on this one, except for that time I ate at San Loco. Never eat at San Loco.
4. Dark urine
   - No, but I do have fluorescent urine when I take my multivitamin.
5. Memory loss, short-term memory, brain fog
   - Definitely.
6. Swollen lymph nodes
   - Not sure where my lymph nodes are.
7. Headaches
   - Yes. Almost everyone I know gives me one.

8. Anxiety/Depression
   - Yes, yes, yes! In fact, I'm getting even more anxious as I go down this list.
9. Ringing in ears
   - Yes! And I thought it was tinnitus from too many loud concerts.
10. Chronic fatigue
    - Yes.
11. Intermittent twitching
    - Not really. I did have an eye twitch that lasted for a week, but my doctor said that was just stress.
12. Nosebleeds
    - No.
13. Night sweats and hot flashes
    - No, but I do get overheated when I eat spicy foods. Indian food makes me sweat like a major-league baseball player in a steroids inquiry.
14. Hair loss
    - Yikes! Every time I wash my hair I lose enough to make a Barbie-doll wig. I go through two bottles of Drano a month to clear up the hair clogs. I should start saving the hair and actually make the wigs. If Mattel ever makes "Cancer Barbie" and sells her in all her bald glory, my wigs will sell like hotcakes. And I can use the money to pay for the mold removal.
15. Weight change
    - Yes. I go up and down daily. I gain five pounds between breakfast and lunch. This is bad. How many yeses do I have now?
16. Infertility
    - Knock on wood, I haven't gotten pregnant. I use condoms. Well, they use condoms. Unless . . . oh, great. For all I know, the condoms could have broken, and I never got pregnant because I'm infertile.
17. Heart attack
    - Not yet.

18. Rash, hives, bloody lesions all over the body
    - Ew! No.
19. Heart palpitations
    - Yes. Right now, in fact.
20. Death in some cases
    - Not yet.

So I have at least ten, possibly eleven of these things. I could be dying right now and not know it. Which brings me back to my point about getting married in eighteen months.

I guess I never really explained that. When I said before that I am engaged, it wasn't exactly the whole truth. I'm not actually engaged. Now before you go off thinking I'm some kind of compulsive liar, I'm not. Because I *am* engaged to be married in eighteen months. I'm just not engaged to anyone in particular.

In eighteen months, I'll be twenty-seven. Twenty-seven is the age at which all of my musical heroes died. Jim Morrison? Dead at twenty-seven. Kurt Cobain? Dead at twenty-seven. Jimi Hendrix? Twenty-seven. Janis Joplin . . . twenty-seven. Coincidence? Maybe. But for some reason, I've always thought I was going to be dead at twenty-seven, too. Unless I got married. Don't ask me why I think this. I just do. It's just something I know in my gut. If I get married my destiny changes, and I'll live a long and happy life. If not—there's always my funeral to look forward to, which you know I'm already making preparations for. But let's not go there. I have every intention of being married within eighteen months. Or dead. Don't get me wrong—I'm not going to settle. I'm not looking for any old schmuck to put a ring on my finger and save me from my disastrous fate. It has to be the right schmuck. And I'm picky as hell. So understandably, this is a very precarious time.

• • •

Brady

I decided to paint one wall in my new place dark blue. It will be an accent wall. A friend of mine has one wall painted red, and it looks pretty cool, and *he* called it an "accent wall." I can't copy the accent wall *and* use the same color, so I'm going blue. Navy. Not really navy, but kind of navy. More midnight blue. Which will make it tempting to put those little plastic glow-in-the-dark stars up, but that would be lame so I'll refrain. Maybe one star. No, no stars.

The building is pretty nice. It's wedged in between a twenty-four-hour Duane Reade pharmacy and a little bakery that always smells like buttery frosting. Can't be mad at that. Unless you're on Atkins, which I'm not. For some reason, my metabolism is pretty good. I guess that's God's trade-off for the mass exodus of my hair, which seems to be relocating to my chest . . . and nose . . . and ears. Christ, even my knuckles and the tops of my toes. In fairness, it's not so much a mass exodus as a gradual but unmistakable departure to warmer climates south.

I've been thinking I need a new career. I've always wanted to be an inventor like Uncle Stu. I'm always coming up with new ideas. Always have. And not pot-high–induced ideas that are remarkably stupid upon coming down. And yes, I've had my fair share of those, too. I'm talking knock-'em-outta-the-ballpark, great fuckin' ideas. Ideas that would make me the millionaire I was born to be. But every time I come up with one, I do one of three things: a) I don't act on it and eventually forget what the idea was; b) I don't act on it and later come to see it invented by some other prick and get pissed off; or c) I store it away in the back of my mind until the day I decide to go for it.

I had the idea for the toilet bowl brush with cleaner in the handle years ago. I let that slide and then one day . . . I'm cruisin' down aisle five, and there's my idea: The Ready Brush. Lysol Fuckers. Same thing happened with packaged foods with built-in Ziploc closures. Used to be—and still is sometimes—once you open some product you bought, it's exposed to air. Then you either have to fold the plastic bag over and put the contents in something else, or say fuck it and just eat the whole thing. Nowadays, nuts, dried fruit, deli products, lettuce in a bag . . . they all come in bags that have the Ziploc option. *That* was also my idea. Come to think of it, there are still products that *really* need it and aren't utilizing it. Like potato chips. Once you open the bag, what then? My Integrated Zippers would be supergenius and save many a person the trouble of eating the whole bag in one sitting. Which could also aid in solving this country's obesity problem.

Point is, I have all these great ideas, and I sit on them and watch other people make fortunes off them. I always say, "Someday . . ." and put it off.

I think that day is here. And though the majority of my aforementioned million-dollar ideas have already been done, I still have a couple grand-fucking-slams.

As for my day job, I am the proud owner of Sleestak Records along with my partner, Phil. We're basically reshaping the music industry along with our very small staff. Which actually consists of Phil and me. My days used to be productive but have devolved into . . . well, let's see. I listen to shitty demos, hoping and praying that *one* of the bands will excite me. I brood. I file e-mails. As if organizing them into categories will somehow make my life better. I call the same people I called the week before on behalf of my bands. I Google celebrities' breasts. There's something about celebrity boobs that's better than regular ones. I go on Hotornot.com and give fat girls good scores to make them feel better about themselves. I drink coffee. I wait for the next big thing to happen. But mostly I check out celebrity boobs.

I walk into the office and Phil is looking at an executable file he downloaded which shows President Bush's head superimposed onto a lingerie-clad model, which then morphs through a series of lingerie-clad bodies and eventually turns into a monkey. All this to the background of "Freedom," a George Michael song.

"Is it wrong that I got a little aroused when I watched that?" he asks.

"Yes. Yes it is."

"I'm just kidding," he says and closes the file. We both know he's not kidding.

"You ever have an idea that you know is gonna make you a millionaire?" I ask, not because I think he has, but because I want him to hear mine.

"Huh?"

"Like an invention," I say. "You ever think of something and think if you just got a patent on it and actually went for it, you'd be set for life?"

"I don't think that much."

"No, you don't, do you?"

"Nah," he says. And this resonates for a second. He's serious. And it breaks my heart because he's so earnest. "I do like to draw, though," he adds.

"Well then, there's that."

"Yeah."

"I'm looking into getting a patent."

"Yeah?" he says. "Cool. What does that mean?"

"Means I own the idea."

"So what's the idea?"

I walk to the door and shut it even though I know nobody is listening to us. I do it for effect. Sometimes I do things like that because, as I've mentioned, my life is like a movie to me. And the songs I hear are, of course, my personal soundtrack. And my character in my movie would have shut the door. So I did, too.

"Cinnamilk," I say tersely.

"Huh?"

"Cinnamilk," I say, just as tersely but louder in case he didn't hear.

"Which is?"

"Exactly like it sounds. You ever eat Cinnamon Toast Crunch cereal when you were a kid?"

"Of course," he says with what appears to be genuine pride.

"What's left in the bowl after you run out of cereal?"

"I pour more cereal."

"Right," I cut in. "But before you do that or after you've poured your second bowl, as it were, you're left with the milk. The sweet cinnamon-laden goodness."

"Yeah, that is good," he says, and I lose him for a minute to his cereal rumination.

"I'm telling you! They have chocolate milk, strawberry milk—*why, I don't know*—but no cinnamon milk. An untapped market—just dying to get out to the masses. And the name—Cinnamilk—rolls off the tongue."

"Cinnamilk," he says, nodding slowly with a curious smile.

"Cinnamilk," I echo.

Phil is killing me. We've worked together for seven years, but the last few months I feel like everything he does is a personal affront. Like right now he's playing video games on his computer, and it's pissing me off. He should be working. Granted, I've played my share of video games, but he does it all day long. I mean, even though we're partners in this label, we started out with my inheritance from my uncle Stu. And we've been steadily losing money for the past three years. So it makes me think he needs to stop playing Pong. My life savings are going the way of the VCR, and he's mocking me by playing. I'm already supposed to be rich.

In addition to believing I was meant to be rich, I also think fame is inevitably in my future. I've always thought this, though there's nothing I'm pursuing to achieve it—except, of course, my inventions. I don't mean that in a lazy, I-deserve-fame-for-no-reason kind of way either. I mean that I am not really creative, nor have I ever been. Yet I know I'll be famous for something.

So much so that whenever I've broken up with someone in the past, my one comforting thought is always, "Boy, will she be sorry when I'm famous." I also temper my behavior at times because of it. Not so much in day-to-day things, but big things. Like I always make certain if I make sex tapes with my girlfriends, that they never leave my house. The tapes, not the women. Christ, I'm not Rick James or anything. And I always record over them to be sure. All to make sure that when fame does come my way, the tapes don't get out. Not that there's anything really deviant on them. There's not. Mostly, just your plain old run-of-the-mill sex stuff. That's not to say I'm a boring lay either. I'm not. I'm quite fun, actually. The point is, I'm protecting my persona, as it were.

"Even though this game is like a hundred years old, I still love it," Phil says.

"It's not a hundred years old, Phil."

Then it hits him. "We should get a Ping-Pong table here."

"Ya think?" I say.

"Totally!"

"We're not living in a dorm anymore."

"Ping-Pong!"

"Phil?"

"Yeah?"

"What do you think I'm about to say?" I ask.

"That I should stop playing video games because it's making your ass itch."

"Very good."

"Brady?" he says.

"Yeah, Phil."

"I think your milk idea really is good."

"Thanks."

"And if you make money with it," he says, "I hope you'll buy us a Ping-Pong table for the office."

"I'm sure you do, Phil."

• • •

Heaven

I got my mold test kit in the mail today. Along with some other guy's mail, which I opened. His name is Brady, and apparently he neglects his grandmother, because she says she never hears from him. She sent him a ten-dollar bill, which I left in the envelope, of course. He also has a psycho ex-girlfriend who sent him his toothbrush back, accompanied by a nasty note. I think the mail might be for my new retarded neighbor.

I open my mold test kit and there's not much to it. It's a petri dish and some sticky honey-like stuff. I think it *is* honey. Weird. Supposedly I leave it out in the open for an hour, then seal and keep it in a dark place for three days. Then I mail it back to the lab, and they'll give me my analysis in ten days to two weeks. For an extra five dollars, they'll rush it.

I pour the honey gunk into the dish and let it sit. It even smells like honey, and it's making me crave something sweet, like a Krispy Kreme. After two minutes I'm desperate for a doughnut, and I'm scouring my entire apartment for loose change because I don't have any cash to buy one. Seventy-three cents. Shit. Hmmm. I remember the ten-spot that Retardo's grandmother sent him. What harm would there be in borrowing it? It's for a good cause.

Downstairs in the deli, the anticipation of the first bite of my tasty glazed doughnut is making my mouth water. I stand there looking at my three Krispy Kremes and large coffee, almost enjoying the moment, but I sense someone else's gaze, which is ruining it. I look up to see some guy waiting in line with an egg-salad sandwich, staring at me and my three doughnuts, and he's making me self-conscious.

"They aren't all for me," I lie with a dismissive wave at the doughnuts. But my fingertip catches the chocolate icing on one of the Bavarian Cream Filled, so I lick the icing off my finger while I read his T-shirt. It says "667 . . . the neighbor of the beast." "Funny shirt," I say. He's got really, *really* blue eyes.

"You have an eyelash," he says.

"Hopefully, I have more than one," I say in an attempt to be clever. But before either of us can enjoy my wit, he reaches up and wipes the eyelash off my face and smiles.

"There," he says. I'm boiling. I'm fuming. I could kill this egg-salad–eating asshole. I don't care *how* blue his eyes are.

"What did you just do?" I ask with all kinds of attitude.

"I wiped off your eyelash," he says with all of the nonchalance of . . . well, of any other day in the life of someone who just wipes an eyelash off someone's face with complete disregard for the consequences. I look around, and I don't see my lash anywhere.

"And where is it?" I ask, knowing full well that he doesn't know.

"It's off your face."

"That was a wish."

He furrows his brow and squints his eyes a little. "Pardon?"

"A wish. You just stole a wish from me."

"I'm sorry."

"I really could have used that wish."

"Really, I'm sorry. I just thought . . ." he stammers. "I don't know. It was stupid, I don't even know you. It was just sitting there on your face and . . . I don't know. I'm sorry."

"Well, you should be," I snap.

"I am. Jesus!" he says, suddenly all *what's your problem?*

"What, are you going to be mad at *me* now? I didn't steal *your* wish."

"I wouldn't care if you did."

"Well, I wouldn't."

"Look, I'm sorry," he says. "Okay? Really." I start to feel bad about going off on him. A little.

"It's okay . . . wish stealer." He laughs. I crack a smile, too, but secretly I am pissed.

"You can have one of mine," he says. "I'll yank one out right now."

"No, that won't count. It has to be a lash that naturally falls out." He gets on his knees and starts looking for my lash.

"Maybe I can find it," he says.

"Just forget it."

"No, maybe it's here somewhere. I'll bet I can find it. Here, look. I've already found a string bean and a Sprite cap. Your lash can't be far behind."

"Okay, that's just gross. Get up."

"No."

"Forget my lash."

"I feel bad," he says as he scours the floor.

"The floor looks a little sticky there. God only knows what you're kneeling in."

"I'm standing up now," he says. He wipes off his knees and comes face-to-face with me, and for the first time I really get a look at him. And he's cute. Kind of. Hard to tell. I can't see that well with my missing eyelash. But he does have those blue eyes. Looks like he has a good body. Not like a bodybuilder, but in shape. Cute smile.

"I'm sorry about your lash," he says. "Really, I am. And I've learned my lesson. I won't ever be so careless with someone else's wish again."

"Good," I say, and I leave without looking back.

• • •

Brady

I met a cute girl today. Or at least she started out cute. Then she opened her mouth and her head all but spun around. Had the nerve to tell me I stole her wish, whatever the hell *that* was about. Talk about high maintenance. And psycho. She had like seventeen doughnuts in her hands. Nice ass, too. It's probably expanding right this second.

I sit on my couch in my otherwise empty apartment and take out my egg-salad sandwich. Just as I'm about to take my first bite, there's a knock at my door.

I open it. To my surprise—and horror—it's her. The crazy doughnut-eating, eyelash-wishing girl from the deli downstairs.

"Hi, I'm your neighbor, and I have some of your mail," she says. Then she realizes it's me. "You? You live here?"

"Yes, I live here."

"You're the *retard*?"

"The what?"

"Nothing."

"So, we're neighbors?" I ask in a please-don't-let-this-be-true kind of way.

"Yeah. So . . . yeah. Here's your mail," she says. "You should pay more attention to your poor grandmother. And if I were you I wouldn't use that toothbrush."

She opened my mail?

"You opened my mail?"

"Kind of."

"Yeah, looks that way." She didn't just open my mail. She tore it open. Wasn't even careful about it. It looks like a dog went at it in search of a Milk-Bone. "That's a federal offense, you know."

"Oh, and I borrowed a tenner," she adds casually.

"What?"

"Your grandmother sent you ten dollars. And I borrowed it because I was famished. But I'll pay you back. Promise."

"I'm sorry, I'm just a little shocked. You opened my mail *and* stole money from it?"

"I didn't steal it, I *borrowed* it. I said I'd give it back, didn't I?" She's got this entitled air, like it's my fault for exposing her to the temptation of the *tenner.*

I look over her shoulder, as if some explanation might be trailing just slightly behind her. "That's just so odd," I say.

"Not really. It's not that odd. If I took it out and peed on it and then gave it back to you, *that* would be odd. I simply borrowed it and will give it back. I can go to the ATM right now if you want."

"It's okay."

"I even have a doughnut left. I'll give you your ten bucks back and a doughnut's worth of interest."

"You can keep your doughnut."

"Fine," she says.

"Fine," I say back.

"And you're welcome for your mail."

And she storms back into her apartment, which happens to be right next door to mine. What a freak!

• • •

Heaven

What a creep! They say no good deed goes unpunished, and it's true. That's what I get for doing him the favor of delivering his mail. A bunch of attitude. Attitude from the jerk that stole my wish, I might add. The wish that very well could have been the most important wish of my life. I could have wished on that lash for the man I'm going to marry, and maybe that was the lash that would have brought him. Now I'll never know. Because of him. Or I could have wished for a root beer fountain in my apartment that would never run dry. He has some nerve getting mad at me.

I notice my petri dish sitting on the table. It's time to close it and hide it under the bed. The directions said to put it in a suitcase under my bed but I'm sure a shoe box will suffice. I'm reminded of "The Princess and the Pea" and get to thinking . . . What kind of a girl is going to feel a pea under her mattress? And furthermore, what kind of a man is going to find a girl who is so distressed by a measly little pea and think, "Now *that* is the woman for me." I think if a man found himself a woman that tossed and turned all night because she had a pea under her mattress, he'd run for the hills. That is some high-maintenance woman right there. I myself can sleep with all kinds of things under me, or around me. Like a remote . . . or a book . . . or some recent magazines. Sometimes it's easier to just leave things rather than move them. I remember one time I had so many things piled up all over my bed there was barely enough room for me to sleep in it. But I did it. Uncomfortably, sure. But I slept. And would have done it again the next night had Sydney not physically removed said items when she came over the next morning to drag me out of bed for coffee. She was mortified by my very few inches of sleeping room. The point is: I am not high maintenance. At least not in the *pea* sense. In fact, not in most senses. Sure, I like my share of attention, but I'm pretty easygoing. For the most part.

Sydney and I go to Starbucks for our daily morning coffee get-together, and she is wearing a beret. This is Sydney's newest attempt to deflect attention from what she perceives as a flat chest—some people have crosses to bear, this is Sydney's.

"What is on your head?" I ask.

"Hair?" she quips.

"Okay, Monica."

"Don't give me that. I think it's cute."

"It's not. Berets don't look good on anyone. They're stupid."

"They are not," she says, indignant. "I'm not letting Monica Lewinsky spoil it for me. Plus, you said you liked her. Didn't you wait on her once?"

"She didn't spoil anything. There was never anything remotely okay about wearing one. They're awful. And yes, I liked her a lot. Very nice girl. And were she my friend back in the day, I wouldn't have let her wear one either."

She slurps her coffee, then stops mid-slurp. "What about Prince?"

"What about him?"

"'Raspberry Beret'? You may recall a certain mega-hit about a certain fruit-colored chapeau?"

"You may recall the lyric? 'A raspberry beret? The kind you find in a secondhand store'? That's because they've been out of style so long that you can't find them in a normal store. And because they are hideous."

"So I'm supposed to believe that the entire country of France is wrong?" she says.

"Oh, don't get me started on the French."

"You're just jealous I can pull it off," she says, turning her face away.

"Sweetie, if anyone could pull it off, I promise it's you. But a beret is not okay. And that even rhymes so you can remember it easier."

"I like it, and I'm wearing it."

"Okay then. All you," I say. She pouts for a minute and then takes the stupid thing off.

"Thank you."

"You're not welcome."

"It's only because I love you. I wouldn't let you walk around with poppy seeds in your teeth. I wouldn't let you walk around in jeans that made you look fat. And I will not let you walk around in a beret. That is my credo. And so it is written."

"And so it shall be done. And so you shall be buying our second round this morning due to all this unnecessary stress I've suffered."

"Fine," I say and go to the counter to order.

When I sit back down with our coffees, Sweet'n Low, and stirrers, I start in on my jerk neighbor and tell her what happened. What the hell kind of name is Brady, anyway? Sydney, of course, asks if he's hot. And no, he is not hot. She asks if he's passable. Again I tell her no. She's asking because if he is, then one of us needs to date him. Even if he was, it certainly wouldn't be me, and I wouldn't let him have her either. We deserve perfect princes. And him? The wish-wrecking neighbor from hell? He should end up with a troll.

"Oh! I didn't tell you the latest," she says. "I got set up on a blind date with this guy named Ed, and he kept making this face on our whole first date."

"What kind of face?"

"He kept doing *this*," she says, making this fish face. She's sticking her lips out like she's either puckering up or making fish lips. "After the first date I thought *no way,* but then I decided not to be shallow and that I'd give him another chance."

"And?"

"So I did. We went on three dates, and he was a perfect gentleman. He even picked me up at my apartment before our date!"

"Syd?" I say. "That's what guys are *supposed* to do."

"Well, they never do it for *me.* And he didn't even try to kiss me on the first date. And then he was also a perfect gentleman on our second date. He wouldn't come upstairs. And I *offered.*"

"I have no doubt."

"So on our third date—" she begins.

"Wait—was he still making the fish face all the time?"

"Yes! And it got *worse,*" she says. "He'd be telling me a story and then make these dramatic pauses, and the face would hold for the entire pause. It was awful! But I looked *past* it, and on our third date we finally had sex. Three times."

"To make up for the first two dates."

"Something like that," she says. "But get this . . . here I am, sucking it up, not being shallow . . . giving old fish-face a chance—and he blew me off! Never called me again! What's up with *that*?"

"That's weird," I say.

"I know! And you wanna know what's *really* weird? I don't think he came when we had sex. All three times."

"Well . . . usually you know. I mean, you *know.*"

"I'm telling you!" she practically shouts. "He *acted* like he came. Full on! But after . . . when I went to throw something away, I looked at the condoms in my trash can . . . and there was *nothing* in them."

"Okay—why are you digging condoms up out of your trash?"

"I wasn't," she says defensively. "They were just there, and I noticed they looked empty."

"That's weird."

"He pretended like he came. All three times. Why would a guy pretend to come? Do guys fake orgasms, too? Can you imagine if we were *both* faking?"

"Were you?" I ask.

"No, I came. But the real point here is that he never called me again! I threw him a bone and he blew *me* off. Maybe he was gay," she says, sipping her coffee.

• • •

Brady

I have two main friends I've had for as long as I can remember. One is Phil, with whom I share an office, a company, and far too many hours. The other is Zach, whom I spend considerably less time with but have many more quality conversations with. However, this is not necessarily one of those times. Zach is a substitute teacher/karaoke host. Put the man in front of a mic and he'll bring a smile to your face, a tap to your foot, and *your* girlfriend to his bedroom.

Zach is too smart for his own—or anyone else's—good. Then again, Zach thinks I'm too smart for my own—or anyone else's—good. Like me, he puts himself into every movie character he likes. Except, where I'd be the flawed but lovable fuck-up who triumphs, though barely, at the last hour—the Hugh Grants and John Cusacks of the world—Zach would be the good-looking hipster loose-cannon type. The Jack Nicholsons and Rock Hudsons. Well, the young Jacks. And the straight Rocks.

Zach spends most of his free time trying to plan the perfect crime, which he has every intention of pulling off one day.

I'm sitting with him at this Mexican restaurant called Lucy's. It's equidistant from our offices, and we meet here for lunch at least once a week. It's murder on my digestive system but better than fighting over who traveled farther last time. Zach's drinking a Mojito and keeps referring to it with a bad thick Spanish accent, making it sound an awful lot like Cornholio.

"What's not to love? Sugar, mint, lime juice, rum, ice, soda . . . it's like a glass of happiness," he says, adding "Mojito" once again in the Spanish tongue.

"Can you not turn into Phil, please? This is my lunch break. My reprieve."

"Sorry."

"I'm going for the patent."

"Cinnamilk, or the Catch-It Cone?" he asks.

"Cinnamilk," I say. The Catch-It Cone is another of my little brilliances, but I can tackle only one invention at a time. More on the Catch-It Cone later.

"Good stuff. I'm sure it'll be a smash. Though you can always cross over to the dark side. Be the Sundance to my Butch."

"Why does that sound dirty?"

"It might if we were lesbians," he says. "I could see the correlation there. However, today we are not. Therefore, it is not dirty."

"I stand corrected," I say. Zach and I think alike. We take turns being the straight man. (There has to be a better way to say that.) It's only fair. That was a layup. "How's the quest for the perfect crime today?"

"Not so loud," he says. "It's not a quest. I'm not searching for the Holy Grail. Well . . . I guess metaphorically I am, but it's not like that. I'm not out there searching in the hope of one day finding the perfect crime tucked away in the attic of some old lady who forgot she hid it there when the Alzheimer's kicked in." He takes a sip of his Mojito. "This is years of thought. Planning. Precision. And I'm almost there, my friend. Almost there."

"That would have had the desired effect," I say, "had you not stopped to delicately take a sip of your fruity little drink."

"Fuck you," he says. Then he leans close. "Okay, try this one: You kill a farmer's wife. Then just before harvest time . . . set her out in a wheat field on one of those huge corporate farms, covered in straw . . . and have one of those enormous combines take care of her. Chopped up in a million pieces, and served up on tables across this great land of ours. Not a chance of IDing the body."

I look at him quizzically, then down at the bread basket. "That's just a means—very *unsettling,* I might add—to dispose of a body," I say. "Why would you kill the farmer's wife? What's the motive?"

"Okay, okay," Zach says. "You get a gig as a butler to a wealthy couple. After ten or fifteen years they totally trust you. You've got access to everything. So you pull off an inside job. Snare all the jewels . . . all the art . . . all the collectibles—"

"But wouldn't you be an obvious suspect?" I ask.

"That's the perfect part," he says. "You stay on the gig for another ten or fifteen years to avoid suspicion."

"So when do you get to enjoy the fruits of the heist?" I ask.

"I said I worked out the perfect crime. Not the perfect getaway." And he slumps back down in his chair.

"How are the ladies?" I say, broaching another great crime—i.e., his charmed love life.

"Beatin' 'em off with a stick. And you? Heard from Psycho Sarah?"

"Yes, actually. She was kind enough to send me my toothbrush and a note requesting I die nineteen times. And then actually wrote 'call me' after she signed her name."

"In blood?"

"No," I say. "Not this time."

"Damn."

"Oh, and get this. My nutty new neighbor from hell delivered the letter to me . . . opened . . . and commented on it."

"She hot?" he asks, with a raised eyebrow and a grin that veers dangerously close to the outskirts of juvenile city.

"No. Kinda."

"Knew it." He laughs, which annoys me.

"How?"

"Because she is your 'nutty' new neighbor from hell as opposed to your 'psycho' new neighbor," he informs. "Nutty implies *wacky, quirky,* Kate Hudson meets Drew Barrymore meets Christina Applegate meets—"

"No, no, no. She's psycho. She is. I was just being polite."

"I gotta meet her," he says, and as he says "gotta," his head jerks forward like Dustin Hoffman in *Rain Man.* "Gotta."

"Really, you don't."

"One of us needs to."

"I already have, and it was as unpleasant as could possibly be. I have to *live* next to this girl. So forget it."

"Fine."

"Good," I say. But something tells me that everything is not good. I can still hear the wheels turning in his head. If I start counting backwards I doubt I'll get to seven before he pipes up again. Ten . . . nine . . .

"She got a nice rack?"

"Zach!"

"Rhymes with rack," he says, looking off and pondering this as though he's just chanced upon Newton's First Law of Motion. (For those who need a refresher, Newton's First Law is: Objects in motion stay in motion. And objects at rest, like Zach, stay at rest. Come to think of it, Zack would never ponder Newton's Laws. So to that end, Zach looks as if he's contemplating building a chair out of Cap'n Crunch, and whether he'd actually be able to sit in it.) "Never thought about that. Coincidence?"

"Yes, unless you're planning on growing some man-breasts."

"Please. With breasts I'd be unstoppable. It almost wouldn't be fair."

• ● •

Heaven

I'm not crazy. I've been to a therapist, a psychiatrist, and a shaman healer, and all three have confirmed I'm not. The shaman was at the suggestion of my friend Zoë. She told me this woman would cleanse my aura and cut the imaginary strings that were attaching me to my negativity. I lay faceup on this massage table and watched her actually miming a pair of scissors as she cut the imaginary strings. I wished I paid her in imaginary money.

I visited the shrinks on occasion; at times I thought that I might have, in fact, been crazy. But each time I went they told me I'm not. The thing is . . . I have this book called DSM-III-R. It's a quick reference guide to diagnostic criteria from the American Psychiatric Association. I got it at a flea market from a guy who looked like he'd stepped directly from its pages. I think they're up to DSM-IV by now. So mine's outdated, though I doubt it's changed all that much. In it are diagnoses for every possible mental illness out there. The problem is, sometimes the descriptions are so vague you can convince yourself you have every mania known to mankind.

For example:

307.52 Pica

A. Repeated eating of a non-nutritive substance for at least one month.

B. Does not meet the criteria for either autistic disorder, schizophrenia, or Kleine-Levin syndrome.

When I read that it sent me into a tizzy. I have definitely been known to repeatedly eat non-nutritive substances. It's what I do. I find something I like and eat it. A lot. It becomes my phase. For a while, I was in my pretzel phase. Then it was muffins. Then peanut-butter frozen yogurt. There was a pickles and coleslaw phase. No, I wasn't pregnant, and it had to be that kind of slaw with caraway seeds. I'd search high and low for it. Only the best delicatessens have it, but when it's good . . . it is good. Right now I'm in an oatmeal phase. Odd, considering I'm a carb-conscious eater. But I eat oatmeal every morning without fail.

My phases usually last a month. Sometimes six months or even years. But when I stop, I stop. And rarely do I go back to it. So you can imagine my fear after reading the diagnostic criteria for pica.

That time I read the diagnosis for pica I made an appointment with a psychiatrist. After an hour of telling her my fears of pica and possibly worse, she informed me that while pretzels and coleslaw aren't the most *nutritious* foods, people who suffer from pica eat non-food items altogether. When they say non-nutritive substance they mean:

Chalk
Kleenex
Xerox paper
Etc.

Anyway, you can imagine my relief. But then she hands me this bill for a hundred fifty bucks! I almost told *her* to eat it. But then if she actually did, *she'd* be the one with pica, and her diagnosis of my sanity would count for nothing.

The other times I happened upon mental illnesses with descriptions I might fit, the psychiatrists assured me that I was sane as well. Apparently, my handy quick reference guide to mental health omitted the details that prove it. So I am not crazy. And the only common problem that each of them found was that I had no business reading a psychiatric diagnostic book.

However, certain things *do* make me crazy:

1. People who are mean to animals
2. People who are selfish and self-centered
3. People who abuse their car horns, which is a major problem in New York City

These are things that are *allowed* to make me crazy. They are legitimate gripes.

Here's an example of something that might make you crazy, but is not legitimate: You're on an elevator, zooming up to your desired floor, when suddenly it stops and someone gets on. Then they get off on a different floor. All during *your* ride, which you got on first. Some people might get mad at this. As if their own personal elevator had just been invaded by someone with the audacity to need also to be somewhere that required the use of the elevator. Granted, this has pissed me off on occasion too, but I *know* that it's wrong, and that is key.

• ● •

Brady

I don't lie much, but when I have to, I'm alarmingly good at it. Sometimes it's best to go big or go home. I need time to write out the business plan for Cinnamilk. So when I tell Phil my grandfather in Florida has broken his hip and needs assistance, and I'll be taking the week off to visit him, he believes me and understands.

Phil's understanding is not of the situation as I presented it, however, but it's as Phil sees it in Phil's world.

"Goin' to Florida, eh?" he says.

"Yup," I say.

"Will maintenance?"

"Huh?"

"Making sure you're there in the end so you get good placement in the will?"

"He's not dying. He's just got a fractured hip."

"We're all dying, dude. And he's in Florida. He's halfway there." This is true. I've always called Florida "God's Waiting Room," but what he's saying is just plain wrong. I wouldn't go visit my grandfather just to angle for his will. Plus, he died three years ago.

"How was your date last night?" I ask him.

"I think I blew it."

"Why?"

"When the bill came, I didn't have enough money," he says.

"What about a credit card? Don't you have a credit card?"

"Maxed out. Shit, I maxed that puppy out the first month I got it."

"So what did you do?"

He doesn't answer at first. Then he tries to throw a balled-up piece of paper at the wastebasket, arcing it high, like he's LeBron, and missing *badly.* "I had to ask her for money."

But this miss is so far off the mark. The clock has run out. The game is over. There will be no postseason for this relationship. "Oh, Phil."

"Did I blow it?"

"I don't know the girl."

"She was pretty pissed," he offers.

"Then yes."

"I knew it," he says, pressing his palms to his forehead like it's just hit him. "Fuck. But she had no right ordering the duck anyway. It was like forty dollars. That's just mean!" he adds, like a wounded child.

"I don't think she meant it as a personal affront."

"I think I love her."

"It was a first date."

"And?"

"Never mind," I say. I can't be bothered to get into it with him. There are days I can, and days I can't. This is one I can't. I can't because today I'm troubled.

I'm troubled because I had a dream about John Ritter again last night, which involved the entire cast of *Three's Company,* including both landlords. I wasn't going to mention this. The only other person who knows about it is Zach—and he's sworn to secrecy.

What started out as a funny anecdote to tell your friends at cocktail parties has turned into a guilt weighing so heavy on me that I almost feel like I need to apologize to his family. But I guess this is confusing you, so I'll just go ahead and explain.

A few months ago, while having drinks at Temple, this new hip restaurant that Zach insisted we check out, I playfully tossed an olive from my martini glass at Zach. But he ducked and it missed him and hit John Ritter instead. Three days later John Ritter died.

Of course, maybe I had nothing to do with it—and God, I

hope I didn't. But I keep having this recurring nightmare where Mr. Furley blames me, Mr. Roper blames me, and Chrissy and all her replacements start circling me, as in *Lord of the Flies*. Then there's Janet and Larry. They're all pointing at me and telling me I killed him. They all start throwing olives at me, and it hurts! It feels like they're olive bullets being shot out of an AK-47, and it fucking hurts. So I'm all crouched down trying to block them, and then I wake up with my heart racing, and well . . . this was one of those mornings.

So I think I'll start my week off this very second. I grab my shit and leave.

"Hi, this is Brady Gilbert. I missed your call, but *you* missed a scintillating moment with me. If you'd like to try to recapture that moment . . . leave a message, and I'll call you back." Beep.

When I get home there are seven messages on my answering machine from Sarah. Five hang-ups and two actual messages. Call me an analog geek, but like one of those people who swears on his life that he can hear the subtle nuances of music better on vinyl than on CD, I prefer the warmth and hissing and popping of this old cassette recorder to a digital machine. Plus, I've been able to assemble a truly uproarious *Sarah's Greatest Hits* tape to play at poker games and parties.

But now that red blinking eye has become my tormentor, bringing ill tidings into my home on a daily basis. It's bad enough that I have to listen to that detestable outgoing message of *mine* every time—now I have her clogging up the airwaves. In one message she reminds me of the time—and it was a brief time, I'll have you know—when I was having some "troubles" in the sex department. Fact: Every guy at one time or another has a problem. I am no exception.

It started when we were first dating. I think it was partly because I was so nervous about performing that I just couldn't get it up at all. Plus, she insisted we get AIDS tests first. So it was like a month before we even had sex. It created such a buildup that by the time we were all checked out and ready to go, I couldn't do it.

Then the next time I was so freaked out about the first time that again I couldn't do it. She told me to relax. But then she suggests fucking Viagra, which only made matters worse. I mean, I did *not* need Viagra. I was suffering from nerves. Normal first-time jitters. I do not have a *problem*.

So I took the Viagra. And it worked. If by *working* you mean I got cold sweats, hot flashes, and felt like I was going to have a heart attack. But yes, I was also able to have sex. To some extent it was a relief—yes, the little bastard still worked—but it was also terrifying, because what if that was the only way I'd ever be able to have sex?

As it turned out, I didn't need the little blue pill after all. I *was* able to "perform" on my own. And I really don't like to brag, but for the better part of the last two years I made her scream so loud that my next-door neighbor used to actually give me the thumbs-up every time I'd see him in the elevator.

Sarah's message was as follows:

"Hi, asshole. Remember when you couldn't get it up? And I stuck by you, you pathetic piece of shit! How many girls do you think would have coddled you and nurtured you through that? None. But I did. And this is how you repay me? I don't know why you think you're better than me or that you can possibly do better than me, because you can't. And your little penis problem? It will come back. And if you think I didn't know you were taking that yohimbe every day, you're sadly mistaken." Beep.

Thankfully, my machine cut her off. But then there's part two. There's always a part two.

"Your stupid machine hung up on me," she continues. "Anyway, yohimbe is herbal Viagra. Not a vitamin supplement like you said. You are a sad, pathetic loser who can't get it up without popping pills. Call me." Beep.

This message, in and of itself, is not exactly what I'd call a feel-good message. But worse, that dumb neighbor from next door has pushed her way into my apartment and caught the last bit of the message.

Now, every day is humbling in its own special way. In fact, I like to think I'm building character. Lots and lots of character. You might even say my cup of character runneth over. But that nuisance of a girl walking in at that exact time . . . it took my humility to a whole new level.

"Hey, lots of guys have, um . . . trouble," she says.

"I don't have 'trouble,' and what the hell are you doing in my apartment?"

"You left your door open."

"It wasn't an open invitation. This isn't a dorm."

"Don't take your sexual malfunctions out on me. I'm just here to deliver your mail."

"And it better be unopened." She doesn't say anything for a minute. She looks around my apartment, focusing on my one blue wall.

"Are you painting your whole apartment that color?"

"No, just that wall. It's an accent wall."

"Okay, Martha Stewart," she says.

"Is my mail unopened?"

"Do you want it or not?" she says. And as she says this, for a moment I almost believe it's entirely possible that if I don't behave, I won't be receiving today's mail. Then I look at the mail she's waving before me and see that it is indeed already opened.

"I can't *believe* you."

"Look, at least I'm giving it to you."

"Can you please stop opening my mail?"

"Can you please stop having your mail end up in my mailbox?" she says.

"I'm not having it end up there. It's a mistake. Which the post office needs to fix."

"Agreed." We stand there for a second. She still hasn't given me my mail. I hate that she heard that message. I want to say something about it, but I don't want to even bring it up. Fuck you, Sarah.

"So can I have it?" She finally hands it over. Opened.

"If you don't mind my saying," she says, knowing full well that I'll probably mind, "your finance charges are really high on your credit card. You should call them and try to get them lowered. I'm only suggesting this because I did it with mine. Those credit card companies totally fuck you if you let them. I mean . . . provided they've taken their yohimbe that day," she says, completely deadpan.

I want to punch her. "Is that funny?"

"*I* thought so," she says and laughs. "Lighten up, I was kidding. Was that the toothbrush girl? Sarah?"

"You shouldn't know her name. You shouldn't know anything about her."

"Well, it would seem that I do. And now I know a little more than I bargained for."

"You didn't bargain for anything, and you don't know anything," I say. "That woman is insane. You two should meet. You have a lot in common. I'm sure you'd get along famously."

"Well then, maybe we *will* meet. Maybe the next time she sends you one of your shoelaces back or something, I'll save her address and write her a note inviting her over for tea."

"Perfect." She's still standing there. Does she think I'm going to invite her to sit down? Go away!

"Okay then," she says. And yet she still stands there.

"Is there anything *else*?" I ask.

"No, that's all your mail," she says, looking past me into my apartment. "Well, that's not true," she adds. "I kept your Victoria's Secret catalog. They have these really cute pj's I want to order. Plus, you don't need it."

"You *really* have problems."

"What? I let you keep the Pottery Barn one. And it looks like you can use it. Ever hear of decorating? I mean, aside from your 'accent wall'?"

"I just moved in," I say. "Why am I explaining myself to you?"

"I don't know, but I'm leaving," she says, and I notice she's picking absentmindedly at her fingernails.

"Pity. I hate to see you go." I inch the door closed, taking her up on her offer.

"Was that some of that newfangled sarcasm thing I'm hearing so much about?" she says with a crooked smile and enough gall to fill my very empty apartment.

"Good-bye."

"Good-bye," she sings, flouncing out like nothing happened. Like she didn't just totally invade my space, overhear my own private nightmare, and steal my fucking Victoria's Secret catalog.

• ● •

"Did you have a brain tumor for breakfast or something?"

—Heather, *Heathers*

"Fuck off, *fur shur* . . . like totally!"

—Randy, *Valley Girl*

Heaven

Some people are so rude! That guy needs to get his head checked. No wonder he's single.

As I sit and think about what an ass he is, I suddenly remember I still owe him ten dollars. He's kind of in a bad mood today, so I'm not sure if I should go back there now to return it. But I can tell he's the kind of person who'll hold it over my head if I don't, so I take a ten out of my wallet and knock on his door.

"Who is it?" he yells.

"It's me," I yell back.

"Why, God? Why?" I can hear him say. And I stand there thinking he is coming to the door, but it doesn't seem that he is. I press my ear against his door to see if I can hear him moving toward it, and at that exact second he opens it. I fall inside his apartment, taking him down on my way.

Suddenly I'm lying on top of him. It's odd making physical contact with someone for the first time. Especially horizontally. Even if it's only for a split second, like this is, you feel every contour—the good ones and the bad ones. You're exposed to that person in his totality. This is an unexpected contact, however, and although my chin seems to fit perfectly into that crook between his collarbone and neck, I feel panicked because maybe it doesn't belong there. He smells like the plastic you tear off a brand-new CD, and I purposely don't look in his eyes. Then he starts laughing, and my body moves with him for an instant as his stomach tightens. It feels a little like body surfing. Then I wipe out and fall off.

"You're it, aren't you?" he says. "You're my karmic punishment for some bad thing I did."

I get up and brush myself off, trying my best to pretend I wasn't just superimposed on him. "I came back to give you the ten dollars I owe you."

"That you *stole.*"

"Borrowed."

"What*ever.*"

"Do you want it or not?" I say.

"Yes, I want it," he snaps back, snatching it out of my hand. "Does this mean you'll be returning my Victoria's Secret catalog as well?"

"No."

"I'm not moving," he says.

"What?"

"If this is some ploy to get me to move out so your best friend can move in next door to you or something, it's not going to work."

"Jeez! Talk about paranoid!"

"Well, what other reason could you possibly have for wreaking havoc on some poor stranger's life?" he asks. I'm almost insulted, but a little bit proud at the same time.

"Is this havoc? Seriously?"

"Kind of."

"I'm just being friendly."

"This is how you act friendly?" he says incredulously.

"Neighborly?"

"Neighbors open other neighbors' mail, steal money and catalogs—"

"*Borrow.*"

"Whatever!" he shouts. Then closes his eyes in an attempt to get back a little self-control. Only partially successful. "It's a little much, don't you think? Life is short! Who has time for all this?"

"Actually, that's not actually true. Life is not short," I say. "Life happens to be the longest thing that you are ever going to do." And for once he is quiet.

"Who *are* you?" he asks.

"Is that rhetorical, or are you asking me my name? Which you haven't done, by the way."

"It was rhetorical," he says. And then there is a long moment before he adds, "What *is* your name, anyway?"

"Heaven."

"Is that the name you were born with?"

"Yup."

"Hippie parents?" he says.

"Not really."

"Well, it's an unusual name."

Was that a compliment? I wonder. No, it wasn't. Unusual means *unusual.*

"It's very pretty," he adds. I notice he's not looking at me and won't. Was he just reading my mind? If *no,* then his timing is damn good. If *yes,* then I'm getting the hell out of here.

"Thank you," I say.

"You're welcome." We stand there for an awkward moment. I guess there's nothing else. I've given him his money, so I should go.

"Okay then," I say. "Have a good night."

"You too," he says, and I go back to my apartment.

Today I discovered a new noise I can make with my mouth. I do it by curling my tongue up and pressing it against the roof of my mouth. Then I sort of click it or suck it or do something. It's still new, so I haven't quite worked it out yet—but it is loud and fun, and I can't seem to stop doing it.

At first people at the restaurant were amused by it, but now, after an hour of hearing me do it, I think—not so much. It sounds sort of like a chipmunk. And the face I have to make in order to get the sound out involves sticking my lips out, open, and slightly flaring my nostrils. I don't know if I have to flare my nostrils, but I do it anyway. I can't see myself when I do it, but I can see my protruding lips if I look down, and I think I might look like a monkey. I'm too scared to look in a mirror and do it. I'm fairly certain, whatever the face is—it's not attractive. If I actually caught a glimpse of myself doing it, I'd probably never do it again—and it's way too much fun for that. If this sounds odd, I can only liken it to sex. I'm sure you make some doozies of faces when you're in the throes of passion. If you ever actually saw what you look like, you might not want to do the evil deed again. But sex, like my new noise, is fun. Both things do not need to be scrutinized in a mirror. Unless you find yourself in one of those motels with mirrored ceilings.

I'm clucking away, polishing our silver with our cheap vodka, when it occurs to me that maybe I should pour a little in my coffee. Our coffee sucks anyway, and this place is boring as hell, so it can't hurt. I instantly realize it's a mistake, but now I'm too lazy to go and get another cup, so I just finish it and make a mental note to myself: Coffee + vodka = bad.

Some people dream in color—I daydream in PR. Case in point: I'm lazily looking over a flyer for the prix fixe we're having for Valentine's Day when it hits me—this has the potential to be a little *too* successful. Three courses, choice of our best entrées, coffee, tea, and dessert . . . for *how much*? It's Valentine's Day, for crying out loud. The night when every man tries to compensate for what a slouch he seems like the other three hundred sixty-four days of the year. We can charge double this and *still* pack 'em in. Where's the thinking here? The profit potential is proportional to the market potential. And in this case, we'll have more comers than tables all night long. Regardless of the prix. If I cared about this place, I'd offer them this nugget. But I don't, so I go back to making my sound.

I *stop* making the sound when Brett, our new busboy, storms past me. "I'm gonna torch this place," he mumbles, kicking the swinging door on his way into the kitchen. Brett's been with us for three days, and he's pretty odd. He's supershort and really goofy looking. He has a very thin mustache, which looks drawn on, and he's constantly disappearing during his shifts.

His first day here he didn't speak. Not to anyone. I tried to spark up a conversation but didn't get much in return. Then midway through his second shift, he was all kinds of talkative.

Basically doing stand-up. It was the most bizarre thing I'd ever seen. Until it hit me that he was probably just on coke.

And the next day, after one of his many disappearing acts throughout his shift, all was confirmed when he actually came back with white shit on his nose.

Now, three days in, he apparently wants to "torch this place." I myself am not a fan of the place either, but sheesh! Torching the place? Our new busboy just might be a few inches short of normal. A few hundred inches.

Meanwhile, I notice Bruce outside, jumping up and down like a maniac. He's tapping on the window furiously, motioning for me to come over. I make my way over to the window—he's pointing at some woman quickly walking away up the street, and he's yelling at me to get out there. So I walk out the door.

"Grab that woman!" he shouts, pointing to the woman again.

I look at her. "Why?"

"Because she just stole all of the toilet paper from the bathroom and shit all over the seat and the floor!"

"That's *disgusting*!" I say.

"Grab her!" he yells, waving his hand in her direction as though he and it have become unhinged.

"Why? What do you want me to do with her?"

"Get our toilet paper back!"

This is one of those "what am I doing here?" moments that I have, probably, once per shift. I really need to get a regular job again. Though I swore to myself I would never work in an office again after I once spent three hours organizing my former boss's PEZ collection, only to have her yell at me because she likes them arranged in such a way that no two same-color stems are next to each other.

"*You* grab her," I say.

"I can't. I'm a man. I'm a triple black belt. I don't want to come off as attacking her."

"Then let it go."

"No," he blasts. "She stole our toilet paper, and it's not the first time she's done it."

"Is she a customer?"

"No! She just walks in and goes straight to the bathroom."

"Did somebody clean the bathroom up yet?" I ask, glancing with no small amount of dread in that direction.

"Will you get moving? She's getting away!"

"I don't know what you want me to do, Bruce. I'm not going to go and grab that woman."

"If you want to keep your job you are," he says with his chin out and his eyebrows raised. This is total bullshit. I'm supposed to chase some freak of nature down the street? Some freak of nature who has just shit all over our bathroom and stolen the toilet paper? Because Bruce can't spring for a couple extra rolls?

So I start after her down the street and catch up to her. Sure as shit (pun intended) she's got all of our toilet paper in her tote bag.

"Excuse me," I say.

"Piss off," she says.

"I don't want any trouble, ma'am. But my boss would really like his toilet paper back."

"I don't have your fucking toilet paper. Leave me alone or I'm calling the police."

"I see the toilet paper in your bag, ma'am."

"*Aaaaaaaah!*" she screams at the top of her lungs, which scares the hell out of me. She also has a few longish hairs growing out of her chin. I look back at Bruce, who gives me the thumbs-up. This woman is insane, and I want to go home. But if I don't come back to Bruce with some toilet paper I'm going to, once again, be out of a job. This is total bullshit.

"Look," I say. "Can you just give me one roll? If I walk back to the restaurant with nothing, I'm going to get in trouble. I'm not even asking you to split it with me. Just one roll is all I ask." I look at her pleadingly.

"Eat shit, you little tramp!"

I take a breath. Inhale . . . exhale.

"One roll," I ask again. She starts walking away again. I don't want to touch her, but I can already hear Bruce yelling at me, "Why didn't you grab her?" Blah, blah, blah. I don't know what to do. So I grab the bag, and it becomes a tug-of-war. She screams some more. People are turning, looking to see what the commotion is. Then I see Brady, my neighbor. He too is looking at me—at what apparently looks like me trying to steal this woman's bag.

"Help! Police!" she screams. Brady's watching this with the most confused and horrified look on his face that I've ever seen. The kind of look that tells me, if he wasn't sure before, he's now 110 percent positive that I'm insane. And why shouldn't he think that?

I've had it. This woman is making a scene and making *me* look even worse. Bruce is tapping his foot, which I know means nothing good, so I just decide, *fuck it*. I've already got one hand on the tote. I reach in, grab two rolls of toilet paper, jerk my hand back as she tries to bite me, and storm back to the restaurant. As I'm walking back, I see Brady's jaw drop. So I do the only thing I can think to do, which is give him the finger, and then I walk back into the restaurant.

• ● •

Brady

Oh my God. There are no words to describe what I just saw. She is totally insane. And a kleptomaniac. And it just so happens that the restaurant my neighbor walks into after stealing toilet paper from an old lady is Temple. The same restaurant where the John Ritter incident took place. That place is nothing but bad news, so if *she* works there, it's fitting.

I sneak over and peer into the window. Lo and behold, there she is taking an order. What was that hideous display I just witnessed? A mini break to mug a bag lady and loot some Cottonelle?

She spots me and ducks. But a second later I guess she thinks better of it, because she walks straight over to the window and says, "What?" I can't hear her, but I can read her lips. And even though there's a glass partition between us, I'm fairly certain her tone wasn't warm and welcoming. Frankly, I don't know why she's giving *me* an attitude. I didn't do anything except witness her thievery. Which reminds me, I want to listen to the Thievery Corporation CD when I get home.

I just walk away. I shake my head and walk away. This girl is a menace. On my way home I walk right past porn legend Ron Jeremy. I tell ya, nobody can wear tube socks like that guy.

I get home, throw on the *Sounds from the Verve Hi-Fi* CD, brew myself a cup of coffee, and plan my strategy. I'm starting big. Hershey's makes chocolate milk and they'd be lucky to have my Cinnamilk. I Google Hershey's and find their Web site. Incidentally, I think it's fascinating that Google is a verb. Here's something that didn't exist a few years ago, and now there it is, noun, verb—and something I, frankly, can't live without. And if it's not officially a verb, it is now. You're welcome.

I get the phone number off the Web site and place the call. The conversation is as follows:

"Hershey's customer satisfaction, this is Darlene, how may I help you?"

"Hello, Darlene. I'm looking to get in touch with the main headquarters. Do you happen to have a number I can call?"

"What is this regarding?"

"It's regarding a new product idea."

"I can forward your comments to the corporate office, and they'll get in touch with you."

"I appreciate that," I say. "But I kind of need to speak to someone directly."

"You're speaking to me," she says. Is that the tiniest edge I hear creeping into Darlene's formerly sweet voice?

"Yes, I am. And while I do appreciate your time, *Darlene,* I really need to speak to someone about setting up a meeting. This is a potential gold mine here. And someday you can say you were part of that first phone call. *So* if you'd be so kind as to point me in the right direction—"

"I'll tell you what I'll do . . ." she says, shaping up.

"What's that?"

"You can tell me your questions or comments, and I will forward them to the corporate office, and then someone will get back to you." This is the same canned response that she gave me thirty seconds ago. Not only do I want those thirty seconds back, I want Darlene to be fired.

"It's not a question or a comment, Darlene. It is a product idea."

"Then tell it to me, and I'll pass it along. And someone will—"

"Right, I know. Someone will get back to me. Here's the thing. I'm sure you're a great gal, Darlene. I am. But I don't know you. This is a multimillion-dollar idea. Do you think it would be wise for me to discuss it with you?"

"That's how we do it," she says flatly.

"Well, I can't tell you."

"Then is there something else I can help you with?"

"No."

"Have a Hershey's day," she says and hangs up. I want to punch Darlene.

Well, that didn't work out quite as I'd intended. Maybe a trip to Hershey's headquarters is in order. Or maybe I'll just call Knudsen, Tuscan, Borden, or Parmalat.

I'm about to look up their Web sites when I hear drumming on my door. It's Zach. He knows I'm not really in Florida. I let him stay out there and drum for a few minutes, but then he breaks into song.

"Josie's on a vacation far away . . ." he sings in a high-pitched voice that actually does the song justice. Then again we're talking about *The Outfield,* a one-hit wonder if there ever was one. He does this to embarrass me, and because he knows I'll get off my ass and open the door. And I do. 'Cause if I don't, I know that "Sister Christian" can't be far behind.

"Perfect crime," he says as he breezes past me and opens up my refrigerator.

"I just got off the phone with Hershey's."

"I was in the record store the other day," Zach continues.

"Hey, Hershey's?"

"In a sec," Zach says with a wave of his hand. "I'm just about to walk out with my DVDs—"

"Your porn DVDs," I interject.

Zach does not even acknowledge. "And this girl walking in sets off the shoplifting alarm with something in her bag. Here's the plan: we figure out what sets off that alarm, equip somebody with it, stuff a backpack full of *Lord of the Rings* trilogies, then time our departure to coincide with the arrival of our confused friend—who can't figure out why this thing he's bringing *into* the store has set the alarm off. The embarrassed security guard, not wanting a lawsuit, waves everybody ahead."

"Shoplifting—is our coup de grâce?" I say. "What are we, a bunch of troubled high school *sophomores*?"

"Okay . . . how about this? I send you a letter in a resealable envelope, and you stick your reply inside, reseal it, then write 'Return to Sender' on the front. Full round trip for the price of a one-way."

"That's great, Zach," I say. "We'll make our fortune by bilking the government thirty-five cents at a time."

"For your information, it's more like thirty-seven . . . or *thirty-nine* cents now. Okay, now what's *your* thing?"

"Just got off the phone with Hershey's."

"And?" he asks.

"Bitch wouldn't help me at all and told me to 'have a Hershey's day.'"

"That's a little Disney-ish."

"It's something-ish."

"Ish," he says.

"Hey—guess who I walked past on my way home?" I ask. And then I answer, because he's not going to guess. "Ron Jeremy."

"That guy's fucked like every girl in the world."

"Well, every porn star," I say.

"I never got that. The guy is *ugly.* He reminds me of a guy I used to get pizza from. The pizza guy'd show up, and we'd have bad dialogue for a couple seconds, and then the next thing I knew we were fucking. Wait a sec . . . he was a girl. And there were two of them. Yeah, that's it."

"Really," I say, "how is it that guy got all those parts?"

"I think it was that one *big* part," he says. "But maybe back then it wasn't so much about the looks as it was about the . . . sex."

"Or maybe it was about who was willing to fuck in front of a camera for fifty bucks."

Zach nods in solemn agreement. "That's a good sighting. I'd say you're in the lead, but I had a good one the other day too, and forgot to tell you . . . who was it?" He taps his chin. Then his finger rises in discovery. "Oh! It was the woman from the Palmolive commercials."

"Madge?"

"Yes, Madge!"

"Nice," I say. "How'd she look?"

"Dude. It's not like she was ever hot. What do you mean how'd she look? She looked like *Madge.*"

"True. Madge might beat Ron Jeremy."

"Could be a tie," he offers.

"I think you're in the lead," I admit. Zach and I have this ongoing competition of B-list celebrity sightings. Anyone can see Britney Spears or Harrison Ford. Living in New York, that's shooting fish in a barrel. To us, it's much more exciting to see someone like Gary Coleman or that guy from *Bosom Buddies.* Whatever his name is. The one who didn't have Tom Hanks's success. The one who's probably bitter as hell right about now.

"Come downstairs," Zach says. The bar he works at is conveniently located right down the block from my apartment, and tonight is a karaoke night.

"Can't. I'm planning my strategy."

"Come have a Jameson and then plan your strategy."

"Because *that's* good advice," I say.

"C'mon," he says, brushing off the sarcasm as though it were dandruff. "Just hang out for a little bit. You know I get the ladies in there. You can have some of my spillover."

"I'm out of the business. No ladies for me. You know that."

"Because of stupid Sarah?" he asks.

"No, because I'm done. I don't want a relationship. This is *me* time. Maybe in five years or so, I'll think about it."

"Five years? What the hell are you talking about? You're not going to have sex for five years?"

This throws me into a profound, if momentary, contemplation of five years without sex. And to give you some idea of my weakened mental and romantic state, the prospect *almost* sounds enticing. Think of it: No more praying to God that she doesn't roll over and face the wall when I give her the subtle "Can we?" signal by placing my hand on her right breast. No more transforming my tongue into a ragged scrap of sandpaper over the course of an interminable journey toward an elusive orgasm. No more testing the condom, post-coitus, for signs of leakage. God forbid any of the fruit of my loins should test the fragile wall of her uterus and leave her baking up a Brady Junior to one day cure cancer or solve the energy crisis. No more returning to a half-asleep body whose only epilogue to the rapture is to mutter, "And don't go hogging the comforter."

"I said nothing about not having sex," I say. Because when all is said and done, were there a pair of breasts and a taut naked stomach staring me in the face, I'd gladly ride that toboggan straight back down to hell.

"Then come out."

"Sex isn't my main priority right now. I'm trying to start a company. Invent things . . ."

"Is this because of the 'little problem' you're having?" he asks, and I feel my temperature rise about twenty degrees. Zach is my best friend. I tell him everything. But I *never* told him about that.

"What are you talking about?"

"Sarah told me."

"Oh my God, is *that* what this is about?"

"You need to get back on the horse," he says, drawing near and threatening to put his arm around me. But with a single look I back him off. "Shit, man. Sarah was such a miserable bitch, I'm sure I couldn't get it up for her either. You're lucky she didn't turn you gay."

"Dude! There . . . is . . . no . . . problem."

"That's not what she says."

"And when did you talk to Sarah, by the way?"

"I didn't," he says. "She left me a message on my answering machine. I'm pretty sure she's leaving the same message on everybody's answering machine."

"That's just fucking great." *Now* I need that Jameson.

We go to the bar and I have not one, but two Jamesons. I explain the whole situation to Zach, and how it was only in the very beginning of the relationship, blah, blah, blah. But he doesn't care. He tuned me out as soon as the Twister Twins walk in. Tara Clean and Darling Nikki.

Tara Clean got her name because she carries around the most recent copy of her AIDS test everywhere she goes, and Darling Nikki's been called that since the eighties when "Purple Rain" came out and it was every girl's favorite song. They're the "Twister Twins" because Zach's bar has a dance floor designed like the game Twister, and Nikki and Tara usually go out there in revealing clothes and start everyone off. Before long, everybody wants in. It's become the main attraction at the bar. The girls get a small cut off the net in exchange.

I check my messages at home, and there's this message from Phil:

"Hey, man. I guess you're on the plane or something. I just wanted to tell you that Sarah called me. She said that . . . well, it doesn't matter what she said. But listen . . . I have a Viagra. It's been in my wallet for like four months, but you can have it if you want it. I got it because of that twenty-four-year-old that I was seeing, but she changed her number." Beep. My machine cut him off. Of course he calls back. "I don't know why she changed her number. We were getting along so well. Anyway, she did. So I never got to use it. And you can have it. But we can talk about it when you get back. Have fun in the Sunny State," he says, and hangs up. It's the *Sunshine State,* Phil. And right now I hate Sarah more than Billy Joel hates sobriety.

"Another shot, please?" I say. Zach hits me with a double this time, pointing out a beautiful girl who just walked in with her two friends.

"Check her out. She's fuckin' hot."

"Wedding band," I say.

"She sings in one?"

"No, jackass. She's wearing one."

"Good catch," he says. I'm so pissed right now, and I need to leave. I pull out a twenty and slap it on the bar. "You know your money's no good here. And where you going?"

"Home," I say, getting up quickly because I know he'll try to talk me out of it. I have a giant headache. Plus two fat girls are on the mic singing "Girls Just Want to Have Fun." "Look," I say as I point to the two girls. "Two more reasons to hate this song." And when he turns to look at them and starts laughing, I make my hasty exit.

Of course I run into Heaven in the elevator. What a misnomer *that* one is. This is the last thing I need right now. I don't even say anything. I think maybe if I don't say anything *she* won't say anything, and maybe we'll never have to speak again.

"You don't say *hello*?" she spews.

"Hello."

"Look, about what you saw—" she starts to say.

"I don't want to know," I say, interrupting her.

"Why not?"

"Because it's none of my business. You are none of my business, and I'd like to keep it that way."

"That's rude," she says.

"Oh, really? And what would you call coming into my apartment uninvited, opening my mail, which is not only rude but illegal, *borrowing* my money without asking, and attacking that woman today?"

"I didn't attack her and you're right . . . it's none of your business."

"That's right, it's not."

There's another moment of totally palpable silence. Then she comes out with "I have your mail." Fuck. Of course she does.

"Which is none of *your* business."

"Whatever," she says. This means she read it. Again!

"You've *got* to stop opening my mail," I say seriously. "Seriously. You can't just open anyone's mail all willy-nilly like that."

"Willy-nilly?"

"Just . . . don't."

"It's in *my* mailbox," she says.

"Look at the outside of the letter before you open it."

"That takes extra time," she says, greatly pained. "Time that I don't have."

"Yes, I know you have a very busy schedule, stealing things."

"I beg your pardon?"

"My ten bucks, that poor woman's freakin' toilet paper . . . what's next? Stealing Legos from children?"

"You don't know what you're talking about," she says dismissively. "And you weren't interested in hearing about what happened because it's none of your business, remember? So here's your stupid mail, and you can feel free to go fuck yourself." With that, she hands me my mail.

"Thank you," I say. "For the mail. Not the freedom to go fuck myself. But thanks for that too, I guess." She doesn't say anything. We're on our floor. She gets out. I get out. "Don't you want to crack wise about the content of my mail now, or something?"

"There was nothing good today." And she opens her door and goes into her apartment. Doesn't even say good-bye. Not that I expected her to, but I don't know. Maybe she's having a bad day, too. Why am I now feeling guilty? I don't need this shit. I'm not going to think about her. Fuck her.

Of course there has to be more to the story. She's not really a maniac. I know that. Or at least I *think* I know that. I just assed off because I'm pissed Sarah is making my life, and reputation, a living hell. Now I feel bad.

Maybe I should go and apologize. Or maybe not apologize, but at least find out what the hell is up with that woman. And then there's a knock at my door. She saved me the trouble. Good.

I open it, and holy shit. It's not Heaven standing before me, but Sarah. Satanic Sarah and her devil-may-care diarrhea of the mouth.

"Hi, Brady," she says. "Can I come in?" No. No, you can't

come in, vile woman. I crack the door a little more and motion her in. I'm such a pussy.

"What can I do for you, Sarah?"

"I was in the neighborhood and I found your E.T. lunch box and thermos under my sink. I thought you'd want it."

"I thought I lost that!"

"Oh yeah. No," she says. "It was never lost. I just didn't want you starting a collection of kitschy lunch boxes all over the apartment. You and your stupid eBay habit. So I hid it under the sink where I knew you'd never find it. God forbid you'd actually hunt down a cleaning product."

How did I stay with this woman for two years? Well, in her defense, she turned into megabitch only when I broke things off. Prior to that she was just your garden-variety bitch. Bitchy during PMS, which is part of the rules, I get that. And bitchy every third or fourth day.

"Nice to see you," I lie. "And thanks for the lunch box back." Feel free to leave now.

"Nice place."

"Yeah, I like it."

She peers around the place. "There's only one bathroom."

"I'm only one person." Unlike you, you multiple-personality psychopath. Nice ass, though.

"Look, Brady. We both know we're going to get back together. I don't know what you're trying to prove with this moving-out thing, but enough is enough."

"Sarah . . . we are not getting back together."

"You are a loser," she says matter-of-factly. "And if you think you can do better, you're sorely mistaken. And wasting time. And risking me being with someone else when you finally realize this and come crawling back."

"I'll take my chances."

"Fuck you, Brady."

Just then the door is pushed open by Heaven, who sashays in and over to my refrigerator. Both Sarah and I are watching her. I don't know what the hell she's doing but she's doing it, and that's all that matters.

Heaven takes my orange juice out of the refrigerator, pops the cap, and takes a huge swig directly out of the jug. Then she puts it back, turns around, and smiles this killer smile that I didn't even know she owned.

"Hi, I'm Heaven. OJ?" she asks Sarah (who's about to have a nervous breakdown).

Heaven is my new favorite person.

"Who is this?" Sarah asks me.

"She just told you her name," I say. "Heaven is my neighbor. Heaven, this is Sarah. An old friend."

"Friend?" Sarah hisses. "I'm his ex. His very recent ex. And you should know that he has a wee bit of trouble getting it up."

"Really?" Heaven says. "I never noticed."

I think I love Heaven.

Sarah's head looks like it's going to explode. I swear to God, she's beet red. And maybe I've just watched too many cartoons in my day, but I think I actually see steam coming out of her ears.

"Well, you wasted no time, eh?" Sarah says.

"I gotta go," Heaven says, planting one on my lips before making her exit. "See ya later. And hey . . . nice meeting you, Sarah." And she's gone.

Sarah's eyes turn to little slits. "I'm leaving, too."

"Thanks for the lunch box," I say cordially.

"You're an asshole."

"So you've said."

And she leaves, too. I go to my refrigerator to pour myself some orange juice, but the carton is empty. She knew it was empty. She not only put back an empty carton, but she knew full well that it was empty when she offered it. She also knew Sarah wouldn't take it. It was just for effect. I owe her, big.

• • •

Heaven

He owes me so big. Like . . . huge.

• ● •

Brady

Did she just *kiss* me?

• • •

Heaven

I hope he doesn't think that I *like him* like him. Christ, I don't even *like* him.

I think I'm going to be fired. If not, then I am definitely one table closer to being fired. The tables at Temple are numbered. Table 23 gets the hex today. Doug, our bartender, wishes "ass cancer" on rude customers and customers that show up when we have no more customers and are about to close. Then we have to stay open for—at least—an extra hour plus, just for these jackasses—and they always come. So when I tell Doug about Table 23 he walks over and gives them the "ass cancer hex." I don't know what it entails because I've never seen him do it. But just knowing that he did makes me feel better already.

These two women had a hard-on for me from the minute they sat down, and they're making my night a living hell. First they yell at me for how long they've been sitting there. They claim they've been there for fifteen minutes, which is impossible, but since the customer's always right I just nod, apologize, and offer to take their order. But they continue to berate me for not coming over sooner. I can't help zoning out and focusing instead on the small bumps all over this woman's face. It's unbelievable. She is like a giant pale gherkin. Finally I say, "Look, I'm here now. So, would you like to order your dinner because I'd *really* like to take your order." Fake smile. Fake smile. Plastered-on smile.

And it works. They give me their order. One woman orders a chopped salad with no dressing to start, and they will share one order of lemongrass chicken. I ring in their order and bring the lady's salad to her.

"I want a side of blue cheese," the mouthpiece says.

"All right," I say. "I'll go get it for you." I go and get a side of blue cheese dressing and bring it back to her.

But she gets angry. She huffs and rolls her eyes, and has this look on her face like she smells something really bad.

"This isn't what I wanted. I was here before and they brought me dry crumbled blue cheese. I don't want just plain old blue cheese dressing." I guess I had my mind-reader turned off. Shame on me.

"Okay then. I'll go get you the dry blue cheese." I go back to the kitchen, get her a side of dry blue cheese, and bring it to her.

"I need the oil and vinegar that comes on the salad."

"Okay," I say, and I go get her a side of our vinaigrette.

I return with the vinaigrette, place it on the table, turn to walk away, and I'm stopped short. This lady has grabbed onto my shirt. "This is not what I asked for!" she yells. "I asked for oil and vinegar. I wanted separate containers of oil and vinegar. Not this. This is mixed. I don't eat oil!"

"So what you wanted was vinegar."

"Yes."

"My apologies," I say with all of the warmth and affection of Joan Crawford. "When you said you wanted the vinaigrette I understood that to mean you wanted the dressing that normally comes with this salad. Which is what you asked for. Next time you just want vinegar, perhaps you can just ask for vinegar. I'll go get you the vinegar."

"We also need plates. We're sharing this salad. Can't you *see* that? We need plates to share," she says as I go right around the corner and grab the vinegar for her. When I hand it to her, she looks like she's going to explode.

"Where are the plates?" she blasts out like a trumpet.

"Ma'am" (and when I say *Ma'am,* I mean *you stupid whore*), "the vinegar was closer, and it seemed to be your most immediate concern. I was just going to go and fetch you some plates as soon as you were satisfied with your vinegar."

"And you didn't bring us a serving spoon to serve the salad."

"No, I didn't. Salads don't come with serving spoons."

"Well," she says, "if you were a good waitress you would have brought one."

"Well, I'm not. So this is what you got."

"I'd like to see the manager." Shit. Saw that coming. But I can take only so much. I tell Jean Paul that the customer has a complaint. He takes his sweet time going over to their table, which does my heart good.

I hear her complaining about me, spitting nails, and when he obsequiously asks if there's anything else he can do, she says, "Well, you can have that girl bring me a cup of decaf." This is one of the times I'm happy about our Magic Coffee.

We have something I like to call "Magic Coffee" at our restaurant. Here's what it is: plain old run-of-the-mill coffee. And it's not good. Management knows it's not good, and they like it that way. Why? Because if it *was* good, people would stay and enjoy a second or third cup. Coffee doesn't cost anything, and they want to turn tables and make money on new customers. So they make sure it's bad, so people have their one cup and get out.

But the reason it's called Magic Coffee is because we have no decaf in the restaurant. None. Never have, never will. If someone wants decaf, we imagine it's decaf and suddenly, POOF, it's decaf. At least as far as they are concerned. This is immoral, you might think. And yes, it is. But they don't care. When I first started working here I was shocked. And concerned. I happen to be one of those people who cannot have regular coffee after a certain hour. It will keep me up all night. If I were the person being duped into drinking fully caffeinated coffee, I'd be livid. But worse, what if it's some old person with a heart condition. I mean, it's *dangerous*. Yet they don't care.

Personally, I don't serve it. That's how my conscience deals with it. As a server, I take the food and drink orders and deliver the food and drinks. That's it. After they've eaten dinner, the busboy takes the coffee and dessert order, delivers it, and *lies*. They'll often ask, "Which one is the decaf?" And the busser will say, "This one," and go so far as to point one out so they're reassured. It's all very sneaky. But I'm not involved in that part. I'm not the one lying. So I deal with it.

Meanwhile, all of this time running back and forth has caused me to ignore a couple at another table. The two of them also ordered salads with blue cheese dressing. He's nearly finished, but her plate is barely touched. A full glob of blue cheese is sitting right on top. I go over.

"I don't like this dressing," she says. "I'm done."

"All right," I say. "Let me get that out of your way." I reach down and pick up her plate, but as soon as I lift it, it slips from my hand, which has oil on it from stupid Table 23. I try to catch it, but my effort only makes matters worse, and I end up essentially hurling the salad right onto her. All over her blouse. All over her skirt. A renegade piece of lettuce in her hair. Blue cheese everywhere. What is it with fucking blue cheese?

I'm just as shocked as she is. We're both stunned and silent for a minute. Then:

"I guess you *really* hate that dressing now, huh?" I say. I mean, what do you fucking say? This is a nightmare. This is seriously a nightmare. I wouldn't be surprised at all if I woke up right now and called Sydney to tell her about it. But I don't wake up. Because I'm awake. And this hell is just another night at my workplace.

Amazingly, I don't get fired. Not yet, at least. The couple's meal is comped, and they'll send us the dry-cleaning bill. And that woman . . . probably put the "ass cancer hex" on *me*!

Back at Table 23, Pickle-face has devoured her "decaf." Knowing that she'll be up all night with the jitters because of it, I actually feel good about our Magic Coffee. So much so, I even personally deliver a refill after I've closed out her check. Yeah, I know it's wrong. I'll live with it.

On my way home, I'm listening to The Clash on my iPod and I see a dog tied to a street sign. He's scruffy and adorable, and he looks cold. I need to get home and take a bath, but I don't want to just leave this mutt tied up there alone. I look at his collar and there are no ID tags. I can't have a dog. A dog is a lot of responsibility. I can barely take care of myself. And God help me if I get near any blue cheese dressing. I pet him and start on my way home again.

I don't even get two blocks away before I turn around and go back to check on him. I just want to make sure he's okay. Was he even a *he*? I walk into the Ray's Pizza—one of about a thousand Ray's Pizzas in New York that claim to be the "Original Ray's."

So I ask the guy behind the counter if that dog has been tied up to the pole long.

"Depends," he says. "Is four hours long?"

"Jesus Christ," I say. "The poor thing's got to be freezing."

"I see it all the time. People don't want their dog anymore, and they leave it at a dog run or tie it to a pole."

"People are assholes," I say. He nods and sort of chuckles.

"Yeah, and they hope a sucker like you will take pity on the thing and give it a home."

"Ugh!" I groan and walk outside to check on him. When I get there he starts wagging his tail like he knows me. You don't know me, stupid dog! Don't wag your tail at me. And then he smiles. I swear to God, the fucking dog smiles at me. I will not take this dog home. I am not going to become a dog owner. There *is* a sucker that will take pity on this dog, but that sucker is not me. I need a long bath. I need to wash this day off me, and I do not need a dog.

I have a dog in my apartment. He's clumsy and adorable, and I'm calling him Strummer, after the recently departed Joe Strummer. Plus, he seems to like The Clash, too.

I sit at my desk and check my e-mail and my CNN home page announces that the "Condom in Soup Lawsuit Is Settled." You better believe I click on *that* link. Turns out this California-based seafood chain, McCormick and Shmick, settled a lawsuit with a woman who found a condom in her clam chowder. The woman also claimed she was treated rudely by the waiter, whom she'd asked to take her soup back to be reheated. When she began to eat the soup she encountered a chewy, rubbery object, which she first thought was calamari or shrimp. She spat the offending object into her napkin and, lo and behold, discovered it was a rolled-up condom.

Now, I know this is truly disgusting. It is. But knowing what I know, waiting tables and dealing with asshole customers, I find this story gives me pause. I have to wonder what the woman *really* did to her waiter. How badly did she treat him? And it also begs the question, "Was this waiter actually practicing safe soup sex?" Perhaps the waiter thought he was doing a service by wearing a condom when he stuck his dick in her soup. How many times does a dick end up in a bowl of clam chowder without a condom? Personally, if anyone is fucking my soup, I'd prefer they do wear a condom, but that's just me. And I don't like clam chowder anyway.

Classic crisis-management opportunity in *my* mind. There's got to be a way to turn that bad PR into something good. Well . . . it's actually a bit of a challenge . . . their *sticky* situation. They could always see the humor in it and make fun of themselves. They could put right on the menu, "Our chowder is condom free." Or do a month-long Seamen Celebration: free clam chowder with any entrée. But I'll tell you this—if they were paying me, I'd have chowder sales back up and rock solid in no time.

I call Sydney and tell her to come over. I tell her I have someone here that she needs to meet. She whines that it's too cold, but she comes anyway.

It takes her an hour to get here, even though she lives only three blocks away. She got all dolled up thinking it was a guy that I wanted to introduce her to. And it is. But this particular little guy has four legs.

"What did you do?" she asks.

"He was homeless. Some idiot just left him tied to a pole."

"Oh, Heaven."

"I know. But I couldn't leave him there. Anyway, he's here

now and he's mine. And you're an aunt. So say hello to Strummer."

"Strummer?" she says, not getting it.

"Strummer."

"Like strumming a guitar?"

"Yes, but it's actually after Joe Strummer."

"I don't know who that is," she says.

"Blaspheme!"

"Is this one of your hip musical references?"

"Hardly. But it's okay. Anyone who enjoys the *Blue Crush* soundtrack as much as you is exempt from knowing who Joe Strummer was."

"Whatever," she says. "It's a really good soundtrack."

"I know you think so, sweetie."

"You have a dog."

"This is my point."

"Well, I don't know what to say." She squinches up her face. "Congratulations?"

"Thank you." Strummer walks over to me and rests his head on my knee. It's quite possibly the cutest thing I've ever seen. It is in this instant that not only is my taking him home validated, but I decide that I love him.

Love is pretty much a decision anyway. Just like happiness. You can decide to either love someone or not, be happy or not. The rest is just commitment to the idea. I am now committed to this dog.

"I think I'm pregnant," Sydney says.

"You're not."

"I'm late."

"You're late every month," I say. And it's actually not true that she's late every month. Just that she says it.

"Well, I don't have unprotected sex five times in one night every month."

"With a stranger, you forgot to mention."

"I knew him," she says defensively. "I met him once. A year ago. But thanks for making me feel better."

"Sorry, but you still should have used a condom."

"We meant to."

"Well, you're not pregnant," I say. "I know because you've been in a very bad mood all week, which means you're clearly PMS-ing."

"Promise?"

"Yes."

"Good," she says. "What's going on with *you*? You haven't had sex in a while."

"I haven't had a *date* in a while. No dates equals no sex."

"Not true," she says.

"For me, it's true." Sometimes I wish I could be the kind of person who has one-night stands, and instead of feeling guilty about it feels empowered by it. But I'm not. That's Sydney's role. I just can't do it.

There's a knock at my door. Sydney looks at me funny.

"You expecting someone?" she says.

"No, but it's probably Brady."

"Who's Brady?"

"My neighbor." I open the door, and it is indeed Brady.

"Hi," he says.

"Hi," I say back. Strummer runs to the door, and Brady starts to pet him.

"I didn't know you had a dog."

"I didn't. Just got him."

"What's his name?" Brady says.

"Strummer."

"Cool. After Joe?"

"You got it."

"Wow." He smiles. "Good name."

"Ahem," Sydney says.

"Sorry," I say. "This is Brady. My neighbor."

"The retarded one?" Sydney asks before I can stuff a pair of thick woolen socks in her pie-hole.

"What is it with this *retarded* thing?" he asks.

"Nothing," I say. "So, what's up?"

"I just wanted to say thanks. You know. For what you did. With Sarah. It was really cool." After a moment he walks to the elevator and presses the call button.

"You're welcome. She's a real peach, that one." The elevator comes and he gets in.

"Yeah. No kidding. Anyway, I'm on my way out. I just had to tell you that what you did . . . was perfect. And that kiss. Nice touch," he says as the elevator doors start to close.

"No problem," I say. And just as the doors shut I add, "By the way, I have mono."

• ● •

"It's really human of you to listen to all my bullshit."

—Samantha Baker, *Sixteen Candles*

"You aren't dying, you just can't think of anything better to do."

—Ferris Bueller,
Ferris Bueller's Day Off

Brady

I know she's kidding. She better be kidding. She *is* kidding. I know it.

I feel a tickle in my throat. I swear to God, I do. I hate her.

I've called just about every dairy company and none of them want to hear my idea. This morning I called Knudsen. Who transferred me to Santee Dairy. I told them I needed to speak to someone about a new product idea. They said the person I need to get in touch with is a Lydia somebody. So I called this Lydia. She directed me to their Web site, and suggested that I click on the link to their customer comments section and leave my comment there.

I don't have a fucking *comment.* I have a million-dollar idea. Don't they get this? I explain to Lydia I don't want to just submit my idea at random. What I am offering is a business proposition, and I'd want to be involved. She stutters a bit and puts me on hold.

When she comes back she informs me that she doesn't think she can accommodate me with what I am looking for.

"Why not?" I ask.

"Because we don't do partnerships," she answers.

"This is a really good idea, Lydia," I say, thinking that using her name will somehow help matters. I think I can feel her caving a little bit. But not enough.

"I'm sorry. I really don't think I can help you."

"Fine," I say. I'm tempted to add, "But don't come crying to me when this thing goes double-platinum." But I don't.

I need a cup of coffee. Lucky for me there's a Starbucks on my corner. In fact, there's a Starbucks on just about every corner in Manhattan. I know what you're thinking, but I like my coffee to be consistent, and Starbucks is nothing if not consistent. Plus, they filter their water. I won't make coffee from my tap at home. I know they say New York water is the best water, but who *really* knows? Maybe the water is clean, but the pipes are nasty. There are all kinds of good minerals, bad minerals, too many minerals, chemicals in some cases, contaminants, carcinogens, and well . . . cancer-flavored coffee tends to taste bad.

And this just in . . . it was recently on the news that Orthodox Jews can't drink water from the tap because there are shellfish in the water, which makes it not *kosher.* For those who don't know, kosher is only kosher because it passes a rigorous inspection test. Since my body is made up of like 80 percent water, I'm gonna make sure it's the purest form of water known to mankind. If that means kosher water fits the bill . . . that's what I'm going for. And I'm not even *Jewish.* But if something that goes into my body as frequently as water does can't even pass a *kosher* test . . . I ain't drinkin' it.

So I'm standing in line deciding. That seems to be a big part of the experience. Decisions: Cappuccino or Frappuccino? Tall or Grande? Or Venti? And then there's the fixins: Whole milk or skim? Chocolate or vanilla? Nutmeg or *cinnamon*? Then it hits me. *This place is the answer.* I need to get in touch with Starbucks. This would be a great market for Cinnamilk. I don't know why I didn't think of it before. I even read the book *Pour Your Heart into It: How Starbucks Built a Company One Cup at a Time* by Howard Schultz. He's the guy who founded Starbucks. He needs to hear from me. And he will. I'm calling him as soon as I get home.

Not as easy as I thought. All I can get is the customer service line. Can you believe that the phone number is 1-800-23LATTE? How precious. I tell the woman I need the headquarters and she tells me that I've *reached* the headquarters.

"Are you in Seattle?" I ask.

"Yes, I am."

"Well, I need to speak to Mr. Schultz."

"Regarding?"

"Regarding a business idea."

"Do you have a proposal written up?"

"Yes," I lie.

"Then I can give you the address that you should mail it to, and someone will get back to you if they are interested." This is, basically, the same as the questions/comments link on a Web site. But I'll get the address at least.

"Fine," I say. "What's the address?"

"P.O. Box—"

"Wait—it's a P.O. box? That's not an address. That's not where Howard Schultz is."

"That's where all proposals go," she says.

"And to whose attention do I put it to?"

"Just to the P.O. box."

"Perfect," I say. My sarcasm is lost on her.

"Okay. The address is P.O. Box 3717-L-UE1, Seattle, Washington 98124-3713."

"Excellent."

"Anything else I can help you with?"

"No," I say. You haven't helped me at all. What do you mean anything *else*? Of course I don't say this *out loud*. I just hang up.

I walk into the bar. Zach's on the mic emceeing. The kid really is smooth. His stage presence is like a get-laid guarantee. It's the equivalent of a fat bank account or Brad Pitt looks. If he wasn't my best friend, I'd hate him.

They're all warmed up, and he turns the mic over to three girls who are doing "Summer Nights" from *Grease*. Not only the most overdone song, but it's a duet. For a man and a woman. Not three girls. But that's not my problem.

"Let me ask you something," Zach says. "Why is it that every time a girl says the phrase 'I'll try anything once,' I always think she's talking about anal?"

"Because you're a twisted fuck. But I admit, my mind tends to wander there, too. There are actually *two* things that my mind goes to . . . anal, and having another girl join in. I think they do it on purpose."

"Shit, yeah."

All of a sudden I think about Heaven, and I swear my glands feel swollen. No, I wasn't thinking about anal sex with her. Although, now that it's on the table, I guess I am. But not because I *want* to. Because the last person I want to have anal sex with is Heaven. Or any kind of sex. I think I have a fever. She better not fucking have mono.

"Do I have a fever?" I ask Zach.

"No," he says.

"You didn't even feel my forehead." He reluctantly feels my forehead.

"No, you don't."

"Phew," I say. But I'm still convinced I can feel something coming on. I pound a shot of whiskey, and all of a sudden it hits me. I know what I need to do. "Do you want to go to Seattle?" I ask Zach.

"I thought you're supposed to be in Florida."

"No, I mean for real."

"Grunge is dead, dude," he says. "It died with Kurt."

"I'm serious. I'm going to Seattle. You wanna come? I could use the company."

"No, I don't." He's serious. And he's rarely serious. "What the hell's in Seattle?"

"Howard Schultz."

"Who is?"

"The founder of Starbucks," I tell him.

"And you want to go see him . . . why?"

"Because sitting on my ass, looking milk companies up online, and then calling them and talking to idiot secretaries is getting me nowhere. I need face time."

"Why him?"

"Why not him?" I ask. "He took fucking coffee and made it an event. The guy, bless his heart, has made it okay to charge five dollars for a cup of fucking coffee."

"Mine's four-sixty," Zach says.

"People used to go to coffee shops to get a cup of coffee. Not some exotic trendy milkshake. He's revolutionized a bean—a silly little bean—and made billions. Not to mention the freedom of expression he's created."

"Huh?"

"People are sheep. Consumers. They eat and drink what you put in front of them. But this guy Schultz . . . he's given them their one shot at individuality. With all the many ways they can order their latte . . . decaf, extra hot, no foam, breve, soy milk . . . he's provided the people with one way to stand out and define themselves. And I'm here to offer a new choice for their coffee: *Cinnamilk.* I think Howard may be the only person who will listen to me. But I need to meet with him . . . *in person.*"

"Maybe you *do* have a fever," he says and reaches out for my forehead.

"No, man. Maybe I've just finally hit on the path to my destiny." I play with the skull ring I'm wearing, my homage to Keith Richards. Zach looks long and hard at me.

"Dude, I hate to say it, but you are one bad career move away from working at the Guitar Center."

"Fuck you," I say and cringe inside because he's totally fucking spot on.

"I've gotta get up there," he says. "If I don't go wrangle some more people, the Jersey boys will take over and it'll be a medley of 'Bohemian Rhapsody,' 'American Pie,' and 'Margaritaville.'"

"We can't have that."

"No, we certainly can't." He gets up and takes over the mic. I stick around for a few more songs, then walk home.

The next night I'm passing by Heaven's door, and I almost knock. But I don't. I decide to go back to my door. Fuck it. Who needs the hassle? Then I go back to her door. I stand there for a moment and then laugh to myself. Because I'm *knock knock knockin' on Heaven's door.* I pull my shirt over my face so I won't breathe her germs. She answers in a mask. A green facial mask. No shame whatsoever.

"Hi," I say.

"What are you doing? Why are you burying your face?"

"I just had to make sure. You were kidding about the mono thing, right?"

"No," she says with the best poker face I've ever seen. Then adds, "Of course I was kidding, you doughnut."

I expose my face. "I knew that. I just had to make sure. And what's with this retarded thing? Why did you and everyone you know think I'm retarded?"

"Whether you are or not is still debatable."

"Seriously, what's the deal?"

"It's a long story," she says. "And it's time for me to remove my mask. I have to leave in fifteen minutes."

"It's a good look, by the way."

"Thank you. Anything else?"

"No."

"Good night, Brady."

"Good night, Heaven." Where is she going?

• • •

Heaven

Why is he still standing there?

• • •

Brady

"Where are you going?" I ask, even though it's none of my business.

"I'm going out with my vet."

"You have a vet?"

"Yes," she says.

"You just got a dog. Like yesterday."

"And I got a vet. Like today."

"Huh."

"Yeah," she says. "I needed to get Strummer checked out, so I took him to a vet."

"And now you're going on a date . . . with your vet?"

"It's not a date," she says as though she believes her own bullshit.

"It is *so* a date."

"It's a platonic date. He's new in town. Just started his practice. He needs friends."

"Right." You've gotta hand it to the guy. Playing the "new in town" card. I've done it myself, but coupled with the great humanitarian angle of a veterinary career . . . that's a tour de force. "So this is going to be your boyfriend? A vet."

"He's not going to be my boyfriend."

"Well, at least you'll have all your shots," I say, feeling pretty good about the line.

"Cute." See?

"Where are you going?"

"I don't know. We're meeting downstairs."

"This is such a date. I'll bet he's getting groomed right now."

"Funny," she says. "I'll give you a dollar if you stop saying it's a date. It's annoying."

"You can keep your dollar."

"Good, because I'm short on cash."

"That's okay. Vets make good money."

"They do?" she innocently asks.

"Think about how much you paid. Unless he didn't charge you."

"If he doesn't charge every hot girl that walks in there, he's not going to make a very good living."

"I'm glad you realize you're hot."

"Hey—I got charged," she says defensively.

"Now *that's* funny."

"Can I go now?" she says, making a little fist and digging it into her thigh.

"Who's stopping you?"

"Good night, Brady. Again."

"Good night, Heaven. Again."

• • •

Heaven

I go downstairs and wait for Chris, my vet. I guess Brady was sort of right about it being a date. But I wasn't really looking at it that way. He *is* kind of cute and I *do* admire what he does for a living, but I genuinely just want to show him around. It's hard to move to a new city and try to start a life and make friends.

I mean . . . *should* I consider this a date? The first time I met Chris, the majority of our conversation involved ringworm. We determined Strummer's probable age and his likely place of birth, and we clearly established that he'd never been to Asia and therefore had a zero percent chance of having contracted a Malaysian bird flu. And *then* he chased me out onto the sidewalk to make sure I'd taken my complimentary pen. And *then* . . . he asked me if I "know of a good place to eat, in your neighborhood, that you wouldn't mind eating at, possibly with me."

I've never understood why guys have to wait until the elevator doors are almost closed before blurting out some awkwardly phrased solicitation for your company. Go ahead and ask! I'll probably say no . . . but at least we won't have wasted the time. Dating is like pushing your tray along in a cafeteria. Nothing looks good, but you know you have to pick something by the time you reach the cashier.

Chris shows up in khakis and a sweater, and in that instant it becomes no longer a date. I'm sorry. Call it what you will, but I hate khakis. It's the weekend uniform of the uninitiated. I don't like to stereotype people, I really don't. But I'm just not interested in the khaki armada. I don't worship Dave Matthews, and I never play Hacky Sack or Rollerblade. This is not my husband.

I take Chris downtown, and we hit this tiny sushi restaurant that hasn't yet been discovered by the masses. The women that work in this place all wear these geisha getups. They look so uncomfortable that it's almost uncomfortable to watch them. And they have these weird-looking packs strapped to their backs, and I have no idea what they're for. If it's for fashion . . . somebody needs to clue them in.

Chris is sweet and genuine. He tells me about the time when he was eleven and a half years old and his doctor asked him if he was sexually active. He said yes because he wanted to look cool, and then had to sit through an embarrassing forty-five-minute lecture on safe sex and how to properly use condoms.

After dinner we walk around the Lower East Side, and I show him some of the *cool* places to go and some places he'd be wise to avoid—like the Third Street block governed by the Hells Angels. Then I take him to this cozy little tea shop that I love, and we sit and drink chocolate mint tea.

I begin to wonder if Chris thinks this is a date. The clues: The pointless chair reposition, so now he's a little closer but no longer facing me. The arm touch—I've counted two, and I swear if I say anything else even mildly funny, he'll use the opportunity to make it three. I begin to feel nervous. Not really nervous, but guilty. I hate that awkward thing when one person doesn't feel the same way about the other. I know what I'll do . . . I'll fix him up with Sydney.

And just then, my suspicion is rewarded. He leans in, his face centimeters from mine, and tries to kiss me. I pull back and put my hands up like one of the Supremes. Stop, in the name of . . . whatever this is.

"Whoa."

"Not okay?" he asks, face still directly in my face. It's now not centimeters away, but still inches from mine, and *way* too close.

"Well . . . I just thought—I don't know. I thought we were going to be friends."

"Friends kiss," he says.

"They do." Like hello and good-bye! "But I really need a good vet." And you're wearing khakis.

"And you've *got* a good vet."

"But if this doesn't work out, then I'll be out a vet. And a good vet is hard to find. You come highly recommended." And you're wearing khakis.

"I think the phrase is, a good *man* is hard to find. Probably harder to find than a good vet. And if it'll help, I can get recommendations from some of my exes."

"I'm sure they'd be thrilled to do that."

"I really like you," he says. "I mean, I don't *know* you. But I thought we clicked today."

"I like you too." God, I hate this.

"Not gonna happen, huh?"

"Sorry . . ." I say.

And now comes the awkward silence. I hate this part, too. And while we're sitting there in awkward silence, I start to think about Brady. God knows why, but I do. I think Brady was jealous about my going out with Chris. At the time I thought he was just being his usual annoying self, but now that I think about it, he was definitely jealous.

When I get home, Brady's Pottery Barn catalog is under my door. The one I generously let him keep in exchange for keeping his Victoria's Secret catalog.

There are a few pages earmarked, and when I turn to those pages there are Post-its with question marks on them. I think he's asking my opinion. Does he have no friends? Are *we* friends now? And no, he cannot get that stupid fake antique phone. I can't believe he's even *thinking* about it. I skim through the catalog and look at what else he's picked out. It's not the worst stuff, I guess.

I'm tempted to knock on his door and give him my opinion, but I'll wait until tomorrow. Let him sweat it out, not knowing when I came home from my non-date, which he thinks was a date—and which Chris thought was a date, too. Apparently, I'm the only one who didn't get the memo.

The truth is, Chris is a good-looking guy. He's smart and funny, and a doctor. I'd probably go out with him any day of the week at any other time. But if I'm really going to be honest, I guess I'm still hurt. Not hurt, but a little gun-shy. I haven't had the best luck in love, which we've never gotten into and don't need to. And khakis had nothing to do with it. I think I'm scared. Which is extremely inconvenient because, as I've already told you, I need to be married in . . . well, *now* in only fourteen months. Ugh.

When I get to work, I'm informed Bruce and Jean Paul want to meet with me. Just the three of us. Which usually means bad news. When I find out they want me to come in early tomorrow for this meeting, I'm sure—it's *definitely* bad news. Okay, fine. But as angry as they are, I'm pissed now, too. That I have to come in an hour early just to get bad news. Fuck that. It's *my* spare time. My *free* time. My time away from this *hellhole.* And for added enjoyment, I get to dread this meeting for all of tonight.

I see Marco in the kitchen putting the bread baskets together. I walk over to him and make a face.

"What is this face for?" he asks.

"I think I'm getting fired," I say.

"I think perhaps, too."

"Really?" I say, now completely freaking out. I thought maybe they'd at least give me a *warning* first.

"Why do you think you are getting fired?"

"Because Jean Paul and Bruce want to meet with me. In the morning. Why? What did *you* hear?"

"They don't tell me anything," he says. And he squeezes the bread to check it for freshness.

"You must know something. You agreed with me when I said I thought I was getting fired!"

"I know that Bruce has spoken of your many conflicts with the customers. It seems you have had several conflicts, yes? Many scandals?" I guess by conflicts, he means problems. Which is close, I guess. Maybe that's even a better way of describing it. I'd just say my customers are assholes who want to feel superior, so they treat me like crap, but yes, I guess I have "conflicts" with them.

"Yeah, I *have* had a few," I say and sort of laugh. Then that seems stupid, so I stop.

"Don't let the customers make you nervous and collapsed," he says. Marco says "collapsed" instead of "upset." I've tried to teach him, but he hasn't gotten it yet.

"Upset . . . angry," I say. "Not collapsed and nervous."

"Yes. Angry. Mad. Don't let these customers get you mad."

"I try." Then I sigh. "I'm not a waitress, Marco," I say. It's the first time I've said this out loud. It freaks me out because, yes, I'm not a waitress—so maybe that makes my behavior okay . . . sort of. But really because . . . I *am* a waitress. This is what I do. For now I am a fucking waitress. It's the only thing that's paying my bills. Without this, my nest egg would be scrambled in no time. And as much as I don't want to admit it . . . it's the cold, hard truth. Maybe I need to shape up and try harder not to fuck up. It's not a question of skill, really. It's basically an attitude adjustment. Or *maybe* it's time to quit procrastinating on what I've wanted to do since the moment S&M PR showed me how *not* to run a PR agency—start and run one of my own. That's the one good thing that came out of that job, I guess. They taught me that I don't want to work for corporate America anymore. And I sure as hell don't want this either.

"I know you are not a waitress," Marco says. "This is why I like you. I don't like a woman who can carry more plates than me."

I smile. "It's not just how many plates I can carry. It's a mentality thing," I say, not sure if I'm talking above his level of understanding.

"I know this, too. I understand you, Heaven. Better than you think," he says. I adore him. Not in a want-to-throw-him-up-against-the-refrigerator-and-have-crazy-sex-with-him way . . . but in a sweet way. He's one of the good ones. I know he can tell what I'm thinking because he says, "Who is your favorite Albanian?"

"You are," I say, and I give him a squeeze.

"Yes," he says. "But unfortunately I don't have any competition."

"Marco, if everyone who worked in this place was Albanian, I promise you—you'd still be my favorite." He smiles, which shows off his missing tooth. It's not right in the front, but on the side. He's quite a vision with the eye patch and the missing tooth, but it just makes him that much more lovable.

"Albania . . . it sucks. We have nothing," he says. "Even Bulgaria won an Olympic medal, but it was stupid."

"Why was it stupid?"

"Because it was for weight lifting. And then they got kicked out for drugs. I don't understand this weight lifting. It is stupid sport. Why do people watch this? To see one man pick up a piece of metal? This is not very interesting to me."

"You have a point there, Marco." I laugh.

There's an older man sitting by himself, eating Canh Chua soup, and he clears his throat. He does it again. And then once again, with more effort.

The next thing I know, Marco lifts the man out of his seat and starts to shake him. He gets behind him and starts to do the Heimlich maneuver. I'm stunned, as is everyone else. No one is as stunned as the poor man, though.

Marco's now standing behind him, his hands together in a fist, which he is hurling into the man's stomach. He's literally lifting him off the ground with each hurl. Tossing the man around like a rag doll. The man is actually trying to speak, in between each punch to his gut.

"What . . . [punch] are . . . [punch] you . . . [punch] doing? [punch]"

"I am saving your life," Marco says. "I have had extensive training in Albania for just this thing!" he announces, heaving his doubled fist once again into the man.

"I . . . [punch] don't . . . [punch] need . . . [punch] the Heimlich!" the man says.

"Marco!" I say. "The man can speak! If he can actually say *Heimlich,* he doesn't need it!"

Marco puts the man down and looks at him. "Are you okay?" he asks.

"No!" says the man. "I was just clearing my throat and you beat the living crap out of me!" Marco looks like he's going to cry.

"We are incredibly sorry, sir," Bruce says. "Our busboy is new to the country. He's very stupid and very sorry."

"Yes," Marco says. "I am terribly sorry. I thought perhaps you had one shrimp from the soup there inside of your throat."

The man throws his napkin onto the table.

"Your lunch is on us," Bruce offers meekly as the man storms out. Bruce then whirls on Marco. "Don't *ever* do that again."

"And if he *was* choking?" Marco asks.

"Let him die!" Bruce yells and storms out after the old man to do damage control.

I get home and Brady's blasting music so loud I can hear it while I'm still in the elevator. I get out and go straight to his door. He's listening to Massive Attack. I bang on his door. No answer. I bang again. Nothing. I should know by the choice of music that maybe I shouldn't just barge in, but the door is slightly open. So, I think, *Fuck it.* I go in.

And *fuck it* is exactly what I walk in on. Brady is fucking *it*—that monster of an ex-girlfriend of his. She's on top, riding him like a cowgirl. In the middle of his living room. On the floor. I should, of course, turn and leave immediately, but I'm so shocked that I actually stay and watch for a second. Literally a second. Which is all it takes before Psycho-girl sees me, and the next thing I know Brady is howling in pain and I am out the door.

• • •

Brady

Sarah shows up at my apartment in those wrap-around-the-ankle, all-the-way-up-to-the-knee, fuck-me heels and . . . what do you want me to say? You've seen those shoes.

Honestly, I wasn't even going to go there, but she had this take-charge thing going on and just pushed me down onto the floor and began having her way with me. Believe me, she'd have preferred a bed with 800-thread-count sheets, but we were on the floor because I still have no furniture.

Sarah was never all that adventurous in the bedroom and rarely spent time on top. This time was definitely an adventure. I think, partly because she's trying to win me back, and partly because, as I said, we were on the floor—and she'd be damned if she'd be on the bottom.

So there she is, putting on quite a performance. Touching herself to try and get me hotter as she rides me into my hardwood floors. I should really get an area rug. Anyway, she starts really getting into it. She's thrusting up and down, up and down, harder and harder. You know how it is when girls really start going at it. That kind of raw, animalistic, your-cock-means-more-to-me-than-chocolate-or-even-diamonds-right-now kind of way. First off, forget about the twinges of pain in places I don't need to have pain, but there's always that chance she goes up too high—and it pops out. And then she comes crashing down on you. Down comes a hundred-and-twenty-pound bag of flour onto your cock. It's like running into a wall at top speed with a hard-on. It fucking kills. People don't talk about it, but I think most guys are terrified of this happening.

But she's off . . . going higher and higher. All I can think is: Please don't go up and down so hard, please don't go so high, please for the love of God be careful. Shit, I wonder if it can break. I mean, I know there are no bones in a boner . . . but as hard as it is, maybe it can snap. And man, would that hurt.

And just as I'm picturing my dick snapping in two, Heaven comes prancing into my fucking apartment, and every single one of my fears are realized. Sarah sees her, which throws her off her game. I pop out, she comes crashing down, and bones or no bones . . . I think she broke my dick.

Sarah is gone, I am sitting on the floor with a bag of frozen peas on my dick, and I want to cry. Then *she* knocks on my door.

"Go away!" I yell.

"Can I come in?" Heaven asks.

"No," I yell again. And then it gets quiet. I think for once she's listened to me. Maybe she's gone back into her lair.

"Captain Kangaroo died," she yells through the door.

"I never liked him anyway," I yell back. "Him and his freak-of-nature walrus mustache."

"That's not very nice," she says.

"I'm not a nice person," I say. "Look, can you come back another time? What you did—you have no idea what you did," I say. I look at the quickly thawing bag of peas and wonder if I should actually see a doctor.

"I'm sorry," she says.

And then she's quiet again. Peace. I start to draw a glass of milk. I'm going to make a presentation to show Schultz when I get there, and I think a mock-up is a good idea.

"Did you know that the host of *Romper Room* got mugged last week?" she now yells. "She did. And they stole her mirror. The one she'd look in and say who she saw. She never saw me. I used to wait for her to say my name. She never did. I used to cry when it ended because she'd never see me. 'I see Tommy and Mary . . . and Lucy . . . and Kevin . . .'"

I can't take it any longer. She's not going to fucking shut up.

"'And Karen . . . and Lisa . . .'"

So I get up and open the door.

"What do you want?"

"They stole her *mirror*!" she says. "The muggers."

"Okay. They mugged the *Romper Room* lady and Captain Kangaroo is dead. I hear you. I understand. Bad week for kids' TV. Too bad Mr. Rogers died last year. Could have had a hat trick. Does this conclude your morbid update of children's TV hosts of yesteryear?"

She looks at the bag of peas in my hand.

"Cooking?"

"No."

"Look—I'm sorry about before. Your door was open."

"That doesn't mean *come in,*" I say. "It means I—or someone else—didn't close it properly."

"Someone else like Sarah? That *was* Sarah your crazy ex, right?"

"Yes, it was Sarah."

"Guess you two are on better terms today," she says.

"What do you *want*? What did you want when you came barging into my fucking apartment?" I say, waving my arm for effect. And then, *smack,* I end up hitting myself in the crotch with the bag of peas. "Fuck!" I yell.

"What is *wrong* with you?" she asks.

"Nothing," I say, one whole octave higher.

"Seriously, are you okay?"

"I would be if you'd leave me alone."

She pauses. "I only came back because I heard her leave."

"And?"

"I was going to give you my opinion on the stuff in the catalog. The Pottery Barn."

"I don't care anymore."

"Then why did you shove it under my door?" she says.

"Because . . . God, you are annoying! Can you just leave it alone? I don't want to talk about the fucking Pottery Barn right now."

"You're very hostile," she observes. "Is this a side effect of that herbal stuff you take when you want to have sex with

Sarah? Who you supposedly hate? Funny way of showing it, by the way."

"We're done here," I say, starting to close the door.

"Fine," she snaps. I slam the door in her face. Hard. I'm fuming. I stand there for a minute, then open the door again.

"It's yohimbe," I call out. "I don't take it regularly. I haven't taken it in months, in fact. And not that it's any of your business, but right now I wish I *did* have problems getting it up. If I'd been *Mr. Softy* today when you came barging in, I wouldn't be in the massive pain I'm in right now. But I wasn't soft. I was hard as steel, baby! And it was all *natural*." But . . . she doesn't respond. I peek my head out, and she's not there. But our other neighbor is. This fat Polish nanny who watches the kids across the hall. She looks somewhat shocked and not even a little bit amused. She shakes her head in disgust, and I meekly smile at her and then duck back into my apartment. I hate Heaven.

I'm back at the office, and Phil wants to know how Florida was. I feel bad. But not bad enough that I don't spend the first twenty minutes filling him in on the elaborate details of my trip.

The truth is, I don't feel like I did enough to get the ball rolling on Cinnamilk, but it's not easy. My buddy Jonas, who's a graphic artist, offered to make some sample ads for me so I'm looking forward to seeing what he comes up with. Anything remotely professional looking will further the cause.

"Get any?" Phil asks. Which reminds me that I did get some, and worse, reminds me of the pain in my crotch. I actually took Advil this morning before leaving for work. It's not helping.

"I don't kiss and tell," I say.

"You dirty dog. Tell me everything."

"Nothing to tell." Except that my dick is now broken. What do they do to fix it? What *can* they do? Did I really break it? Is that possible? What's the cure? Surely not a cast. Viagra for a week? Keep it hard and in place? I don't even want to think about the options.

"Fine," he relents. "I want you to hear this band. I think I found our new saviors."

"Who are they?"

"Superhero."

"No," I say. Honestly, when he said the name, it didn't even register, I had my "no" cocked and loaded, and would have fired at whatever he said. Such was my state.

"You know them?"

"We don't need another band with 'Super' in the name. There's Supergrass, Supersuckers, Supertramp . . . far too many in the universe already."

"Aside from the name," he says.

"Superdrag . . . Superchunk . . . Super Furry Animals—"

"Forget the name!"

"What are they like?" I ask. Because the truth is, we really do need a good band, or we're going to have to call it a day with this record company thing.

"Catchy songs, good harmonies, bluesy rock. Three kids from SoCal. Seventeen, seventeen, and the drummer is fifteen. He's sick. I swear the kid just shreds."

"Did you just say 'SoCal'?" I ask, turning to face him in disbelief.

"That's what they call it." He pops in the demo, and surprisingly they're *really* fucking good. The first song has a great hook. They've got this kind of Wilco-esque wit and depth, MC5-ish unrehearsed energy—the raw impact of the Replacements, the heart of a young Nick Drake, and the soul of the Cure (without the doom). None of that Screamo bullshit that's been clogging up the airwaves.

"Where'd they come from?" I ask, surprising myself by saying this aloud when I had been dead set against showing Phil even a drop of interest.

"My cousin goes to school with them. Nobody knows them yet. It's a beautiful thing."

"Can we get them to change their name?"

"Maybe," he says. "They're playing next weekend."

"Here?"

"No, not here," Phil says. "In California. They're still in school. They're not on a national tour."

"Not yet," I say and smile at him. I'm smiling for two reasons. One, I am going to go to California next weekend to see what these kids can do live. If they're half as good as the demo they recorded, this is our next signing.

And two, California is right next to Seattle. Sure it's an hour or two by plane or . . . well, I don't know how many hours in a car, but it's right there. I can check out the band and then head up to Seattle to meet with a certain someone. I hope Jonas has the mock-ups done. And I really need to figure out the real address of Starbucks Corporate.

And like a gift from up above, I hear the ding on my e-mail. It's from Jonas.

Subject: Re: Ad Mock-up
Date: 1/25/2004 5:54:39 PM Eastern Standard Time
From: Jonas_Richardson@usmeal.com
To: BradyGilbert@Sleestakrecords.com

Dude—it's rough, but it's a start. Tell me what you think.—J

I click on the attachment and it starts to download. We'd discussed what it should be. A hearty breakfast sitting next to a big tall glass of Cinnamilk. Eggs . . . toast . . . waffles . . . bagels and cream cheese, maybe?

The download finishes and it's . . . different. There's a girl stretching in the background wearing workout gear. I like that. Nice touch. The Cinnamilk looks good, too. But what is that on the breakfast table? I can't be certain. There are some nice-looking tomatoes. And then some kind of bread with a smear of something on it, and then rolled up . . . something. Some kind of meat. Whatever it is, it looks like nothing I'd want to eat, and more important, it sure as shit doesn't look like breakfast.

I don't want to make him feel bad because he's doing this

out of the goodness of his heart, but fucking hell. I write back, trying to focus on the positive.

Subject: Re: Ad Mock-up
Date: 1/25/2004 7:24:41 PM Eastern Standard Time
From: BradyGilbert@Sleestakrecords.com
To: Jonas_Richardson@usmeal.com

Jonas—

Nice work, man. Excellent color on the Cinnamilk. Not too brown, not too white. Just the right touch of color to really look right. (hey, I rhymed) Well done, brother. And I love the workout girl. Really great stuff. Thanks so much. Hey—just wondering . . . we'd talked about having the ad feature the Cinnamilk with "breakfast." I wasn't quite sure what we had there in the forefront. What exactly was that?

Subject: Re: Ad Mock-up
Date: 1/25/2004 7:31:32 PM Eastern Standard Time
From: Jonas_Richardson@usmeal.com
To: BradyGilbert@Sleestakrecords.com

Thanks for the compliments. It's fresh tomatoes, and bagels with lox.

Subject: Re: Ad Mock-up
Date: 1/25/2004 7:36:06 PM Eastern Standard Time
From: BradyGilbert@Sleestakrecords.com
To: Jonas_Richardson@usmeal.com

J—

Again—really nice work. I gotta say, though . . . that doesn't look like bagels to me. Or lox even. Are you sure? Didn't we talk about . . . like bacon and eggs or something?

Subject: Ad Mock-up
Date: 1/25/2004 7:41:43 PM Eastern Standard Time
From: Jonas_Richardson@usmeal.com
To: BradyGilbert@Sleestakrecords.com

Dude—so sorry. Upon closer look I think it's prosciutto on like some sort of focaccia bread. Not really breakfast fare, I guess. Ironically, and this is just a coincidence . . . Italians actually consider prosciutto a "breakfast meat." I'll work on the bacon and eggs.

Breakfast meat? If I were to pick out the absolute last thing I'd want to devour with a tall glass of Cinnamilk, it might very well be prosciutto.

But Jonas is awesome, and the fact that he's taking time out of his busy day to create this thing for me far outweighs his inability to differentiate between an Italian snack and an all-American breakfast.

Anyway, the copy on the ad right now reads "You may outgrow sugar-coated cereals, but you'll never outgrow Cinnamilk." It's cute. Fun. But I'm not married to it. I'd like to have a few different taglines for options. And I need something really clever. I need the guys who write the *Real Men of Genius* Bud Light commercials. Hell, I need a lot of things.

• ● •

Heaven

I go to work an hour early to have my "meeting," and Jean Paul and Bruce are already there and wave me into the office. This kind of formal sit-down isn't good at all. It tends to bring out the Eddie Haskell in me. I mean, of *course* I'm going to be on the defensive. It's already them—and apparently every person I've ever waited on—against me. They read aloud every complaint I've received and then have me sign each one at the bottom, to acknowledge that I understand and agree. What kind of crap is that? I may understand what they are saying. I understand because they are reading it to me in English, my native tongue. But agree? Uh . . . no. I most certainly do not fucking agree. And who even knew they wrote all these complaints down?

All of my complaints were transcribed by the managers into this *incident book* I didn't even know existed. They seem to relish letting me know I am the only one who's made it into this little book. Quite an accomplishment. The book should just have my name on the cover. There is even one complaint typed on law-firm letterhead. They have to admit . . . I am popular!

So they're sitting there reading me these complaints aloud, one after another. It doesn't matter that there are just three of us in the room. I feel like I'm on trial and the charges are being read against me in front of a jury—full of people I waited on and pissed off. I, of course, have a comment for each and every one of these complaints.

Jean Paul starts. "Table Eleven. A Mrs. Feldstein: 'She—'" and he lifts his eyes up to me, "that means you—'was very cold and rude. Bad service.'"

"Bad service how?" I ask.

"They didn't get into it."

"Didn't you want to know?"

"Here's the next one . . ." and he flips the page. "From Mr. Giorgio: 'Rude behavior. Bad service. Had been warned by the people at Table Seven not to sit in her section.'"

"What? Who was at Table Seven?"

"I don't know," he says, "but they warned him not to sit there."

"Did Table Seven complain to you, too?" I ask.

"No. They complained to Table Eleven."

"Table Eleven is nowhere near Table Seven," I say, which is true. "And that's insubstantial hearsay," I proclaim. And all three of us seem to stop, marveling at my TV trial lawyer moment. "Unsubstantiated," I correct myself quietly.

"Table Nine," Jean Paul continues. "'Rude. Said to us, and I quote, I only have two hands.'" I look at Bruce and Jean Paul and actually hold up my hands.

"But it's *true,*" I say. "I do. I only have two hands. See?"

"You obviously are missing the point," he says condescendingly. "We *all* only have two hands, but you can't go saying that to customers."

"And you don't have to have an answer for everything," Bruce adds. "Like this one . . . 'When I complained that my food was cold, the waitress told me that cold was the new black!'" And so on, and so on. They ramble on about my bad behavior, misheard communications, misunderstood facial expressions, and the occasional cussword, *never* intended for customers' ears. After a few minutes I sort of tune them out. Thank God they don't know about the spitting incident—which I do still think about and feel terrible about. Suddenly all these random thoughts start popping into my head, like the time my friend Franklin was on tour in Europe and he made it his mission to learn how to say "eat a dick" in as many languages as possible. I think he told me the French say, *mange a bitte.* The thought makes me get the giggles because Jean Paul is French, and now I have this sudden urge to say it. I don't, of course, but now I've got this panicked *what if* thing going. Like, what if I suddenly get Tourette's and just blurt it out.

"I don't know *what* you are doing out there, Heaven," Bruce says. "But something has to change."

"Well, what would you suggest?" I ask. Someone once told me that one way to avoid conflict is to ask the person what he or she suggests.

"I suggest you try harder to cater to your tables. Treat the customers like they are guests in your home."

"Guests in my home wouldn't treat me like shit the way these people do."

"If this is how you talk to us—your superiors," Jean Paul heaps on, "I can't imagine what you do at those tables." My superiors? Oh my God, I need a new job. You manage a *restaurant.* You are not superior to me. Of course I don't say this. But I have to bite my tongue this time to keep it in.

"I am speaking to you with candor, as my colleagues," I say. "Believe me, if I did so at my tables you'd have a lot more complaints," I say.

"I think you *already* have a lot of complaints," Bruce says. "Look, we are in the service industry. This is the career that we chose. It's nobody's fault but our own when people treat us badly. And they will, every day. It's what we chose. So you just need to learn how to deal with it better. Much better. Because nothing is going to change. The customer is always right."

I want to scream. This may be what *they* chose, but it's sure not, not, *not* what I chose. I do PR. I have a career. Things just got a little slow. I want to tell them this, but of course I don't. I can't. Because they *did* choose this as a career. This is their ceiling, pretty much. They're managing a hip, successful restaurant. What more could they want . . . besides my discontinuation of routinely offending their customers?

The end result of the meeting is I get a warning. Well, six warnings, if one were counting. And then a seventh, letting me know the next time I commit a restaurant sin (that they hear about, at least), I'm out. I'm actually shocked that they didn't fire me, but I guess like they do in all professions these days, they're keeping a paper trail in case they do let me go to prove I'd been warned and wasn't fired unjustly.

Oh, and in case you should ever need it, "*Essen der Gockel*" is "eat a dick" in German.

We're well into the night when Jean Paul sits these three ugly forty-five-year-old women at one of my tables which is a six-top. Three women at a table of six already qualifies as *not cool,* but to make matters worse they're splitting everything. They're splitting the spring roll appetizer three ways, two of them are splitting the lemongrass chicken, and the other one orders Ca Chien, which is a whole fried fish.

It's one of their birthdays, and honestly, it's a sad, sad situation. Here are three aging, lonely, and bitter women who have come to the über-hip restaurant hoping that maybe there will be a table of three hot single guys who will send over a round of drinks, and from there it will be true love.

But this doesn't happen. And every time they order another pinot grigio, they get a little more depressed.

I'm pretty nice to them all night long, trying to make them feel special and being extra attentive. It seems most of my complaints come from women, so on the offensive, I'm "killing them with kindness." And then it comes time to serve their main course.

I have all three plates balanced on my arms. I give the two women who are splitting the chicken their plates first. The one who got the fish is sitting tucked into the corner, as far away from me as she can be. Remember, this is a table for six people, so it's a big, round table—but it's positioned against a wall, and it's impossible for me to walk around it. There is no way I can reach her to put the plate in front of her, so I lean forward and try to hand it to her. She doesn't budge.

I raise my eyebrows a bit to say, "Okay, ma'am, this is your cue to take the plate." Nope. Nothin' doin'. She should have to manually accept a plate from me? No, sir. I will have to be the one to place this platter of fried fish in front of her, or she shan't eat it.

So I reach over and stretch and manage, balanced on one leg, to place her plate before her.

Unfortunately, her fish manages to slide itself off the plate. Of course it does.

But it only lands on the pristine white tablecloth. I'm at a total loss. I don't know what to do, so I quickly stab it with a steak knife and put it back on her plate. She's not happy.

"I'm really sorry," I say. "I had been trying to hand it to you to avoid this, but . . ." She's just staring at me with this icy stare. "I'll bring you a new one." She squints her eyes at me, giving me a dirty look that could rival even my best high school dirty looks. She still doesn't say anything. I ask her, "Do you want me to bring you a new fish?"

"You mean do I want to sit here and wait for another half an hour while my friends eat? No."

"Okay then," I say.

"I would like another plate, though." Huh?

I take the fish and the offending plate back to the kitchen and put it on a new plate. I even sprinkle a little parsley on it to make it look nice. I'm totally confused why she'll eat the fish but wants a new plate. Nothing was wrong with the plate except for the light skid marks that the fish made on its hasty departure. But *the customer is always right,* so I do what she asks.

I bring the fish back on the newly decorated plate, and before I can put it down, she tries to take the fish off the plate and put it on the bread plate she used for her spring roll.

"If you just hand me that plate," I say, "I'll put this one down. There's more room on it."

"No," she says. "If you can manage to simply hold that plate for a minute, I'll just take the fish."

So I stand like a good monkey and hold her plate. Once her fish is safely transferred, I take the new plate back to the kitchen and move on to another table.

But I feel the back of my head burning, and I turn around to see the fish woman glaring at me. I walk over and smile.

"Is there anything else I can get you?" I say with as much cheer as I can.

"Um . . . yeah! A new *knife*?"

And in her hand she is holding the steak knife. The one that I had temporarily borrowed to stab the renegade fish and put it back on the plate.

She can't possibly use a knife that I touched—one that has already pierced the flesh of her fish.

"Of course," I say. And I take the knife from her and return with a new one, held in a white cloth napkin to preserve its current pristine status. I walk away laughing to myself . . . if she only knew the reality of our dishwashers.

For the rest of the night I go out of my way to be kind. I bring them more drinks. And at the end of their dinner I even gather up all the other waiters and bussers and we all sing "Happy Birthday" to the birthday girl.

They tip me just under 5 percent. American dollars.

But the kicker is, they don't even have the decency to duck out quickly after doing so. They are not ashamed at all. They walk over to the now-empty bar and stand there having after-dinner drinks, which by the way are on Doug the bartender, because he's so desperate for a date at this point he'll buy anyone a drink.

So these hags stand there drinking their free drinks. And stay for another half hour. I write on a piece of paper and hold it up so Doug can see:

> They only tipped me 5%.
> Cunts.

At that minute—in the mirror behind the bar—I catch the reflection of one of the women. She is reading what I've written.

• • •

"She is the only evidence of God I have seen, with the exception of the mysterious force that removes one sock from the dryer every time I do my laundry."

—Kirby, *St. Elmo's Fire*

"Did you know your foot's as big as your arm, from your elbow to your wrist?"

—Vivian, *Pretty Woman*

Brady

I'm standing on the sidewalk outside my apartment when a car full of pretty girls slows down and they do a double take. I look behind me to see if they're looking at someone else. Nope. Nobody else there. They start to back up. I try to fix my hair without them noticing. Then one of them rolls down her window and smiles.

"Is that your car?" she asks.

"No, I don't have a car," I say. "No" would have sufficed. She doesn't need to know I don't have a car.

"Oh," she says, disappointed. "We were hoping we could take your parking spot." Ouch. Boy, do I feel like an idiot. But they drive off so quickly I don't have time to think about it much.

I decided to have a poker game at my place tonight. I need a win. I haven't won a hand of poker in two months, and it's not because I don't know how to play. It's the deck, I'm sure of it.

Anyway, Phil and Zach are coming over, and Jonas, too. He has new artwork to show me. I'm psyched. I even bought some of those mini-pizzas to commemorate the occasion. The oven is already preheating when there's a knock at my door.

"*Entrez-vous,*" I say in my best French.

"*Mange a bitte,*" a female voice says back. The unmistakable female voice of—you guessed it . . . Heaven.

"Huh?" I ask.

"Whatcha doin'?" she says as she strides in, surveying the place.

"Getting ready for some friends to come over."

"Cool," she says, sensing a slumber party in the making. "What are you guys gonna do?"

"Play poker."

"Fun." And now I can see in her eyes . . . the slumber party is *on.* "Can I play?"

"No."

"Why not? I know how."

"It's guys' night," I tell her. "Just like you like to stay in on Sundays and watch *Sex and the City* with your friends, we like to drink beer, play poker, and fart."

"First of all, *Sex and the City* has been over for a long time, and second of all . . . you're gross."

"Good, then you won't have a problem making yourself scarce." I put the little pizzas in the oven.

"Why can't a girl be there?" she says. Why is it that every girl who ever hears about a poker game tries to invite herself? "I'm sure I'd have plenty to talk about with your friends," she adds.

"See, that's the thing. We just want to play poker. We don't want to talk."

"How do you know? You speak for them?"

"Trust me on this one. It's a fact."

"Really, now?" she says with this face that is just begging for trouble.

"Yes," I say. "Fact."

"Documented somewhere?"

"Actually, yes. *Men's Health* magazine says that men speak thirteen thousand words a day. Women, however, speak twenty-five thousand words a day. But here's the kicker." And I frame the revelation with my hands. "Men speak twelve of those thirteen thousand during business, leaving one thousand for the rest of their talking. But the women speak ten thousand during business, leaving fifteen thousand miserable words for the rest of the time. Fifteen thousand variations of 'Do I look fat in these jeans?' I tell ya, God plays a strange game."

"Whatever," she says.

"What? Don't give me 'whatever.' I just gave you documented fact proving my point."

"No," she says. "You summarized what you read in a sad men's magazine."

"I didn't need a magazine to tell me what I already know. I know the fundamental differences between men and women."

She puts her hand on her hip. Why do girls always do that? As though a hand on a hip constitutes a valid argument? "And you get this from how much we want to talk?" she asks.

"It's not just how much. It's also *content*," I reply. And for some reason, as though I'm about to count the ways, I start enumerating on my right hand. "Talking about feelings? We don't want to talk about feelings. We don't even want to talk. We only have a thousand words. So we choose them wisely." Now I look at my hand and it occurs to me that I've only counted one.

"Ha. And what else do you know?"

"You really want to know?"

"I wouldn't be asking if I didn't," she says.

"Okay . . . sushi. We don't like it. We know *you* do. Oh, you girls *love* sushi. Where do you want to go for dinner? Sushi! Nine times out of ten you want sushi. And it's expensive. They're not even cooking your food, and it's the most expensive meal you can get."

"Uh-huh," she says. "What else?"

"Wine. We don't like wine. We like beer. Clothing? Do you think we really care? We don't. Shoes? Forget it!"

"Some men do care about clothes and shoes. Men with taste."

"*Gay* men. And what about *bathrooms*? Your bathrooms are a mess. Here's what we have in our bathrooms: a toothbrush, a razor, and a towel."

"True," she says. "Who needs toothpaste, soap, or deodorant when you're gonna be alone all your life?"

"You ladies, you have about three hundred products, two hundred and ninety-four of which—we have no idea what they are."

"You don't wear makeup," she defends.

"There's a lot more than makeup going on in there. It's a war zone."

"I've heard enough," she says, contemplating her fingernails again. "You can have your little *man party.*"

"Oh, thanks for your permission."

"You're welcome."

"Did you come here for something?"

"Oh yeah," she says. "Almost forgot, I got your mail."

"And? What are the lowlights?"

"How should I know? I didn't read it."

"Really?" I say in shock.

"No, I read it. You got some CDs. They're not very good."

"You listened to them?"

"Yeah," she says, "and they suck."

"They're probably demos. So yeah, they probably *do* suck." I'm beyond getting mad at this point. I just assume that she's going to read my mail. She's Heaven. It's what she does.

"Are you in the music business?"

"Yeah, I own a label."

"Really? That's cool," she says, kind of lighting up. "Do you put anything out that I'd know?"

"Doubt it. Our most popular release was a compilation we put together of cover songs. It's the *only* thing generating any income, and I think that stream may be drying up soon."

"Why?"

"Because I just read on this Web discussion board where someone wrote, 'Right, asshole, do that and I'll pay you back with a Christmas present of that played-out compilation disc from Shitstack Records.'"

"Shitstack? *That's* a memorable name," she says.

"It's Sleestak, actually."

"What's the name of the compilation?"

"*Looks Like We Re-Made It.*"

"Manilow? *Hilarious.* What are they covering? Songs to retch by?"

"No, cool seventies songs that the kids today don't know but would love if they were done by bands they *like.* 'Baker Street' . . . 'Seasons in the Sun' . . . 'Bad, Bad Leroy Brown'—"

"I *love* that song," she says, and she gives me this obnoxious slap on the arm that actually hurts, but I don't show it. "All of those songs. What else?"

"'Crosstown Traffic'—"

"Hendrix?"

"Of course."

"He died at twenty-seven, you know," she says. I'm surprised that she knows that.

"Yes, I know."

"So did Kurt Cobain."

"I know."

"And Jim Morrison and Janis Joplin." She seems to know her dead players.

"Do you know the ages of all dead musicians or just the ones who died at twenty-seven?"

"Just those," she says. And then she adds in an almost embarrassed mumble, "It's sort of a thing I have."

"What kind of thing?"

"Just a thing," she says, looking distractedly across the room. "Nothing you need to know."

"You seem to need to know everything about *me* . . ."

"You'll think it's crazy."

"I already *know* you're crazy," I retort, and she makes one of her faces at me. Then she sort of squints her eyes at me. Like she's deciding if I deserve to know.

"I've always thought that I was going to die at twenty-seven—" she finally blurts.

"God, that's really morbid. Why?"

"Well, you didn't let me finish. Not conserving your thousand words," she says with a smile.

"Finish," I say.

"I've always thought that unless I do *something* before I'm twenty-seven that I'm going to die. But if I do *something,* then I won't."

"Like make a mark in the world? I hate to say it, but all of those people made pretty big marks, and they still died."

"No. Not like that."

"Then what?"

She opens her mouth wide and rolls her eyes way up in their sockets. I've seen this before. It's what people do at altitude to make their ears pop. But we're only on the fourth floor. Then she comes back down to earth. "Get married," she says—like, no big deal.

"If you get married you won't die?"

"Yes," she says matter-of-factly. In fact, she says it with such conviction I believe her. At least I believe she believes it.

"Huh," I say, because I don't know what else to say. Kurt was married, but I don't want to bring that up. I don't think it's about whether or not they were all married. I think it's just something she believes, and I'm not going to argue with her about it. For the first time I don't want to argue with her. It feels kinda weird. She reminds me a little of the dog she just rescued. Helpless, but happy. Not hopeless. And I almost want to take care of her. Almost.

Just then Zach shows up, and Phil marches in right behind him. I think Phil has always looked up to Zach—or at least wished he and I had the friendship that Zach and I have. But Phil also realizes that he's the Joey to our collective Chandler.

"Do I smell mini-pizzas?" Zach asks.

"The nose knows," I say.

"It's a beautiful thing," Zach says.

"How can you smell the difference between mini-pizza and regular pizza?" Phil asks. Nobody responds for a minute, then we all start laughing. All of us, that is, but Phil.

Heaven looks at me. "I think I get it now," she says and starts for the door. "I'll catch you later."

"Sure you don't want to stay?" Zach asks.

"No, thanks. I have plans," Heaven says.

"No you don't, loser," I say.

"Yes, I do," she insists. "I have plans with Sydney."

"That's why you were just begging me to let you play poker with us," I say.

"I wouldn't say I was *begging,*" she replies. "And I was only asking you to see what your response would be."

"Right."

"You're so funny when you think you're right. It's kind of sad, actually. Love to chat, but Sydney is probably waiting in the hall right now wondering where I am. By the way, Hi . . . and bye," she says to Zach and Phil.

"By all means, invite Sydney," I say, calling her bluff, wanting to watch her squirm a little. Which is mean, I admit.

She opens the door and smiles.

"Hey, girl! Come in here for a second." She's either taking this *way* too far or I'm a huge idiot. Once again.

Sure enough, I'm a huge idiot. In walks her friend, Sydney. The one that called me retarded. Idiot, retarded—six of one, half a dozen of the other.

"This is Sydney, everybody," Heaven says. "I'd introduce you gentlemen, but I don't know your names."

"Where are my manners?" I say. "Zach and Phil." And then Jonas walks in. "And Jonas."

"Nice to meet you," Sydney says.

"You're so burned," Heaven says. Then she slowly walks up to me and gets really close. It's almost sexy. Who am I kidding? It is *very* fucking sexy. And she whispers, "But not as burned as your mini-pizzas," and she cracks up, dashing out and dragging her friend with her. I turn around and see smoke coming from my oven. Zach's jaw drops after she leaves.

"Dude," he says. "Totally holding out. What's up?"

"Nothing." I run to the oven and open it, letting out a giant cloud of smoke. "Shit."

"Salvageable?" Zach asks.

"Definitely," I say as I pull out the sheet of burnt-to-a-crisp mini-pizzas. "If you mean, can we still use them for *something.*"

"Poker chips!" Phil offers.

"So, uh . . . that Heaven chick? She's hot, man," Zach says. "What's going on there? I detected a little sexual tension."

"Nothing going on. She's just the local pain in my ass."

"Then may *I*?" Zach asks.

"No, you may not," I say.

"Knew it," he says.

"What about the friend?" Phil asks. "She looks like she'd take it in the poop chute like a champ . . . if you catch my meaning."

"No, Phil," Zach says. "We have no idea what you mean."

"What is *wrong* with you?" I ask. "Never mind."

"I have some stuff to show you," Jonas says, and he pulls out his latest incarnation of the Cinnamilk mock-ups. It's much better. No sign of the mystery meat. Bacon and eggs. Some buttered toast. And Cinnamilk. Glorious Cinnamilk.

"Love it," I say. "I need a tagline. You guys got any ideas?"

"How about . . . 'Who needs the cereal when you have the leftovers?'" Phil offers.

"It's not about cereal," I say.

"You said it's like the milk left over in the bowl after Cinnamon Toast Crunch—"

"But it's about the *milk*. Chocolate milk may resemble the milk after a bowl of Count Chocula, but they don't talk about Count Chocula in the ads."

"Okay, I got it," Phil says. "'Because you're too young for fiber.'"

"What does that have to do with anything?" I sigh.

"Fiber cereals!" Phil explains.

"I know, Phil. So we're back to cereal. Cereal I just said I didn't want to use. And by the way, you're never too young for fiber."

"Dude, no shit," Zach says. "I didn't eat enough for dinner last night, and the first thing I ate this morning was pretzels. It was like a giant fist trying to come out my ass."

"Not helping the plight," I say.

"Okay," Zach says. "How about, 'Cinnamilk! Two of the worst bad-breath creators . . . together at last!'"

"Fuck you," I say. "Cinnamon is good. They make mints . . . gum . . . cinnamon freshens breath."

"I've always hated cinnamon gum," Zach says.

"This isn't gum!"

"'Cinnamilk! When you're done . . . smack your lips and gums! It'll sound like two beavers fucking.'" This gem comes from Phil. Then he walks over to my refrigerator and swings the door open. "Dude . . . *speaking of*—the typical protocol is to chuck the milk *before* it goes brown."

"Ah, but not just any milk," I say. "*Cinnamilk*—that's it. Want a sip?" Phil shrugs and begins to lift the plastic container to his mouth. "DUMBASS," I shout. "That's okay for me, but I have home-field advantage." I grab down a motley assortment of glasses, at least two of them clean, and pour three samples. Zach is the first to bite the bullet.

"You know something?" he says.

"What?" I say excitedly.

"That tastes exactly like cow piss." He sees I take this seriously and quickly corrects. "Kidding. Brady . . . you may be onto something."

Jonas nods his head. "I wouldn't give up regular or chocolate milk for it, but not bad," he says.

Seeing the others' reactions, Phil downs his. "Yes, indeed. Definitely . . . very good. Really. I'd pay for this shit." Then he returns to the refrigerator. "But let's move on to that other brown beverage I saw in here." And he pulls out four beers. All in all, very positive, considering the generous helping of negativity and humiliation these guys normally dish out.

"Hey, thanks for the new artwork, man," I say to Jonas.

"No problem. We'll think of a tagline. Don't worry," he says. "Hey, Jenny and I are selling our living room carpet, since she's forcing me to remove anything manly and stylish from our apartment in favor of more feminine furnishings. Before I post any flyers in our building or at work, you want anything? You know that killer rug I have? It's in great condition. Be perfect here, dude. Looking for around ten thousand dollars, but that's highly negotiable. I'm thinking around fifty bucks."

"As much as the offer's appreciated," I say, "I think I'm going to pass. I am intent on getting a nice Persian rug."

"To allow for some nice Persian rug burns," Zach chimes in.

"Suit yourself," Jonas says.

"Dudes . . ." Zach says, "try this one on for size—"

"Oh, God," Jonas says. "Here comes another imperfect crime."

"You establish a fake museum in a country that doesn't exist," Zach says. "You go all around to the great museums toting these phony programs for past sold-out shows, hyping your exhibition to the curators, pissing them off that *every other guy's* best Impressionist piece is going to be in your show, but not theirs. They'd be *throwing* the stuff at you. Van Goghs . . . Monets . . . Manets . . ."

"Mayonnaise," Phil chimes in.

"Renoirs," Zach continues, ignoring him. "Anyway . . . you'd get these great works of art delivered to your door."

"What's the address of this imaginary country," I ask.

"It's actually a warehouse in the Bronx," Zach says.

Phil, Jonas, and I all simultaneously roll our eyes. Then Jonas, thankfully, changes the subject. "I made a reservation at Brother Jimmy's on Ninety-second for Thursday's game." Jonas went to Duke with Phil and me. Zach went to Carolina. Thursday's game is Duke/UNC. "Thursday night, Brother Jimmy's. Good vs. Evil. You in?"

"Go to hell, Heels," I say. "Yeah, I'm in."

"Oh yeah, Tarheels," Jonas says. "I was, of course, referring to us vs. Zach, but I guess the Good vs. Evil applies to Duke/UNC as well." Zach tosses a burnt mini-pizza at Jonas.

"Hey!" I say. "No tossing of food items. Especially after the olive incident." Zach and I bow our heads simultaneously and say, "Rest his soul." Phil and Jonas look confused but don't ask.

"All right," Jonas says. "Count on Scott Mulcahey coming along as well. I think you guys have met him before. He's the asshole who blew the curve in every class I took freshman year. Lady Zachary, pending the outcome of any bets that may or may not be placed, should I make ready your corset?"

"No need for that," Zach says. "However, after you're done with your impotency pills, I'm sure Brady'll want some."

"Those things don't work," Phil says.

"No shit," Zach says. "I'm taking like ten Levitra a day and I still can't throw a football through a tire."

"That's okay," Jonas says. "I'm loaded up on Cialis and can't even find my rubber ducky."

"I don't have herpes," I say. "But those Valtrex commercials sure do make it seem like a hell of a lot of fun."

"Are we playing poker or what?" Zach asks. And we settle into a poker game that lasts till some time between three and four. In the end I'm too tired to look. Or too depressed. I lose. Again.

• • •

Heaven

Everybody is just waiting for me to fuck up again at work. I can feel it the minute I walk in, and it doesn't go away. It's like I'm in an alternate reality watching myself go through the motions and even *I'm* waiting for me to fuck up. This is not a good feeling, and I can't shake it.

So I start thinking about the worst possible scenarios and imagining how they'd play out. And I write a fake letter of complaint about myself just to ease the tension and make a joke out of it—an example of how asinine some of the customers are. Here's how it turns out:

February 2, 2004

Temple Restaurant
ATTN: Manager
575 Mercer Street
New York, NY 10003

Dear Sir and/or Madam:

I have had occasion to dine at your establishment approximately six or seven times during the last few months. I think it is fair to say my wife and I are "regulars." Though the service and food are generally exemplary at Temple, I regret to inform you of our most recent—and decidedly unsatisfactory—visit to your restaurant.

On the evening of January 21, my wife and I arrived for dinner at 7:30. We were seated in the section of a young woman who appears to still be "learning the ropes" of the restaurant business. This is by no means reflective of a sexist attitude—my wife and I share a joint checking account, in fact.

This young lady introduced herself as "Heaven"—an unusual name, which I assume is fake to go along with the "Temple" restaurant theme.

In an attempt to get things started "on the right foot" I made a joke, arguably inappropriate, in which I mentioned that my wife was menstruating—an event which generally heightens her appetite. "Better get her fed quickly, Heaven. This time of the month, she's ravenous!" Heaven seemed annoyed by this comment—even though I was talking about *my own wife's* menstruation—to which I have a right. I'm sure you'll agree? In any case, it was no excuse for the events which followed.

My wife asked what wines you offered by the glass and she told us merlot, cabernet, chardonnay, pinot grigio, and white zinfandel. My wife asked for the white zinfandel and this waitress returned with a glass of pink wine. Pink!

"I asked for *white* zinfandel," my wife said.

"That *is* white zinfandel," Heaven replied. Does this woman think we are stupid *and* color blind? This wine was no more white than the majority of your staff.

The salads arrived in short order and were excellent. I tried to extend an olive branch to Heaven by quipping that there'd be "no more menstruation comments—*period.*" I thought this rather clever, but it did not improve her mood. When our entrées arrived late, Heaven told us that the kitchen was a little backed up. I pointed out that, given my dodgy colon, I too am often "backed up," but I wouldn't use it as an excuse for poor service. Well. In an angry tone, which was highly inappropriate, Heaven told me that she had no interest in hearing any more about my colon or my wife's vagina. Let me repeat—*your waitress mentioned my wife's vagina.*

Finally—the pièce de résistance. As we drank our coffee at the end of our meal, I found myself needing to blow my nose. Generally I carry a handkerchief, and certainly I *should* have had one with me. But, alas—I did not. Since our tablecloth had been somewhat stained by my wife's spilled glass of "white" zinfandel (Ha!), I assumed your establishment would have the need to launder it after our departure. Given that fact, I couldn't see what difference it made if the cloth was a little more soiled. Although I'm not proud of this fact, I was in great discomfort, so I discreetly blew my nose into the tablecloth.

Unfortunately, Heaven had singled us out for her wrath on this evening. She must have been watching me from across the room because she stormed over and asked me if I "needed a tissue." Can you believe the nerve of this girl? I found this to be highly impertinent and, frankly, embarrassing. I told her, "No, thank you—just the check."

Not content to leave bad enough alone, Heaven pointed out that I had left "a big bloody booger" on the tablecloth.

A "booger."

Sir or Madam: Zagat's gives your restaurant their highest rating. And you risk your reputation by having a waitress who uses crude language to customers. Appalling.

Naturally, I was quite indignant. I told her that as far as I was concerned, that "booger" could serve as her tip.

This seemed to (finally) put her in her place. She flounced off without another smart-alecky comment.

I'm sorry to complain, but—really—what are things coming to when a man can't spend a dignified evening enjoying some fine dining with his wife without a churlish (although attractive) trollop ruining the evening with her gutter mouth?

I would be happy to accept one year's free dining as compensation for this nightmarish experience (provided we can sit in someone else's section!). I sincerely hope to resolve this matter absent the threat of litigation.

Sincerely,
Royston Felcher, Jr., Esquire

* * *

I enjoy my composition so much and think it's so funny, I print it out and mail it to the restaurant as a joke. I can't wait till they get it.

I see Brady on my way out of the apartment building, and he's got a cactus in his hand. It appears to be dead.

"You managed to kill a cactus?" I say.

"Yeah. I remembered the no water bit but forgot the plenty of sunlight part."

"Sorry. So what are you doing with it?"

"Honestly?" Brady says. "I don't know. I felt bad throwing it away. I couldn't do it. So I thought I'd . . . I don't know. Lay it to rest somewhere out here. Maybe near a tree or in a bush."

"That's really sad," I say, because it is. It's also kind of heartbreaking. And sweet.

"Yeah, I've kind of been wandering up and down the block looking for the right spot," he says.

"Maybe it had a great life. All plants die," I say, trying to make him feel better. "It's a living thing. And all living things die." That didn't come out as uplifting as I'd wanted it to. "So cheer up," I add. "Because today it was just a cactus. Someday it'll be you." Yeah, that wasn't much better.

"What's next? You gonna tell me Santa Claus isn't real?"

"Worse—you know how they tell you when you go to the Olive Garden, you're family? You're not *really* family."

"That hurts."

"Love to stay and chat, but I gotta go to work," I say. "Sorry again about your cactus."

"Thanks," he says, pretending to wipe a tear the way Letterman sometimes does.

I've decided I'm going to speak with an accent at work today. I think this is a good idea for two reasons. One, it's a good way to entertain myself, and two, it may help me stay out of trouble. If I'm busy focusing on the accent, and therefore in character (somewhat), I won't react to bad customers in my normal fashion.

It's a toss-up between Australian and white-trash Southern, but I go with Australian. There is a big difference between Australian and British, though to the layman they sound quite similar. I can do Australian perfectly. British too, for that matter. In addition to my keen sense of smell I've got this uncanny knack for accents and imitations. When I was little I was like a mynah bird. It caused all sorts of trouble. I'd constantly repeat things I heard—often at inappropriate times.

Like once when I was seven years old I overheard the dental hygienist arguing with my dentist. And when I walked out into the waiting room I proudly said, "For fuck's sake, Gerald, I don't blow you for my health. Either you leave her or I'm going to shove her PTA boat up her ass."

The whole office got quiet. My mom took my hand and walked me outside, where she said, "It's a PTA book, not boat. You can't shove a boat up someone's ass." To which I replied, "I must have heard her wrong." My mom was always very cool.

So I'm Australian today, and so far so good. When people ask, I tell them I'm from Sydney, and I really love being here. I just hope I can renew my visa when it runs out.

Brett the not-so-new busboy has been mumbling to himself all day. He won't stop. It's definitely a mumble, not a hum. I've heard the word *fuck* at least thirty-two times. He's always pissed off. It's kind of amazing how he's never been anything but irate. I don't know what they were thinking when they hired him. I don't know how he's managed to stay around.

Table 4 has been asking me questions about Australia all night, and I've been playing it up. But they seem to know a lot about my "homeland" already.

"So do you think you'll win another Equestrian?" one guy asks.

"Pardon?"

"You've won three in a row at the Olympics. This would be your fourth consecutive gold medal."

"Oh, the Olympics. Right. Yeah, we have some good horses," I say. "Can I get you anything else?" I ask, trying to change the subject.

"No, I'm great. This soup is fantastic. Bet you don't have anything like it down under," he says.

"No, we don't have much soup there," I say, which is completely lame, but what the hell am I going to say.

I entertain these people for the better part of my night, taking time away from other tables, because they've been the nicest. They also have the biggest check, which translates, hopefully, to the best tip.

When they leave, they wish me well and hope that I can extend my visa. I open their check and they've left *no* tip. This makes no sense whatsoever. They were way too nice to do that.

Brett sees the expression on my face, walks over and takes a look at the check.

"Motherfuckers!" he says, seemingly more angry that I am. In fact, I'm not mad at all. I'm more shocked than anything. Brett, being the busboy, gets a percentage of my tips—so he's taking this personally. He's steaming. But then he smiles this giant grin. He reaches onto their table and picks up their digital camera, which they've left.

"They'll probably come back for that," I say. "They know where they had it last."

"Better believe they will," Brett says, putting the camera in his pocket and walking away with it.

"They were my table," I say, walking after him. "You can't keep it. I'll be the one to get in trouble."

"I'm not gonna keep it," he says, continuing into the kitchen.

About fifteen minutes later the customer comes back. I assume it's for his camera, but it's not.

"I'm so sorry," he says. "I meant to leave cash when I signed my credit card. I don't leave tips on my credit cards, and I guess I had too much wine. I completely forgot."

"No problem," I say. And he takes some cash out of his wallet and hands it to me. See? I knew they were too nice to stiff me.

"Here you go. Thanks again. You were great," he says and turns to leave.

"Wait," I say suddenly. "You forgot your camera."

"Oh my God! I didn't even notice," he says.

"Hang on, let me get it," I say and go into the kitchen to find Brett. He's not there. I look all over, but he's nowhere to be found. I panic, thinking he decided to finally quit and take the camera with him. But finally I spot him coming out of the bathroom and breathe a sigh of relief.

"Brett, I need the camera. The guy came back." Brett smiles this really strange smile.

"He was commenting on the soup, right? He really liked the soup."

"Yeah," I say as I take the camera from him.

I race back to the guy and return his camera.

"Here you go. This is a nice one. Don't go leaving it at your next stop," I say with a wink.

"I won't." He winks back. "Thank you so much."

Brett walks over to me. He looks annoyed.

"You were awfully chummy with the guy that stiffed us," he says.

"He didn't. He didn't even come back for his camera. He came back because he realized he forgot to tip."

"How do you forget to tip?" Brett asks and now he seems even *more* angry that the guy came back and tipped us than he was when he thought he stiffed us.

"I don't know. It happens. He's drunk. He paid with a credit card."

"Fuck," Brett says.

"What?"

"You're not gonna like it."

"What?" I say.

"The guy was commenting on the soup, right?"

"Yeah?"

"I heard him saying how much he liked it."

"Yeah?" I say impatiently. "And?"

"I just took a picture with his camera. Of me pissing into a bowl of soup."

"You what? You peed into soup?"

"Yes."

"And took a picture of it."

"Yes."

"What is *wrong* with you?" I fairly scream in his face.

"I hate people. It's fucking cold outside. I'm thirty-seven years old, and I'm a busboy. How much time do you have because I can go on and on—"

"Brett! I can appreciate all that . . . but you just did something really bad."

"Hey—I didn't know he was going to come back and tip us."

I feel sick. I feel clammy and sick. I can't believe he just did that. I'm mortified. Partly because I can't fathom how someone could do such a thing. And worse, I'm *one* of them. I can't believe I spit in that guy's Caesar salad a month ago. I feel awful. Granted, it's not pee, and I didn't take a picture of myself doing it, but I feel truly awful just the same. Sydney was *so* right. Forget karma paying me back—my own guilt and shame are doing plenty for that cause. I hate myself for doing that. What have I become? I know that nine out of ten waiters have spit in food or much worse, but I could have been the one that didn't. And Brett doesn't even think what he did was wrong. Except in the context that the guy came back. If he hadn't tipped us Brett would feel perfectly justified.

"Look," he says. "If it comes up, just say you don't know how it got there."

"If? *If* it comes up?"

He grabs his crotch. "It's obvious *you* didn't do it. A *guy* had to do it so you're off the hook."

"They can figure out who was working tonight, you know."

"What are they gonna do?" Brett says. "Make us all pull out our dicks in a lineup?"

"Who knows?"

"Just don't worry about it," he says and walks away.

• • •

Brady

This morning I wake up feeling a little confused and a lot hungover. Heaven is sitting on my bed, and my reality seems a little distorted.

"Hi," I say, not sure how many beers I drank last night and wondering what the hell went on.

"Morning," she says, and she doesn't seem happy at all. Did something happen between us? I'm going to hope for *no* if this is her reaction to it.

"What's wrong?" I ask hesitantly.

"Everything," she says. She falls onto my bed and buries her face in the pillow. "How did this happen?" she asks. At least I think that's what she asked. Her voice is so muffled with her face in the pillow.

"Too much alcohol?" I offer, now thinking that maybe we had sex.

"Huh?" she says, and sits up.

"I don't know," I say. "I'm hungover. I may still be drunk, in fact. Speak slowly, and start at the beginning."

"It's not that I've failed—really . . . it's not. I mean, I *do* the job. I do what I'm supposed to do. Sure, I may have had a few 'conflicts' as Marco likes to say." Who is Marco, and what is she talking about?

"Uh-huh . . ." I say, trying just to listen and appear to know what we are talking about.

"I think it's just . . . you know what it is?"

"No, I don't," I say.

"I failed to adapt. I entered a world I didn't know, and I just didn't adapt." She sighs. "And for whatever reason, I can't. People make changes in their life, and they blend and assimilate. They find a way to make it work. That's where I've always taken the wrong turn. By not taking a turn at all."

"I'm sorry, what *are* we talking about?"

"Work," she says. "The restaurant. I wasn't always a waitress, you know."

"So we didn't have sex?"

"What?" She sits straight upright and looks at me like I've got three heads and one of them is wearing a sombrero.

"I don't know. I just woke up, and you were here."

"Zach let me in on his way out!"

"Ah. Okay then."

"Gross!" She recoils. "You think I'd have *sex* with you?"

"Gross?"

"And you wouldn't remember it?"

"I'm still stuck on the gross part," I say, scratching my neck and squinting.

"Believe me, if we had sex you'd remember it."

"I'd like to think so."

"But we won't," she says quickly.

"Fair enough. So back to you. You didn't adapt."

"Exactly," she says. "And I hate feeling like a failure."

"You're not a failure. You're just not a very good waitress."

"But I could have faked it better."

"Well, what happened? Did you get fired?"

"No," she says glumly. "But I got a warning."

"Okay. So, that's not the end of the world."

"That was before Brett peed in my customer's soup."

I'm sure I've heard what she said. Every word. Clear as a bell. Yet it seems essential to add, "Pardon?"

"Not his actual bowl of soup. It's not something I want to talk about."

"Okay . . ." I say quite happily because I'm still half asleep, and the last thing I want to think about right now is pee soup.

"I don't even know why I'm here," she says.

At that moment I feel something on my foot. It's cold and wet, and it freaks me the fuck out.

"What the *hell*?" I say. I jump out of my bed and see Strummer at the foot of my bed. "Oh . . . didn't know he was here, too. I felt something under my covers, which was apparently a nose. Hi, Strummer."

"Sorry." Heaven's really down. I don't know what to do, but it seems like it's on me to cheer her up. So I put on a sweatshirt and jeans and grab my keys.

"Come on," I say.

The Central Park Zoo is one of those places that people who live in New York City don't take advantage of enough. It's right here in the middle of Central Park, and it's got everything you could possibly want from a zoo. Most important, the monkeys. It's nearly impossible not to enjoy monkeys. I think their sole purpose is to act foolish for our entertainment. Never mind the fact that they are merely imitating us humans, so who are the real fools?

As we walk up to the admission line I turn around and discreetly put on a pair of dark sunglasses.

"Give me Strummer and hold on to my arm," I tell her.

"Why?" she asks. Of course. Never content to just do as I—or anyone—asks.

"Just do it," I say. And she does.

"No dogs allowed," says the woman at the window.

"This is my Seeing Eye dog," I say. The woman looks as if she's trying to look at my eyes through my glasses. "I'm blind."

"That don't look like a Seeing Eye dog to me," she says.

"Well, being that I can't see, I don't know what he looks like," I say, a little miffed. I turn to Heaven, who can't believe what I'm doing. She looks like she's about to burst out laughing. I kick it up a notch and start to act upset. "What's this woman saying to me? Did they give me a cheap Seeing Eye Dog? What did they give me, a fucking poodle?"

"Your dog is fine," Heaven says. "He's a perfectly acceptable Seeing Eye dog," she adds. And then she whirls on the woman in the window. "Are you trying to give this man a complex? He's already *blind,* for Christ's sake!" The woman is now very uncomfortable and embarrassed.

"No, ma'am. I just never seen that breed before. I apologize." And she starts to fumble as she gets out our tickets.

"I think you should only charge us for one," I say. "Since I won't actually be able to *see* anything."

"Um . . . of course," the woman says, clearly never having been in this type of situation before. "That will be twelve dollars," she says. And I pay her. And Heaven, Strummer, and I walk into the zoo.

"Nicely done," Heaven says.

"Well, you weren't so bad yourself."

We do the zoo as much as one can do before getting exhausted. There are only so many animals you can look at. Heaven falls in love with one of the monkeys, and she insists we go back and visit him once more before we leave.

When we get there, it seems her fickle monkey friend has found another. He snubs Heaven for a four-year-old boy with a banana. The kid wants to share his banana with the monkey, but his mother tells him he can't. So the kid starts screaming, and then the monkey starts screaming, and we decide it's time to go.

Heaven's mood is decidedly improved, and I'm glad for that. I would have loved to take her to Serendipity for frozen hot chocolate, except now that they used it in that God-awful movie, I feel like I can't. The next best thing is s'mores at DT-UT, a coffeehouse on the Upper East Side. But we can't take Strummer in there, and I don't want to pull the blind thing again—so as a last resort I buy Hershey bars, marshmallows, and graham crackers at the corner deli and head back to my place.

We're in my kitchen—which, if you've been to New York, you know is small. But more relevant to the situation, my stove is electric, as are many stoves in New York City apartments. My great s'mores idea is a bust.

Heaven cracks up, and that alone makes it totally worth being the monkey that I feel like.

"So, what's the worst thing about your job?" I ask.

"Besides everything?"

"Yes, besides that."

"The customers. They're just so rude. Or worse, stupid. And annoying . . ."

"Example?"

"Okay," she says. "Yesterday I had a woman ask me what kind of salad dressings we have. I told her we have sesame soy dressing, spicy lime vinaigrette, and blue cheese. She made a face and asked, 'Is that all?' 'Yes,' I told her, 'those are all of our dressings.' 'You don't have *any* other dressings?' she says. I mean, what the hell? What does she think? That I'm holding out? I was tempted to say, 'No, we actually have an entirely different assortment of dressings that I don't tell people about the first time they ask, because they don't deserve these great secret dressings. But now that you have proven your worth, I will show you to the VIP room, where the array of salad dressings will dazzle and delight you.'"

Heaven is funny. I always knew she was funny, but I'm usually so caught up in her being annoying I don't give her credit where it's due.

"I got nothin'," I say. "I wish I had a silver lining to offer, but customer service has never been my bag. All I can do is empathize."

"That's plenty," she says. "And speaking of which, feel free to throw some of that empathy my way right now, because I have to go to work."

"Really?" I ask, knowing that she's clearly not lying. Suddenly I feel like the salad dressing lady, and she has every right to make fun of me for it but doesn't. And I realize I'm disappointed that our hang time has to come to such an abrupt end.

"Yes, really," she says. "Thanks for today. Seriously. You totally cheered me up."

"No sweat," I say. "Hey—" I add before I even know what's coming out of my mouth. "You wanna leave Strummer here when you go to work?"

"Really?" See, she just did it, too.

"Yes, really. I miss having a dog. I haven't had one for years. Strummer and I can bond a little."

"Yeah, that would be great!" she says. "I'm sure he'd love it. Just don't teach him any bad habits. I've finally got him to put the toilet seat down."

There's a dog in my apartment, and I'm listening to sappy Elvis Costello songs. She's been gone for three hours, and there is still a giant smile on my face. This is all her fault.

• ● •

"A little nonsense now and then is relished by the wisest men."

—Willy, *Willy Wonka and the Chocolate Factory*

"Okey dokey, Doggie Daddy."

—Alabama, *True Romance*

Heaven

This is *so* not cool. I just left Brady's apartment after spending the entire day with him, and now everything seems different. He was actually nice to me, for once, and now I don't know what to think. Not that I really need to think about it. I mean, I don't. That's stupid. He's a neighbor. And maybe a friend. That's that.

I walk into work, and Marco tells me I look happy. It's not what he says, though . . . it's how he says it. Like he's perplexed by it.

"Do I usually look unhappy?" I ask.

"Yes," he says. He's not intending to be insulting, just stating what he assumes to be the obvious. "But now you are smiling. You are much prettier when you smile."

"Thank you," I say.

"These fucking assholes!" Brett says as he walks past, waving a knife at us and mimicking a customer. "'My knife isn't clean—*waaaa*!'"

"I'm not like *that,* am I?" I ask Marco, motioning to Brett.

"Nobody is like that. I have fear that he will kill somebody. I just try to stay out of his way," he says. We watch as Brett dips the knife into a water pitcher, wipes it with a napkin, and brings the same knife right back to the table. I hate to say it, but this is actually common practice. Waiters use the water pitchers to clean dirty silverware all the time and then pour the same water into people's glasses. This is why I always spring for the bottled water when I'm out. And I advise others to do the same.

Midway through the night, I start to smell something. I mean something really bad. At first I think someone has devastatingly bad gas, but it doesn't go away. It's no secret that I pride myself on my keen sense of smell, but this smell is so wretched that I'd gladly give up my olfactory sense just to avoid experiencing it.

It's centered on Table 19, which happens to be the closest table to the bathroom. I wonder if maybe there's a problem in there.

"Do you smell that?" I ask the guests at Table 19. "It's *terrible.*"

"I don't smell anything," the older man at the table says. But there's no way he can't smell it. The woman scowls at me, so I assume that she *can* smell it and isn't pleased by it.

"I'm really sorry about this. I can't imagine what it is," I say. "Maybe we're having a problem with our toilets. I'll try to have it taken care of."

I'm really embarrassed about it, and I know Bruce and Jean Paul would have a fit if they knew that the restaurant smelled like a sewer. So I go to the bathroom to check it out. It's fine. In fact, the farther I walk away from Table 19 the better it gets.

I walk back to Table 19 and there it is. The God-awful smell is front and center. I can't stand it. I can't wait on this table. Maybe one of them stepped in dog shit and dragged it in here—whatever that dog is eating is lethal. I don't know how to bring it up, but it seems the only way to do it is just to politely ask.

"Excuse me," I say. "I'm sorry . . . I know this is rather awkward, but . . . does anyone think that perhaps they may have *stepped* in something outside?"

They look mortified. And now so do I. I don't know what to do. It's awful. And the weird thing is—now they are ignoring me. I don't know what to do.

"Hello?" I say, and they all look down, not answering me. "Hi," I say again. Am I losing my mind? I am speaking out *loud,* right?

"Excuse me," I say. "I'm your waitress, remember? I brought you your drinks before?" Still nothing. "Look, someone here has stepped in something," I say. I'm circling their table, sniffing it out like the bloodhound that I am. Finally, I zero in on the older woman, and I know for a *fact* that it is her. Well, almost for a fact. I haven't seen her shoes. I start to kneel down—

"Get away from me!" she screams and bursts into tears.

"What is going on here?" Jean Paul says, suddenly appearing out of nowhere.

"This woman is harassing us," the man says. Jean Paul starts shaking his head in disappointment.

"I'm not harassing them," I say. "I was trying to help! It smells like the outhouse from hell over here, and I was just trying to—"

"That is *quite* enough," the man says. "My wife has a colostomy bag. And apparently it has sprung a leak. It *happens.* But this woman wouldn't leave us alone about it."

There are no words for how I feel right now. If I could crawl under her colostomy bag and die, I would. I am horrified. I want to run out of there, but my legs feel like jelly.

"I am terribly sorry, sir," Jean Paul says. "Your meal will, of *course,* be on us."

"We're not staying," he says, throwing his napkin down for effect. He helps his wife up, and their two friends follow, scowling at me on their way out.

I look around for Bruce, and thank God he doesn't know this is going on. I see him over at the bar, reading the mail. When he finishes what he's reading, he looks up at me and points.

"Me?" I mouth.

"Yes, you," he says at the highest volume that I've ever heard him use in the restaurant—and that's saying something. "Get over here."

I walk over to him, and Jean Paul follows.

"Yet another complaint about you," Bruce says.

"I didn't mean to—" I stop. What do I say? How can I possibly justify what just happened? But I really wasn't trying to be rude or offensive. I was honestly trying to help.

Then I look at the letter in his hands, and I realize he's not even talking about what just happened. I mean really, how could he have been? He was reading mail way across the restaurant when it was happening. But *this* was even worse.

He was reading my letter.

FUCK.

"Oh, that?" I say.

"This is abominable," Bruce says.

"It's a joke," I offer meekly.

"A joke? You think telling someone they got bloody boogers on the tablecloth is a joke?"

"Well, yeah," I say. "The whole thing was a joke."

"Well, this man didn't find it very funny, and neither do I," he says.

"No, no, no," I say. "That letter isn't *real,*" I try to explain. "I wrote it!"

"Heaven, we've put up with a lot of crap from you, but pointing out something like that to a customer . . . it's completely out of line."

"Are you not hearing me?" I say.

"Are you not hearing *me?*" he says back.

"No, you don't get it," I say.

"No, *you* don't get it," he says. "You're fired."

I don't even argue. I can't. There's no point. I take off my apron and walk out the door.

I'm only four or five paces down the street when a pigeon shits on my head. *Perfect.*

So that's it. I'm fired. I knew it was coming, and yet it's still a little shocking. I'm not really angry about it. I don't wish ass cancer on Bruce or Jean Paul. But it doesn't feel good—being fired never does. I have failed—and officially been told so. It's like a big red stamp came down and plastered FAILED on my forehead. And when I look in the mirror, there it is. Although it says ᗡƎ⅃IAꟻ because I'm looking in a mirror, and mirrors always reflect images backwards. But I still know what it means. I think the normal things that people feel after being fired are anger, guilt, and shame. Me? I feel like having several drinks.

I think it's safe to say that I'm drunk. I'm with Sydney at Dos Caminos and I've had several margaritas. I called her when I got fired, and she insisted that we go out drinking.

"And did I tell you I got shat on? By a pigeon?"

"Several times," she says. "And I told *you* that it is supposedly good luck."

"Then let them shit on *you*. That kind of good luck, I don't need."

What I *do* need is some fresh air. I finish my drink and walk outside. We walk up Park Avenue and cut over to Third. I spot the Rodeo Bar a couple blocks up and insist we go in. Sydney hates country music of any kind. She doesn't get alt country or rockabilly or psychobilly. She's not in touch with her inner redneck. I drag her in anyway.

There's a band onstage. A three-piece country/rockabilly band and Sydney can't stand it.

She immediately chimes in, "I just don't get this music. It's twangy and whiny—"

"I love twangy. Twang is good," I say.

"Twang is not good. And what are they singing about? Every song is like, 'My girlfriend's cousin raped the cat.'"

"Somehow, I missed that lyric."

"It's just the whole mentality. I hate it," she says as she downs her drink. She's switched from margaritas to tequila shots. Patrón Silver. No lime, no salt, because only wusses do that. "And why is he all tattooed? The tattoos don't go with the plaid shirt. It's dissonant. He's either the tattoo guy who is wearing the plaid shirt because he's trying to pretend he likes country because that's the only kind of music that he's good at . . . or he's the country guy who came to New York and felt like he had to fit in, so he got all the tattoos. Either way, they don't work."

"No, it *does* work," I explain. "That's a look. He's rockabilly."

"He's what?"

"Rockabilly."

"What is that? Like Hillbilly Rockstar?" she asks. I crack up.

"It's a music style. And a lifestyle. The tattoos and pompadours . . . hot-rod cars . . . hollow-body guitars . . . pin-up girls. And the girls all want to be Bettie Page. Well, Bettie Page with tattoos."

"But why mix country with the fifties?"

"Why not?"

"Because I don't get it."

"Oh . . . in that case," I say.

"Sorry," she says. "I'm just not a little bit country. I'm all rock 'n' roll. And speaking of—this sucks! 'BROWN-EYED GIRL'!" she yells out. I can't believe it. I know it just happened, but I still can't believe it.

The band looks out at us and I sink into the floor. "No, don't do that," I say.

"Why not?"

"Because they're not taking requests," I say.

"How do *you* know?" she says. The band suddenly starts walking off the stage. I think it's because of her yelling, but it's actually because they've finished their set. And at this very moment, a cowboy takes his cue.

One of the band members took the "Brown-Eyed Girl" shout-out as a mating call, and saunters over to Sydney and me. He's not *totally* inked, but the tats peeking out from his cuffed plaid shirt promise more to be discovered. Looks like he's ripped under that shirt as well.

"'Brown-Eyed Girl,' huh?" he says. "Haven't heard that one in a long time. At least a couple of minutes." I get it *immediately,* but Sydney seems to be listening more with her eyes, so she doesn't make out what he's saying.

"You guys sounded really . . . really good," Sydney gushes. "What was that last song?" Oh God.

"It's an original of mine," he says, smooth as a Jack Daniel's milk shake.

"Who wrote it?" Sydney replies. All I can do is smile at him as if to say "she tries." But he's way ahead of me.

"What about *you*?" he says to me. "Did *you* like our set?"

"Yeah," I say. "You guys are really good." I sip my Seven & Seven and sort of look away. Sydney's eyes widen a little bit as if she's sensing I'm not into him, and she doesn't want to let this one flop off the hook.

"Yeah, she liked it a lot. She loves *rock-a-hillbilly.* We both do. The whole thing . . . the lifestyle," she says. In that moment he looks at her outfit and I'm thinking, Yeah, you're in head-to-toe Prada. You're a regular cowgirl.

Picking up on her eagerness, he not-so-subtly drops, "I've got a '56 Chevy Stepside parked right out front. Wanna check it out?"

"Stepside?" Sydney echoes uncertainly, not knowing what the hell he's talking about. He takes this as girlish awe and leads the way. Sydney follows him outside to his truck, and I trail behind.

"Wow . . ." she says. "That's so cool!" Sydney coos. And I have to admit, chromed out with cherry-red metallic paint, which shines like lip gloss, bumper to bumper . . . it is decidedly cool—calculated cool—one bad-ass motherfucker.

"Wanna take her for a spin around the block?" he offers. I know Sydney doesn't know how to drive a stick, and Sydney sure as shit knows she doesn't know how to drive a stick.

"Sure," she says. As I watch her take the keys to his classic car, it's as though it's all happening in slow motion.

"Sydney . . ." I say with all the reproach I can stuff into my voice.

"*What?*" she says, almost angrily.

"Use your blinkers." I smile.

Sydney jumps in on the driver's side, and he slides in on the passenger's side. I slide in next to him. The responsible thing at this moment would be for me to explain to this innocent country boy (probably Brooklyn born and bred) that he's risking his pride and joy on someone who's already well past tipsy—and can barely ride a bike on a good day. But I've got three drinks in me, I'm preoccupied with my own bad day, and those fuzzy dice he has hanging from the rearview mirror are making me feel lucky. Besides, I'm in that weird place that alcohol takes a person to, where ideas like a late-night bacon and broccoli sandwich start to sound brilliant.

Sure enough, Sydney's first act in her inaugural run with a

manual transmission is to grind the gears raucously—SGRRRRAAAAAKKKKK. For a split second he looks alarmed, but then he's like, "Hey . . . happens to everyone," and he relaxes again into a studied slouch.

"Ready?" Sydney says with a nervous smile, and I detect a warning. Then—bang! All hell's afire, the pickup lurches forward on a sharp angle into a raging stream of Third Avenue traffic. Taxicabs are swerving left and right, horns blare at us from every direction, and I can actually read the "What the fuck . . ." on the lips of the driver to my immediate right. Abruptly Sydney makes her correction, wheeling to the right at just as sharp an angle. And I am sure I will not make it to twenty-seven . . . or marriage . . . or tomorrow—because barreling toward us is a gigantic garbage truck, resembling a charging prehistoric rhino. Its full-throated foghorn is trying to blast us out of the way.

I hear a high-pitched scream, and I think at first it may be *me,* but then I realize it's the manly cowboy to my left who has just turned instantaneously into a bug-eyed, dashboard-grasping Don Knotts. Now we're stopped dead in the middle of Third Avnue.

"Where to *now*?" Sydney asks, delightfully unabashed by the predicament and the chorus of car horns urging us to a decision.

"Out!" he yells. "Get out!"

I survey the situation, and honestly, jumping out of the pickup into moving traffic on Third Avenue seems safer than continuing on Sydney's road trip. I grab her hand at the front of the car, and we Frogger our way to the sidewalk.

"Wait!" Sydney screams. And I'm thinking some irate driver has decided to run us down. "I didn't give him my phone number!" she says.

"Don't worry," I say. "He'll never forget you."

I check my mailbox when I get home, and I find my mold test results. And something from American Airlines for Brady. Where is *he* going? I tear open my letter from Mr. Mold, and it says my test was inconclusive. In-con-fucking-*clusive*? What the hell is *that*?

So I may or may not have the black mold. All of a sudden I've got a headache. It's probably the mold!

I go upstairs, and once I'm inside my apartment I open Brady's mail. It's a plane ticket to California. What's in California?

I can't think about this right now. I'm drunk, I have a headache, my apartment is infested with poisonous mold, and my dog is missing. Where is Strummer?

"Strummer!" I call out. Nothing. "Struuummmmer . . ." In the middle of the second syllable I remember he's next door at Brady's.

I walk out and bang on Brady's door. He comes to the door in 3-D glasses.

"Can I help you, madam?"

"I've come for my dog," I say.

He sniffs the air around me. "Has someone been drinking on the job?"

"No," I say. "Someone got fired, shat on by a pigeon, and embarrassed at a honky-tonk. And went drinking."

"Come in," he says. And I do. "You got fired?"

"Yeah," I say as I slump into his beanbag. Which is new. "When did you get this?" I ask.

"Jonas donated it. Wanna talk about it?"

"No. Lots of people have beanbags."

"I mean the job," he says. "Or lack of it?" Strummer comes and sits on top of me.

"What's in California?" I ask.

"Huh?"

"You got a plane ticket."

"Oh!" he says. "Should've known. A band. I'm going to check out a band we might sign. Then I'm going to Seattle."

"What's in Seattle?"

"Howard Schultz."

"The *Peanuts* guy?"

"No, that's Charles Schulz," he says.

"Why do you want to see the *Peanuts* guy?"

"I don't. And if I did, I'd be shit out of luck because he's dead."

I look aside. Had I heard that? I guess so. So many people seem to be dying. I was almost one of them tonight. "Oh. Then why are you going?"

"You *have* been drinking, haven't you? I'm going to meet Howard Schultz."

"Who is he?"

"The founder of Starbucks."

"I love coffee." I beam.

"Me too," he says. "And you could definitely use some right now."

"No, I need sleep. But I can't go home."

"Why not?"

"Because I have the *mold.*"

"The what?" he says.

"The mold," I say. I fall asleep on the beanbag with Strummer's head resting on my leg.

• • •

Brady

Heaven is asleep in my apartment. She spent the night last night curled up in a ball on my beanbag with Strummer. It's actually pretty darned cute.

I'm drinking coffee when Strummer yawns a giant lion yawn and walks over to me.

"Hey, boy," I say. "Good morning."

"Morning," Heaven says.

"You're up?"

"I'm not sure," she says. She sits up, revealing a crease from the seam of the beanbag etched in the side of her face.

"You had a rough night, huh?"

"Yeah," she says.

"Were you just really drunk last night, or is there something wrong with your apartment?"

"Oh," she says as if she's remembering. "Oh, no. I forgot about that."

"Yeah, you started talking about the mold last night, and then you just zonked out."

"Yeah . . . the mold."

"Care to elaborate?"

"I think I have black mold," she says.

"What is black mold?"

"Toxic mold."

"What makes you think you have this?"

"The tests came back inconclusive. I don't wanna stay there."

"Well, then you'll have to come to California with me," I say (of course kidding).

"Okay," she says.

"Fantastic," I say, not taking her seriously. I hand her a cup of coffee.

"I'll go pack."

"Seriously?" I say, now wondering if she's serious.

"Yeah. I *seriously* don't want to stay in *my* apartment. And for all we know, you could have the mold here, *too.*"

Holy shit, she's serious. "I was kidding. What would you do in California?"

"Whatever *you* do. I don't have a job anymore. I'm free to go."

I cannot believe she's serious. She can't come with me. I mean, sure she could come to California to check out the band, I guess, but I have important business to deal with—and no way is she coming to Seattle. I can't have her there messing things up. She does seem to have a knack for getting into trouble, whether she tries to or not. No, absolutely not. She cannot come with me.

"I don't think that's a very good idea," I say.

"Why not? You could use the company. And Strummer has never seen California."

Strummer? She can't be serious this time. "Strummer definitely can't come."

"Why not?"

"This is getting out of hand. We're not seriously discussing this, are we?"

"Yes, we are. Why can't Strummer come?"

"Because," I say. "He can't."

"Doggist bigot," she says.

"You can't come either."

"Why not?"

I want to come up with a really adult-sounding and final answer. "Because I have important business to take care of."

"I heard that part. What does that have to do with me and Strummer?"

"You just can't come, okay?"

"Fine," she says.

"Fine," I say with finality.

* * *

I'm on American Airlines Flight #3 on my way to California, and Heaven is sitting next to me. Strummer is in a crate under the plane. His ticket cost a hundred bucks. Apparently Heaven likes the aisle seat, too. But I booked my flight first, and I'm not budging. She could have sat somewhere else. Not my problem. What *is* my problem, though, is the fact that she's milking it for all that she can. She's gotten up and climbed over me about seventy-five times since we boarded. She demanded I give her my Smokehouse Almonds because she thought she was *gypped* in her bag. And she's listening to the Chinese channel on her headset and trying to repeat what they are saying. This is even less amusing to the Asian person sitting directly behind us.

I get up and go to the bathroom. As I wash my face, I notice the sign telling me to please wipe the washbasin after my use for the next passenger. Which I do, though I'm not sure I really understand why. Sure, if I was shaving or something—but if all I do is wash my hands or face, I don't know why the inside of the washbasin has to be wiped dry, just so the next passenger can wet it again. Which gives me a thought: What about a self-drying sink? Maybe it could have holes like Swiss cheese that air could blow through. Even better . . . so much air that if you waved your hands in front of it, they'd get dry . . . which would eliminate the need for those separate air dryers. But then how would the water stay in the sink? Bad idea.

And then the flush—the flush is quite possibly the loudest toilet flush I've ever experienced. It gets me thinking about all toilet flushes. They're really unpleasant—loud, obnoxious. Unsettling, really. At that second, it hits me. What if I designed an MP3 player Flush Button. It would play music when you flushed instead of the imposing *whoosh*. It wouldn't have to play a whole song. That could get annoying—but maybe the chorus, or a clever line, even. "Water of Love" by Dire Straits, "Big Balls" by AC/DC, "Smells Like Teen Spirit" by Nirvana, "Tush" by ZZ Top . . . even Sinatra's "My Way." I'm sure Old Blue Eyes would be honored. Then again, maybe not. Maybe he'd turn over in his grave, in which case I'd sample the Sid

Vicious version. The possibilities are endless. I am a wealth of inventions. This one could even top Cinnamilk—and the Catch-It Cone. Not just because of its genius, but because it involves my first true passion—music.

I come back to my seat and find Heaven in it.

"What are you all smiley about?" she asks.

"Move it or lose it," I say.

"Make me," she says. I lift her up out of my seat and place her in her own, where she sits and pouts but quickly gets over it. "What were you smiling about? Have a wank in there? You know, you're not officially a member of the Mile High Club unless there's another person involved."

"Hmm," I say. "So what club is it when there are *two* other people involved and they're both flight attendants?"

"The Masturbatory Fantasy Club?" she offers. "Seriously, what happened in the bathroom that was so grin-inducing?"

"I came up with another idea, that's all."

"What kind of idea?"

"I can't tell you."

"What," she says. "You think I'm going to steal it?"

"No."

"Then tell me."

"I can't, not here at least. Too many people around."

"Fine. But I'm going to make you tell me later," she warns.

"Okay."

"And I'm not going to forget, either."

"I'm sure you're not."

"I don't forget things," she says.

"Of course you don't."

"Especially things like this."

"Uh-huh."

"I do forget where I put my keys."

"We all have our faults," I say.

"I wouldn't consider that a fault."

I notice that she's made a list on the vomit bag in my absence. "What is *that*?" I ask.

"It's my updated funeral persona non grata list."

"I see," I say.

"A plane is dangerous. Might as well have an updated version with me."

"So there are *other* versions?" I say, craning my neck in a half-assed attempt to see if my name is on the list.

"Yes."

"And you want your final version to be on a throw-up bag?"

"It's as good a place as any," she says, checking up and down her list.

"And if we have some kind of tragedy on the plane, don't you think that list will be destroyed along with the rest of us—and the plane?"

"Perhaps."

"Perhaps. But you're thinking some other tragedy that would just take you and leave your list unharmed."

She thinks for a second. "It's a precaution," she says.

"It's ridiculous."

"Nobody asked you."

"Fair enough," I say and open my duty-free shopping catalog to see if anything new has shown up since my last flight.

We arrive at Long Beach Airport. The band's playing in Costa Mesa, so we flew into Long Beach instead of LAX.

We're reunited with Strummer, and I swear that dog smiles at us when he spots us. I didn't fully understand until this moment—this dog has a soul. And a fantastic smile. He jumps up on Heaven, and she's giddy with love for this mutt. I pat him on the head and try to play it cool, but I gotta say, I've fallen for him, too.

We get in my rental car, and Heaven pulls out a CD mix she made for the trip. The first song is by Spoon, which just happens to be one of my favorite bands. The second song is a Wilco song, another near-perfect band. Then she's got Franz Ferdinand's "Come on Home" going straight into "Heart of Glass" by Blondie, which blows my mind because I thought I was the only one who noticed the similarities between those two songs. I'm afraid that if the rest of this CD is as good as its beginning I'm going to have to ask this girl to marry me. And that is definitely not in the cards. As soon as I think this, "Little Guitars" by Van Halen comes on. Seriously proposal-worthy, so we'll just keep this between us.

We drive straight to the nearest Fatburger, which is my obvious first stop. Truth be told, I'd prefer an In-N-Out Burger—which are the best burgers in the world—but Fatburger's closer, and it's the next best thing. We'll hit In-N-Out Burger tomorrow. I haven't been to L.A. in a while, but I used to spend a lot of time here, and I know where the burgers are.

Or at least I used to. Unfortunately, the Fatburger I picked out has been replaced by a strip mall, and the next closest one is a few miles away in Orange. So we drive—or shall I say crawl—in traffic for a half hour. During which time I marvel, once again, at Heaven's choice of placing Soul Asylum's "Somebody to Shove" back to back with Adam Ant's "Beat My Guest," a B-side from *Stand and Deliver.* Both songs begin with almost the exact same guitar riff, and this track selection leaves no doubt in my mind that this girl knows her music. Maybe she should be a DJ instead of a waitress?

We finally get to Fatburger and I order a Double Fatburger, Fat Fries, and a vanilla shake. Fatburger makes the world a better place. I tell Heaven that she has to also order the Double Fatburger, which she does, but she orders the Skinny Fries. Girls.

"Don't you think they could have come up with a better name for this place?" she asks.

"The name is great," I say.

"No, it's not," she says. "They might as well call it 'Increase Your Ass Burger.'"

"No, see . . . back in 1952, when this place opened, *Fat* meant you had really made it. 'Fat City,' 'Fat Times,' 'Fat Cat . . .' It was a good thing."

"Like *phat* with a 'ph' now," she surmises.

"Exactly."

"So when phat—with a 'ph'—came out over the last few years, they were totally copying the fifties. It's totally unoriginal. Someone should call them on that."

"You go ahead."

"I might," she says.

"I have no doubt about that."

We get an extra burger for Strummer and sit on the grass at this little park across the street. It's nice not to be wearing a winter coat. Los Angeles is a really nice place. If it weren't for the smog . . . and the earthquakes . . . and the people . . . and the traffic—

Okay, not that nice, but the weather's good.

"This is a really good burger," she says after her first bite, as if she's surprised.

"As if I'd steer you wrong?"

"Well . . . you know . . ." She cracks a crooked smile.

"Yeah, yeah," I say. And we settle into a comfortable silence as we eat our Fatburgers in sunny California.

• • •

Heaven

Today is discreetly-give-everyone-the-finger day. Some girl on the plane was reading a book called *This Book Will Change Your Life,* and when she got up to use the bathroom, I picked it up. Of course Brady told me to put it back, but I didn't. I mean, I did in time for her not to notice, but I flipped through it first.

Basically, it gives you something to do with all three hundred sixty-five days of the year. Talk about having too much free time on your hands.

Anyway, the book had entries like "Do Something Nice for Someone Else Without Them Knowing Day" or "Compliment Someone Day." Most of the Days were boring, but I happened to flip to a page that said: "Discreetly Give Everyone the Finger Day," and I thought, Now *that* is my kind of day!

So Brady and I are sitting on the grass eating Fatburgers and flipping people off. So far I have flipped off seven people without them knowing, and nine total. Strummer got his own Fatburger and I think he enjoyed it, although he ate it so fast I'm not sure it even happened.

So far Los Angeles is a lot of traffic and fake boobs. Maybe there's something in the water. I think I've seen Paris Hilton about thirty-seven times. Must be the look they're going for right now. Kind of like in *Fast Times at Ridgemont High,* when Jennifer Jason Leigh points out to Phoebe Cates a girl who looks exactly like Pat Benatar. And Phoebe informs Jennifer that there are *three* of them at Ridgemont.

And there's a lot of sky. I'm not used to there not being tall buildings everywhere, so the sky just seems to be limitless. But it's not blue. I guess that's where the smog comes in. I heard that everyone who lives in Los Angeles has low-grade emphysema, which is pretty scary. So scary that I take a deep breath and hold it.

"What are you doing now?" Brady asks. I'd answer, but I can't because I'm trying to hold my breath. I point to my cheeks to show there's a lot of air in there trying to stay put, and clearly I cannot speak. "I see," he says. "I'll just wait then."

Finally I exhale. "I was decreasing my chance of catching cancer."

"You don't 'catch' cancer," he says with this look that just says, *Duh!*

"Well, technically, no. You don't catch it the way you'd catch a cold from someone else's germs, per se, but . . ."

"This should be interesting . . ."

"The level of smog in Los Angeles is so high—" I start to say, but he interrupts.

"And you think that holding your breath is going to spare your lungs."

"Absolutely."

"That one time?"

"Surely not," I say. I take another deep breath and hold it. Strummer is panting away, so I grab his snout and hold it shut for a moment to spare his lungs, too. Then I motion for Brady to hold his breath with us.

"No," he says. I bulge my eyes out at him, insisting that he hold his breath. "Uh-uh," he says again, shaking his head back and forth at me. I frown. He takes a deep breath and holds it.

We meet the band at their rehearsal studio, which also doubles as Justin's parents' garage—though a Saturn and some kind of bulbous SUV thing have been forced out. The guys are all really excited to have us there—or should I say *kids*. It's shocking. The dead at twenty-seven thing aside, I don't think of myself as old . . . I don't feel old . . . but next to these kids I feel almost like . . . a grown-up. There's Sam, vocal and lead guitar, who's got jet-black hair, pale, pale skin, and a safety-pin lip piercing. Perhaps a spare for his diaper. Then there's Ethan, the bass player, with brown dreadlocks and an Atari T-shirt, and Justin, the drummer, who resembles Tanner from *The Bad*

News Bears. His longish dirty-blond hair and cherubic face looks too young even for acne. All three show the signs of spending *way* too much time together, constantly looking at each other with these silly inside-joke smiles.

They offer us a Red Bull before we settle in to talk. People out here are really big on Red Bull. Brady asks them how long they've been playing and tells them about his label. He's so passionate when he talks about it that I almost don't recognize him. He tells them most labels claim they're "artist friendly" and then stab their artists in the back. He promises them he is not one of them. That's not how he operates. And then laments *that's* why he has no cash, which may not have been the brightest thing to say in that moment—but there's an earnestness as well as a business savvy that he's got intermingling, and it's really something to see. I sit back and let him do his thing, and when all is said and done, he tells them he's really looking forward to seeing what they can do live.

We get to the club about a half hour before they go on, and Brady stakes out his spot. Not right up front, but not all the way in the back with the wannabe hipster, trucker-hat–wearing idiots who are too cool to even nod their heads along with the music.

The band goes on, and I'm nervous. I know this is important to Brady, and I really want them to be good. And they are. They're really good. And I can tell that Brady likes them because I've noticed that when Brady's excited, he gets this glassy, happy twinkle in his eyes. He smiles, and he's got that twinkle. He looks over at me, and I nod at him. The nod is like an entire conversation. I know he's just decided that this band is his future. He knows that I approve, and I think—even though he made up his own mind—the fact that I approve means something to him as well. He smiles at me, and goes back to watching the band.

The room is packed, too. The kids are singing along to their songs, which is always a good sign. I look around—and not only is the place packed . . . it's not the ordinary semi-bored army of eyes wandering, looking for cute skinny guys or girls with belly piercings. *Everyone* in the room is locked onto the band. There's a girl wearing a DIY "Superhero" T-shirt. I walk over to her.

"Hey, cool shirt," I say to her.

"I made it myself," she says.

"Cool," I say back. Then I notice four more girls with four more homemade shirts, and one with "I Heart Superhero" painted on her jeans. It's a little following. And something tells me it's going to get much bigger, soon—which gives me an idea.

I look around the room and spot a neo-hipster standing in the back in a trucker hat. Trucker hats are the silly fad made famous by Ashton Kutcher, where by wearing a mesh-back hat you are somehow saying, "I am supercool, I am down with the white trash, look how ironic I am." Sadly though, just like every other fad, this one has seen its time, and this dolt doesn't know any better. The rest of the hipsters have moved on to the shrunken old Rolling Stones T-shirt and blazer. Maybe the memo hasn't reached L.A. yet. I feel for these people. Having to change your musical tastes and wardrobe and move to a different neighborhood every two years must be exhausting.

Then I get this feeling in my stomach—the same feeling I get when I'm caught in a lie or run into a long-lost ex-boyfriend when I didn't have time to fix my hair. Because this is not just any out-of-touch dolt: It's none other than Darren Rosenthal. Darren was my college boyfriend, and every one of my girlfriends wanted him. Tall, wavy dark brown hair, white teeth, just enough stubble, and a boatload of his parents' money. He was the coolest guy in our class. He definitely should know better. He should at *least* have the rocker T and blazer in effect. But, despite the hat, he's looking pretty darn good.

I walk over to him and knock the hat off the back of his head. This would annoy anyone, but especially someone wearing one of *those* hats, because that type will not want to be seen with the aftereffects of the trucker hat, which is really bad hathead. He whirls around to see who the asshole is that knocked his hat off. And he's blown away when he sees it's me.

"Heaven?" he exclaims. "Oh my God, how *are* you? What are you doing in Los Angeles?"

"I'm here with a friend checking out this band," I say, instantly aware of how dumb that sounded.

"They're great, aren't they? I've got a good feeling about them," he says. "I might sign them." Uh-oh. I realize that he's there doing what Brady's doing, and all of a sudden I get protective.

"I don't know," I say. "They're not doing anything really *different.*"

"You don't think?"

"Nah," I say. "There's already a dozen bands just like them out there, and three dozen more camp followers have been signed, who'll probably be dropped before their records come out," I say with complete authority, even though it is total bullshit.

"You in the business?"

"Sort of," I lie.

"Still a girl of mystery, I see," he says. I catch Brady's eye. He waves me over.

"I'll be right back," I say, walking over to Brady.

"Who are you talking to?" Brady says.

"Darren Rosenthal."

"Darren—*cokehead, asshole; I never had an opinion of my own, but I made a fortune off everybody else's opinions; look at my fake tan, I'm such a dick*—Rosenthal?"

"Well, he never mentioned his middle name."

"You *know* that guy?" he asks.

"He's my ex-boyfriend."

"You've got to be kidding."

"Nope."

"I've lost all respect for you," he says. "That guy is the biggest scumbag in the business."

"It was a long time ago," I say uncomfortably.

"Still."

"And I didn't sleep with him."

"Thank God for that."

"Not for at least two months."

"Oh, come *on,*" Brady says. And he covers his ears, even though I already said all I had to say. I remove his hands from his ears.

"It was in college. Jeez!"

"He's an *asshole.*"

"So you say."

"You didn't tell him we were here for Superhero, did you?" he asks anxiously.

"Yes. I said you wanted to sign them, and you were offering them a deal as soon as they got off the stage tonight."

"Please tell me you're kidding."

"I'm kidding," I say.

"Are you telling me you're kidding because I just told you to tell me that you're kidding, or are you really kidding?"

"I really am. I'm not an idiot, you know." I turn and walk over to the bar to get another Red Bull and catch up with Darren some more.

After the show we hang around and watch the crowd say their hellos to the band. Brady waits until they've done all of their schmoozing before he moves in to do his own schmoozing.

By the end of the night the band has a record-deal offer on the table with Sleestak Records, Brady's label. I really hope they sign with him.

We go to The Coffee Bean and Tea Leaf, which is L.A.'s competition for Starbucks. Apparently it's been around for a long time, and they seem to have a devoted following. Many of them are even directly across the street from Starbucks, and neither seems to suffer for it. I guess you are either a Coffee Bean person or a Starbucks person.

I order a Vanilla Blended, which is quite possibly the best thing I've ever consumed. As I'm taking my second sip I notice a bottle of water they're selling. At first I think I can't be seeing right, but when I walk over to the counter I find that my eyes were not deceiving me. They are selling bottles of "Fat Free" water. No, really. This is true. You can go in there and see for yourself. Now, this is not like Vitamin Water, or any of the fruit-flavored waters, some of which have a calorie count and additives that might make you question what you were drinking. This is just plain water—God's own water. But here it is bottled and labeled as "Fat Free." Unbelievable. And it is at this moment that I truly realize that I am in L.A.

• • •

Brady

I leave Heaven at The Coffee Bean, where she's marveling at the Fat Free Water, and I tell her I'll meet her back at the hotel in a few hours.

I head out to meet the band so we can talk about my offer. I think I'm lost. We're meeting in Hollywood at this Mexican restaurant on Sunset Strip called El Compadre, which the band is particularly fond of. I realize I've gone a little too far into Hollywood when I get to the corner of *Crack Whore* and *Gangbanger,* so I make a U-turn and finally spot the place.

As I'm going around the block looking for a place to park I give Phil a quick call on my cell phone, because I realize that I didn't check in with him after the show last night.

"Hello?" a female voice says—a voice that sounds remarkably like Sarah.

"Sorry, I think I have the wrong number," I say. I hit End as fast as I can because I think I called Sarah by accident. She laughs as I'm hanging up the phone—probably because she thinks I did it on purpose. I'd call her back to tell her I didn't, but it's not even worth it.

I close the phone and open it once more, just to make sure we're disconnected. Then I scroll through my phone book and find Phil. I hit Send and watch as it says "Calling Phil" and then "Connected to Phil."

"Hello?" the female voice says again. I pull the phone away from my ear to look at it and make sure that it indeed still says "Phil."

"Sarah?" I ask.

"Yes, Brady?" she says back.

"Sorry, I'm trying to call Phil."

"You've succeeded."

Huh?

"You're with Phil?" I ask, completely confused.

"I am."

"Okay . . . can I talk to him?"

"He's in the shower," she says with this breezy, I-just-fucked-your-oldest-friend tone in her voice.

"I see," I say. And there's an uncomfortable silence. Do I ask her to have him call me back? Do I react to this extremely fucking strange situation? No. I'm just going to play it cool. It's none of my business.

"We're fucking," she says.

"I thought he was in the shower," I say.

"He is. I just mean, in general. We're fucking."

"It's none of my business," I say with a calm, cool tone that even surprises *me*.

"Hmm," she says. "Did you know that Phil's dick curls to the right?"

"What part of 'it's none of my business' did you not understand?" I say, now sounding much less cool.

"I heard you. I just think it's funny."

"That you're fucking my friend, or that his dick curls to the right?"

"Well, both, I guess."

"Fair enough," I say. "No, Sarah . . . I did not know that Phil's dick curls to the right. But could you have him give me a call when he gets a chance?"

"Sure," she says.

"Fantastic," I say. I hang up the phone, turn up the radio, and floor the gas as the Violent Femmes sing about blisters on the sun.

Once I'm parked, I sit in the rental car for a few minutes to process the conversation I just took part in. Sarah is evil. This we know. Phil is stupid. This we also know. Therefore, both behaviors are to be expected. Okay, not expected—but understandable. Definitely not expected.

Still, I gotta say . . . it chafes my ass to even think about it.

I don't give a shit about *her.* I really don't. That said, were I to ever have a weak moment and feel like having sex with her, I can now never do that again. I will never put my dick where Phil's crooked fucking dick has been. That is just a fact. So, yes . . . I am disappointed in Phil, as a friend. But worse, I'm pissed off that he has just permanently cock-blocked my guaranteed booty call. And on top of *that,* now I'll have to think of his bent dick whenever I look at him. This is precisely why guys *don't* look at another guy's junk in the bathroom. You never want to picture a guy's dick when you're looking at him. Every which way I turn, this just fucking sucks.

I walk into El Compadre and they're already drinking margaritas. Though it occurs to me that the drummer is closer to twelve than twenty-one, I keep my trap shut and order one for myself.

Sam is the mouthpiece for the band, and as I take a tortilla chip and pop it into my mouth he casually says, "Wanna hear something crazy?"

"What's that?" I ask.

"Looks like we have *two* record deals on the table. Darren Rosenthal met with us this morning, and he offered us a deal. Our lawyer is looking over both."

Fuck.

Not only do I choke on my chip, I scratch my throat. This is turning out to be a really bad day.

Sam looks at me to gauge my response after he casually drops the Rosenthal bomb. I play it cucumber style.

"That's cool," I say. "Anyone who's heard you would be a complete moron not to want to sign you." This answer works twofold. It shows that I am not deterred by Rosenthal's offer, and it strokes their ego, which every band feeds off of.

"Thanks," he says, and I know my response was correct. The only problem is, I'm practically shitting in my pants. Darren *motherfucking* Rosenthal works for a major label. I can't compete with that. The only thing I can do now is pray to God they don't fall for his schmooze. Well, that and tell them some cold, hard facts about the business.

"Here's the thing," I say as I sip on my much-needed margarita. "Major labels are sexy. They're powerful and exciting. You look at some of the bands on their roster and can't help but be awe-inspired."

"Totally," he says.

"And you'd be psyched to be on the same label as them."

"Absolutely," Ethan tosses in.

"I know. I was where you are. I used to be in a band."

"What did you play?" Sam asks.

"Guitar."

"Right on," he says. We clink our glasses to our shared talent. "You just got sick of trying to make it?"

"Sort of," I say, and I take another sip before I go in for the kill. "My band was called Crooked, and we were signed to Warner about six years ago."

"You were?" he says, totally surprised by this.

"Yeah," I tell him, setting my glass down as if to suggest I've got something incredibly important to reveal at this moment, for his ears only (though I've tried it on ten other rising stars like him). "We had a three-record deal and they sold us all this bullshit about us being the next Stones."

"So what happened?" they all ask.

"What, you never heard of Crooked?"

"No," they say.

"Exactly. What happened? I'll tell you what happened." The whole band is now on the edges of their seats. "We signed the deal and went into the studio to cut our album. We recorded all of our best songs and made a kick-ass record. The only problem was they'd signed about seventeen other bands at the same time as us and didn't want to put a lot of money into promoting us. Any of us, really. They already had their star bands, and with the rest of us it was pretty much: *Let's see how many records you can sell with no help from us.*"

"That sucks," Sam says.

"Yeah, it does, but that's what happens at the majors. One in a hundred bands make it. Labels just snatch everybody up because they don't want to miss out, but they don't take the time to nurture a band and really help make them successful. And if you don't produce in, say, six months or a year—and really, how can you—you get dropped. Not only do you lose your deal . . . you lose your best songs."

"Jesus," he says.

"Yeah, and by the way . . . those advances you get? They're recoupable. Which means that if you don't make back the money they spent on you—you'll end up owing them all kinds of money that you don't even have." Okay, maybe I'm laying it on a little thick here.

"Fuck," Sam says.

"I know. It sucks. That's why I switched to the other side of the business," I say. I start to sense something I don't believe I've even seen before. Not hero worship, but maybe an unwitting or unconscious respect for someone who's *been there.* Even the drummer looks up for the first time. I have all of their innocent faces looking up at me. They look so young that for a split second I don't know if I want to coax them into a contract or offer them chocolate milk. I stand up, and they're transfixed. At this moment, someone needs to start humming "The Battle Hymn of the Republic."

"To actually help other bands, I do what I was once promised back in the day: nurture them and help them grow. Help build fan bases and set them up for a long career, not just a three-month shot and then *fuck you.* Overnight success is rare. Sometimes it takes a couple records to truly figure out exactly what you're about. My thing is . . . I give bands that time. I'm not in the immediate results business. I'm in the business of putting out music that I love. Music that I believe in and I think other people should hear." All of the guys are looking at each other and nodding.

"Totally," Sam agrees.

"I like to think so. So I can't offer you the slick contract at the giant corporation. But I can offer you loyalty. And if you sign with Sleestak, you're making a home for yourself for as long as you want. And we will continue to put your records out for as long as you want us to. We'll give you 200 percent of our attention and do everything in our power to make you rich and famous."

I leave the restaurant feeling better than I did when I first sat down, but there's still this nagging feeling that Darren can woo them with money I just don't have. I hope what I said to them sinks in. Hope is really all I have right now. That, and, as I mentioned earlier, my talent for lying when I have to. The truth is, I exaggerated my whole band scenario. And "Crooked"? Well, I guess that was an homage to Phil's fucked-up dick. Don't get me wrong—I was in a band, and I did get screwed by a label. But not to the extent that I described, and it certainly wasn't Warner that had signed me. Anyway, everything I told them happens every single day in the music business, so even if it didn't happen exactly that way to me . . . it really could happen to them.

When I get back to the Hyatt, which is where Heaven and I are staying, Heaven is nowhere to be found. For the first time it occurs to me—wow, we're sharing a room. But at the same time the voice also says—wow, at these rates it's amazing we're not sleeping in the park, sharing a bench with a crack addict.

So I wait.

Three hours later she is still not back. Her cell phone is going straight to voice mail, and I'm starting to get worried. The girl is a menace. God only knows what kind of trouble she's gotten into, and we are in a strange city.

Five hours later she comes tiptoeing back into the room to find the lights on and me with a scowl on my face.

"You're up?" she says.

"No, I'm sleeping," I answer. "Where have you been? I was worried."

"I'm sorry," she says. "I thought you'd be busy with the band."

"Didn't I say I'd meet you back here in a few hours?"

"I guess."

"Right. Well, what that meant was that I would meet you back here in a few hours. Which in layman's terms equals one hundred eighty minutes."

"Gotcha," she says.

"Right," I say. And then I just sort of look at her while I wait for her to tell me where she was. But she gets up, walks into the bathroom, and starts washing her face.

I walk in after her. She comes up from the sink all wet-faced, and I hand her a towel.

"Thank you," she says and takes it.

"So where were you?" I ask.

"With Darren," she says, and I snatch the towel back. I don't know why, but I do.

"Can I have the towel, please?" she says, almost laughing. I fail to see what is so funny.

"You were with Darren?"

"Yes."

"Rosenthal?" I ask, knowing full well it's Rosenthal.

"Yes."

"Why?"

"He called me," she says, stretching and unstretching her hair scrunchie but refusing to meet my gaze. "Wanted to hang out. Catch up."

"I'll bet he did."

"Yeah," she says. "He did."

"Yeah. I'll bet," I say again because I don't know what to say right now. I mean, it's really no big deal, so I don't know why I'm even freaking out. They dated a long time ago. She wouldn't actually *do* anything with him. Not a chance. I'm certain of it.

"Would catching up involve nudity?"

She chucks the scrunchie back into her makeup bag. *"God,* Brady."

"Would it?" I pursue.

"Well, I can tell you this," she says, spinning to face me.

"Either I forgot what it was like with him, or he's picked up some new moves in the past few years."

"No, you *didn't* just say that," I say, suddenly channeling a trailer-park baby momma on the *Jerry Springer* show.

"Yes, I did," she says, rubbing moisturizer into her face a little too aggressively. I half expect to hear her say, "Out, damned spot! Out, I say!" If I wasn't absolutely certain to the contrary, I could *almost* swear that with this motion she wipes away a single tear. "I'm so glad I came out here with you. I am *really* enjoying this trip." And with that she walks out of the bathroom and plops herself down onto her bed.

"Well, I am really not enjoying *you* right now," I say and stomp out after her.

"What's your deal?" She's playing it tough, but there's a slight tremor in her voice.

"My deal?"

"Yes," she says.

"I'll tell you what my deal is."

"Please do."

"God! I can't *believe* you!" I say. It occurs to me, in all the emotions she's ever inspired in me, the anger or mock anger I felt was never really rooted in actual feelings. Until now.

"What?" she says. "Can you please explain what your issue is here?"

"Look, I don't care what you do or who you have sex with. I don't. It's none of my business," I say for the second time today, when both times I've felt that it was *absolutely* my fucking business.

"Good. Because it's not."

"Right. See, the thing is . . . the person with whom you have just done things that I don't care to think about is the same person that offered Superhero a record deal this morning."

"What?" she says, all surprised.

"Yes, he did," I say. "So in essence, he's actually just fucked both of us. Only I didn't bend over by choice."

• • •

"My God . . . I haven't been fucked like that since grade school."

—Marla, *Fight Club*

"Try not to suck any dick on the way to the parking lot."

—Dante, *Clerks*

Heaven

Some people pick the wrong things to say all the time. I am one of those people. I also happen to pick the wrong men, jobs . . . you name it. I don't *mean* to do it. Of course I don't. But if there was a cartoon bubble over my head at all times, and everyone could read my thoughts, I can safely say that 87 to 90 percent of the time, it would say "Shit!" or maybe "Fucking shit!" or simply "Oops." Those seem to be the three major thoughts that arise after I do or say something regrettable—most often a combination of the three. It may start out as an "Oops," but quickly turns into a "Shit" or a "Fucking shit" without fail.

It seems that I am Lucy. I don't know how or when it happened, but I do everything short of crying, "Ricky, why can't I be in the show?"

Here I thought I was having a perfectly innocent sex-with-an-ex moment, and it turns out I've just completely fucked Brady over. But did I know it at the time? No. And if Darren hadn't offered the band a deal, Brady probably wouldn't even give a crap. This was not supposed to make me feel bad. So why do I feel like my new puppy just got hit by a car? Because Darren *did* offer them a deal? Which means I have now lain down with the enemy? Although, truth be told, there was actually very little lying down involved. Honestly, I kind of thought that I'd swayed Darren the other way when we were watching them play. I had no idea that he offered them a deal. So Darren offered them a deal. That's life. I still think Brady will win them over in the end. But he's all pissed, and I don't know what to feel right now. But I'm feeling it.

"I'm sorry," I say quietly.

"Whatever," Brady says.

"I really am. I never would have . . . I *wouldn't* have, if I thought he would in any way mess things up for you."

"I know," he says without looking at me.

"Do you?"

"Yes, I do," he says, and this time he looks right at me. "You may be a bit of a nuisance and a gigantic pain in the ass—"

"No offense taken—"

"—but I know that you wouldn't willingly jeopardize my deal."

"Well, I *didn't* jeopardize your deal."

"No," he says, "but you slept with the person who did." I've seen Brady up, and I've seen Brady down, but I've never seen or heard him be this . . . vacant.

"And we didn't exactly sleep."

"Your semantics aren't helping." He sighs.

Oops, says my thought bubble. See?

"Just out of curiosity, what part of your brain thought it was a *good* idea to say that?" he asks.

"Wow," I say.

"Wow, what?"

"I was just thinking that."

"You were thinking what?"

"That I seem to have this uncanny knack for saying the wrong thing all the time."

"And doing," he adds.

"Yeah, that too," I say. And start to genuinely feel awful. I mean, I felt bad before, but now I'm starting to think that I may need a muzzle.

I get up and grab my jacket.

"Where are you going?" Brady asks.

"Just for a walk." I grab Strummer's leash, and he jumps off the bed, putting his paws up on me to assist the attachment of leash to collar.

"Why are you making *me* feel guilty?" he asks.

"I'm not. I'm just taking Strummer for a walk."

"Fine," he says. "I don't feel guilty, you know. I'm not going to feel bad because *you* feel bad that you had acrobat sex with Darren Rosenthal."

"Good. I don't want you to. *I'm* the one that feels bad about it, okay?"

"Okay," he says. And Strummer and I head out for a walk down Sunset, and over to the Starbucks where we can sit outside.

It's 6 a.m. and people are starting their day. I haven't slept yet, but that's okay.

A guy walks by and smiles at Strummer. He tells me how cute he is, and I thank him. As if I had something to do with it. I watch people get their coffee, and there's an almost physical change that happens when they drink it. If they are uptight or pissed off or just plain tired when they walk in . . . you can see an improvement the minute they are handed their triple shot, no-foam latte—and then when they're done at the *fixings* bar and actually take their first sip, it's like all is suddenly right in the world. Shoulders become un-hunched. People look around and actually notice that other people are there. It's a helluva thing to watch.

Then a guy who looks an awful lot like Ben Stiller walks in. I'm sitting out on the patio, and when he passes, he looks at Strummer and smiles. When he comes back out he walks over and I can see that he is indeed Ben Stiller.

"Hi," he says.

"Hi," I say back, a little in shock that Ben Stiller is talking to me.

"Great dog," he says.

"Thanks," I say. Again, I think about how funny it is that we take credit for compliments to our dogs. But then again, if Strummer had green dreadlocks, and I dressed him in a tutu, it would sort of be my fault—so conversely, the fact that he is a good-looking, non-dreadlocked, undressed dog . . . is to some extent my doing.

"What's his name?"

"Strummer."

"Hi, Strummer," he says. "Is he friendly?"

"Totally," I say. Ben leans down and starts petting him.

At which point, Strummer lifts his leg and pees on Ben Stiller. I can't believe my eyes. I'm mortified. Ben jumps back and sort of squeals.

"Whoa, what the fuck?" he says. In his little dance to get out of the way and shake the pee off, he knocks his coffee over.

"Oh my God. I'm so sorry," I say.

"Jesus!" he yells. "You could have warned me that your dog pees on people!" He's pissed off—and now pissed *on*—but it's not *my* fault. I've never seen Strummer do anything like that before. How could I know that Strummer was going to pee on him?

"I said he was *friendly* . . . I didn't say he was *potty trained,*" I say in my defense. *Strummer's* defense.

"That's great. That's just great," he says. "Thanks a lot."

"I'm sorry!" I say. "I've never seen him do that before. He didn't mean anything by it."

"Whatever," he says as he tries to shake the remaining urine off his pant leg.

"I'll be happy to pay for your dry cleaning," I offer.

"That's okay," he says.

"And if it makes you feel any better, it's probably good luck."

"Yeah?" he says. "How do you figure?"

"Well, if a pigeon shits on you it's supposed to be good luck. I can only imagine that a dog peeing on you would bring you some sort of . . . something."

"I don't think it works that way," he says, and he's probably right. By my logic, an eight-hundred-pound gorilla taking a dump on you would surely bring you fame and fortune. Okay, so it doesn't exactly make sense. But it *sort of* does. To me, at least.

"Okay, well, I hope it does. Bring you good luck."

"Thanks," he says.

"Can I at least buy you a new cup of coffee?" I ask. But as the words are coming out of my mouth, the barista from inside walks out with a fresh cup of coffee for him.

"Hey, Ben . . . I saw you spill your coffee," he says. "Here's a fresh one."

"Thanks, Adrian," Ben says and takes the coffee from him. I guess Ben is a regular here. And I guess I should probably never show my face here again.

Ben starts to walk away, and I can't help but think I need to say something. Anything.

"By the way . . . I'm a really big fan of your work," I call out, and Ben sort of guffaws and shakes his head. He doesn't even turn around. I *am* a fan, though. I really do like his work.

When I get back to the room Brady is a heap under the covers, and the lights are out. I sit on my bed and look over at him in his.

"You sleeping?" I ask, but he doesn't answer. "You asleep?" I ask again, and he sort of groans. I jump off my bed and climb onto his.

"What do you want?" he whines.

"I had my first celebrity sighting in Los Angeles."

"Good for you," he says, and he rolls over.

"Don't you want to know who it was?"

"Not right now," he says.

"It's now or never," I say.

"Then it's never," he says, pulling his pillow over his head.

"It's a really good story, though," I say.

"I'm sure it is," he says.

"And I mean it. If you don't let me tell you right now, I will never tell you."

"I'm okay with that."

"I mean it."

"Okay."

"For as long as I live," I assure him.

"Understood."

"You're no fun."

"All righty then," he says, and it seems like he's fallen back asleep. Just like that. Not even the *least* bit curious about my story. Unbelievable.

Well, I'm not going to tell him when he wakes up. I don't care if he begs.

I climb off his bed and get back on mine. But I can't sleep. For starters, I just drank a cup of coffee. But even if I hadn't, I just have so much nervous energy right now that I can't stay still.

So I don't. I get up and leave. Of course, I can't go too far because I don't want to take our rental car. Plus, it's 7 a.m. so it's not like there's a lot happening on the strip. The stores aren't open, so nobody will be out, and I can't exactly people-watch.

So I decide to just sit in the lobby. And it's there that I meet a man who claims he was once in a famous rock group.

"Hi," he says. I look up from the window I've been peering out of to see a red-faced older man. "Hello," he says again.

"Hi," I say back.

"Are you staying here at the hotel?"

"Yes," I say. "You?"

"No. Just visiting friends in town from London. What brings you to L.A.?"

"A band," I say. "My neighbor has a record company and he's scouting a band. I just tagged along."

"Wonderful," he says. "I used to be in quite a famous group myself."

"Really? What band?"

"Manfred Mann and His Earth Band," he says proudly. At first it doesn't click.

"Wow," I say.

"I'm Manfred."

"Nice to meet you."

"You know us?"

"Um . . . no," I say apologetically.

"You must. We had a big hit." And then he starts to sing it: "'There she goes, just-a-walkin' down the street, singin' do wah diddy diddy dum diddy do.'" When he gets to the "do wah diddy" part he sort of nods and motions for me to join in. I don't. But I do know the song.

"That was you?"

"Indeed it was," he says proudly. Then it hits me. Manfred Mann! "Blinded by the Light," source of one of music history's all-time misheard lyrics.

"This is amazing," I say, jumping up in my seat. "You can solve something that's bothered me since I was born."

A curious look comes over his face. "Well, I'll try but I don't know—"

"Of *course* you know!" I shout back, aware that I'm talking way too loud for 7 a.m. in the lobby of the Hollywood Hyatt. "Is it: 'Blinded by the light . . . dressed up like a *douche* . . . I'm gonna run her in the night'?"

Out of the corner of my eye I see Brady storming over. "Please don't do that," Brady says to me.

"Do what?"

"Disappear," he says.

"I'm right here. This is Manfred," I say.

"Nice to meet you . . . Manfred," Brady says. "C'mon, we're getting breakfast," he says to me.

"I thought you were sleeping," I say.

"I was, but when I woke up and realized that you left, I couldn't sleep anymore. God only knows what trouble you'd get into."

"Well, I look forward to chatting some more," Manfred says as Brady pulls me off.

"Wait!" I say. "What about the lyrics?"

Manfred cocks his head and gives me a sly wink. "That's the fun of it," he says. "It's open to interpretation."

"What?" I say to Manfred, but Brady's pull on my arm is too strong. I mean, really. He's almost yanking the thing out of its socket.

"Do you know who that was?" I whisper.

"Uh . . . Manfred?" Brady says.

"Yeah! Manfred Mann. He sang that *do wah diddy* song!"

"No he didn't."

"Yes he did! And he was about to solve one of life's eternal mysteries. You know, was it 'dressed up like a douche, I'm gonna run her in the night'?" He looks at me with a Joker face—exactly like the Joker from Batman.

"Dressed up like a douche?" he laughs derisively. "First of all, it's 'revved up like a *deuce,* another runner in the night.' And B, Manfred Mann was English. From England—accent and all."

"Are you sure?"

"Yes, I'm sure. God, you'll believe *anything*! I can only imagine who you *think* you saw earlier."

"Oh, I don't think I saw someone. I *know* I saw someone. We had an interaction, in fact."

"I'll bet," he says.

"And I'm not telling you who."

"And I'm still okay with that," he says. Then he mocks, "Manfred Mann . . ."

Well, really. Why would he lie about that?

• • •

Brady

Heaven and I grab breakfast at a place called the Griddle Café. We both order pancakes. The tablecloths are paper, and they have crayons on the tables for those who want to color. Naturally, Heaven picks up a crayon and starts to draw.

When the food arrives, there is an ungodly number of pancakes before us.

"And there are people starving," I say.

"Then we shouldn't waste any."

"I am *not* going to eat all of this."

"I'll bet you I can eat more than you can," she says.

"I doubt that," I say, knowing full well my capacity for food intake greatly outdoes hers.

"And faster," she adds.

"I'm not racing you," I say. "I'd like to just enjoy my pancakes if you don't mind." But before I can even finish my sentence, she's shoveling pancakes in her mouth like a chipmunk.

And it is *on*. I start shoveling food in my mouth too, but I'm at least chewing. She has so much food in her mouth that there's no way she can possibly fit more in. Yet she does. In goes another forkful. It's like nothing I've ever seen.

"Chew," I order with a mouthful of food myself.

"I am," she says. At least I think that's what she says, even though it sounded like "ugn-aaahn." But by deductive reasoning and a keen talent for understanding people with too much food in their mouth (having lived with crooked-dick Phil for four years), I am fairly certain that she said "I am."

And when all's said and done, I'm mortified to say that Heaven out-ate me by a landslide. She sits there all smiles and rubs her imaginary Buddha belly. She has syrup all over her face and a few pancake crumbs stuck on there as well.

"You're a mess," I say. She licks her tongue around her mouth, trying to clean it up a bit, but it's a lost cause. I dip my napkin in my water glass and wipe her face off. And she lets me. She just sits there, face forward, eyes scrunched shut, jaw tilted up, and lets me wipe her off like a little child. In that moment she seems so innocent, and as I'm doing it I feel protective of her. I feel almost like I've known her since she was that little child. And then I think, This sweet little child fucked Darren Rosenthal last night, and my stomach flips.

"Let's go," I say, throwing some money on the table. She reaches into her pocket, takes out some money, puts it on the table, picks up the money that I put down, and shoves it into my pocket.

"Pancakes are on me," she says.

"No, they *were* on you. I think I wiped most of them off," I say, poking her in the rib cage.

"Don't," she says as she laughs.

"You don't have to buy," I say.

"You're paying for the hotel," she says.

"But I'd be paying for it even if you weren't here."

"Whatever. I'm buying the pancakes," she orders. "Plus, you didn't even get to enjoy them."

"True. And I guess loser *should* buy," I say, knowing full well that she kicked my ass.

"Pardon?" she says.

"You heard me."

"Oh, I *know* you didn't just say what I think you said."

"I think you heard exactly what I said."

"Funny," she says. "I guess we'll have to have a rematch at lunch."

"Lunch? After what we just ate? I'm good until at least dinner. Maybe even until next Tuesday." She starts to cluck like a chicken. I just ignore her.

My cell phone rings, and it's the lawyer I hired during my week off telling me that the trademark for Cinnamilk has gone through. This is my first bit of good news in a while. Then the air conditioner in our rental car dies. Does *everything* have to be a trade-off?

Heaven and I walk into Ralph's Supermarket and I'm stopped dead in my tracks. They have Jolt Cola. This was my favorite cola in the eighties, and I haven't seen it since. There it is, row after row. There are certain discontinued foods and drinks that I miss more than I probably should. Aspen Soda was an apple-flavored soda which was almost like apple 7-UP. It was made by Pepsi as a test beverage, and I fell in love with it, only to have them discontinue it within the same year. I went around buying it up from every store I could find it in. There was Quisp Cereal . . . Team Cereal . . . There was the Reggie Bar, which was a candy bar endorsed by Reggie Jackson . . . Munchos, the light, airy potato chips that came in the bright orange bag . . . Funyons, the onion-flavored potato chips in little onion rings (which occasionally you can still find) . . . and of course Taco Flavored Pizza at Pizza Hut. It's painful to think that I will never have any of these things again. I can almost hear the theme from *Brian's Song* as I remember them.

But here before me is a boatload of Jolt. And dammit if I'm not going to buy up every last can. I go get a cart and start grabbing them off the shelf.

"What are you doing?" Heaven asks when she finds me with half the cart full.

"They have Jolt!"

"And?"

"Don't you remember Jolt? It was my favorite soda ever. It had enough caffeine to wake the dead."

"No, but I miss Tab," she says wistfully. I'm sure that she's now going through *her* mental list of favorite discontinued items. "And Maisie's White Popcorn." See? "So what are you going to do? Buy every can?" she asks.

"Yes," I say matter-of-factly as I continue to load the cart.

"Okay," she says. And without missing a beat she starts to join me in collecting the Jolt cans and loading up my cart. I know that she understands and would probably do the same thing.

All of a sudden the most important thing in the world is for me to find her some Tab.

While we're standing in line with two carts full of Jolt, Heaven turns to me, all excited, with this big lightbulb-over-her-head idea.

"Wanna thumb-wrestle?" she asks. *This* is what had her all excited. The mind reels.

"Here? You don't thumb-wrestle in the middle of the grocery line."

"You don't?"

"No, it's like arm wrestling. You need to be sitting down."

"I didn't know."

"Now you do," I say, immediately starting to move my thumb around to loosen it up for the impending match.

My cell phone rings when we get outside, and it's Phil.

"Hey, buddy," he says.

"Hi, Phil," I say, not sure exactly how I want to deal with the Sarah situation.

"How's L.A.?" he asks.

"Great," I say. I roll my eyes at Heaven, who looks confused because she doesn't know why I'm rolling my eyes.

"So, um . . ." he stammers. "What's up with the band?"

"The offer's on the table. Actually, there are two offers on the table."

"Two?"

"Yeah. Darren Rosenthal made them an offer."

"Fuck," he says.

"Yeah," I say. "So now it's just a bit of wait and see."

"Fuck," he says again.

"Yeah," I say. And we go quiet for a minute. There's a giant pink elephant balancing on a ball, singing show tunes, but neither of us is mentioning it. And I'm not going to be the one to say anything.

"All right then, bro. Call me when you hear anything," he says.

"That's it? You're not even going to address the fact that you're fucking Sarah?" So much for me not saying anything.

"Oh," he says, and there's a long pause.

"What?" Heaven yells. "He fucked Sarah? Your Sarah? Psycho Sarah?"

"Shhh," I say to Heaven, waving her away.

"Dude, what can I say?" Phil says. "It happened."

"Yeah," I say.

"Oh my God!" Heaven says. I shoot her a look to shut up, and she just covers her mouth with both hands and looks shocked.

"Look, it just sorta *happened,*" he says. "I don't blame you for being pissed. But remember in college when I was all about Marnie Williams, and you wound up dating her? Or . . . or . . . what about that time that we both saw that blonde at the Village Idiot? The one who took her bra off and left it on the bar?"

"Which you stuffed in your pocket when she went to the bathroom? Yes, I remember."

"Well, exactly," he says. "I got the bra, and *you* wound up taking her home."

"Phil, this all has nothing to do with anything. Let's not kid ourselves. All these things you're mentioning are serving no other purpose than to not so thinly veil your shitty judgment and blatant disregard for our friendship. It's like a guy going to the grocery store and buying twenty dollars worth of groceries he doesn't need, to cover up the fact that he's there to buy tampons for his lady. Be a man. Walk up to the cashier with nothing but a giant box of Tampax, and I'll at least have *some* respect for you."

"Sarah needs Tampax? That's weird because—"

"Oh, man," I say. Analogies are always lost on Phil. I don't know why I bothered.

"Are you pissed?" he asks.

I think about it for a minute. And the truth is, I'm really

not. Sarah was a nightmare, and to be rid of her is actually a relief. She was great at first, like most girls are, but her oasis of greatness was quickly revealed as a mirage. And I spent the next couple of years parched—wandering in the desert of bitter, occasionally racing like a madman after the ghost of some happy moment with her, but reaching out to find handfuls of sand. Now? After being with Phil, I know she wouldn't have the nerve ever to try to come back. And that in and of itself is a new lease on life.

"No, I'm not. I'm really not. If she makes you happy, then I'm happy for both of you."

"Good. That's good to hear. That's why the Tampax thing was so weird because if she needed them, then we'd be in a whole other scenario."

"What are you talking about?"

"Sarah's pregnant," Phil says, and immediately my heart starts racing. I think back to the time she and I had that accidental—really bad judgment on my part—stupid, stupid, stupid sex, and rack my brain to think about whether or not I used a condom.

"How pregnant?" I ask.

"Come on, man. You know how that goes. Nobody's ever a little bit pregnant. You either are or you aren't."

"I meant, how many days . . . weeks . . . please God, not months?"

"Good question," Phil says. I feel dizzy.

"I gotta go, Phil."

"Okay. But are you mad at me?"

"No, I'm not mad at you," I say. I hang up the phone and think I'm going to throw up.

• ● •

Heaven

Brady is green. And I don't mean green in the *young* or *inexperienced* context. I mean, Brady is green. Like the color. And he looks like he's gonna throw up.

"Do you know what 'vagina dentata' is?" I ask him to distract him from whatever it is that's bothering him.

"Huh?" he says in a complete fog.

"Vagina dentata," I say again.

"Um . . . wasn't that a Police album?" he says, still able to crack wise under duress.

"No, that was *Zenyatta Mondatta,*" I say.

"Then no. I do not know what 'vagina whatever' is."

"Dentata. It's a fear that men have. Where they think that vaginas have all of these sharp teeth in them. So they're scared to put a penis inside one because they think it will bite it off."

"That's delightful."

"I didn't make it up."

"What about it?" he asks.

"Just wondering if you've ever heard of it."

"Because . . . why?"

"I don't know. Seemed like you needed a distraction," I say as I read the ingredients on a Jolt can.

"So you tell me about vaginas with teeth?"

"Uh-huh," I say.

"You know what? That kind of distraction—I don't need."

"Fine. Sorry. Jeez," I say. "Wanna thumb-wrestle *now*?" I ask.

"No." He opens the trunk and starts loading up the Jolt. So I help.

"I have thirty teeth," I say as I lift another six-pack of Jolt into the trunk. "Not in my vagina, obviously—in my mouth." Brady doesn't say anything. "Most mouths have twenty-eight teeth. But an untouched mouth has thirty-two teeth. And four are removed when the wisdom teeth come out."

"Yeah?" Brady says, feigning interest.

"I used to have thirty-two teeth. And then I had one wisdom tooth removed, so I had thirty-one. And I hated it. It was uneven. I just felt off-kilter for that whole year. I think that was 1998. But then in 1999 I got the other side done, and everything was better."

"I'm so glad."

"Like feng shui of the mouth."

"Right."

"But I never got the other two taken out to make me have the average mouth of twenty-eight teeth. Which is okay. I'm happy with thirty." Brady still doesn't say anything. "Sharks have multiple rows of teeth—"

"You've gotta stop," Brady suddenly says. "I can't hear any more about teeth. I don't want to hear about teeth in your mouth . . . teeth in your vagina . . . shark teeth . . . no more discussion of teeth."

"I don't *have* teeth in my vagina," I say, rolling my eyes at him. "Did you know that I was born at 5:21 p.m.?"

"What are you doing?" he asks.

"What do you mean?" I ask back.

"You keep talking about ridiculous things. Why?"

"I'm just making conversation."

"Well, don't," Brady says. And we finish loading up the last of the Jolt and get into the car.

There's a dog beach out here, and it's something I think Strummer needs to experience. For starters, he's only been to dog *parks* before, never dog *beaches*. But I also don't know if he's ever even seen a beach.

Brady and I start heading west, and when we finally get to the beach it's like nothing any of us have seen before. Dogs upon dogs. More dogs than I've ever seen in one place. And Strummer is having a blast.

"That little man is in doggie heaven," I say to Brady, who is watching Strummer and smiling.

"So this guy walks into a vet with his dog and places him on the examining table," Brady says. "The doctor looks at the dog and says, 'I'm sorry, sir, but your dog is dead.'"

I look around immediately to see if there are any dogs within earshot, and indeed there is a border collie about three feet away.

"Shush!" I say to Brady. "Don't talk about dead dogs here. You're going to upset the poor pups."

"It's a joke."

"Dead dogs aren't funny."

"You didn't let me finish."

"Does the dog come back to life?" I ask.

"Can I finish?"

"Fine," I say.

"So the vet says, 'I'm sorry, but your dog is—'" and Brady whispers, "'—dead.' And the guy says, 'I want a second opinion.' So the vet opens up a cage and lets out a Labrador. The Lab sniffs the dog, paws him a little bit, and concurs that indeed the dog is dead. So the guy says, 'I demand a third opinion.' So the vet opens up another cage and lets out a cat. The cat walks around the dog and looks him over. When he's finished, he also agrees that the dog is dead. 'Fine,' the man says. 'So what do I owe you?' 'Fifteen hundred,' the vet says. 'What? You're going to charge me fifteen hundred just to tell me that my dog is dead?' 'Hey,' the vet says, 'you're the one who ordered the Lab report and the cat scan.'"

I laugh a little, even though it was silly. And then we're quiet for a while, just watching the dogs play. Strummer seems to be scared of the water. He runs along the edge, but he recoils every time the wave comes in.

I roll up my jeans and go in a little to show him that it's okay, but he won't budge.

Until he sees this bird. Some seagull comes swooping down, and Strummer starts to chase it, chasing it all the way into the ocean. Of course the seagull is flying, so Strummer has no chance of actually getting near it, but he doesn't know this. The next thing I know, Strummer is paddling away in the water, and it's the cutest thing I've ever seen. I feel like a proud parent, and I hear Brady hollering from where we were sitting.

"Whoo-hoo! You go, Strummer! Thatta boy!" he yells. I turn around to see Brady jumping up and down with a similar sense of pride. I wave him over, and he walks down and joins us in the water.

Now Strummer is having so much fun he doesn't want to get out. We splash and play for at least another hour, and it's like we've forgotten all of our problems. For this moment it's just the three of us, playing at the dog beach in sunny California.

And then Brady's cell phone rings.

"Hello?" he says. "Hey, Sam! How are ya?" I watch his expression turn from excitement to frustration in about five seconds. "Uh-huh. Uh-huh. Wow . . . yeah, that must have been really cool. Yeah, Eddie Vedder . . . he's big-time. Then again, all of his recent stuff is crap, but that's another story . . ." He listens a little more, picks up a rock from the sand and chucks it as hard as he can. "Look, just meet me later today, okay? Don't sign anything with him. Promise?"

Brady is sweating, and I hate to see him look this stressed out. He hangs up the phone and looks like he's going to explode.

"What happened?" I ask.

"Your boyfriend took the band out drinking last night with Pearl Jam."

"He's not my boyfriend."

"Whatever. Darren Rosenfuck arranged it so they got to hang out with Eddie Vedder all night. I mean, how the fuck am I supposed to compete with that?"

"Fuck Pearl Jam," I say. "Who cares?"

"They did! You should have heard how excited he was."

"Are they meeting you later?"

"Yeah," he says. "We gotta head back into Hollyweird."

"Good. Look, it's not over till it's over. I have every faith in the world that you are gonna get this band. I know things."

"Yeah?" Brady says with about as much belief as a thirty-year-old being told that the Easter Bunny exists.

"I do. I'm clairvoyant. I am. I always have been. And I know that you are going to sign this band. So have a little faith. I promise you."

"If you say so . . ." he says reluctantly. And we get our things and take off.

On our way back to the hotel we stop at a 7-Eleven because I want a Slurpee, and Brady, all of a sudden, gets on his knees.

"Oh my God!" Brady exclaims. "No freakin' way! This is like my birthday and Christmas all rolled into one!"

"What are you talking about? Get up!" I say and pull Brady up off the floor.

"Look!"

"What am I looking at?"

"Munchos! And Funyons! You can't get these things anymore."

"Apparently you can," I say.

"This is unbelievable," he says as he starts taking practically every bag of chips off the rack. "What's the deal? This is the city of gold! Is Los Angeles like the land of the lost snack foods?"

"Oh, no. Please tell me you aren't going to buy up all of these too."

"Damn skippy, I am."

"Christ," I say. And then I help him grab the rest of the Funyons and Munchos.

The car is now practically sagging in the back. We have a four-door rental, but there is no room for any other person or snack food/beverage in this car. We're also going to be leaving in the morning for Seattle, so I'm not quite sure what Brady is planning to do with all of this stuff.

My cell phone rings, and it's Sydney. I haven't spoken to her since I've been out here, and she's pissed.

"Um . . . hi. Remember me?" she asks.

"Sure do, missy!" I say. "What's shakin'? Holding down the New York fort?"

"Yeah. You could call me, you know!"

"I'm sorry. We've just been running around nonstop."

"Guess what I just did?" she asks.

"I can't imagine."

"I just set up a PayPal account."

"To buy things off eBay?" I ask, because this is why *I* have a PayPal account.

"Nope," Sydney says, totally serious. "Guess again?"

"I really have no idea."

"I've just set up a Boob Fund," she announces proudly. I take the phone away from my ear and look at it. Why I do this, I don't know. I guess to amuse myself. When I put the phone back she is still talking. "—so for my twenty-sixth birthday, as a gift to myself, I've decided to buy myself a new set of boobs."

"Oh my . . ." I say.

"But I don't have enough money, so I've set up a Web site where people can donate to the Sydney's New Boobs Fund and I put a link to it on my Friendster page and my MySpace page."

"You've got to be kidding."

"Nope, I'm totally serious. And people have already donated! Can you believe it? There's $153.67 in the account."

"No, I really can't. And who would donate sixty-seven cents, is what I wanna know."

"Who cares? It's so cool. Why didn't I think of this before?"

"Because you were *sane*?"

"Pot . . . kettle . . . *hello,*" she says. "Anyway . . . how's la la land?"

"It's good. We're having fun."

"If you can call having Darren Rosenthal parade bloated rock stars before your potential band *fun,* it's fun," Brady shouts.

"What's he yelling about? Darren Rosenthal, *your* Darren Rosenthal?" Syd asks.

"No, not *my* Darren Rosenthal, but yes, the one you know."

"Oh, yes it is *her* Darren Rosenthal," Brady contests. "You'll be happy to know that Heaven and Darren were reunited!" and he starts singing the seventies song by Peaches and Herb, "'Reunited and it feeeels so gooood!'"

"What?" Sydney asks.

"Can you shut up?" I say to Brady. "It was nothing," I say into the phone. "Look, Brady is meeting with the band in a few minutes, so let me call you back."

I hang up the phone and stare at Brady, who is driving and looking straight ahead.

"What is wrong with you?" I say.

"Besides *everything*?" he says back.

"What did I tell you before? Stop stressing. You're gonna get this deal. You will walk away from this meeting with a deal."

"Yeah . . . so you say."

"I believe in you," I say, and he looks over at me for the first time. "It's gonna happen. I promise."

"Thanks," he says. We pull into the Hyatt driveway, where Strummer and I jump out, and he drives off to meet the band.

• • •

Brady

You know how you see those movies about the music and entertainment business and you think, Wow, that seems like a really cool job. Well, it's not. It's nearly fucking impossible to have any kind of success. There's *one* Lester Bangs for every trillion wannabe music critics. There's *one* Clive Davis or David Geffen for every zillion A&R dudes. And any way you look at it, Cameron Crowe is just one lucky motherfucker. Sure, he's talented as shit, but who gets to write for *Rolling Stone* magazine at age fifteen? Who gets to write genius movies like *Fast Times at Ridgemont High, Say Anything, Singles,* and *Almost Famous*? Ever hear of a flop, Cameron? And my *God,* the guy even got to marry the hot chick from Heart! (Oh, I forgot about *Vanilla Sky.* Guess Cameron Crowe *isn't* untouchable. Still . . . the dude's had a pretty good run so far.)

Well, I sit on the *other* side of the fence, in the house on the *wrong* side of the tracks. (Cue the soundtrack from *Some Kind of Wonderful.*) Where I sit, I have three hundred sixty-four dollars in my business bank account, a psycho-woman who may or may not be carrying my child, no Top 20 albums on my label—or even Top 1,000 for that matter—and I'm pretty sure I'm losing my hair.

I pull up to where I'm meeting the band, and they're all peering into my car.

"Dude . . . what the fuck?" Sam says.

"Oh, this?" I say when I realize they are talking about the many bags of snacks that have taken over the car. I explain about my long-lost foods, and they all start cracking up.

"How are you getting this stuff home?" Justin asks.

"I guess I need to ship it. Because from here I'm actually going to Seattle."

"What's in Seattle?" Sam asks. I don't want to tell him about Howard Schultz and my Cinnamilk get-rich plan, because I want him to think I'm committed to the label. And I am. If he would just give me a reason to *stay* committed. I'm pretty much hanging my hopes on this band. But that's too much pressure to put on them. I get out of the car and walk with the band into their rehearsal space.

"Just visiting some friends up there," I say.

"Cool. So listen," Sam says. "Darren offered us ten thousand dollars to record some demos."

"That's a lot of money," I say as my heart sinks into my stomach and the bile crawls up my throat.

"Just so I understand correctly . . . is that an advance that he's offered to *pay* you guys or is that money he's going to put into studio time?"

"Studio time," Sam says. "Look, we all really like you," he goes on to say, and I feel like I'm getting dumped. It always feels the same. Suddenly I'm in the fifth grade, standing on the playground in my orange and blue plaid pants, and Danielle Boranski is telling me that Stuart Armstrong gave her his peanut butter and jelly sandwich, so she's going to be his girlfriend starting right after lunch. "But the thing is, Darren has the money to back up the promises." And I'm wishing I had a peanut butter and jelly sandwich to offer Sam. "We really do like you, though, dude."

"Thanks," I say. I mean, what do you fucking say when you have only three hundred sixty-four dollars in your business account? "Look . . . I know it seems really cool that you got to hang out with Pearl Jam last night, and that Darren is all slick and trying to give you a taste of the good life," I say. "But the fact still remains that Darren is going to have to walk into his boss's office at the end of the year, and if you haven't met the quota they had in mind—you're done." They look at each other and start to get uneasy. This is the one thing I still have going for me. My loyalty.

"Yeah, we know," Ethan says. "That's the one scary thing."

"Well, that's not going to happen with me. As I've told you, I'll start from the ground up and make it happen for you guys. I have faith that we'll make it on the first time out, but if not, there'll be a second and a third chance. As many as it takes. When you're done recording, I'll get you set up with a good booking agent. Plus, with my contacts, I have no doubt I'll be able to get you set up on some good tours and *that's* where you'll develop a wider fan base."

"We're into *that,*" Sam says, and they all nod in agreement.

"I'll set up a big grassroots, street-team marketing campaign all over the country," I continue. "And as far as the record goes, I'll get it into all the stores, targeting the places you need to be . . . all of the major online retailers, all major chains, and the super-cool indies. And mom-and-pops too, which major labels sometimes neglect. Plus, I'll place the record in overseas stores and retail programs, and we can also secure separate overseas deals for you—which could mean more advance money that goes directly to you guys."

"That sounds cool," they all agree.

"Plus, I don't know if you're into it, but we could place your music in TV or movies—"

"Car commercials?" Justin says.

"No car commercials," Sam says. And then he adds, "Unless the price is right." They all high-five. "Brady, we totally dig your vibe. For real. But seriously, dude, it's the ten grand."

All of these things are the same as what Darren is offering them. But the difference is, there's a chain of command in Darren's world that's nonexistent in mine. He has to answer to someone, and I don't. Therefore, if Darren's boss says to get rid of them . . . he will. I've got loyalty to offer. A guaranteed home. Everybody wants to feel safe, and that safety is the one thing that I can offer that Darren can't.

"Are you telling me that if it wasn't for Darren Rosenthal offering you guys ten thousand dollars worth of recording time, you'd sign with me?"

"Absolutely," Sam says, and they all nod to back him.

"Really?" I ask.

"Totally," they all say. I think about it. I think about it long and hard—for at least thirty-seven seconds.

"I'll match it," I say. "I'll put ten grand into recording your demos, too. And I can even pull some favors and get enough studio time to record your whole album."

"Cool," Sam says. "Then we're in."

"Yeah?" I say, so happy that I want to cry. Finally something is going right. So what if I just promised ten grand that I don't have.

"Yeah," Sam says. "We were hoping you'd say that. It wasn't at all about you. It was just that we needed to make sure we could have the same opportunities in the studio."

"I'll do you guys proud," I say. "I promise." And when I say "I promise," I think about the fact that those were the last words Heaven said to me before she got out of the car. She promised me it would work out with the band, and she was right. I don't know how *she* had so much faith, because I was barely hanging on by my fingernails, but I can't wait to tell her.

I start wondering if she's even in the hotel room. The last time I left her she wound up in bed with Darren Rosenthal. My heart starts racing at the thought of it. It's fucking nuts. I'm either keeping an eye on Heaven so *she* doesn't end up with Darren or keeping an eye on the band so *they* don't end up with Darren. This dude is a serious pain in my ass.

But Superhero just agreed to sign with me, so at least I know I can relax about that. Fuck. It's like I can finally exhale on that one.

"And, dude . . ." Sam says. "You're driving around Los Angeles buying up all the Funyons and shit. We could just have my mom send you a box of them once a month, so you don't have to be like this crazy guy with all these groceries in his car."

"That would be awesome. I'll just take a few for the road then."

"Whatever you need, bro," Sam says.

And then I say something before it even occurs to me that

I'm thinking about Heaven. "Hey—this is kind of random, but—do you happen to know if it's possible to get Tab out here?"

"Yeah, my mom drinks that," Justin says.

"Really?"

"Yeah. I might even have some in the house. You want a can?"

"It can't be that easy," I say aloud, though it was really to myself.

"You want it?" he asks again.

"Could I?"

"*I* don't drink the shit. Sure." Justin takes off and shows up moments later with a pink/maroon can with the white Tab logo on it. That logo really is one of the coolest logos ever created. But it's even sweeter to look at, knowing how excited Heaven is going to be when *she* sees it. That is, if she's not having sex with Darren right now.

When I drive away from the band there's about seven seconds where I'm totally elated. I got the deal. They're signing with *me*. They are my band. Life is good.

And then it sinks in a little more clearly. I just promised ten thousand dollars that I do not have. But there's *got* to be some way. Think, Brady . . . think. A loan . . . but *how*? What do I have of value? Aside from things banks don't have any way of appreciating . . . like my signed Johnny Cash train whistle or my original-issue *Land of the Lost* lunch box.

I'm starting to get that clammy, sick feeling again. So I try to think of things that make me happy. Puppies? Paychecks? Heaven? *Bacon*. Bacon is a safer bet. I love bacon. I love bacon so much that I could write a poem about it. I'm also a big fan of cheese. A world without cheese . . . that's a world I just wouldn't want to live in.

This isn't working. I'm sweating, and I have the AC on full blast. Of course the AC doesn't work. It's just a massive gust of air pouring in my direction, and it's not helping. Everything is fine, I just need to breathe. And calm myself down. I know this business. You can talk about deal points, publishing, advancing gigs, and booking tours until you're blue in the face, but it all means nothing without a good relationship with the artist. There needs to be respect, open communication, and an overall good vibe between you and your band. To me, this is the only way it can work. And so far, I think I have that with Superhero. Minus, of course, the whole thing about me lying about being in a band back in the day. And having ten thousand dollars.

It's like back in school when the teacher would say, "You're all starting with an A. Now all you have to do is keep it." We all have an A right now. The band has an A. I have an A. Everything is cool.

Until I'm up at all hours of the night listening to why their girlfriends don't want them to go on tour. Or when right before the start of a tour they all of a sudden want a *tour bus* as opposed to an Econoline van . . .

So they get the freakin' bus. And then they bitch about the *hotel room* . . .

Now enter alcoholism and drug addiction . . .

And how the fuck am I going to come up with ten thousand dollars?

• • •

Heaven

I read somewhere, maybe in that DSM-III-R, that an average person is someone who is ordinary and represents most people. Meaning that if an average person eats two chocolate bars a week, then some people will eat more, and some will eat less—but most will eat about two bars a week.

I really don't eat chocolate bars at all. So by this reasoning, I am not normal. Or not average, at least. And as *American Beauty* taught us, there is nothing worse than being average. Well, they said there was nothing worse than being *ordinary,* which is essentially the same thing.

Now, celebrating is something average people do when they've accomplished something. The average person will cook a nice dinner or take someone *out* for a nice dinner. That would be expected. Typical. I—being *not* average—decide that I want to do something different to celebrate Brady getting the band, because I know in my heart of hearts that he will return with good news.

But we're leaving in the morning, and we don't have much time. My first thought is to take Brady's favorite things and make him a cake. But I don't have an oven. So I think . . . maybe a drink. Maybe I'll take some Munchos and Funyons and mash them into a glass of Jolt and make this his celebratory beverage. I could call it Munyon Cola. Munyon. It's even fun to say. See? I'll bet the average person wouldn't have the inspiration to concoct this delicacy. I'll bet the average person wouldn't want to *drink* it either. I'm going to include Brady and me in that one too, as it may be the most disgusting thing I've ever thought of. So on second thought, I'm *not* going to make it. Munyon Cola will never be, and I'll just leave the drink inventions to Brady.

But I want to do *something* to celebrate. Brady's been so stressed out, and we need to do something fun. Not just because he's stressed out, but because, let's face it . . . I'm on a vacation from life right now. When I get back, I have no job, no way of making rent without dipping into the rainy-day fund, no man, and no obvious means of securing any of the above. When it comes to worrying, usually I don't have my priorities straight. Maybe this is what worrying *should* feel like. Normally, I'd just worry about the fact that my hairdresser is going on maternity leave this week, so God only knows how long it'll be before I get a decent haircut—which is true.

We need to have a party. Too bad we don't know anyone in L.A. You know what? A party is a party. Most of the time you don't know people at a party, anyway. That's what parties are *for*—mingling. Making new friends. This is an excellent idea. I'm going to invite all the cool people at this hotel to our room. To celebrate.

Brady walks in and our room is wall-to-wall people. He actually walks out and checks the door to make sure it's the right room. And when he walks back in he spots me in the corner. The music is blaring, and everyone is drinking and having a good time. I wave Brady over, and he squeezes through the crowd to get to me.

"What is going *on*?" he asks.

"Surprise!" I scream. And I blow the party blower thing that the people in Room 801 were kind enough to bring.

"What is this?"

"It's your party! This is Brady," I say to everyone in the general vicinity. Everybody raises their beer bottles.

"Congratulations, man!" one guy says, putting up his hand to high-five Brady.

"Who *are* these people?" Brady asks me.

"Don't leave him *hanging*!" I say to Brady, who looks at the guy still standing there with his hand up waiting for him to respond. Brady finally high-fives him, and the guy turns back to whatever he was doing.

"Are you ready to have an *Effen* good time?" I ask Brady.

"Heaven!" Brady says. "What *is* this?"

"It's your party," I say. "We couldn't stay in a hotel dubbed the 'Riot House' and not oblige. Plus . . . we're celebrating!"

"Celebrating what?"

"Superhero! Them going with you."

"How did you know?"

"I knew. I had faith," I say. "I was right, *wasn't* I?"

"Yeah, you were," he says as a big grin spreads across his face. I jump up and hug him.

"But what if they *hadn't*?" he asks.

"Then this would be a *come cheer Brady up* party."

"And I ask again . . . who *are* these people?"

"Neighbors," I shout. "People staying in the hotel. Cool people I saw downstairs going to Chi, which Justin Timberlake owns, by the way. Did you know that? The place right downstairs is his new restaurant bar."

"I didn't know."

"Well . . . he's busy. He couldn't attend."

"You invited Justin Timberlake?" he says.

"No, he wasn't there. But Kevin Dillon was."

"Who's that?"

"Matt Dillon's brother. He's actually over there," I say, pointing. "In the red bowling shirt. Next to the girl with the fake boobs. Wait—that's every girl in this room." I hand Brady a beer. "Drink up, bud. It's our last night in L.A., and this party is in honor of *you,* my friend."

"You did this in a matter of hours—"

"Yup. I pretty much just gave out the room number, and the rest is history."

"You are a strange and wonderful creature," Brady says. He takes the beer, and we clink bottles. "I take it this party was B.Y.O.B.?" he asks as he looks around and sees all the alcohol. Then he notices the table full of Effen Vodka. "And where did *that* come from?"

"Jon," I reply.

"And Jon would be?"

"Only the coolest guy ever! I was downstairs, and I saw these two guys hanging out by the restaurant, so I invited them. Turns out one of them founded this new vodka called Effen Vodka. Cool name, huh? Anyway, I sat down with them for a half hour and we got to talking about launch strategies—kind of a specialty of mine. I threw out a couple ideas they fell in love with—"

"Like what?"

"'Effen Cool' merchandise and wearables, an Effen-sponsored worldwide poker tournament . . . stuff like that. His guys were doing a little promotion downstairs at Chi that didn't seem to be generating much heat, so I found them a ready-made, targeted audience of qualified prospects."

"Meaning?" he says.

"I told him they'd be suckers if they didn't supply free booze for your party. So . . . we are among the first to try Original and Black Cherry Effen Vodka."

"Effen unreal," Brady says. "Only *you* could pull this together and manage to somehow get a liquor company to sponsor it." He shakes his head in amazement, and we spend the next five hours making new friends and hyping Brady's new band.

We both wake up with black cherry hangovers. The phone rings to deliver our wake-up call, and it's akin to a megaphone pointing directly in my ear. We went to bed approximately seventy-eight minutes ago.

"Make it *Effen* stop!" I say. Strummer looks at me like I'm talking to him, and he cocks his head to the side. "Not you, boy."

"Hello?" Brady moans into the phone. "Thank you," he says and hangs up. "Get up. Time to go. We have to be at the airport in an hour."

"Ugggh," I groan, dragging myself out of my bed.

I hear the shower turn on in the bathroom, and I walk over to the door and push it open.

"I'm coming in," I say and head to the sink to wash my face.

"In here? That's new," he says.

"No, dumbass. You *must* still be drunk. I'm just washing my face."

"Well, I'm glad that we're comfortable enough to share a bathroom now," he says, oozing with sarcasm.

"Not like I can see anything in there. Or *want* to. Do you pee in the shower?"

"No," he says vehemently.

"Liar," I say back.

"Whatever," he says.

"Madonna does," I say.

"She told you this?"

"No, I think I saw it on Letterman. She told Dave. Apparently it's good for you. She said it is."

"This should be interesting," Brady says.

"It prevents athlete's foot."

"Okay then."

"So . . . that's all I'm saying. Were you so inclined to pee in the shower . . . it may be gross, but it could be beneficial."

"I don't have athlete's foot," he says. "But thank you for the newsflash."

"No problem," I say. And then I add, "You're probably peeing right now. Make sure you aim at your feet."

"You're *retarded,*" he says. I leave the bathroom and start to pack my bags. I pack four six-packs of Jolt for Brady at the bottom of my bag. Not that he'll go through all of them in Seattle, but he'll have the option—which is nice.

When we get to the airport, we have a little time to kill. So we check in and see if they'll give us a free upgrade. They won't. And once again, Brady has an aisle seat. He won't budge, and I don't want to be stuck in the window again. So I ask if there's another aisle seat available. Turns out the aisle seat right in front of Brady is open, so I switch my seat.

When we board the plane nobody is sitting next to Brady,

and I have some thinnish droopy guy sitting next to me. He's not overweight, but he looks like at one time he was very overweight. He's got that Jared-from-the-Subway-campaign thing going. I can almost see him proudly holding up a pair of pants that were ten sizes bigger and then stepping out in his new svelte form. Speaking of which . . . the new Subway ads have Jared with his shirt untucked—possibly hiding something?

"Well, how's it going?" he asks. "I'm Evan." He smells like chicken noodle soup.

"Fine," I say. And knowing that my name rhyming with his will spark all sorts of hilarity in him, and at least thirty more minutes of conversation, I decide not to tell him my name. "I'm Belinda."

"Well, that's an unusual name," he says. And I immediately wish I'd gone with Jane . . . or Mary . . . or Cathy. Maybe Sue. "You know this is the bulkhead seat, right, Belinda?"

"Yeah," I say. "More room for us. And by the way, you misheard me. My name is Sue."

"Well . . . oh," he says with an odd look. "But listen . . . when the stewardess comes by she's going to ask us if we're okay with opening the emergency door and helping people exit the plane if there's a problem." And then he leans in. "Just say yes," he says.

"Okay . . ." I say.

"Well, a pilot buddy once told me that if we crash . . . the emergency exit door is useless, anyway. Plus, there are going to be so many cracks in the fuselage that we'd be better off just crawling out through one of the cracks."

"Um . . . okay," I say, not exactly sure why he's discussing this with me moments before we take off. I'm wondering why everything he says begins with "well," and starting to get the feeling that all is *not* well with this man.

"And as far as helping the other passengers . . . I say—" And he doesn't actually say anything, but he dismisses all of humanity with a wave of his hand. What is *wrong* with this man? I can hear Brady snickering behind me too. With his damned empty seat next to him.

"Thanks for the tip," I say. I open up the in-flight magazine and pretend to read an article about Queen Latifah so he'll stop talking to me about plane crashes. Of course, this doesn't work.

"Well, when they go into their little *demonstration* about flotation devices? Just plug your ears and go *la la la,* because if we torpedo into the ocean . . . well, your seat cushion is about as useful as—well, it's not very useful. If we crash into the water, we're all dead. Flight 21 Soup."

Okay . . . there is a certain way to behave on an airplane. There's a little thing I like to call "Jetiquette," the rules that govern appropriate behavior whilst flying on an airplane. I don't know what kind of egg this Evan was hatched from, but apparently good breeding and social graces were not high on his family's list of priorities. And just as I'm about to get up and reclaim my seat next to Brady, the fattest woman I've ever seen comes and sits next to him. She barely squeezes herself into my would-be seat. And the cherry on top is . . . she's got an infant with her. Splendid.

• • •

"I've worn dresses with higher IQs, but you think you're an intellectual, don't you, ape?"

—Wanda, *A Fish Called Wanda*

"No, no, you've always had that wrong about me. I really am this shallow."

—Will, *About a Boy*

Brady

I'm sitting next to the fattest woman in the world. This is no exaggeration. There are rolls of fat overflowing into my seat, touching my arm, and I think I may very well get sick. She's got a baby on her lap, and I genuinely fear for that child. What if she falls asleep and crushes it? One wrong move and that little tot is a pancake. And then if she gets *hungry* . . . oh, the horror! All right, that's just gross. But she's really fat. And I'm really wishing Heaven and I didn't change our seating arrangements.

"They make these seats so small!" the woman exclaims, and I bite my tongue. "I hate flying," she adds.

"I do too," I say, and I pull out my iPod.

"God, this is a tight squeeze," she continues. Does she really need to keep bringing this up? The *Suez Canal* would be a tight squeeze for you, lady! "Did you know that Southwest Airlines actually makes heavier people buy two seats? *Two* seats?" she scoffs. And I'm thinking, two . . . maybe *three*. Then again, it's not such a bad idea. She is clearly in my personal space. "Do you think that's fair?"

How am I supposed to handle this one? I feel Heaven's eyes on me, and indeed they are. She is peering through the seats in front of me with this shit-eating grin, just waiting for my response.

"Um . . ." I say, "no, I guess it's not fair." And I should have stopped it there, but of course I'm a little miffed, so I keep going. "If it's not their fault."

"Oh, so if I'm what society calls *fat*, and it's because my thyroid doesn't work properly, then I *shouldn't* have to pay for two seats . . . but if I'm fat because I just can't stop stuffing my face then I *deserve* to pay double? Is that what you're saying?" I look at Heaven, who is nodding her head *yes*. She's egging me on, but she doesn't have to sit next to this woman.

"Sort of?" I say, and I almost wince like she's going to hit me or something. I regret it as soon as I say it. In fact, I even tried to stop, but it just came out. I think Heaven may be rubbing off on me. This is not a good thing.

"Well, that is a violation of my rights as a human being," she says. "Do they make people with body odor pay for two seats because the person sitting next to them is uncomfortable having to smell their stink?" Sounds good to me.

"I don't know. Until now, I didn't even know they made . . . *larger* people pay for two seats."

"Well, they don't. There is no *smelly* penalty. I mean, I'd rather sit next to a fat person than someone who hasn't bathed since the Reagan administration."

"I'm with you there," I say. But you *are* obese. So why would you mind sitting next to someone who is obese, is what I'm thinking.

"You're with me there, but you still think I should have bought two seats," she says with some attitude.

"No, no, not you," I say. "I wouldn't put *you* into that category." Here I go, trying to worm my way out of this one. "You shouldn't have to pay extra."

"Oh?" she says.

"No!" I say in a way that totally dismisses the silly possibility that she could be overweight. She puffs up a little like a happy bird. Heaven is mouthing something, and I'm trying to make it out. I can't. So she turns to the annoying plane-crash guy sitting next to her.

"I wonder if they'll have *chicken* on this flight," Heaven says, bulging her eyes out at me. So that's it. She's calling me chicken. Fine, I can live with that. I'd rather be chicken than have this woman hate me for the next two hours and thirty-seven minutes. Thank God this isn't a cross-country flight. How much can go wrong in two hours?

"Well, thank you," the fattest woman alive says. "I do struggle a bit with my weight, but I've lost some weight recently. Maybe it shows." Damn right it shows. But if you pulled your pants up a little, it might *not* so much. And she lost weight? You mean to tell me she was fatter?

"Well, I didn't know you before, but you look great," I say, and Heaven actually laughs. I kick her seat in front of me.

"This is Henry," she says as she smiles at the baby boy. "I think I just put on some baby-weight." So when are you due, I wonder. And how many are you having? "He's just two months old," she says proudly.

"He's really cute," I say. And I browse through the artists on my iPod, close my eyes, and start listening to Bright Eyes.

Within fifteen minutes I feel something on my arm. It's warm and fleshy, and I think it's got to be one of her folds of fat—but she was wearing long sleeves. I can't imagine what it is. I open one eye and immediately shut it. I squeeze it so tight that I also inadvertently start holding my breath because I'm in something of a state of shock.

This woman has whipped out her big fat tit and is breast-feeding! I know, breast-feeding is a beautiful thing, and blah, blah, fucking blah. But her giant tit is resting on my arm, and that is not okay. It's *wrong*. I'm sorry. It is just . . . plain . . . *wrong*. And I don't care how hungry little Henry is. Can't he wait two hours to eat? No, of course he can't. What—*wait to eat*? That's a concept that his mother certainly never seems to have wrapped her head around. *Fuck*. My eyes are squeezed so tight that I'm giving myself a headache. And it's not like if I don't look at it, it's going to go away. It's *on* me. Her bare boob is touching me. I feel it. Something must be done. I take off my iPod and look at her, hoping she'll notice that we are in a bit of a *situation* here.

"You like that? You like it?" she is saying to baby Henry, and it's almost obscene. She's got nipples the size of kneecaps and she's cooing and *ooh*ing while Henry is feeding from her massive breast. It's making my stomach turn.

Forget the fat penalty or the stink penalty . . . there should *definitely* be a penalty for this shit. And she ought to fucking pay *me*!

• • •

Brady

By the time we land, I'm so happy to get off the plane that I jump up, grab my bag from the overhead bin, and grab Heaven's, too—because the faster we're out of here, the sooner I can put this flight out of my mind forever.

I think I get a hernia lifting Heaven's bag.

"What the hell?" I groan. "Why is your bag like eighty times heavier than it was in L.A.?"

"Oh . . . I packed some Jolt—for *you*."

"Did you pack *all* of it?"

"No, just a few six-packs."

"Thank you," I reluctantly say.

"You're welcome," she says, completely oblivious to how heavy her bag is. No wonder the flight attendant seemed a little put off helping her get it up there. Luckily it's on wheels, so we can get it out of there without too much effort. We get Strummer from the cargo, and I think both Heaven and I envy *whatever* circumstances he flew under. That's probably a first. But it couldn't have been worse than what *we* endured.

When we get outside we make a pact not to switch seats like that ever again. Heaven even offers to take the window seat from Seattle back to New York. As long as I don't mention plane crashes, natural disasters, or for some reason the words *moist* and *panties*. I ask her why, and she just shudders and says she hates those words. A few seconds later she adds *enthused* to the list.

We get our rental car at the airport, and the first thing I do is transfer the Jolt cans from Heaven's bag into the trunk of the car so I don't have to lift that bag ever again. They gave us a white Ford Focus, which is certainly an improvement from the hideous gold one we had in Los Angeles. And what's with the Ford Focus? It seems to have the market cornered on rental cars for people who can't afford rental cars.

We're in Seattle. It's sixty-two degrees and sunny. This is not the rainy Seattle that I've heard about. We're staying at the Ramada Inn downtown. It's conveniently located seven blocks from the Convention Center, seven blocks from Pike's Market, and seven blocks from the Space Needle. I'm also fairly certain that it's near the Starbucks corporate office—which I will find.

Heaven and I check in, and the clerk at the front desk is abnormally cheery. I know it's part of customer service to act friendly, but this woman is borderline psycho. You know those commercials for the antidepressant Zoloft? With the happy little bouncing-ball character? She's like that ball in human form. Times a thousand. Her name is Annie, she's originally from Ohio, and she'll be happy to help us with anything we should need.

"I'll be right here, manning the decks. So if you need something . . . you just pick up that phone, and guess who's gonna be there to help?" Annie says.

"You are?" I say, playing along.

"Exactly," she says with this confusing conspiratorial nod. Like she'll be there *always*—day or night. I pick up the phone . . . she's gonna answer. She doesn't sleep . . . she doesn't eat. She's happy Annie and she's here to help. She's starting to really freak me out, so I tug on Heaven's sleeve and we go upstairs to check out our room.

Our room is average. Twin beds, like at the Hyatt, but no restaurant/bar downstairs. Well, there is one, but it's not exactly the same as the one under the Riot House. No celebrity sightings here. But that doesn't matter. Because Howard Schultz is in Seattle. And I am going to become a rich man, very soon.

The phone rings, and Heaven picks it up. It's Annie.

"Hi, Annie," she says and gives me a look. "No, so far we've found everything okay. Okay . . . thanks a lot." Heaven hangs up the phone. "That woman sure likes her job."

Heaven and I are unpacking, and all of a sudden she pulls

out a picture of Kurt Cobain and one of those big white candles like you see in church. She props the picture up next to the candle and then lights it. This is new. She didn't do this in L.A.

"Um . . ." I say. "What do we have here? A little altar?"

"You could say that."

"What's goin' on?"

"You don't know what tomorrow is?" she asks with wide eyes.

"Monday?"

"April 5, 2004."

"Should this mean something to me?"

"It's ten years to the day since Kurt Cobain killed himself," she says.

"Wow. I can't believe it's actually been ten years."

"I know . . ." she says and she looks really sad.

"Not to be morbid, but weren't there a few days that went by before he was actually . . . found?"

"Yes," she says.

"So is tomorrow—"

"April 5, *tomorrow,* is the day that he killed himself. April 8 is the day that Gary Smith, that *electrician,* found his body."

"Ah," I say. I know this is a big deal to her—and frankly, it's kind of a big deal to me, too. I mean, I've never thought I'll end up dead at twenty-seven like she does, but Kurt's death really bummed me out. Like Elvis or the Beatles . . . when Nirvana came onto the scene, they pretty much *saved* music. And sadly, I think that for a number of years now everyone's been waiting for someone else to come along and do it again. Don't get me wrong, there's some really good stuff going on in music lately. In fact, I'm more excited about music *right now* than I have been for years. But still, Kurt . . . he was something special.

"There's going to be a vigil to mark the ten-year anniversary of his death."

"Really? Did you know this ahead of time?"

"Uh-huh," she says.

"So were you going to come out to Seattle anyway?"

"No, probably not. I would have had my own little ceremony at home. But it just worked out perfectly. Plus, maybe Dave Grohl will be there and propose to me.

"He's married," I remind her. "Where is it?"

"The original one was at the Seattle Center, so I'm thinking probably there," she says with astonishing authority. "But some people will probably go to the Young Street Bridge, or to the benches at Viretta Park near his house, where some of his ashes are scattered. So sad . . ."

"I know," I say empathetically. She gets quiet and looks at her picture of Kurt. Strummer can sense her sadness, so he walks over and rests his head on Heaven's knee.

Every morning when I wake up I am humbled by the realization that I am not a rock star or an astronaut or a fighter pilot/international spy/gladiator/wealthy jet-setting playboy et cetera. I'm just an average guy who has to get up and drag his ass to work—and is way too dependent on coffee. That said, I *do* understand that my *average* life is still far less mundane than the suit-and-tie guys that push paper all day long.

But this morning is different. I wake up and practically jump out of the bed. And as far as my dependence on coffee? Well, that can only serve me well today because I don't care if I have to hit every Starbucks in Seattle to find him . . . Howard Schultz and I are going to have a sit-down.

This sounds ill conceived, I know. But it's really more a case of wanting the whole experience to happen naturally . . . magically . . . without too much forethought or calculation. Cinnamilk is a long shot, albeit an inspired one. And my business plan makes a pretty good case for it. But if it's going to be part of standard fare at Starbucks the world over, I'm gonna need a lot of luck. So my plan all along? Don't plan too much.

I look in the yellow pages for the corporate headquarters. But there's no listing. I try calling information again, and I even call the 1-800 number again and try to trick them into giving me the address—but no dice.

Heaven is still asleep and I don't want to wake her, so I tiptoe around the room and get dressed. I watch her sleep for a minute, and I'm struck by how beautiful she *really* is. It's not even a matter of opinion. She's lovely. She stirs in her sleep and stretches. She opens her eyes, yawns with her delicate hand covering her mouth, and then rubs her chin for a minute.

"Morning," I say.

"I think there's a hair growing out of my chin," she says.

• • •

Heaven

Waking up in hotel rooms is always awkward. For starters, sometimes you don't know where the hell you are. And even once it kicks in, there's still no real comfort in that . . . no familiarity. That said, I love hotels. I love them. I don't love that the bottom sheet is never fitted, or that they tightly wrap that filthy blanket in between the sheets instead of washing it, but I *do* love that they make no apologies for it. Some people get pissed that there's a price tag on everything from the minibar to a toll-free number . . . but you have to—at least—respect the earnestness and lack of pretense that comes when everything within view is striving to hoover out your wallet.

I wake up in our room at the Ramada, and Brady's at the little desk, presiding over a bowl with a spoon—like a wizard—waving around his magic wand. He's got quite a little mess going. I walk over and peer over his shoulder. At the bottom of the bowl is a shallow puddle of milky liquid in an uncertain color.

"You're up already?" I say.

"I'm not just up. I've been to the store, bought the necessary ingredients, whipped up a batch of Cinnamilk, packaged it—"

I look across the desk. "In baby bottles?"

"It's all I could find with a seal," he says.

"And who doesn't love babies?"

"Here," he says, offering me the bowl. "Taste it."

I accept. And feeling a little like I'm seven years old again having just finished a *ginormous* bowl of Lucky Charms, I tilt the bowl toward my face and drink the leftover milk. Brady's watching me with expectant eyes, and when I emerge from the bowl with Cinnamilk on both of my cheeks, I don't say a thing. It's mean, I know, but I just want to watch him squirm—plus, it's good practice for when he's in the room with Schultz.

"*Well?*" he screams. "C'mon . . . what do you think?"

I can't hold it any longer. I break out into an embarrassingly huge smile and tell him, "It's awesome. Seriously. I can't believe it's not already shoulder to shoulder with the two-percent and one-percent and no-percent milks of this world. Anyone who could market this would be a fool not to hand you a check right now."

"Really?" he says, more vulnerable than I've ever seen him. "You're not just trying to make me feel good? Not that you'd ever do that *intentionally.*"

"Nope. Totally legit. It's a hit," I say, and Brady instantly picks me up into a giant bear hug. I squeeze back, and then he quickly sets me down, stepping back awkwardly.

"Anyway, it's game day," he says. "This is why we're here."

"So . . . what's the plan?"

"Finding Howard Schultz . . . making him see the beauty of Cinnamilk."

"Right," I say. "But how are we going to find him?"

"We?"

"Yes, we. I'm gonna help."

"I don't know . . ." he says.

"Well, I *do*. I'm coming," I say as I walk into the bathroom. "Why don't you take Strummer out for a walk while I shower? By the time you get back, I'll be ready to rumble."

I turn the water on and quickly get in so he doesn't have time to argue.

The first Starbucks we hit is on Fifth Avenue. Brady orders a latte while I case the joint. I see an unsuspecting barista refilling the milk containers, so I sidle up to him and turn on the charm.

"Hi," I say with this wide smile that's usually reserved for traffic cops.

"Good morning," he says.

"How many times a day do you have to refill these things?"

"Oh . . . you know. As many times as they get empty."

"Huh," I say. And I think about what to say next because I hadn't exactly planned this out. "So, isn't the corporate office right around here?"

"Um . . . yeah. Sort of," he says. And leaves it at that.

"Yeah, I thought so. What is it, five blocks from here?"

"No. It's . . . well, yeah, there's a few blocks, but it's only one avenue over."

"Right. So it's on . . . Fourth? No . . . Sixth?"

"No, you were right the first time. It's on Fourth," he says and goes back behind the counter. I catch up with Brady, who hands me a latte.

"Thank you."

"Anything?"

"Yup. It's on Fourth Avenue. That's one street over."

"Nice work." We clink our paper coffee cups and walk out the door. We drive over to Fourth Avenue, and when we get there we come across *another* Starbucks. Why shouldn't there be another Starbucks here? If they're on every other corner in every other city, then I'd imagine the founding city would just be one huge Starbucks. In fact, I'm surprised they didn't hand us a Frappuccino when we walked off the plane.

Brady walks in, and I follow. He orders another latte, and I begin to wonder if he's going to get a cup of coffee at every Starbucks we hit on the way to finding Mr. Schultz, which would probably not be the best idea.

He talks to the barista at the counter and comes back looking sideways at me.

"What?" I say defensively.

"That guy just told me that the corporate office is on First, not Fourth."

"Well, the guy that *I* spoke to seemed like he knew what he was talking about."

"Apparently not," Brady says. He walks out, dumping his latte onto the sidewalk.

We drive back from Fourth to First Avenue and turn right.

"Did he tell you a cross street?" I ask.

"Yup . . . Lander."

"Do we know which way Lander is?"

"This way," he says. I can tell he's nervous because he's being a little short with me, and he's not usually like that. I mean, usually he's annoyed or flustered or pulling his hair out. But he's never really short for no reason. And I understand. He's got a big meeting in front of him. That is, if he can even get in to see this man—which is a completely different story. I sit quietly alongside him for the next few blocks because I don't want to stress him out any more than he already is.

When we get to First and Lander, there really is no sign of the corporate office. I guess we look lost because a skinny woman with a hair color not found in nature offers her assistance. Brady rolls down the window, and she walks over to us.

"Do you need help?" she says. "Is there an address I can help you find?"

"Yes," Brady says. "We were told that the corporate offices of Starbucks were here, but I can't seem to find it."

"Well, there's a Starbucks a few blocks down the way . . ." she says. "But I'm not sure about the corporate headquarters."

"Okay. Thanks anyway," Brady says and continues driving in the direction she pointed.

"Are we going to the next Starbucks?" I ask.

"As many as it takes," he says. And we drive a few blocks until we see another one and pull over.

Brady walks up to the counter and smiles at the girl in the Starbucks cap. "Hi there. I'm supposed to have a meeting at the corporate office, and I seem to be lost. I thought it was on First and Lander . . ."

"No," she says, "it's on Fourth and Lander." As soon as I hear her say Fourth I want to give Brady an *I told you so,* but I don't. I refrain. Brady thanks the girl and walks over to me.

"Go ahead," he says.

"What?"

"You *know* what! You were right. You know you want to gloat."

"I do not," I say defensively. "I'm just happy that we know where it is now."

"Uh-huh . . ." he says in this I-don't-believe-you sort of way. But I still keep my trap shut, and we get in the car and drive *back* to Fourth Avenue. Before we get there we pass *another* Starbucks, and there's an employee standing outside taking a smoking break. Brady pulls over to him. "Hey," he says to the guy. "The corporate office is up this way?"

"Yeah," the guy says. "It's on Utah."

"Utah?" Brady says, a little exasperated.

"Yeah," he says as he takes a super-long drag off his cigarette, "2401 Utah. It's in the old Sears building."

"I thought it was Fourth and Lander," Brady says, and he gives me an I-knew-you-were-wrong look, even though I kept my mouth shut during the whole First Avenue thing.

"Well, it *is* Fourth and Lander," he says, and I give a satisfied look back to Brady. "The cross streets are Fourth and Lander, but it's actually *on* Utah. It's just up that way, 2401. You can't miss it. It's a big brick building with the Starbucks logo on top."

"Thanks, bro," Brady says, and we drive until we see it: the big brick building with the Starbucks logo as the cherry on top.

We pull up front and both get out of the car.

"This is it," I say, and I give him a giant bear hug. "Go kick ass."

He starts to walk away and then runs back to the car.

"Wait! I can't do it!" he shouts. I'm genuinely touched by his reluctance, his indecision. His fear of the unknown. He's come all this way only to be seized by self-doubt.

"Yes you *can*!" I shout. And sensing the need for some encouragement, Strummer leaps up and bumps his head into the closed passenger window.

Brady looks at me oddly, reaching past me into the back of the car. "Not without *this* I can't," he says, grabbing the business plan and a Cinnamilk baby bottle.

I get in the driver's seat, give him a wave of encouragement, and pull away. Strummer hops into the passenger seat and we crank up the radio. I told Brady I'd wait for him to go over to the vigil so we could go together. He said he'd call me when he was done, but I don't know how long he's going to be, so I just drive around checking out the local sights. I pass Pike's Market, with all of the fish throwers and the fruit stands, and I get out to buy a bag of cherries. I was going for the run-of-the-mill red ones, but the guy at the stand talks me into Rainier cherries, which are white-ish and pretty tasty. Whatever the color, the real fun of eating cherries is spitting the pits out the window. It's a little-recognized art, and one that I'm a master of. I notice that Strummer is eyeballing me, and I feel bad not being able to share with him—but they have pits, and I don't want him to swallow one. I don't want to be responsible for a cherry tree growing in his stomach.

I spot a convenience store a block away and head over to get Strummer some dog treats.

On my way in, I pass three white kids from the suburbs on a Free Tibet hunger strike. It's apparently Day 15 of the strike, and they don't look happy. They're camped out on this makeshift bed, and they look tired, weak, and hungry. I'd bet *they'd* like some cherries.

It takes a lot of willpower for me not to try to sneak them some, but I don't. I'd probably get blamed for all Tibetan suffering, and I get blamed for enough as it is.

I walk into the convenience store and they've got Seattle's classic rock station on with "Fly Like an Eagle" blaring. I wonder what would happen if they banned certain songs or retired them permanently. It seems that classic rock boils down to like five songs on heavy rotation. Boston's "More Than a Feeling," Eagles—it's a tie between "Hotel California" and "Life in the Fast Lane"—Bad Company, "Feel Like Makin' Love," Led Zeppelin's "Stairway to Heaven," and every single Steve Miller Band song. I reserve the right to lump them all into one song. If a moratorium were suddenly declared on all those songs, it is my assumption that classic rock stations would all go under.

I scan the aisles for dog treats as "Fly Like an Eagle" fades into "The Joker," and my point is proven. They have only the shitty kinds of dog treats made of garbage and nasty by-products, and I don't want Strummer eating that crap, so instead I get him a ham and cheese sandwich. They also have Slurpee machines, only they don't make *real* Slurpees. The flavors are Cherry and Blue Ice. I mix both. It's not the worst, but I prefer the Cola flavor.

I also spot the Pringles and realize that I haven't had Pringles in a very long time, and I'd like some. When I was younger I remember eating Pringles, and how I'd stack them before I'd eat them, so I'd end up eating four or five at a time. I wonder how many Brady can eat. I hold up a can and start measuring it out in chunks, figuring out how many stacks it would take to kill a can. As I'm counting, I notice a tall good-looking guy in a Cubs cap hovering over by the magazines, watching me. So I try to explain.

"I'm seeing how many handfuls it would take to polish off a can."

"And what have you come up with?" he says as he looks out the window. He seems a little nervous.

"I'm thinking seven," I say. "Maybe six."

"Ambitious," he says, and then looks out the window again. "Did you know that cat piss glows in the dark?"

"Uh . . . no. I didn't."

"Well, it does," he says as he puts one magazine down and picks up another. He may want to work on the non sequitur, I'm not sure. Either way, I'm suddenly all the more glad that I have a dog. "I got black lights and replaced the bulbs in every room in my apartment so I could have a look-see, and it's everywhere! Fuckin' cat piss!"

"Okay . . ." I say. Nothing I can or really want to add to *this* stimulating conversation. So I grab seven cans of Pringles because I've decided that Brady and I are going to have a contest to see who can finish a can faster.

I end up with three gallons of bottled water, seven cans of Pringles, Strummer's ham and cheese sandwich, my Slurpee, and a funny pair of Foster Grant style sunglasses. I realize after

I pay that I'm out of work and still buying things like I'm gainfully employed.

I drag the bags out to the car two at a time, and pop the trunk. While I'm loading the bags, the cat-piss guy comes over.

"Let me help you with those," he says.

"Thanks," I say. "The water was actually killing me." I go and throw the rest of the stuff up front.

"You got it," he says. He loads the water in the trunk, comes back into view, and smiles. "That it?"

"Yes," I say.

"There you go, then," he says and shuts the trunk. See? Now, this is a good guy. Sweet. Helpful. Guys in New York aren't like that.

"Thanks so much," I say. I maneuver my way out from the front seat, but I don't even know if he heard me because he's already walking down the street. Okay then.

I give Strummer his sandwich, and once he's devoured it we take a walk down the block. We walk past a Rite Aid and a coffee shop called Tully's before we get to Union Street, where we make a right. We stop to listen to a street performer who is playing his guitar and singing a medley of Nirvana songs in honor of the anniversary of Kurt's death. Strummer and I listen as he sings, "I feel stupid . . . and contagious / Here we are now . . . entertain us."

Strummer gives me a tug, so we start walking back. Several cop cars speed past us on our way. When we get back to the car Strummer sniffs it out to see if there's any sandwich left, and I open a can of Pringles. Two cans are for the contest. Two are for when he loses and demands a rematch. And the other two are in case he wins that one, and we need a tie-breaker. The seventh can is my practice can. I grab a handful and pull away from the curb. As I'm driving back toward Fourth and Lander a bunch more cop cars with lights flashing speed past going the opposite way. I'm tempted to flip a bitch and see what the action is, but I refrain and stay my course, back to Brady.

• • •

Brady

I walk into 2401 Utah Avenue South, and it's pretty much exactly what I expected. Yes, there is a Starbucks on the ground floor, and yes, it's a corporate building sparsely populated with people in suits and the occasional bike messenger—all coming and going, all in a rush. I scan the directory for Schultz. His office is on the eighth floor.

When I walk over to the elevator banks, nobody stops me to ask where I'm going. I'm in. Just like *that*. The elevator opens up on the eighth floor, and there is actually another lobby—only the coffee is free in this one. There are pots of coffee along a ledge, with all of the fixings you'd find in a Starbucks, naturally. Behind the reception desk there's a smallish guy wearing a button-down shirt with a V-neck sweater over it. He's got glasses on, and he's got this look on his face like someone just spoon-fed him some motor oil.

"Good morning," he says. "Can I help you?"

"Yes, I have a meeting with Howard Schultz."

"Your name?" he asks, looking me over and then wrinkling his nose as he notices the baby bottle.

"My name? Yes. My name is Brady Gilbert."

"One moment," he says as he buzzes what I assume to be Schultz's secretary. "Hi . . . Brady Gilbert?" he says to her. My heart starts to pound so loud I'm worried that he can actually hear it. "One sec," he says and covers up the phone with his hand. "Where are you from?" he asks me.

"New York," I say. Which is true.

"Right . . . what company?"

"I'm . . . I . . ." Fuck, I think. What the hell do I say? "Sleestak Records" isn't exactly going to get me in the door. "Cinnamilk" will give away my brilliant idea. "I'm from the Make-a-Wish Foundation," I say. It just comes out.

"Very good," he says. "He's from the Make-a-Wish Foundation," he repeats into the phone. "Uh-huh? Okay. Great." He hangs up and looks at me with this thin-lipped smile. "I'm sorry, but they don't have a record of any appointment."

"There must be a mistake," I say.

"Mr. Schultz has two assistants back there. Not one . . . two. They *together* constitute a highly effective machine who are employed to make certain that there *are no mistakes.*"

"Well, there's always a first," I offer meekly.

"I'm sorry, but you have no appointment. You can feel free to leave your literature with me, and I'll send it back."

"No," I say, checking the pleading tone in my voice. "You don't understand. I need to see Mr. Schultz today."

"Not going to happen, my friend," this little man with the big attitude says. I can see I'll have to change my approach. But first I need a cup of coffee.

I step away from the big desk and make my way to the coffee. Dammit if I'm not going to have some free coffee while I'm here. I take a sip of my coffee and pace. He's watching me, so I sit down. Then I stand up again.

"Look, I need to see him. The truth is . . . I'm not from the Make-a-Wish Foundation. I'm sorry. I don't know why I said that. I just thought it would help."

"Yes, lying about working for a company that grants the wishes of dying children is an excellent idea. I can see why you'd think it would help." He opens up a magazine and starts to flip through it, like I'm not here.

"But I came *clean.* That's got to count for something."

"What's next?" he says. "Begging me for a milk refill for some starving imaginary baby?"

I don't get what he means at first, but then I see he's looking at the baby bottle. "Oh, this? This . . . this is my lunch."

"How nice," he says. "Your mom packed you a lunch. I call dibs on the Fritos."

"Look, I just flew clear across the country to see Mr. Schultz.

I have to talk to him about something that is actually going to make him a *lot* of money."

"Yeah, you and everybody else who walks through that door. Get in the back of the line."

"Well, I would . . . if you'd show me where the line *is*."

"It's an expression," he says, rolling his eyes.

"I know. I was making a joke."

"He already *has* a lot of money. Thanks for stopping by. If you'd like to leave your press kit, or whatever it is that you'd like to speak with Mr. Schultz about, you may do so."

"It's really important," I say. "Can you *please* just tell him that there is someone out here who needs to talk to him about very important things."

He reaches for his pad and picks up a pen. I see him write my name on it and I think I'm finally getting somewhere.

"Okay. Brady . . . Gilbert . . . very . . . important . . . things," he says, holding it up to show me. "Does this look about right?"

"Yes," I say.

He crumples it up and throws it in the trash. "He's booked solid with meetings."

What had been a test of wills transforms into me wanting to test one of the carafes of coffee over the bridge of his nose. I take a breath. "I'll wait," I say.

"For the next seven months."

"I just need five minutes of his time," I say, enunciating every word.

"I know. You have this brand-new idea that is going to make him a zillion dollars—or wait—let me guess . . . you've just reinvented the coffee bean! You think there aren't a dozen of you people a week that 'just want five minutes' of Mr. Schultz's time?"

"But I don't want to reinvent the bean! I just want to talk to him!"

This is *so* typical, this guy. In his little shirt with his V-neck over it. A whiny, overgrown fifth grader who got picked on his whole life and now has this big *position of power.* Don't get me wrong, I'm usually pro–*high school loser makes good.* The losers who were picked on in high school tend to fare a lot better in society than the ones who were popular. The popular kids are all now living culturally vapid suburban lives with white picket fences and SUVs, while the high school losers are now the movers and shakers of society.

But not this clown. This guy has his all-important job as a receptionist. It's his job to keep out all the riffraff. He is the gatekeeper. Him and his David Spade *and you are?* attitude. That's what he is. A poor man's David Spade. As if a rich man's David Spade would be any better. Either of them . . . all of them would be keeping me out, and that is just not acceptable.

I start freaking myself out with mental pictures of this guy and David Spade together, laughing at me. It's that moment that I realize I've drunk *way* too much coffee. He's not going to budge, and I'm going to have to come up with a better plan. A *better* plan? How about *any* plan . . .

"Is there something else I can help you with?" he asks me.

"No . . . nothing else. Just, you know . . . letting me meet with Mr. Schultz."

"Okay then, if there's nothing else, I'm going to have to ask you to leave now."

"Put yourself in my position," I say, taking a breezy new tack, in the absence of that plan I just referred to. "You just flew all the way across the country to see Mr. Schultz. The only thing standing in your way is some guy—some very nice and well-dressed guy—who's just trying to do his job."

"Please leave."

I walk out of the reception area, but then peek my head back in. . . .

"Don't make me call security," he says, and I duck back out. I stand in the hallway for a few minutes, thinking. There's got to be a way. A side door . . . a fire escape . . . something.

A food delivery guy gets off the elevator and heads to the reception area. I stop him and ask if they send him back when he delivers food, or if whoever ordered it comes to reception. He tells me he's not allowed to pass reception. So much for that idea.

I take the elevator downstairs and walk around the main lobby, trying to figure out a new plan. A costume? It works in the movies, right? I can pull a Fletch. Unfortunately, I don't have access to a costume shop, so I'm going to need to improvise.

I walk outside and look around. There's really not much to work with. I actually contemplate breaking a bunch of branches off a tree and going up there as a tree. But this is assuming that the guy has a sense of humor and a heart.

I walk back into the building and spot a janitor. Sure, I could pay the guy twenty bucks to let me put on his outfit, but what's that going to do, besides make me short twenty bucks. Every harebrained idea I think of seems like it's from an episode of *Laverne & Shirley,* and I hate that I'm not better prepared for this. But how do you prepare to meet a man who is guarded behind a 1-800 number?

Then I get this idea. The bathroom! I take the elevator back upstairs to the eighth floor and head straight for the bathroom. The man is going to have to relieve himself at some point, right? I'll just hang out in the bathroom and wait until he comes.

So I'm sitting in a stall with not even a scrap of reading material, and I am bored. Not just bored . . . I'm *doorman bored.* This is a term I coined years ago when I had a summer job as a doorman in a fancy apartment building. Your job is to just sit there and wait for people to come in and out. But I worked on the off hours when people rarely came in or out. And I'd just sit there. And I'd try to entertain myself. Reading wasn't allowed, so it was all down to the imagination. Back then I had it bad for Stephanie Seymour, so I'd just think about her all night. Of course, that would inevitably lead to extreme discomfort. So I'd try to clear my mind and think about nothing. Just sit there, doorman bored.

I wait in my stall, and people come in and out. I peek out, but it's never Schultz. It's been an hour and thirteen minutes, and I've heard things and smelled things that I couldn't even do if I tried.

Two guys walk in, one after the next, and they start going on about some race:

"Hey, are you still going down to Portland for the Nike Run Hit Wonder 10K?" the first guy says.

"You kidding me? I wouldn't miss it for anything! I'm a huge Tone-Loc fan." This person is admitting this out loud?

"Who else is playing?" the first guy asks.

"Tommy Tutone, Flock of Seagulls, General Public, and a mystery band. And Devo is headlining," the second guy says. What's this? Devo? Devo certainly had more than *one* hit, and they are not especially connected to the running world, so I don't understand why they're going to be playing. Why not get Bob Seger? Not a one-hit wonder either, but at least he was all about running "Against the Wind."

"Devo just doesn't get the respect they deserve," I find myself saying out loud, and then I actually cover my own mouth with my hands to physically shut myself up. Neither of the two responds, but they both make pretty hasty exits.

A few minutes later someone else walks in. He gets in the stall next to me and sits down. I recognize the shoes. It's David Spade. I actually hold my breath because I don't want him to know I'm in here. I'm sitting here turning purple, but I don't hear any action on his behalf. Not that I want to hear the guy do his business, but I just find it odd that he's not doing *anything*. I'd suggest he eat some bran, but I don't want to blow my cover.

"Just so you know . . . we know you're in here and have known since you came in," he says.

"Are you talking to me?" I ask, not in the De Niro way, but in an innocent *who, me?* way.

"Yes, you."

I come out of my stall, and so does he. "How's it going?" I ask. Totally nonchalant. I notice that there are two security guards standing at the door as well.

"Listen . . . I understand this is important to you," David says.

"Okay, now we're getting somewhere."

"But the thing is . . . even if I wanted to let you back there to see him . . . it wouldn't do any good."

"Why not?"

"Because," he says, "Mr. Schultz is in Barcelona at the Global Food Business Summit."

"Barcelona . . . Spain?"

"No, Barcelona, Rhode Island," he says.

"He's out of the country?"

"Yes."

"And you let me sit here for over an hour?"

"Yes."

"Why?" I ask in bewilderment.

"I don't know," he says, like he genuinely doesn't. And it comes out so matter-of-fact that I want to punch him in the face.

"You're an asshole," I say. Obviously not the *right* thing to say, because as soon as I say it, the two security monkeys grab me and drag me out. They escort me into the elevator, and just as the doors are almost closed, that Spade wannabe sticks his arm out and stops the door. It opens up again to reveal the smug little prick standing there with his arms now crossed.

"Oh, and by the way . . ." he says. "Mr. Schultz has his own private bathroom here, so even if he *was* in the office . . . you *never* would have actually had your little toilet conference." And he turns and walks away. Just as the doors are closing again, I hear him say, "Who's the asshole now?"

He won. The little bastard won.

When I get to the lobby I see Heaven and Strummer right outside waiting for me. As I come outside, she can tell by the look on my face—and the two security guards attached to either side of me—that things didn't go as intended.

"Did you at least get to see him?" she asks.

"No."

"Did you get to see *anyone*?"

"Yes, his receptionist. And, of course, the coffee teamsters," I say, motioning at the two men who just tossed me at Heaven.

"You were there an awfully long time," she says.

"I really don't want to talk about it."

"All . . . righty, then."

"What about you? I hope you had a better time than I did?"

She crosses her arms in front of her chest. "Well, I had an interesting one. Educational . . ."

"Do tell . . ."

"I learned that cat piss glows in the dark. Did you know that?"

"No, I didn't know that."

"Yeah, me either," she says. I don't know where she comes up with this stuff. Her mind . . . It's like I've come upon this secret vault that science will someday discover—or probably never discover. Which is fine by me. Kind of like when there's a band I really like but nobody knows about them. I want people I like to hear them, but when the whole world jumps on the bandwagon I get pissed. Because I found them first. Unless, of course, it's one of *my* bands . . . in which case the world is more than welcome to jump. But Heaven . . . I'd prefer it if nobody else jumps on her.

• • •

Heaven

Brady and I grab lunch at this place called Honey Hole Sandwiches, which sounds slightly pornographic, but supposedly they make a mean sandwich. It has sort of a gothic bayou theme with a full bar that looks like a run-down bayou shack of sorts. The people that work here are friendly and seem to really enjoy making sandwiches.

After lunch Brady changes out of his nice(r) shirt and throws on his old CBGB T-shirt. We get back into the car and drive over to the Convention Center, but there's nothing going on.

"Hmm . . . that's strange," I say. "I guess it's not as big a deal as I expected."

"Guess not," Brady says.

"Then let's just go to Viretta Park," I say. "It's right across the street from his old house."

"Lead the way," he says, and I pull out our map of Seattle as we drive to pay our respects to Kurt.

When we get to the park, which is right across from Kurt's old house, I get chills as soon as we pull up. The neighborhood is extremely nice. Really big houses. Obviously an exceptionally wealthy neighborhood.

I think we're both surprised by how few people are there. It's certainly not empty, but it's not the thousands upon thousands of kids that were at the Seattle Center ten years ago. Then again, those kids are now grown up and probably have better things to do. We park the car and walk onto the grass.

There are two hippie guys, stoned out of their minds and stinking of patchouli oil, leaning up against a tree. One of them looks at Brady and scoffs.

"Hey, Trendy Wendy," he says.

"Trendy Wendy?" Brady says back, not sure what his deal is.

"Yeah, Trendy Wendy," he says and points at Brady's CBGB T-shirt. "Where'd you get that shirt . . . at the *mall*?"

"I'm from New York. And I got it in New York—where I *live*."

"Poser," the stoner says.

"Um . . . no. I live in *New York*," Brady says.

"Just ignore him," I say.

"Oh, now *you're* the voice of reason?" Brady says to me.

"Yes," I say.

"Fine," he says, because he knows I'm right. And any other day, in any other place, I'd have told the kid to fuck off myself. But not today. Not here.

There are people sitting on the grass, leaning up against the trees, playing guitar and singing Nirvana songs. The bench seems to be an altar. Kids have come here for the last ten years and scrawled messages to Kurt on it, but today it is overloaded with a bunch of candles, flowers, and pictures of Kurt. There are also poems and letters written to Kurt, and there are even a couple Teen Spirit deodorant sticks on the bench, which I think is pretty clever. The kids are singing "All Apologies." As I stand by the bench looking at the makeshift altar, having my own private moment, a tear forms in my eye. I can't help it.

We get to talking to a few of the kids, and I meet a girl who came out here with her mother from Kansas. Just for this. She tells me that they happened to meet Kurt's grandfather earlier in the day, and he invited them over to his house for tea. He actually gave the girl a few childhood pictures of Kurt. That's a pretty cool story—and keepsake.

What strikes me, actually, is the age of these kids. The people you would think *make sense* being here aren't the majority. The majority are younger. There's a little girl in a Nirvana T-shirt who can't be more than thirteen years old, which means that she was three when Kurt died. And they don't seem like depressed or fucked-up kids. They seem like good, intelligent kids who just love the music. They relate to it because they think that Kurt was *real*. And he was. A lot of people are crying.

Others just sit quietly, drinking their coffee. What's weird is everybody here has a cup of Starbucks coffee.

Then this idiot comes from out of nowhere. It's been pretty peaceful so far, but he's some local cable access TV host who's got all kinds of conspiracy theories about Kurt's death. He starts screaming all of this crazy shit . . . rattling off statistics, pointing the finger at Courtney Love, and just making a giant fuss. He has one camera pointed at the crowd and another one attached to his hip, so he can also tape himself. He's making a scene, and it's really uncomfortable.

"Get out of here!" one kid yells.

"It was all a cover-up!" he yells back. "You're all content to sit here and cry, but none of you are doing anything to fix it! What have you done for Kurt?" He starts to follow some of the kids around with his camera, shouting in their faces. When he picks on some poor fourteen-year-old and actually pokes him, Brady steps in front of him.

"Dude, chill out," Brady says. "These people came here to pay their respects to Kurt. They don't need you screaming in their faces."

"Courtney's own *father* thinks she did it!" he yells.

"Shut the fuck up," says the hippie dude that was calling Brady "Trendy Wendy" ten minutes earlier. It's true. Nothing unites people like a common enemy, and Brady and hippie guy, along with everyone else, are now on the same side.

"You're all accomplices then! Murderers!" the wacko yells.

"Listen," Brady says, and he suddenly gets in the guy's face. "There are a lot more of us here than you. If you don't take your little cameras and your big mouth and get the fuck out of here, we will tear you apart limb from limb, and then come back here ten years from now and celebrate *your* death."

Everybody starts cheering, and the hippie guy actually *hugs* Brady. Then everybody goes back to playing songs and singing along.

I walk back over to the shrine and notice a sign that someone made and put under the bench. It reads DON'T FORGET LAYNE

STALEY. He was the lead singer of Alice In Chains, another Seattle band. Layne died of a heroin overdose two years ago this month (bad month for Seattle rock stars) at the age of thirty-four. And almost as soon as I notice the sign I see a three-legged dog walking over to the vigil. I swear to God, this is true. It freaks me the hell out because the cover of one of Alice In Chains's records had a picture of a three-legged dog. The only difference is that the dog on the album cover was missing a front leg, and this dog is missing a back leg, but it's almost like a sign. Like Layne is here with us, too. Or maybe he's with Kurt, and they're both okay.

"What's with all of the Starbucks cups?" Brady says when he notices that there's actually a table full of canisters of Starbucks coffee and coffee cups. "It's like they're here to mock me."

"The dude who owns Starbucks lives right up there," I hear someone say, and Brady and I both turn around.

"You've got to be kidding me," Brady says.

"I shit you not. Howard, I think, is his name. I come here all the time to pay my respects to Kurt. I've met him. He's really cool. He donated all the Starbucks coffee for anyone who was going to show up here today."

"What house?" Brady asks.

"First house to the right," the kid says, pointing.

"Un-fucking-believable," Brady says.

"You need to go over there," I say to Brady. "You must. I mean . . . you absolutely must. This is *fate*!"

"That is kinda weird."

"Totally. You were psychically brought to this spot."

"Wow," Brady says. "Thanks, Kurt."

"Go over there," I urge.

Brady turns to the kid, "That house right up there?"

"Yup," the kid says. Brady looks at me, runs to the car, grabs his proposal and a baby bottle, and takes off toward the house.

I walk back to where the kids are sitting in a circle, singing.

"Can't believe it," some girl says. "Dead at twenty-seven. Too young." And I'm once again reminded of my fear. I still haven't found a husband. I haven't even gone on a date. Unless you count Darren the other night, but we didn't even go out to dinner. I start to get anxious and try to push it out of my mind. I don't want to think about this right now. Or the fact that my professional career in PR is a fading memory. Or that I can't even hold down a fucking waitressing job, let alone a serious relationship. And I'm going back to . . . what?

I try to quiet the inside of my head and just *be* here. Where it's calm, and people are singing and remembering Kurt. But they start singing "Something in the Way," and my brain starts replaying my breakup with Darren and the two failed mini-relationships I had after Darren. And then it fast-forwards into all these little movies—little full-color vignettes of all the stupid things I've ever said or done. Maybe it's giving me examples of why I'm still single? Why I'm unemployed? Why nothing is going my way? Maybe it's all my fault.

But wait—fuck that! I'm single because I'm picky. I'm single because I'm not going to *settle.* Yes, I'll find a job, but not just any job. And yes, I need to get married relatively soon or I will die, but I *still* will not settle. It's *not* all my fault. Stop the tape.

• • •

"I guess we're playing for keeps now. I guess the kidding around is pretty much over, huh?"

—Carl Spackler, *Caddyshack*

"But how can you be sure?"

—Buttercup, *The Princess Bride*

Brady

I walk up to Schultz's house and my Y chromosome kicks in immediately. Instead of focusing on the task at hand, I start comparing his house to my would-be millionaire's mansion. This place is *impressive* and everything. But I'd have at *least* five cars out front—just like any self-respecting rap star does. And I'd have someone there making sure they are waxed to perfection. Daily. I know . . . I've seen too many episodes of MTV *Cribs*. But you know what you *don't* see on those MTV *Cribs* episodes, where they flaunt famous people's wealth? Moats. When I make *my* money I am going to build a moat in front of my house. Just because. Because someday when Howard Schultz and I are hanging out, shootin' the shit, doing those things that guys do—rating supermodels, berating pro-sports coaches, debating who has more hair—I'll always have my moat. My trump card. Oh yeah, Schultz? Well, you don't have a moat! Take *that*!

Just as I'm standing there nodding this very self-satisfied, moat-having nod, I'm snapped out of it when a gardener walks onto the property and leaves the gate wide open. Now I'm not a person who believes in signs and all that. But if *Heaven* were standing here, she would insist that that was a sign. And that I am supposed to just walk in behind the gardener. So I do.

Okay, the guy may not have a moat, but his house is pretty fucking nice. I don't know exactly what to do here, so I just start walking up the lawn with my proposal. And that's when I hear this shrill Mexican woman's voice come out of nowhere.

"What you want?"

I don't even know where to look, but I answer like I'm talking to Oz.

"I just . . . have something for Mr. Schultz," I say as I raise the proposal and baby bottle over my head to show that indeed I have something.

"Mr. Schultz no home. You no invited! You trespassing! I call the police!"

"No, no need for that!" I say, still wondering whether she's invisible, or perhaps communicating through some tiny speakers implanted throughout the lawn.

"I call police NOW!" she says, and I hear a snap. At first my panicked brain thinks it's a gunshot. But no, it was more like a door slamming shut. Anyway, I'm pretty sure she means business. And then there's the matter of the gardener striding toward me with a menacing look in his eye and an enormous metal lawn rake in his hand—so I take off across the lawn, through the gate, and down the hill over to where Heaven is talking to a couple of little kids.

I'm out of breath when I reach her, and I bend forward with my hands on my knees and just pant for a few seconds. Strummer comes over and licks me on the face.

"What happened?" she asks. "Did you see him?"

"No, I saw his gardener and got yelled at by what I assume is his housekeeper, unless he's married to a very high-strung lady who doesn't speak very good English."

"You never know," Heaven says. "Maybe she's really nice but overly caffeinated. I'm sure they have an endless supply in that house."

"I'm going to go with a *no* on that. I think it's safe to say that *nobody* is married to that woman." She looks at my hands holding my proposal and the baby bottle.

"What's *that*?" she says. "Why is your proposal still in your hands?"

"Did you miss that last bit? The high-strung lady, the gardener . . . his rake?"

"Ugh, give me that," she says. She grabs the proposal and bottle out of my hands and marches over to a stoner kid. The next thing I know, he's peeling off his hipster bowling shirt and handing it over. She turns it inside out and puts it on, ties her hair up into a bun, and marches up to Schultz's entry walkway, toward his front door.

"Nice knowing you," I shout.

I can't even look. But since Heaven's life is in jeopardy, I figure this might be interesting. So from behind the car, I peer across the lawn to where she's reached the front door of the hulking Howard Schultz house. I can make out a door opening, and a figure dressed in black, and Heaven speaking to him for what seems like an eternity. Then the door closes. And as if nothing has happened, she returns.

"Brady?" she says.

"Down here," I say from my position crouched behind the car, which now strikes me as a little cowardly. She crouches down. "What happened?" I whisper.

"A guy came to the door . . . I told him I had a very important delivery expressly intended for Mr. Howard Schultz, and I would hold this man personally responsible for ensuring that it reached Mr. Schultz intact and with all due—" and she waves her hand in the air.

"All do what?"

"I forget the word I used," she says, "but he was very impressed with the gravity of the situation. So I think we've got at least a fifty-fifty chance."

He's not the only one impressed. Success or not, it seems like such a Heavenly thing to do. She pulls me out from behind the car, and we come face-to-face with this twelve-year-old boy wearing a Nirvana T-shirt and a black motorcycle jacket.

"Cool jacket," I say to him. "You're like the Fonz in that thing."

"Who's that?" the kid says. I don't even bother putting my thumbs up and saying "Aayyy" to try to jog his memory because he *has* no memory of this. And suddenly I feel like the oldest man in the world.

Right then this cop car pulls up behind our rental car and two cops get out.

"Shit," I say. "That fucking maid really *did* call the cops."

"What's this?" Heaven says.

"We need to just blend," I say. "*Blend.* Act natural." But the cops walk over to our car and start shining their flashlights into it. "Fuck . . . they know it's me. I better just go over there."

I walk over to the car, and Heaven follows.

"Excuse me, Officer, I think it's me you're looking for," I say. "I didn't mean any harm, I just wanted to talk to Mr.—"

"That's her! Freeze! Get down on the ground," they say and draw their guns. "Facedown." And I do. *Fuck.* Schultz must be in really good with this town. But why "her"? How did Heaven get implicated in this thing?

"Both of you!" they say, looking at Heaven. She complies. I feel awful that Heaven is being dragged into this.

"Look, Officer, she had nothing to do with it," I say.

They handcuff us while we're on the ground, and then they walk us over to the cop car and push us up against it with our backs to them.

"Spread your legs," they bark at us. "Are you carrying any weapons?"

"No," we both say. And they start patting us down. Right then about seven other police cars come speeding over to us, lights flashing. One of the cops reaches into Heaven's pockets and pulls out the keys.

"Is that *your* white Ford Focus?" he asks.

"Yes . . . I mean, no . . . it's a rental," I say.

They open the trunk and pull out this big duffel bag.

"What's that?" I ask Heaven.

"I don't know," she says.

One of the cops opens the bag and then looks at the other cops with a look I don't quite recognize. Then he pulls out this gigantic shotgun.

"Oh my God!" Heaven and I say at the same time.

"You have the right to remain silent . . ." he says. As he goes on with the reading of our rights he's being drowned out by the people at the vigil, who are all of a sudden booing and hissing at us.

Many more cops have arrived, and we're being walked through the crowd at Kurt Cobain's vigil, handcuffed, with a cop carrying a shotgun, which he just found in our trunk. They hate us. Somebody actually *spits* at me and then a couple other people follow suit.

"Kurt died for your sins!" some girl screams. And all of a sudden *we've* become the common enemy that everybody has banded against.

"She stole my shirt!" the stoner kid says. And that one has a *special* sting to it, because while accidental . . . that part is true. Strummer starts barking like crazy, and he won't stop.

"How did that get in our trunk?" I ask Heaven.

"I don't know! They're *spitting* on me!" she wails.

"Heaven! Think about it! A shotgun? At Kurt Cobain's vigil? You *do* know that's how he committed suicide, right?"

"Of *course* I know that."

"Well, *I'm* about ready to spit on you, too."

"It's not my fault!" she yells.

"When was the last time anything *was* your fault? Never? Okay, just checking," I say. Then I add, "You are the embarrassment capital of the world, you know that?"

We get to the cop's car. He opens the door and covers our heads as he guides us in, so we don't hit them on the roof of the car. They take Strummer and put him in a separate car. No cuffs.

I'm staring at Heaven, but she won't look at me. She can feel my eyes burning into her, but she won't look back. She's like Strummer when he's misbehaved—he can hear the tone in my voice, but he pretends he can't hear me and won't look at me. "The car is also being impounded," the cop says.

"Of course it is," I say and turn to face the menace on my right. "Okay . . . Heaven?" I say, and she just sits there refusing to look at me. "I am officially raising your national terror alert from *orange* to *red*."

I'm sitting in a cell at the King County Jail in downtown Seattle. Heaven and I just totally disrupted Kurt Cobain's vigil, and we've been arrested for unlawful possession of a firearm and accessory to bank robbery. How this happened, I do not know.

We've just been fingerprinted, and I'm in a holding cell. Heaven is in the cell next to me, and she's taken to singing old chain-gang songs. I roll my eyes at her.

"I'm sorry!" she says through the bars. Then she gets this look, like she's just seen a ghost. "Hey!" she says to some guy in a Cubs cap and cuffs that the cops are walking past us. *"It's the cat piss guy!"* she whispers to me. Not a ghost, apparently. The cat piss guy. Whatever that means.

Then I hear footsteps coming toward us. I turn, and I'm shocked to see that little wank from Schultz's office and a short, heavy Hispanic lady in a housekeeper getup . . . peering into our cell.

"Yes, Officer," David says. "That's him."

"Sí," the Hispanic lady says. "Bad man!"

"You have *got* to be kidding me. Is using the restroom in an office building a crime?"

"No, but trespassing is," the cop says. "You've sure been around today, Mr. Gilbert."

"Somebody pinch me," I say. "Smack me . . . do something. Wake me up from this nightmare." Then I look at the guy who I'm sharing my cell with, and he's suddenly perked up. I definitely need to correct myself. "I don't *really* want to be smacked."

"Who was that?" Heaven says.

"The receptionist," I say.

"Get out of here, you little maggot!" Heaven yells at him. "You'll be sorry when you realize who you messed with!"

"You're not helping," I say to her.

"Sorry," she says and presses her face between the bars so she can better see the "cat piss guy."

"What are *you* doing here?" she asks him. *"Oh my God . . . you!"* she says as if she suddenly realized something. She extends her entire arm through the bars to point her finger accusingly at him. "*You* put that gun in my trunk. And you're the reason all of those cop cars were coming—"

"Say what?" I ask her.

"It's *his* gun."

"Who *is* he?"

"He's the nice guy that helped me put some stuff in the trunk. Turns out . . . not so nice."

The guy doesn't even look at Heaven. He just stares down at his shoes.

It takes the cops twelve hours to confirm our story and do the paperwork, but they finally let us go. Turns out the guy that Heaven charmed into helping with her groceries robbed the Bank of America next to the convenience store about ten minutes prior and decided to ditch his gun in our trunk. All of which was caught on the surveillance camera. They let me slide on the trespassing charges because one of the cops actually went to high school with the David Spade clone (whose name is actually David—you just can't make this stuff up), and he promises he'll "talk the dweeb down out of his tree." The cop refers to David as a "band fag," and informs me that David once passed out onstage while playing his bassoon at a recital. When I was losing my virginity David was praying to a shrine of Captain Kirk. This almost explains his loathsome existence. Almost. But geekism aside, I still want to crush the guy. Or at the very least give him a wedgie.

They take us to Strummer, who is hanging out in a detective's office with a black Lab. He's apparently been having a grand old time, having a play date with this cop's dog, and he's not ready to leave yet.

We drag him outside and stand on Fifth Avenue, where once it's all officially said and done, we look at each other as if to say, "What the fuck was *that*?"

When we get our car out of the impound both of us are starving, so Heaven busts out the couple months' worth of Pringles she bought. But she won't let me have any unless I agree to race her and eat a whole can. This is what I have to deal with. After suffering in *jail* because of this woman. I can't even have a single Pringle.

"Haven't you done enough for one day?" I ask. "Must I condemn myself to a potato fist that will lodge itself in my solar plexus for a week?"

"Maybe your colon, not your solar plexus," she says. "C'mon. It'll be fun."

"Having food races is not fun. I like to actually chew my food."

"'Once you pop . . . you can't stop,'" she sings. This is the Pringles jingle.

"Yeah, but I'm not looking to pop . . . an artery."

"Lame."

"Pringles aren't meant to be shoveled into your mouth twelve at a time," I say, trying to sway her. "They're special. They're meant to be savored, one chip at a time. The ultra-thin texture . . . the crunch. And then the melt-in-your-mouth sensation . . . not too greasy . . . not too salty . . ." Finally I've worked myself up into such a Pringles frenzy that I can't take it anymore. "Give me that," I say as I grab a tube, pop the top, and dig in. Fuck it. "I'm done playing nice with you," I say, mouth full of chips. "I just suffered in *jail* because of you. I think I deserve a chip."

"Hey, you had your own woes in there, mister."

"Did I?"

"Does trespassing and stalking ring a bell?" she says.

"But they wouldn't have sent the entire Seattle police force looking for me. I got dragged into *your* mess."

"Potato . . . po-tah-to," she says. "And by the way, you should *thank* me. At least now, because of me, Schultz will know who you *are*." And she reaches into the tube, takes about seventeen Pringles, and shoves them all into her mouth.

"I'll bet you're gonna be awfully thirsty in about thirty seconds."

"And?" she says, mouth full of chips.

"And . . . you shouldn't speak with your mouth full." Which, naturally, makes her open wide to show me her chewed-up chips. When did I become her *brother*? "And . . . before you started acting like a bratty eight-year-old, I was going to offer you a beverage."

"I really am thirsty," she says.

"Well, it just so happens that I have a certain cola you might enjoy." I pull out the Tab that I've had in my bag since we were in L.A. and hand it to her.

"Oh my God! Where'd you *get* this?" she squeals.

"I traded my cellmate for it. I'll have you know, that cost me three packs of smokes and a hand job."

"Shut up, where'd you get it?"

"I got it in L.A.—I meant to give it to you before, but it just kept slipping my mind. Between Schultz's security throwing me out and doing hard time—"

"Thank you," she says and yanks the pull tab off the soda can. She takes a big sip and *aaah*s. Then she takes the pull tab and puts it on her ring finger like a wedding band. She holds her hand out and looks at it. "Someday," she says wistfully.

"Wow, a soda pop pull-tab ring. You're easy. Most girls want their ring from Tiffany's."

"Well, I'm not most girls." She's telling *me*?

Our flight home is at seven tonight, and at this point I've done all I can do for Cinnamilk, so we have one last day to enjoy all that is Seattle. If we actually make it out of here in one piece, I'll be amazed.

We take a disco nap so we're not totally useless, and then Heaven wants to go to the Experience Music Project, which is Seattle's newest tourist attraction. It's a participatory museum of music, designed by Frank Gehry. I actually wanted to check it out, too, so we head over there. And I'm kind of amazed. Frank Gehry is someone that I really admire. Usually his architecture is so unique and fluid and graceful, but this thing is a fucking *eyesore*. It looks like he just threw up a bunch of steel and sheet metal.

We go inside and check out these electronic kiosks that are basically VH1's *Behind the Music,* minus the commercials.

Jimi Hendrix collectibles were sort of the beginning of this place. Supposedly it started with the guitar Hendrix played at Woodstock and his famous black-felt bolero hat. Now they have guitars belonging to Bo Diddley, Bob Dylan, and of course Nirvana.

They have technology that lets people who have no idea how to play music suddenly jam with their heroes. Heaven rushes off to the Onstage space, a light- and smoke-filled room, which allows people to experience what it's like to play live before an audience of thousands of screaming fans.

She sings an over-the-top rendition of "Wild Thing" to the simulated crowd—apparently fans from a Yes concert in Los Angeles back in the day—and when she finishes, she stands there bowing repeatedly. Just when I think she's done, she takes another bow. I have to physically remove her from the stage.

"Do you mind?" she says.

"Do *you*?" I say back.

"I was having a moment," she says.

"Indeed you were. But then again, when aren't you?" She makes a face at me, and we walk through the rest of the museum. They have a coffee shop in there called The Turntable, and there's a gift shop where they sell CDs and other music-related items. They have what they've deemed the one hundred most essential CDs in rock and roll, and there's some stuff in there that I didn't even know they *had* on CD. This is actually my favorite part of the whole museum.

We leave the joint feeling satisfied that we—at least—did *something* you're supposed to do when in Seattle. And Heaven wants me to see Pike's Market, which she saw a bit of yesterday.

We head over there and find a bar called Powell's upstairs at the market. It's this awesome, smoky, old-man bar with an amazing view. The type of place where people drink in the day-time and everyone's on a first-name basis.

Heaven and I decide to get smashed before our flight home,

but no matter how drunk I get, I will not forget that we made a pact when we landed here. She is taking the window seat on the way back.

"What are you going to do when we get back?" I ask her. And it makes me ask myself the same question. What the hell am I going to do about the ten grand I promised the band? I felt bad enough about lying to them about it . . . but now I feel even worse because when I get back . . . I've actually got to come up with the money.

"What do you mean?" she asks.

"Well . . . not to bring up a sore subject, but you kinda lost your job recently."

"Yeah, I know," she says, obviously overjoyed that I've reminded her. "I can tell you what I'm *not* going to do."

"What's that?"

"Get another job waiting tables."

"Good. You shouldn't," I say. "*Somebody's* gotta need a great PR mind."

She looks at me, and it becomes a stare. I'm tempted to shake it off, to ask whether I have something on my face.

"Yeah . . . I know a certain band that's going to need a big push in a couple months," she says. "And they'll need a boutique firm, not one of those ones with the same old tricks. Somebody who thinks outside the box. Somebody who's newer. Gonna work harder."

"Hmm . . ." I say as I think about this. For maybe the first time in as long as I've known her, I see Heaven without irony. Straight up.

"I'm serious," she says. "What have you got to lose?"

"You definitely have a big *mouth.*"

"If I did Superhero's PR, then you'd be working with me. Could you deal with me on a regular basis?"

"Like you're *going* anywhere?" I say with a smile. "It doesn't seem like I have a choice in the matter. I may as well put you to good use at least."

"What would I call my firm?"

"Good question," I say, pondering.

"Dead at 27 PR?"

"Not the most uplifting . . ."

"Cool firms have cool names . . ." she says. "Nasty Little Man . . . Girly Action . . . Big Hassle . . ."

"Okay . . . it can be a working title."

"I *like* it," she says confidently.

"Fine," I say, knowing full well that this will be the name of her company. And I raise my glass. "To you, and Dead at 27 . . . may you have more success than you ever dreamed of . . . and may you make Superhero famous as fuck and make both of us very, very rich!"

"Hear! Hear!" she says, and we clink.

We get to the airport and check Strummer in. It's always hard to say good-bye to that little dude, but I know we'll see him on the other end of the flight.

Heaven

When we land back in New York, reality quickly sets in. The good thing is, the weather is nice, but I don't want to go back to my apartment. What with the mold and everything. I'd forgotten about the mold. Brady and I retrieve Strummer, and Brady takes off with him for a run around the airport. Two little boys, wreaking havoc in JFK. I find them, both panting, at the baggage claim. My bag comes out first, and Brady's takes six weeks. When we finally get it all together, we grab a taxi and head back to our humble abode.

Our apartment building is the same as when we left it, only our relationship isn't. I mean, nothing happened, but it's been five nights sleeping in the same room with Brady, so it's gonna be weird to split up. When we get upstairs we each walk to our separate doors and look at each other. I know he's thinking the same thing.

• • •

Brady

Finally, some peace. It will be nice to not be responsible for Hurricane Heaven. God, my front door looks good. Brady needs some peace. Brady needs some alone time. Brady knows he needs alone time when he is talking about himself in third person. And I'm not talking hand-lotion-and-a-towel alone time—I just need to decompress. Plus, she still has that Victoria's Secret catalog, anyway.

• • •

Heaven

I put my key in the lock and turn.

"Well," I say, "guess you'll be glad to have your place to yourself."

"Yeah," he says. "Not that you haven't been good company . . . but it will be good to have some personal space."

"Yeah," I say. "Well . . . good night. See ya around."

"I'm sure you will," he says. "Good night." And we both walk into our separate spaces.

I stand in my apartment and look around. Everything looks the same. I walk over to my bed and lie down. Brady was right. It's good to have private time . . . personal space. I take all of my clothes off and run a bath. And as I immerse myself in my tub of banana coconut bubbles, Strummer walks over and rests his chin on the side of the tub. I pat his head and think to myself, This ain't too bad at all.

• ● •

Brady

This sucks. How is it *possible* that I finally have Heaven out of my hair, and all I'm doing is wondering what she's doing? This can't be normal. I must just be overtired.

I wonder what Strummer is thinking. I'll bet *he* misses me. Crazy mongrel with his love that goes on and on.

I need ten thousand dollars.

Wait a second. *On and on* . . . like the love that the compilation keeps bringing to Phil and me and Sleestak records. That's *it*. Or anyway, it's worth a shot. I'll call Phil right now, and we'll go all in. We'll stake the revenue stream from the compilation as collateral for a loan and bet our whole future on an unknown Superhero.

• ● •

Heaven

Breakfast is my favorite meal of the day. So much so, that this morning when I get up I decide that I will eat breakfast for breakfast, lunch, and dinner. I even make a small bowl of oatmeal for Strummer because his nose is twitching while I'm eating mine, and I take that to mean he wants some too. Oatmeal and dogs are not a very good fit. His face ends up covered in dried oatmeal. But he's happy. And isn't that what it's all about?

I'm listening to the Superhero demo that Brady gave me, thinking about marketing ideas for them, when my phone rings.

"Hello?"

"Heaven," an unmistakable Albanian voice says. "I am on break. I must talk with you. If you have time right now?"

"Marco?"

"Who else do you know who sounds like this?" Marco says.

"What's going on, kiddo?"

"Can I speak with you? In person?"

"Sure," I say, and I agree to meet him at the little park across the street from Temple.

When I get to the park I spot Marco pacing, and I notice that he's wearing a blazer, which is very uncharacteristic. He looks almost dressed up.

"Hi, sunshine!" I say and give him a big hug. "How's the restaurant?"

"How do you think? It is awful. Same as always," he says. He lights a cigarette and takes a deep drag. "I have received bad news."

"What is it?"

"My visa is expiring in four days."

"Oh no!" I say, truly alarmed.

"I don't know why I don't have received this paper before now. If the idiots think I can resolve this in four days, I don't know how."

"Will you have to go back to Albania?"

"Eventually, yes," he says.

"In the next four days?"

"No, of course not in the next four days. I can't. And Jean Paul made me a fake social security number when I started, and now when I called for my visa they have two social security numbers—and I have no proof of working, and I can't work in the restaurant without my visa. It is some mess. Why Jean Paul gave me fake social security number I don't know."

"Well, why *would* he?"

Marco sighs. "Because when I was hired I didn't have one yet, and he just said that he made it up to be finished with paperwork."

"How thoughtful of him."

"Yes," Marco says. He lights another cigarette with the one that he's just about totaled.

"I'm so sorry, sweetie," I say. "Is there anything that I can do?" It's in that second that I really regret asking, because Marco gets down on both knees. I think he's about to propose to me, but he *can't* really be about to propose to me, can he? He is. This is awful.

"I am not sure of what is to be proper. Am I to be on both knees or one knee?" he says, and I want to cry. I adore this little dude, and I would really do whatever I could to help him out . . . but there is no *way* I am going to marry him.

"It's one knee, but get up, Marco." He picks up one leg and is now on one knee, looking at me with his one good eye.

"Heaven, I know that this is not very romantic because it seems like it is only because I need citizenship. And it is. But also, I have always thought you were the most beautiful girl in the world."

"Marco, stop . . . really—"

"It is true," he says, and he presses my hand.

"I can't marry you, Marco, so please don't ask me to marry you. I can't. I hate to say no, but I can't."

"When you were sad because you broke up with your boyfriend . . . when you first began to work with us . . . and you cried, and I told you that there were hundreds of mans that would love to be with you—I wanted to tell you that I would be your new boyfriend—"

"Marco, listen . . ." I say, but then he reaches into the pocket of his blazer and pulls out a box. The box is a little bigger than a ring box, but what else can it be? He got a ring? Oh, this is getting worse by the second.

"I can't afford the ring that girls want, but I have this to give you," he says. He opens the box and holds it out to me with the most heartbreakingly earnest expression on his face. And I look in the box.

It's a belt buckle. It's a belt buckle with a rooster on it. It's the most ridiculous thing I have ever seen.

"It's a *rooster,*" I say.

"Yes, do you like it?"

"I . . . I love it! I think it's very beautiful . . . but I can't—"

"Heaven . . ." he says with a long pause that I'm sure seems entirely appropriate to him. "Will you please marry me?"

To say I am stunned by the question would be like saying Michael Jackson's face has been affected by plastic surgery. No one has ever asked me the question before, but much more unsettling is my realization that it was the one question I needed to hear to dispel my looming dead-by-twenty-seven curse. Instantly, a life with Marco flashes before my eyes: rides in tiny carriages drawn by goats, a diet consisting of potatoes and coarse grain alcohol (made from potatoes), a wardrobe consisting of broad flowered skirts topped off by an apron, smashing plates, milking cows, squeezing out little Marcos with overgrown bowl haircuts and little glass eyes that constantly need polishing.

I snap out of my day-mare to see him standing there looking sweet and hopeful, despite the aroma of stale cigarette smoke hanging about him. "No, Marco. I can't. I'm sorry." I hate this. I hate it. This is so unfair. I hate immigration, I hate Jean Paul, and I hate myself.

"I will love you forever, you know," he says. "Not just until I make citizen." I believe him. I'll bet he *would*. And given the fact that I still need to get married soon, this is almost like some sort of test. I don't know what I'm being tested for, because of course I'd never marry Marco, but it still feels like something. And I hope I passed. If I did, then why do I feel so shitty?

"I know," I say to Marco. "Please stand up." I reach my hands out to help him up.

"It is okay. I didn't think you really would, but I had to try."

"I'm sorry. Here . . ." I say as I hand him the box with the rooster belt buckle. "You should keep this."

"No, I want you to have it," he says. "I insist."

"Pardon my ignorance," I say, "but is there a special significance of the rooster in Albania?"

"No," he says.

"Oh. Okay then. Well, it's really . . . really . . . special."

"I am glad you like it. I hope you will wear it often and think of me."

"I will," I say. And now that I've said it, it means I have to wear it because I don't lie. I mean . . . I *lie* . . . but not when it matters. I never lie when it matters, and I never make a promise that I don't keep.

I give Marco a big hug, and I start walking back toward my apartment—with my new rooster belt buckle.

"Tell me *everything*," Sydney says as we settle into our uncomfortable wooden chairs at Starbucks.

"I wouldn't know where to begin," I say.

"Did you hook up with him?"

"Brady?" I say. "*No*."

"Hmm."

"Hmm what?" I say, smelling a notion baking in that oven.

"I just thought for sure you would have," she says. "*I* would have."

"Well, you're a little less discriminating than I am."

"True," she says. And then I lose her to a cute guy that walks in and orders an Americano. "I'm sorry," she says without breaking her gaze. "I'll be back with you in a moment." And she continues to fixate on Mr. Triple Shot until he walks out. "He was gay. Didn't even look over here once."

I cough. Then I let it drop. "In *other* news I got proposed to today . . ." Sydney abruptly stops drinking her coffee and stares at me with fish eyes. "Remember Marco?" I continue. "Did you ever meet him? The Albanian busboy?"

"The one with one eye?" she says. "Gross!"

"Be nice. He's in trouble with immigration. I felt awful saying no. Really awful."

"Well, of *course* you said no."

"But I didn't have anything to offer," I say. "Like, 'No, I won't marry you, but here's a free pass to stay in America.'"

"Ooh! While you're handing out good stuff . . . can I get a key to Gramercy Park?"

"Sure," I say.

"Too bad he's not loaded. I'd do it for the money," Sydney says as she sips her coffee. And then it hits me. Marco showed me pictures of his parents' home in Albania. They *do* have money. She wants new boobs, and he wants to be a citizen. Seems like a fair trade to me.

"Actually I think his family *does* have money . . ."

"What kind of money?"

"The boob-buying kind?" I offer.

This seems to touch her in a special place. She ponders. "Would I have to have sex with him?"

"That's your business," I say, laughing. "I'm a matchmaker, not a pimp." I was only half serious when I brought this up and I *think* Syd was only half serious when she asked about the money. And oddly, that seems to add up to one whole serious proposition. Then my cell phone rings, and I don't recognize the number on my caller ID.

"It's 213," I say to Syd, and then I answer. "Hello?"

"Hey, sexy . . . miss me?"

"Yeah . . . desperately," I say even though I have no idea who it is.

"It's Darren," he says. "I've been thinking about you."

"Hey, Darren," I say, and Sydney's eyes pop out of her head.

"Oh yeah . . . you need to fill me in on *that* one," she says, and I shush her.

"I'm in New York," he says. "I wanna see you."

"You're here? Wow. Okay . . . what's your schedule?"

"I'm free . . . right now."

"Well, I'm with Sydney right now."

"Tell her she's a ditz. Ask her if she's had a substantive thought since last time I saw her."

"Okay, I'll tell her you said that."

"How 'bout tomorrow night?" he says. "Aqua Grill? Like old times?"

"Sure . . ." I say slowly. "Sounds good."

"Great. I'll grab you around seven?"

"Uh . . . fine," I say. I give him my address and we hang up. "He said he misses you," I tell Syd.

"You're seeing him?" she asks.

"I guess so. He caught me off guard."

"Tonight?"

"Tomorrow."

"Oh boy . . ." she says.

• • •

Brady

I wake up to a pounding on my door that can only be Heaven. So you can imagine my surprise when I open my door and find Phil standing there.

"Hug me," he says, thrusting himself into my arms. So I throw my arms around the fucker and hug him back.

"What's up, man?" I ask as I try to break away from our embrace.

"We just need a hug."

"We do?"

"I love you, man," he says. I start looking around and wondering what he wants, because this is frighteningly reminiscent of a beer commercial.

"Okay, bro. I love you, too. It's cool," I say as I pry myself out of his clutches.

"Is it?" he asks. And now I realize that this is about Sarah. He genuinely feels bad, and I'm touched. It still sucks, but at least now I know that he really feels bad about it.

"Yeah, man. It's cool. If you're happy, that's all I care about. But be warned . . . she *is* the Antichrist."

"She just needs love, man."

"Is that what she needs? Funny . . . I thought she needed a lobotomy and a one-way ticket back to hell." And Jesus Christ, is she pregnant with my baby?

Phil eyes me cautiously. "I went to the bank," he says, "and I met with—"

"Wait—you actually did something I asked you to do?"

"Absolutely," he says. "I've got the forms, and I had a good chat with my main man Lawrence at the Prince Street branch." Phil detects his opening. We're back on solid ground. "I'm psyched to get to know the band better, too."

"You'll hit it off," I say. "They're awesome."

The good thing about Phil and me is that there's never a power struggle. I know he'll do what's best for us, and he knows I will, too. We both have *ears,* and when it comes down to mastering and picking the single, we'll probably lean toward the same shit anyway. Having *ears* means having the ability to pick hits. A lot of people can have good taste or are able to listen to something on the radio and respond to it. But few people can pick out what will work as a first single or as the all-important follow-up. You can really make or break a band by picking the right or wrong single, or by introducing the band the wrong way.

Take a band like Jellyfish. I picked them out to be rising stars first time I heard them. Easily one of the greatest bands ever, and one of the least appreciated. You can say they were too ahead of their time, and they were. Years before their time. Bands like Radiohead and Beck also pushed the musical envelope at the same time, and went on to have great careers. And sure, Jon Brion from Jellyfish went on to become a brilliant producer, and Eric Dover sang for Slash's Snakepit (not that *that's* the biggest crowning achievement), but they could have been *huge.* Same with Fishbone. Had they been marketed by the Chili Peppers's team, things could have been a hell of a lot different. And even in pop music today . . . I have a friend who works with the bubble-gum pop stars. He swears that Nick Lachey is an amazing singer. I've heard the tracks and the kid *can* actually sing. But he picked the wrong single and got overshadowed by Jessica Simpson's boobs.

Happens all the time. Brilliance gets overlooked or marketed wrong, and one-hit wonders become megastars. You not only need to be able to recognize talent, but you have to know how to pick the hits. Phil and I *both* have had this ability since we were kids, so as soon as we get this band off the ground, I'm pretty sure the sky's the limit. And I hope the sky's the *credit* limit. Because otherwise . . . we're sunk.

* * *

I bump into Heaven when I'm heading out the next day. She's got a Starbucks cup in her hand.

"Is that to mock me?" I ask.

"Oh, am I supposed to stop drinking coffee now because of all this?"

"No . . . but the *least* you could have done is brought me some."

"Sorry," she says. She unlocks her door, and Strummer runs out into the hall and over to me. I pet him on his head, and he nestles his body against my knees.

"God, I've missed this little guy."

"Yeah, he's good company," she says.

"Maybe we can all hang out tonight?"

"Oh . . . that would be fun . . ." I can tell there's a *but* coming. "But I already have plans tonight."

"Oh . . . okay. That's cool," I say. "We'll do it another time."

"Definitely," she says. "Oh, I spoke to my friend Bart, and I told him I'm starting my own PR firm. And I told him about the band, and he said he'd do their Web site for us."

"Really? That's awesome!"

"Yeah, he's really cool, and he knows his shit. He's even designing my logo for me."

"Very cool," I say. "I can't wait to see it."

"Yeah, me too!" she says. "I just downloaded the forms to start my LLC. Anyway . . . I'm gonna take Strummer for a walk over to Staples to pick up some expanding file folders."

"Wow. Look at corporate you."

"Hey—I'm no slacker. You just met me at an off time. Believe me . . . you just got the best PR firm you could ever have hoped for."

"I have no doubt about that," I say.

"You know, you were *so* right. I've been going over it in my head—all the contacts I already have. This thing is really gonna work."

Heaven puts Strummer's leash on, and I watch them get onto the elevator.

What plans?

* * *

Not too long ago this girl was Satan. Now I can't get her out of my head. I'm so used to being around her that I find myself walking outside about ten minutes later (coincidentally close to Staples), and I bump into Heaven.

"Hey," she says.

"Hey back."

"What are you doing here?"

"Just enjoying the day. Taking a walk. Wanna get some ice cream? I saw that they have Oreo Cookie at Tasti D-Lite." I know this will get her.

"They do? Shit, yes, I want ice cream!" And we head over to Tasti D, which is just around the corner. They have this retarded plastic rim that they put around the cone, and it pisses me off. It's another reminder that I really need to talk to someone about my Catch-It Cone. It's hard when you have so many inventions swimming around your brain.

"See this thing?" I say to Heaven.

"Yeah?"

"I invented it," I tell her.

"You don't say."

"Well, not this, but my own variation of it. Move over here," I say because I don't want anyone to hear me. "It's called the Catch-It Cone."

"Okay?"

"When I invented it they didn't even have these plastic thingies. But mine is the whole cone!"

"I don't follow . . ." she says.

"Okay, my cone, the Catch-It Cone, has *this* plastic rim thing *built into the cone.* And not plastic. In cone . . . wafer . . . whatever the hell they make it out of. So, yes, it does the same job as this thing . . . but mine is edible! More cone. More sugary goodness. No ice cream drips on your brand-new summer tank top. It's a beautiful thing."

"Where do you come up with this stuff?" she asks.

"I have no idea. Or maybe I have *every* idea . . . I don't

know. But then again, none of them ever seem to go any-where—"

"Have you ever talked to anyone about it?"

"No, I was focusing on Cinnamilk. And we saw how well *that* worked out for me."

"Hey," she says. "Don't be negative. You don't know what will come of it."

"I think I do. A whole lotta nothing."

"Well, there are other investors," she says. "Plus, there's your MP3 Flush, and this cone thing. One of them is bound to hit."

"Speaking of hits . . . did they have the folders?"

"Yeah, right here." She holds up the Staples bag and looks down at her arm. "What's that?"

"What's what?"

"That," she says, pointing to something on her arm that I don't see.

"What am I supposed to be looking at?"

"That red spot!" she says with alarm.

"That's a freckle!"

"It wasn't there *before* . . ." she says as she inspects her entire arm.

"It's cute."

"It's not cute."

"Then it's mine," I say. "If you don't like it, it's mine. I'll call it Brady."

"My freckle?"

"Yes."

"You're naming my freckle after yourself?" she says. "And you think *I* have issues?"

"It's like a star. People buy stars in the constellation and name them after people all the time. As gifts."

"So then are you *buying* my freckle? Because I don't know if you can afford my freckle. My freckles don't come cheap, you know."

"I've already claimed it," I declare. "It's not up for discussion anymore. Just eat your ice cream. And don't spill any on Brady."

"Well, I *could* guarantee that I wouldn't if I had a Catch-It Cone . . . but some lazy slob is too busy putzing around to bother *inventing* it."

I'm taking my trash out at 7:29 when I see *Darren Fucking Rosenthal* walking around our hallway looking at the different apartment doors like a simian. At first I'm thinking he's come to congratulate me on beating him out for the band, but the door he stops at . . . is Heaven's.

"Darren?" I say as I push my ice cream back down my throat. *This* is who she had plans with?

"Hey, man!" he says. Man? I'm not his man—or his boy or his bro.

"What are you doing here?" I ask.

"Coming to fetch my girl," he says. My head is instantly on fire, and I want to knock his teeth out. Don't say "my girl." She is not *your* girl. She is not your anything. She may have *once* been your girl. But that time has come and gone.

"Your girl?" I say, still playing stupid.

"What are *you* doing here?" he asks, ignoring me. "Oh, right . . . you're neighbors." And suddenly I'm reduced to a neighbor. We are *more* than neighbors. Way more. Aren't we?

"Yeah, we're neighbors," I say. "Seriously . . . *why are you here*?"

"I just told you. I'm taking Heaven out."

"Why?" I say, suddenly sounding like a bitchy teenage girl whose parents have just told her that she can't spend the night at Becky's.

"Because I want to," he says. "Because she used to be my girlfriend. And who knows . . . she might be again—"

"I don't think that's a very good idea. I mean, there must have been a reason you guys broke up, right? Why move backwards in life? Never move backwards. You gotta move forward."

"I miss her," he says.

Fucker. "Well, you didn't miss her for the past few years. You were *fine* until you saw her in L.A."

"Okay . . . I see what's up. I get it."

"You do?" I say.

"Yeah, man, it's cool," he says. "I mean . . . she's awesome. How can you *not* dig her?" And for a minute I start to feel better. Until he says, "But seriously, dude . . . you didn't think you'd get the girl either, did you?"

Huh?

"I just don't think it's a good idea . . . you and her," I say.

"Well, I *do*."

"Give me *one* good reason."

"Fine," he says. And he thinks to himself and smiles. "Okay . . . here's one. Heaven and I used to practically live together. I mean . . . we were together all the time. And I went home for Christmas vacation, you know—to see the folks."

"Isn't Rosenthal *Jewish*?"

"Yeah," he says. "So? Whatever, winter break—"

"Fine. Go on."

"So I'm gone for like two weeks . . . and the day I get back, I leave the airport and head straight to Heaven's place—where she's waiting for me."

"Uh-huh . . ."

"So I ring her bell . . ." he says, raising his hands in front of him like he's ringing her bell, "and she answers the door, naked. Completely butt naked . . . but with one red rose stuck in between her ass cheeks. I mean . . . how do you *not* love a girl who does that?"

And just then Heaven opens her door, looking *of course* like a twelve on a scale of one to ten.

"I thought I heard voices," she says. "Hey," she says to Darren. "You two know each other, right?"

I walk back into my apartment, and the blinking light on my answering machine is taunting me, giving me its little red evil eye. I resign myself to hearing another humiliating Sarah screed.

I press the Play button.

"Hi, this is Brady Gilbert. I missed your call, but *you* missed a scintillating moment with me. If you'd like to try to recapture that moment . . . leave a message, and I'll call you back." Beep.

"Brady . . . this is Sam . . . from Superhero. Sam. Hey . . . we wanted to let you know that we're really sorry and everything, but we're going to go with Darren Rosenthal. It's not anything with you guys or the contracts, but Darren's thing is just probably better for us now. At this point. And . . . so, anyway . . . sorry. And . . . I guess we'll see you around."

• ● •

"If somebody doesn't believe in me, I can't believe in them."

—Andie, *Pretty in Pink*

"She's gone. She gave me a pen. I gave her my heart . . . she gave me a pen."

—Lloyd, *Say Anything*

Heaven

Darren and I are seated at a table in the back of Aqua Grill. A couple minutes after we're seated, this big party gets put next to us at the prime table, which was no doubt reserved for them. Sean Puffy Combs, or P. Diddy, or Ditty—or whatever we're supposed to call him this week—is in the group. So is Russell Simmons, who goes by Russell Simmons. I don't recognize the other people, but they make a hell of a scene when they walk in. Russell gets seated closest to me.

"How's it goin'?" Russell says to us.

"Good, thanks," we both say.

"Do you know those guys?" I ask Darren, thinking he might since he's in the same business.

"No," he says. "I've seen him out at functions, but I don't really know him."

"Guess he's just really friendly," I say.

We order some appetizers from the raw bar, and they bring us the complimentary salmon tartare on those waffle potato chips that I always end up dreaming about after I've been here. Yes, they're *that* good.

"So this lady dies," Darren says. "And this is a true story—"

"Someone you knew?"

"No," he says. "A friend of a friend. And her family goes to the funeral home and is making arrangements for the woman. The funeral director is asking questions about her, what kind of casket would she like, what kind of flowers did she like, what kind of music did she like?"

"Uh-huh," I say. I'm not sure if I should be eating the tartare or if I'm supposed to hold off because this is a serious story that requires a moratorium on the waffle chips.

"So the daughter picks out a mahogany wood casket, tells

the guy her mother liked white roses, and that she really liked Elvis. So when they come to the wake a day or so later they find their mother, lying in a casket in a white studded Elvis jumpsuit, with muttonchop sideburns glued onto her face and her rigor mortis lips curled into the trademark Elvis snarl."

"No! This has to be a joke."

"No, I'm telling you," he says. "So the daughter pulls a different funeral director aside and asks him where the guy she spoke with is, and wants to know what the hell happened to her mother. The guy she first spoke to isn't there, so this funeral director takes her to the office, and together they look at the work order and they see that the first guy wrote 'Like Elvis' instead of 'Liked Elvis.'"

"That's insane," I laugh.

"It's supposedly true."

"Oh my God."

Darren rips off a piece of bread and dunks it in some olive oil. "So, uh . . . what's up with you and Brandon?"

"Brady?" I ask, knowing full well that Darren probably knows his name, but he's pulling that dick move guys do when they're jealous.

"Yeah, Brady."

"Nothing's up," I say, playing dumb. "Why?"

"You guys more than friends?"

"Nope," I say.

"You just travel together?"

"Yup."

"That's kinda weird, don't you think?"

"We're just friends," I say as a couple of people walk over to the hip-hop table and say hi to Russell. They sort of seem to reintroduce themselves, and Russell is totally cordial. He nods and says "Good to see you," and then as soon as they leave the table he says, "Never seen that motherfucker in my life," and his whole table laughs.

Our appetizers come, and Darren orders a bottle of wine. He knows I get drunk on wine, but I don't object. When the waiter comes back to do the wine service I almost cringe. This is the first time this is being done for me since I got fired, and it brings back all kinds of bad memories. I'm overly friendly to the waiter. I've always been nice to waiters, but now I feel like I'm in the club, so there's a different bond.

Darren holds his glass up, so I raise mine as well.

"To us finding each other again," he says. I give him a look as I think, Well, I've been right here. We clink our glasses and drink.

"So you didn't tell me what you're doing here," I say.

"I'm here a lot. I'm working out of our New York office. I'm thinking about getting a place here again."

"Wow," I say. A *flat* wow.

And then another group of fans, or friends, goes to say hi to the Puffy/Simmons table. This is the third or fourth time people have interrupted them in seven minutes. Must be annoying to be them, I think. But they don't seem to mind. They're having a great time. They're laughing and telling stories, and they're loud. They are *really* loud.

"Do you think I'm losing my hair?" Darren asks.

"No!" I say. When Darren and I were together he used Rogaine regularly, and he wasn't even close to balding. I think he was using it as a preventive thing, but he was always paranoid about his hair, and it looks like he still is. "You have as much hair as you had the last time I saw you."

"The last time in L.A.," he says, "or the last time a few years ago?"

"Both. Relax." I sip my wine.

"So what did Sydney say when you told her that you were having dinner with me?"

"She said what she always says about you."

"Which is?" he asks.

"'He sucks.'"

"Yeah," he says, chomping on a piece of bread, "she never liked me. What does she know?"

"She knows how you treated me."

"I wasn't *that* bad," he says. And then he gives me this innocent look and bats his eyelashes.

Right then someone at Russell's table points to someone sitting at another table. "See that guy over there?" Russell's friend says, and his whole table looks—and so do I. The guy looks like some self-important dude in an Armani suit, which he probably has in every color. He's got his nose stuck in the air, and you can just tell he's a jerk. "Back in the eighties," the guy goes on, "I was in a club chillin' one night . . . and when I went to the bathroom . . . that guy's girlfriend came in after me. I busted a nut in her mouth . . . and then she walked out there right after and kissed that nigga on the *lips*!" The whole table erupts with laughter and high fives.

"Plus, I've grown up since then," Darren continues.

"Oh yeah?" I say, trying to keep a straight face—not because of Darren, but because of what I just overheard. Because that was really fucking funny. Gross . . . but funny.

"Yeah," Darren says. "I'm ready to settle down."

"Really . . ." I put some disbelief in my tone for good measure.

"It's true," he says. "With the right girl. I just think I may have blown it with her a long time ago, and I don't know if she'll give me another shot . . ."

Oh God. If it wasn't obvious before, now it is—he's talking about me. And he's trying to be romantic and sincere, but some guy is in my right ear, still talking about that time he busted a nut in that guy's girlfriend's mouth, and I'm finding it a little hard to focus.

There was a time when I was crazy about Darren, but that was years ago. When we hooked up in L.A., I thought it was just going to be one night of really good sex. I didn't even entertain the idea that we'd ever get back together, so this is all a bit of a surprise. That said, the sex was *really* good. This is so confusing. Then again I don't have anyone *else* in my life, right? Do I? What's to be so confused about? Why do I feel so goddamned *confused*?

When we ask for the bill our waiter tells us that it's already been taken care of.

"By who?" Darren asks, clearly feeling aced out.

"Mr. Simmons, the gentleman at the next table. He knew they were going to be loud, so when he came in he told us he was going to pick up the tab for the tables on either side of him."

Now *that* is one cool dude. We thank him, he shakes our hands, and we walk outside and pour ourselves into a taxi.

Fifteen minutes later, I'm on my couch with Darren. He's kissing me, and clothes are starting to come off. And all I can think about is Brady. *Brady!* What the hell is *this*? This is not supposed to be happening. I try to put him out of my mind but I can't. It's like he's here in the room with us. I push Darren off me and get up.

"What's wrong?" he asks.

"I'm thirsty," I say. And I walk to the kitchen and get some water. I sit on this bar stool just outside the kitchen and slowly drink the whole glass of water.

I don't want to go back to the couch with Darren, so as soon as I finish, I refill my glass and sit back down. Not only do I not want to go back there with Darren, *I don't want to go back there with Darren.* Back to eighteen. Back to nothing mattering but this guy who was going to be a big record producer because of someone his dad knew. Back to relying on anyone or anything else to make me feel like I matter, like I'm going somewhere, like I need anything but my own intelligence and hard work and attitude to make it. Darren is who I *was.* Crazy, half-assed, sometimes brilliant, never-surrender Brady reminds me more of who I want to be.

Darren finally walks over a couple minutes later.

"You all right?"

"Yeah, just . . . thirsty," I say. And out of nervousness, I get up and refill my glass *again.*

"I see that," he says.

"Want some water?"

"Is there any left?" he asks, and I laugh. "What's going on, babe?"

"I don't know."

"I think I do. It's fuckin' Brady, right?" He remembered his name *this* time.

"Kind of."

"I thought you said there's nothing going on," he says.

"There isn't . . . we haven't. But being here with you . . . I feel like I'm *cheating* on him."

"Hmmm . . ." he says.

"I'm sorry," I say.

"It's okay. I was an idiot to let you get away in the first place. But I *did*. So I can't blame anyone but myself if your heart's with someone else now."

"I didn't know it was."

I get up off the bar stool and give Darren a hug. Then he buttons his shirt back up, puts on his shoes, and I walk him to the door.

"No chance at breakup sex, huh?" Darren says with a mock pout. I laugh and shake my head at him. He kisses me on my forehead. "I *have* changed," he says. "And it probably wouldn't have been fair anyway . . . me getting you *and* the band." He turns.

"What?" I say.

"Superhero. They're gonna sign with *me*."

"Since when?" I say, though I'm frozen solid.

"Since this morning. I got the text message when I got off the plane." He buttons his shirt cuffs. "This was shaping up to be a really great day."

"Sorry to ruin your perfect game," I say. And he's out the door. And I'm left standing there feeling . . . I can't even tell what it is. All I know is, I start to cry. I cry for Brady . . . and I cry for me.

I pace around my apartment for a while. I feel like I need to tell Brady that nothing happened, but I don't know if that's even necessary or if he really cares. His mood has to be in the basement right now. No, below the basement. What's below the basement? Mud. And abandoned subway tunnels. And rats.

I knock on his door anyway, but he's not home. I check back a couple more times after that—about thirteen—but he seems to be out for the night. Now I'm wondering where the hell he went. Not that I have a right to wonder. *Do* I have a right to wonder?

• ● •

Brady

To say I am crushed doesn't capture it. To capture it, we would have to invent new words about depression, and hopelessness, and hurt and loss—and then we'd have to ball them all up into one super word. Superhero is gone. And Heaven is out of reach.

Bad enough that she's out with that prick, with his California tan and pearly white teeth, but now I'm saddled with the image of her . . . naked . . . with a fucking red rose between her ass cheeks. And he's—FUCK! I can't even *think* about it. He couldn't come up with a better reason? Who am I kidding? He could probably come up with a million and one reasons. And every one of them would turn my stomach. Because it would be her and *him*. Darren Rosenthal. Winner of the Superhero Sweepstakes.

I call up Zach because I've gotta get my mind off this. He tells me to come down to the bar, and I oblige.

I've been here for six hours, drunk many alcoholic beverages, and sung unspeakable karaoke songs including (but not limited to) Neil Diamond's "September Morn." Thank God, Zach was the only one to witness this display. And I had to promise to pay *him* a hundred bucks not to tell anyone.

The bar is now officially closed, and I think my ass has fallen asleep. I get up off the bar stool and find that my ass is *indeed* asleep, as is the top half of my left thigh. I put my hand on the bar to steady myself, and Zach assumes I've had too much to drink. I *have,* but that's not why I'm walking funny. I'm walking funny because I have pins and needles shooting down my ass.

Nonetheless, Zach tells me to crash at his place since he lives just upstairs. I'm disappointed to find that the pizza place next door is closed at 4 a.m. There's a pizza place on Houston that's open till six in the morning . . . but their pizza sucks, so I just go upstairs to Zach's and eat a half-empty box of stale Wheat Thins.

It's wrong to want to kill someone. This much I know. And yet I want to kill Darren.

"Maybe not kill him," I say out loud. "Just hurt him . . . make his face look like a smashed crab."

"You goin' on about her prick ex-boyfriend again?" Zach says, yawning.

"It's 4:21 a.m. He's gotta be done having mind-blowing, knock-your-dick-into-your-watch-pocket sex with her, and she's probably spooning with him right now. Ugh, it makes me sick. I'll bet he's in front, too, the dick. Anyone would know that Heaven is supposed to be the little spoon, but he's probably making her be the big spoon."

"Dude," Zach says, mashing his face with his hand. "If she's in bed with him it's because she wants to be." Zach staggers off toward his bedroom. He's right. *Everyone* wants to be with Darren. And even Zach doesn't wanna be with me.

"You want the perfect crime?" I call out to him. "Me getting the band *and* the girl."

"Don't be so hard on yourself," Zach says. "You almost pulled it off."

"She doesn't want to be the big spoon. I know that much."

I wake up feeling particularly morbid. Not angry, though, just sad. Sad because as drunk as I was last night, I *heard* what Zach said. And he's dead-on. She's with Darren because she *wants* to be. Which means she *doesn't* want me. Which means I can't want her. I can't waste my time thinking about her when she's thinking about someone else. And even if that guy doesn't understand that she needs to be married in seven months, and I *do,* she's made her choice, and she'll have to live with it.

After four days of watching my own homemade *Gilligan's Island* marathon on Zach's TiVo and eating whatever I could find that wasn't freezer-burned, I've had enough. I decide to quit wallowing in self-pity and join Phil in the office to wallow in mutual pity. I'm hurting and feeling a little lost, but my mind is refreshingly clear for the first time in a long while. It's definitely the end of some things for me, but it's a beginning of something for Superhero, and I owe it to them to lose gracefully. Hell, maybe I owe it to myself even more. I pick up the phone.

"Hey, Sam, it's Brady," I say.

"Uh . . . hey, man," he says awkwardly. "Did you get my message?"

"Yeah, I did. And I hate to lose you guys."

"Listen, it's not—"

"No," I interrupt. "You don't have to explain a thing. You guys are going to be facing a ton of important decisions, sooner than you think. With Darren you've got a great company behind you, but if there's ever anything that bugs you or confuses you, or you just want to talk to somebody who's been there—I'm here."

Sam says nothing for a second. So I go on, "Everyone who starts in this business thinks it'll be different for them, that all the bullshit will go away, just this once, and their ride will be silky smooth. But it's not . . . it's hard. And when you feel like you're goin' nuts . . . call me. I'll be one more person who honestly cares that you guys become the best fucking band you can be."

There's another pause, and I'm half thinking my words are the victims of a lost connection. "Thanks, Brady."

"You're welcome." And then because there's nothing else, we hang up.

As I walk into the office, Phil is standing there like a store manager who's about to celebrate me as the millionth customer.

"Good news," he says.

"That's a first," I say.

"The bank's gonna approve our loan. I just heard from Lawrence. We're getting a twenty-five-thousand-dollar line of credit for Sleestak Records."

I'm astonished. "How did this happen?"

"I made it happen," Phil says proudly. "Your idea got us there. The compilation money proved out, Larry told me. So we don't have it in stone yet, but he says it's a lock."

This time I grab *him* for a hug. "Now all we need is a band to blow it on," I say with a tired laugh.

"I figured it was my turn to step up. We started this company with money from your uncle, which . . . has been dwindling. So this is to help us take a new direction . . . hell, take *any* direction. And to show you that as useless as I am sometimes, I believe in our company and our friendship . . ."

I can't very well hug him again, so I give him a grateful smile and nod my head. "We're gonna do this . . . somehow," I say.

"And when we do," Phil says, "I've got us studio time at Ocean Studios in Burbank." I give him a wondering shrug. "Yeah," he says. "When I heard you got Superhero, I got off my dead ass and made some calls."

"And what did you do when you heard we *lost* Superhero?" I ask him.

Phil ponders for a second. "Started thinking about who you'd find next."

Almost makes me want to cry. My boy is all grown up.

I don't take Heaven's twelve phone calls during the week. I have half a mind to set her number up with a distinctive ring on my cell so I'll know from the first notes of the ring which incoming calls to completely blow off. But for now, it's hear the ring, check the display, and blow off the call.

And it is in this mode that I hear yet *another* ring late in the afternoon, and absentmindedly check the display. But this is different, area code 213.

"Brady," I say.

"Brady?" the voice says.

"Yeah, this is Brady," I say impatiently, in my agitated state of mind.

"Hey . . . it's Sam. Remember me? Sam, from Superhero?"

Just what I need. Probably an early invitation to their first record release party. But I can't be mad at this kid. He just made the right move, that's all. "Hey, Sam. How's it goin'?"

"Well," Sam says. And there's a long silence, like I've lost the call. "Is your offer still on the table?"

On the table? Fuck, yeah, it's on the table. Served up, piping hot, with drinks all around. No ID check. "Absolutely."

"Okay," Sam says. "So . . . uh . . . do you want my dad to overnight the contracts?"

"You're going with Sleestak?" I ask, but the excitement almost chokes the question to death. "What happened? What changed your mind?"

There's another pause. "A couple things," Sam says. "Number one, you. Some things you said about the shitty ride and having someone with silk . . . I don't remember exactly, but we all decided we want to go with someone real."

"What was the second thing?"

"The Stones," Sam says. *Huh?*

"The Stones?"

"Darren called us last night and promised to 'make us the next Stones.'"

Then it comes back to me. *Crooked.* Big-company bullshit. My story about how the label once promised me that we'd be the next Stones.

"We won't make you the next Stones," I tell him. "There's already a Stones. But there's never been a Superhero."

"Yeah, okay, I gotta go," he says distractedly. "We're rehearsing."

"All right. I'll look for those contracts. Take it easy, man," I say. So much for my poetic moment. *But we got the band back.*

I stay at Zach's for the rest of the week. I go commando for the first two days, but I break down when my socks reek so bad that they almost smell like food. (Obviously not a food anyone would want to eat, but not your run-of-the-mill foot stench either. It's kind of an accomplishment, I gotta say.) So when I go and buy my three-pack of socks, I pick up some boxer shorts as well.

I pass a woman pushing a stroller as I walk out of the store, and I get a shooting pain in my left eye. Sarah. The pregnancy. Is it mine? Is it human?

I head over to her place and follow an old woman into the building. When I get to my old front door I'm bitter all over again about losing my rent control, but there are bigger issues at hand. I knock and hold my breath. Sarah opens the door with a glass of red wine in her hand.

"Hi, asshole," she says.

"Nice to see you, too."

"Who said it was nice to see you?" she says.

"Look, something's really been bothering me."

"Wondering if I'm still into you?" she says.

"No. Wondering if my baby is into you. Sarah, I know we had some hard times, but you know I'd always . . . do the right thing . . . whatever it is."

"How about grovel? Would you grovel?"

"If it provided a healthy environment for the child, sure I'd grovel. But . . . is there a child? And if so . . ." There's no easy way to ask this of the last person on earth you'd want to be carrying your baby. "Is it mine?"

Sarah doesn't answer at first. She just looks at me with a smile that holds no maternal bliss and brims instead with eternal hellfire. "First of all, let me say that you are the last person on earth whose baby I'd want to carry." At least we're in agreement. "Second of all, I'm not sure what groveling would do for the kid, but it would do *me* a world of good. And third of all . . . no. I'm not pregnant. I missed a period, but I think it was just my new pill."

And then I say a prayer for Phil and any other man who should stagger into Sarah's life. Please, God . . . don't ever let her forget to take that pill.

* * *

I can tell Zach is sick of babysitting me, so I spend my last night in New York with Jonas and his girlfriend. This turns out to be a very bad idea because I'm faced with a happy couple and I keep thinking about Heaven and Darren. And that fucking rose. The only thing that sustains me is the pending trip to L.A. where we will be cutting soon-to-be-overplayed singles for Superhero (formerly a property of Rosenthal and Company).

Phil and I get to JFK. Neither of us is checking bags. I actually recognize the airport staff since I was just here, but they don't seem to remember me.

When we get on the plane Phil apologizes for sitting in the window seat.

"I didn't do it on purpose," he says. "It just happened that way when they got booked." I guess a lot of people really like to look out the window. I'm just not one of them. I prefer freedom. But that doesn't stop me from guilting Phil for at least ten minutes and working it to my advantage in the form of his bag of peanuts.

The flight is pretty uneventful, but when I'm waiting for the lavatory (why they can't just call it a bathroom, I don't know) I bump into that fucking guy I sat next to last year on my way back from South by Southwest. Old pancake-hands, who wouldn't shut up for the whole trip. He walks out of the bathroom and lights up when he sees me.

"Hey, bro!" he says. "Marc! Remember me? We're like flight buddies or something," he says as he puts his hand out to shake. I can't help but wonder if he washed his hands, and I'm reluctant to shake. But I figure I'm going in next, so I'll just wash my hands really good, before and after.

"Yeah, man. I remember. How are ya?"

"Really good," he says. "I took a job at Virgin. Just moving the last of my stuff out to Lost Angeles. You?" I don't want to get into it. I don't want to tell him anything. I just want to take a piss.

"No news here."

"I saw Sean Combs's Broadway opening last night. *A Raisin in the Sun.* Powerful stuff, man. Really powerful."

"So he's Sean Combs now? Not Puffy or P. Diddy?" I don't even know why I'm continuing this dialogue, so I put the kibosh on it. "Anyway, good seeing you," I say, and I walk into the bathroom, slide the knob to OCCUPIED, and wash my hands twice before I even unzip my pants.

Phil and I check back into the Riot House, and it feels totally wrong. I'm on a different floor at least, but everywhere I turn, I have flashbacks of Heaven. Luckily, I'll be spending most of my time in the studio.

I've deleted all of Heaven's messages. I just can't stand to hear her voice. It makes me lose my focus and think of her and Darren.

I'm in the recording studio in Burbank. Things are really jammin' when they tell me I have an urgent phone call. Without thinking, I pick it up.

"Hi, remember me?" Heaven says, sounding pretty upset. Urgent? I should have figured.

"The voice sounds vaguely familiar," I say, teasing her, trying to keep it light.

"Where have you been?"

"Where do you *think*? I'm with the band. We're recording."

"I know you're there *now*," she says. "But what about the two weeks before now? I didn't know if something happened to you. I mean, you just *disappeared*. You didn't even say good-bye."

"I didn't know I had to check in with you."

"I don't know . . . I would have thought maybe you would have wanted me to come with you."

"I've got it under control . . . I don't need you here."

"Okay," she says. "I just thought . . . I thought you'd maybe at least tell me you were leaving."

"I didn't tell you last time either," I say in a monotone. "You just happened to find out because you opened my mail. By the way, have I missed anything good this week?"

"I'm serious, Brady," she says. "I was worried!"

"Well, don't. I'm not yours to worry about. And you're not mine."

"What's *that* supposed to mean?"

"It means you do whatever you want, and you don't bother explaining to anyone. So don't expect it to be any different for me. I don't owe you anything. I don't need to get your permission to leave town."

"Fine," she says in the smallest voice I've ever heard. She sounds so hurt, and it breaks my heart.

"Good," I say back, because I can't fall under her spell right now. I need to stay focused.

"Well . . . how's the band?"

"Great. Almost done."

"I can't wait to hear it," she says

"Yeah. Anyway, I gotta get going."

"Don't you want to hear what *I've* been doing?"

"Sure." I exhale.

"I got the LLC set up, and Dead at 27 is officially in business."

"That's great, Heaven. I'm happy for you."

"Well, since Zach told me you were back on, all I've been doing is Superhero stuff," she says. "And I already have a lot of things in the works. You're gonna love it. I can't wait for you to see it, in fact—"

"Brady, listen to this playback," the sound engineer says.

"I gotta run," I say to Heaven, and I hang up the phone. I didn't even want to give her the chance to ask when we'd speak next because I just can't deal. I know I did the right thing . . . for me. She's hung up on her ex, or back together with him for all I know. I *definitely* did the right thing. So why do I feel so awful?

When the engineer plays back the last mix, I'm blown away. Everyone, including the band, thinks it sounds better than expected. Phil and I hug each other, then hug the band, and it's a fucking lovefest. We do everything short of holding hands and breaking into "Kumbaya."

* * *

A couple days later I'm driving with Phil down Sunset, and I see all of these posters plastered on buildings, lampposts, boarded-up windows along the way. They look like tricked-up old-time comic book pop art, and each one says only one thing, like SPLAT! or KAPOW! or BAM! I take it as a sign. Those are the kinds of things that you'd find in Superhero comic books. I point them out to Phil, and he smiles.

"Ever think that God is sending you little messages to let you know you're on the right track?" I ask.

"All the time," Phil says.

We're sitting in El Compadre, celebrating with the band, when Sam looks up and says one of my least favorite things, "Hey, Darren!" I look up and see that horse-faced motherfucker. I can't seem to escape him no matter what coast I'm on. He puts out his hand to me.

"Hey, Brady, how's it goin'?"

I change my mind. He's not horse-faced. More like a mule. But either way, still a motherfucker. "Good, man. Just finishing up the record."

"Can't wait to hear it," he says. "You know I'm their biggest fan. Seems you and I have very similar tastes," he says. It takes every bit of my strength not to crush him. But then . . . *then* . . . this fake-titted blond ditz walks up behind him and puts her arms around his waist.

"We'll float you a copy of the record," Sam says to Darren.

"Cool," Darren says.

"Come on, baby, I'm hungry," the blonde says. "Hi, I'm Charity," she says. She smiles a perfect, cap-toothed, pearly smile, then flips her hair. If there were a pole in the middle of this restaurant, I promise you she'd be writhing around it.

Suddenly I'm feeling like a father who's just caught his daughter's first boyfriend cheating on her.

Now, I am not a man of violence. I'm not. In fact, I'm generally against it and have never been one to start a fight. But when I see Darren with this fucking bimbo, and think that he's fucking around on Heaven . . . *again* . . . I can't help myself. Without even thinking, I stand up and punch him in the face. He stumbles backwards, and then blood starts pouring out of the nose on his really confused face. People gasp, and Charity shrieks. And I thought all she was capable of doing was flipping her hair.

"Dude, what the fuck?" Darren says. Charity reaches into her pocketbook and pulls out one of those mini o.b. tampon things. She rips open the little packet and shoves the thing up into his nose.

"Here, baby," she says.

"Why'd you fucking hit me?" Darren asks.

"Why do you *think,* dumbass?" I say, shaking like a ride cymbal but still full of testosterone. "Because you're fucking around on Heaven . . . again."

"What the fuck are you *talking* about?" he says.

"You're an asshole!" I shout. And I storm out of the restaurant because my hands are getting clammy, and I'm feeling about ten thousand different emotions. I can't tell if I want to pass out or do a cartwheel, but in case it's the former I don't want to do it in front of the band—and least of all, Darren. If it's the latter, I'll need the room.

I get outside and just walk. I walk up Sunset and breathe. I breathe and I think. And I shake my hand out a bit because it fucking hurts. I'm a few blocks away when my cell phone rings. It's Heaven. This time I answer it.

"Hi," I say.

"You're an asshole," she says. "Darren just called me."

"And *I'm* the asshole? I did it for *you*. That prick is with another girl!"

"Good," she practically yells. "He has every right to be! *Nothing* happened between me and him that night! You know why? Because of *you*!" She growls, "God, you're an idiot." And then she hangs up on me. I stand there trying to figure out what just happened. I replay the conversation in my head, and even though she just called me an idiot . . . it's the best thing I've heard all week.

I start walking back toward El Compadre, and I come across another one of those expletive flyers. POW! it says. But as I get closer I see something else it says at the bottom, and I do a double take. It says: *"Superhero . . . they're about to save music."*

Are you kidding me? *She's* the mastermind behind this? All of these posters and flyers are Heaven's doing. It's perfect. Almost *all* superheroes have a secret identity. Rather than go with cheesy costumes, she's using their anonymity as the hook. She's a genius. And she's not with Darren. BAM! My heart feels like it's going to explode.

When I walk back into the restaurant Darren is sitting at the bar with blood on his face. The tampon is stuck up in his nose with the little string dangling from it.

"I'm so sorry," I say to him. "It was a stupid thing to do."

"Yeah it was," he says. "Believe me, I've done my share of stupid shit. But be careful . . . that's how I lost her in the first place."

I remember watching Bruce Springsteen get interviewed on *60 Minutes,* and he said something I'll never forget. He said, "A time comes when you need to stop waiting for the man you want to become and start being the man you want to be."

Thinking back on it now, this minute, I believe that's the most profound thing Springsteen has said since: "We learned more from a three-minute record than we ever learned in school." (Certainly more profound than: "Just wrap your legs 'round these velvet rims and strap your hands across my engines.") And curiously, the two lines come together for me now as I think about two things I haven't thought quite this much about ever before in my life. Two things I can't *stop* thinking about. And they're both Heaven.

Suddenly that statement is the most relevant thing in my life. It's time for me to step up. It's not like I ever came out and expressed my feelings to Heaven. I just got pissed off at her when she didn't read my mind.

• ● •

Heaven

The *New York Post* reported a new study this morning, revealing that "poets die young—younger than novelists, playwrights, and other writers, because they're often tortured souls prone to self-destruction." It says that on average, poets live sixty-two years, playwrights sixty-three, novelists sixty-six, and nonfiction writers sixty-eight years. So says the Learning Research Institute at California State University at San Bernardino, at least. It says nothing about PR writers, so I don't know where I stand. This bothers me for the better part of the morning. Then I go downstairs to get the mail.

I get a Citibank bill, a Valpak, and a letter for Brady, who still has yet to change his stupid forwarding address. It's addressed in a handwriting that I don't recognize, and there's no return address.

I stand in my lobby, and for the first time I wrestle with whether or not I should open it. And then I do.

"Dear Heaven," it says. I look at the envelope again to make sure I'm not going crazy. It's addressed to Brady. And then I look at who it's from, and it's *from* Brady. Pretty clever, Brady.

There's also a little envelope—like one you'd get from a florist—stapled to the letter, which says: "Open when instructed to do so." I read the letter:

> Hi, it's me. First of all you *really* need to stop opening other people's mail. I needed to say some things to you, and I thought it best to write them down so I would get it right.
>
> Once you read this, things will have to change one way or the other, so you might want to pause right about now and take one last look around at what you consider to be our current relationship. It's good, right? Maybe even great.

The problem is that I can't be your friend anymore. You've come to mean so much more to me in such a short amount of time. I can't remember what life was like before you, and I can't bear to think of what it would be like without you.

It's not that I can't be your friend, it's that I can't be *just* your friend. I want more. I want it all. I want you. Now and forever, 'til death do us part.

I pray to God that you feel the same way, because if you don't, the dinner I have planned for us tonight is *really* going to be awkward. *Now* you can open the little envelope.

I open it up and inside is a pull-tab ring from a soda can. I continue to read, but tears have welled up in my eyes.

If you feel the same way, please put this on your finger so I'll know. If not . . . make believe you do, and then when I'm not looking, kill me.

Love,
Brady

I'm standing here speechless, just *staring* at the pull tab.

"Are you going to put that on or not?" I hear someone say from behind me, and my heart starts beating a million times a minute. I turn around, and Brady's standing there, leaning up against the elevator. He walks over to me, takes the pull tab, and puts it on my finger.

"Brady . . ." I say.

"I forgot to do something before I left," he says.

"What's that?" I ask, and he grabs my shoulders and *kisses* me. He kisses me like I've never been kissed before. And it's not necessarily that the kiss is any different than any other kiss. On its own merits, it's not that remarkable—two pairs of lips slightly parted, easing together, eyes drifting shut. But what makes this kiss the most impossibly, incredibly, stupendously magnificent chocolate-covered sun-ripened heaven-blessed fresh-squeezed brain freeze of a kiss—the second helping of glorious when you thought there was no more glory left undiscovered in the art of the kiss—is simply this: Those lips are Brady's, and these lips are mine. And now they're together. Parting only occasionally for meals and conversation and yawning and that stuff.

And I kiss him *back*. I kiss him like I want him to be the last person I ever kiss again and the only person I kiss for the rest of my life. And I can feel both of our hearts pounding out of our chests. I pull back from our embrace and look at him.

"And you'd think that would be something you'd *remember* to do," I say with a smile that could swallow the whole world.

"I'll never do it again."

"You *better* do it again," I whisper.

"I meant the forgetting part . . ." he says, and he plants another one on me. "This part I plan on doing with regularity."

"So I'm like fiber now?"

"Stop talking," he says, and he pushes me into the elevator. "And by the way," he says, squeezing the hand with the pull-tab ring, "just because you're not 'most girls' doesn't mean you're not getting a real one."

• • •

Heaven

My name is Heaven Albright. And I'm back in PR. And this time my boss isn't a complete asshole, just sometimes a pain in the neck. Me. Hyping people I *want* to work with (mostly anyway), and working my tail off.

There's Superhero—you know about *them.* But not about the three other bands I'm pimping, or about the hip-hop artist whose clothing line just debuted at the most talked-about show at Fashion Week, or about EnerJewee, "The Chosen Juice," a brand new low-carb, kosher beverage line I just signed on. And you don't yet know about my own version of Heaven, my assistant Heidi, who shows every sign of turning out *way* better than I did. Or about the happy ending for Marco and Sydney. Let's not call it wedded bliss . . . but we'll call it the ultimate marriage of convenience: America gained a new citizen, and Sydney gained two cup sizes.

If I sound different—like a chirpy chorus girl with a face-splitting smile—it's because I am. Maybe it's because this is my first break in a spastic year. And maybe it's because I'm sitting on a plane next to my fiancé, wearing the most gorgeous Tiffany engagement ring *ever.* Superhero? They're on the cover of *Spin* magazine, and Brady and I are on our way to Vegas, where they'll be playing at our wedding. Everything is perfect.

• • •

Brady

My name is Brady Gilbert, and I just gave up the aisle seat. Willingly.

• • •

Brady's Answering Machine

"Hi, this is Brady Gilbert. I missed your call, but *you* missed a scintillating moment with me. If you'd like to try to recapture that moment . . . leave a message, and I'll call you back." Beep.

"Hello, Mr. Gilbert, this is Georgette from Howard Schultz's office. Mr. Schultz would like to speak with you. Please give us a call back as soon as possible at—"

• • •

About the Author

It's five o'clock in the afternoon.

I bring this up mainly because this is about as late in the day that I can still safely drink coffee without wrecking my sleep.

People often say that writing is ten percent inspiration and ninety percent perspiration. This is nonsense, of course. It's pretty much one hundred percent caffeine.

I think the record pretty much speaks for itself. I was born in Hollywood to talented parents—the beloved TV and film star Tina Louise and talk-show pioneer Les Crane, grew up surrounded by *tons* of creative people, graduated from NYU Film School . . . and yet my professional writing career didn't really get moving until I was over *twenty years old,* when I upped my coffee consumption. *That's* when everything changed.

I got a job writing for MTV. From an early age, I reveled in the raucous and spent a good portion of my youth developing tinnitus at countless rock concerts, so it was a pretty good fit. Emboldened by my success, I ramped up to *espresso* consumption and—voilà—I started writing for the biggest shows on the network. Call it coincidence if you want.

I also dabble. I've dabbled in things like the music business and jewelry design. If you come over to my apartment (and you're invited, but please call ahead) you'll be able to confirm my love of music via the meticulously catalogued three million CDs that I've accumulated. If I live to be 140, I MIGHT be able to listen to them all. But don't get any funny ideas about walking out with one of them because my pad is vigilantly guarded by my two faithful pups. All eleven pounds of them.

So, that's where I'm at right now. Dogs, millions of CDs, a somewhat slavish devotion to a treadmill, which I swear is plotting against me while I sleep.

And writing. Screenplays. Stories. And the very book you're holding.

I hope you enjoy it. Have a cup of coffee while you read. After all, it's always five o'clock somewhere in the world.

Keep in touch at: www.capricecrane.com

Top Five Things You Don't Want to Hear on a First Date

1. G.E.D.
2. Custody Battle
3. Rehab
4. Star Wars Sheets
5. Valtrex